EYE OF THE SABER

WHISKEY WITCHES PARA WARS BOOK 6

S.S. WOLFRAM

WHISTLING BOOK PRESS

Whistling Book Press

Alaska

Printed in the United States of America

Published by Whistling Book Press

Whistling Book Press
Alaska
Visit our web site at:
www.whistlingbooks.com

Shifting Heart Romances

by Hattie Hunt & F.J. Blooding

Bear Moon

Grizzly Attraction

Here's the reading order to make it even easier to catch up!

https://www.fjblooding.com/reading-order

Other Books by F.J. Blooding

Devices of War Trilogy

Fall of Sky City

Sky Games

Whispers of the Skyborne

Discover more, sign up for updates and gifts, and join the forum discussions at www.fjblooding.com.

WHISKEY MAGICK & MENTAL HEALTH

S ign up to learn more about our books and receive this free e-zine about Whiskey Magick and Mental Health.
https://www.fjblooding.com/books-lp

THIS is for…
the patient people waiting for this book to come out.
Who gently prodded with a sharp stick. And words.
Also…
obviously my wife belongs here, who is always up for a challenge …
to give me.

Dexx looked at all the eyes staring...at him. Rows and rows of the people dressed in their Sunday best, staring.

Leah had tears in her eyes, her purple bridesmaid gown rumpled in the front where she'd clenched it.

Leslie held her mouth in firm disapproval as she held the bridal broom where she stood next to Tuck.

Others stood there, too. Chuck, Ollie Eastwood, and every one of his surviving pack.

"Well," Sheriff Tuck said, the Bible in hand, "do you?"

Paige narrowed her eyes, her witch hands becoming visible.

Dexx stuck a knuckle to his lips in thought.

Hattie let disapproval roll from her into Dexx. *Cub.*

I'm just having fun.

Do not push it too hard, cub.

He pulled his hand away. "Just playing. Of *course*, I do. Paige, you're the most beautiful, intelligent, and capable person I know."

She relaxed in relief.

"Yes. The answer is, I do." He turned back to Sheriff Tuck. "I do."

Tuck's scent spiked in irritation, but it had a fondness, and a large measure of patience, too. He nodded once and continued on. "And do you, Paige Whiskey, take Dexx to be your lawfully wedded husband…"

Finally, the day had come. Dexx stood in front of Paige and absolutely *everyone* in Troutdale.

They weren't marrying Paige though. *He* was.

If it was up to him, no one but a few people close to them would have been invited. His pack, which included the Whiskeys and Red Star, Tuck, and Chuck, and *maybe* a few others. That would have been *it*.

But no. After the word had gone out, plans and requests and a billion other things had gone on. People coming, going, and whatever else they had on their mind. This entire wedding had sprung up in a matter of *hours*.

There were a few people missing, though. Frey hadn't talked to him in months, though he saw her nearly every day. Roxxie had gone radio silent almost two months ago, and Furiel longer than that.

Balnore had showed up before the ceremony to wish them a lifetime of happiness.

The ones that tore at his heart were gone forever. Boot. Bruna. Alma. Rainbow.

Rainbow hurt him the worst. As he stared into the brown eyes of the woman he loved, he mourned Rainbow, wishing she were there.

Rainbow, ever positive and supportive. The best investigator Red Star had, and the entire department's little sister. She'd left a hole that hadn't been filled. Maybe never would be.

Paige took his hand and squeezed.

Oh, crap. His wedding day came rushing back in. *His* wedding day. To Paige.

He was happy. As happy as he could be with the world in upheaval like it was.

Hattie poked him. *Mates can be like the thornback. And as unsteady as the wind. Give your attention.*

Crap. His fingers didn't have much blood in them, now that Paige had his fingers in a death grip.

Leslie was speaking now, doing the witch part of the ceremony, Dexx guessed.

Dexx showed apologetic teeth to Paige, and her grip loosened.

His memories had all come back, thankfully, but part of him stayed in other places. Sometimes his mind wandered. Easily.

Dekskulta and the undersea city, London, and other places. He'd lived a lifetime away from Paige, but now he was back. In front of her and—

"What?" Everyone had eyes on Dexx, waiting.

Sheriff Tuck leaned in. "Give her a kiss."

Oh, shit. "Yeah. Come here, *vixen.*" He nearly lunged at Paige to get his arms around her for the big smooch.

The kiss may have looked rough to the audience, and the collective inhale agreed, but his grasp was as gentle as picking up Bobby. Before he'd grown up to a tweenie.

Dexx had Paige bent over backward, holding her from falling.

She pulled back just enough to talk. "Now, we can talk about you changing your name to Whiskey."

"How about we table that for a day?" Maybe forever, if he had his way.

"I think it's time you pick me up." Paige smiled against his lips.

Dexx straightened them both and turned to Tuck with a goofy grin.

Tuck returned the grin and looked out to the gathering. "I present Mr. and Mrs. Whiskey."

Dexx pressed his lips together while Paige laughed uncontrollably.

The crowd cheered, and Leah and Mandy crushed them in a hug, with Kate staying beside Rai with a frown on her face.

Dexx and Paige hugged them back.

Rai threw lightning in the sky that boomed and sparkled like real fireworks.

Mandy took control of the fire and rolled it through the sky like an aurora.

Nearly everyone stopped to watch the display.

Dexx tugged on Paige, hoping she'd follow and they could consummate earlier rather than later. With how things were going, they'd probably run out of time to do things right.

She tugged back, not budging.

Well, it'd been worth a shot.

She turned to the guests. "Food and refreshments are over there." She pointed to the tables full of potluck dishes and drinks of all sorts. "We gotta go do photographer things."

Half the crowd descended on the tables, and the other half laughed at the photo shoot.

Danny Miller had a photojournalist friend who had agreed to shoot pictures for the wedding.

Latasha had poses and spots all picked out for the pictures. Some of them were in front of the crowd. Others with just themselves and family.

An hour later, Dexx and Paige were free. "Hey, babe, you want to walk with me?" He didn't wait for an answer. He just pulled her along.

"Uh, sure." Paige had the option of walking alongside or being dragged. She chose walking. "Where are we going?"

"Into the woods." Dexx held her hand and gently rubbed his thumb over her soft skin. He stopped them in front of the grave markers of their fallen family. Rainbow had the latest grave, the soil finally losing the fresh-turned smell.

Paige didn't like to come out here, at least not as often as Dexx did.

"Hey, guys. See, Boot? I told you she said yes. Here's your proof. Alma, I promise to be good to her. Bow, you saved me more than once. I can't ever repay you, but I promise to you too, I'll do for her like you did for me."

Paige said nothing, but she bowed her head to the stones.

Dexx heard the soft steps of someone sneaking behind them. Instantly on alert, he sniffed the air, gathering information.

He relaxed, but not much. Latasha hid behind a tree, snapping pics of the newlyweds.

"You can come out." He could have done without the intrusion, but Latasha was only doing what she agreed to do.

"How did you—"

"It's pretty hard to sneak up on me. We were just talking to our people. Please respect them."

Latasha stepped out of the wooded area, her camera still in hand. "I lost my older sister when Nevada seceded. I think we've all lost someone."

Probably. There hadn't been a lot of fighting yet. That would come soon enough, but they now had about half the total acreage of the forty-eight states, with Alaska soon to join.

"Okay, guys," Dexx said, addressing the headstones, feeling a sense of peace just talking to them, "just wanted to show you we got married. Should be getting back now." He glanced at Paige, then turned.

For the briefest possible moment, he thought Rainbow's soil had a heat signature in it. He spun back, but it was cold.

"What's wrong?" Paige looked worried.

"I thought—it's nothing." He kept seeing Rainbow out of the corner of his eye, or someone who looked like her from the back when he was out and about. His mind just couldn't wrap itself around the fact that they'd lost her. "Let's get back or they'll probably send out a search party. Looking for us to be partying."

"You're gross." Paige punched him in the arm. She might not have Cawli anymore, but she still had a good punch.

"Ow." Dexx rubbed his arm.

The camera snapped off pictures as fast as digital shots could go.

"Where in Nevada was she?" Paige asked as they walked back.

"Las Vegas, in the riot."

"I'm sorry to hear that." Paige sighed a tiny breath.

She most likely *was* sorry to hear it. There'd only been sixteen people killed in the riots immediately after the successful secession of the Western and Southern states, but for Paige, that was enough. She still had hopes the world would wake up and just get along to go along.

Latasha tsked and took in a breath, kicking at the new growth. "I guess a bloodless coup was too much to ask for."

Paige's scent went hot.

Dexx interjected before Paige went nuclear. "We weren't going for a coup. Remember that little piece of paper that said we all had inalienable rights? Yeah. Just going for everyone to have the same ones. Just like two years ago when paranormals were just a myth. Stories." He gave Paige's hand a squeeze.

"I see." Latasha snorted and looked away. "So, you aren't trying to split up the states?"

Paige shook her head. "No. I tried to prevent that very thing. Now we're open to other things. *Worse* things."

"I got an idea." Dexx raised a finger. "Let's get back to the wedding party. Leave all this civil war stuff for another time." He shooed Latasha away with the back of his hand.

They walked the short distance back to the house with the party in full swing. The chairs for the ceremony were scattered in all directions, with circles of people eating and talking.

How many happy days had they had since this had started? Especially after the Registration Act passed shortly after the Confederate States and ParaWest broke away. Too few.

Hattie flared in Dexx's chest when he saw Chuck Deluca. She pushed Dexx to challenge for the high alpha spot every time she saw him. His wife and mate, Faith, stood next to him. As a scarred equal.

Calm down, he told his sabertoothed cat. *We got our spot back. I don't need more responsibilities. We have enough for the time being.* Plus, Chuck wore the regional high alpha spot *really* well.

Chuck raised his chin in Dexx's direction.

"He wants to talk." Dexx led Paige around the crowd.

Paige wasn't an alpha after Cawli had passed. She wasn't even a shifter. But she still held a spot in the regional pack, like a wandering wolf. Or lion, or something. *She* didn't think so, but none of the other shifters treated her like an outsider, which was something she hadn't realized. Dexx had, though.

"Congratulations." Chuck dipped his head to Dexx and Paige. "Even though you have been mated for a good amount of time."

Dexx shrugged. "Yeah, but some people like the tax break, you know." Which reminded him. They were creating their own country and he was going to make a big stance *against* income tax.

"Indeed, some people do." Though, judging on the look on Chuck's face, he was thinking the same thing.

"Hey, thanks for the duds." Dexx thumbed the lapel of the tuxedo. "I don't own anything this nice. And *nothing* that can keep up with her dress." The suit he'd worn in London had been pretty nice, but an expensive tux was as far over the suit as the suit was over sweats.

"You needed to belong in her league." Chuck smiled graciously.

Paige grabbed Dexx's arm. "Thanks. I was worried he'd have to shop *my* clothes to have anything nice to wear."

Dexx spluttered. "Pff, well I don't know about that—"

"Oh, sure. I bet you'd throw something together, all nice and *silky* and pretty."

Dexx opened his mouth, but nothing came out. He was *never* going to live down the *one* time he'd worn her silk underwear...and then ripped them when Hattie'd uncontrollably shifted.

Paige's huge smile kept the laughter back.

Faith cut them off with business. "Have you seen Merry Eastwood?"

Dexx could have gone all day without hearing her name.

Paige dropped her smile and peered around the throng. "No, I didn't invite her."

"She's up to something." Faith crushed her lips together angrily, making the scar pucker. "I had hopes you'd seen her around enough to know what she's up to."

Paige shrugged. "I'm not the one she calls with an itinerary. But I don't think she's up to anything more than normal."

Dexx and Paige had quarreled over Merry for the past five months or so, but Paige had more on her plate than Merry

Eastwood and as long as she was "on their side," Paige was "going to deal with her when the world wasn't as on fire." He could understand that. To a point.

The woman was a blood-drinking snake.

And he wasn't entirely certain Merry was *on* their team.

Dexx felt blood being squeezed into his fingers. His cue to end that line of conversation. "Let Merry be Merry wherever she is. We have a whole wedding to celebrate."

"Of course." Chuck tipped his head with a grin. "Again, congratulations. May your time together always strengthen you."

That was oddly formal. Maybe it was pack slang or something from wherever it was he came from.

Dexx and Paige meandered through the crowd as they ate and talked, sometimes Paige leading, sometimes Dexx. Several people paused long enough to congratulate them, and then quickly returned to their food.

They found a gap in the well-wishing attendees. Dexx had something to say, but he had so often been unable to really express his feelings out loud. He stopped her and pulled her around to face him. He looked into her dark eyes, the most perfect shade of brown. "Thanks for marrying me, Pea. I think I'm better just being around you."

Paige pressed her head against his shoulder. "Yes. Yes, you are." She picked her head up, her earlier smile back. "But I'm better with you, too. We make a pretty good team."

"Jerk. I hate you." Dexx slipped his hands to her waist and pulled her close. "Like *so* much." He bent his head and kissed her.

He looked up and something caught his eye. Something— some*one* at the edge of the house, disappearing around the corner. The afro was a dead giveaway. Of the dead returning.

"Did I—" He didn't want to finish that question.

Paige nodded, grabbed her yellow skirt in two fists and ran toward the house.

Dexx shifted so fast, running by Paige he might have run *through* her. In less than two seconds, he stopped where he'd seen the woman.

Nothing. Nobody anywhere close, and the party had stretched all over.

He shifted back. The tux was unruffled.

Shifting with clothes was the *shit*. Being a shifter and keeping clothes…*now* he could have some fun.

But Rainbow wasn't there. Nobody was.

Paige stopped beside him, turning around, searching and trying to catch her breath.

"Blu? Was that you? 'Cause if it was, we need to talk. *I* need to talk. Come on, buddy."

Dexx listened for her to answer.

Nothing.

He *didn't hear anything.* "You saw it too, though, right?"

Paige nodded then shook her head as she continued to scan the area.

Shit. He turned around to the wedding crowd. Several people were stock-still, frozen. Some still had a bite of food halfway to their mouths.

Oops. He might have wrecked his own wedding.

"Um…"

The closest person to him happened to be an old lady. Like ancient old. She might have had enough wrinkles to put Alma to shame. She smiled, an *old* smile, but her teeth were in good shape. "Youth is wasted on the young. But you should revel in it while you can." Her accent was soft. Sounded like she might be Russian, or at least from an area around there.

"Yeah. We just jump around flaunting it."

She laughed, frail and wheezy. "Don't take the words of an old woman so hard. I was only reminiscing."

People began moving again with no emergency apparent.

Paige looked up at him, her brown eye sad. "Maybe we could get Les?" He shook his head. If Rainbow had the ability to talk to a medium, she would have already. "It's just my eyes playing tricks. Wishful thinking."

"Mine too, then," Paige whispered.

His heart hurt. Alma, Bruna, and Rainbow topped his list of wishes of things he could change. And all the genies he knew were all out of wishes.

The old woman was almost in his personal bubble. "And here is your bride. Introduce me, won't you?"

2

Dexx stood blinking at the old woman. She wasn't familiar at all. How was he supposed to introduce Paige to her? Her soft and frail accent made him think of old Russian paintings, with warm cottages in a snow-laden meadow.

But he also got the distinct impression that he didn't want to insult this woman. "Hey, babe. I want to introduce you to...this lady here." He'd work with what he had. It had worked with the currents. This should work, too. He turned to the old woman. "Young lady, this is my wife, Paige."

The old woman gave him a smile that could have curdled milk and raised the hairs on rocks. "So pleased to meet you. This young man helped me with a problem I had some time back." Her eyes shifted to Dexx as she wrapped her arm around his.

He *should* have pulled away. He *could*, but little old ladies were harmless for the most part. There was something about this one, though, that put him off.

Alma hadn't been harmless.

He had absolutely no clue what he may have done for the woman.

Still, he left his arm in place. "That's right, I did." He turned so the old woman couldn't see his face. He mouthed "I have no idea," to Paige.

She put on a gracious smile. "Did he? I don't know that he told me about it. He helps *so* many."

Wow, she was laying it on thick. Wait. Was she doing that to push his buttons?

"He helped recover a blessing stick." The woman looked up at him, batting her eyes. "It was broken when it was returned, but at least a part of the stick is back in my possession."

"That's so sad. How did it break?"

"I don't believe I was told how, but there was a scuffle with a witch from...Australia, I think they said."

Oooh. *Now* Dexx knew who the woman was. This was the Russian collector the lizard wizard had stolen from. Of all the things that had happened during that time, her broken stick wasn't the most memorable. "I'm sorry about that. We really did try to recover it without the whole explosion part."

"I'm sure you tried your best." She smiled up at him again and, again, her smile looked like it belonged on the Grinch...*before* he grew his heart out.

Paige patted Dexx's other arm. "I'm sure he did, too. Have you eaten yet? It looks *so* good. Please, eat your fill."

"Thank you, darling, but no. I find today's food not as healthy as it was long ago."

Long ago? Sure, the lady might have been over a hundred, but that didn't make them *that* different. "How about the gelatin? At least you won't break any teeth on it." Dexx hoped that didn't sound as snarky as he'd intended.

The old woman shook her head. "I just wanted to

congratulate you both. It isn't every day the most powerful witch and an alpha marry in public, you know."

"I'm not that powerf—" Paige started.

"We're just people—" Dexx shoved in.

The old woman raised her hand. "As I said, I only wanted to see you both. May you live to an old age." She let go of Dexx and tottered off to a waiting limo.

Dexx watched her leave. "Annelle. Annella. Something like that. Cooper stole her blessing stick."

Paige raised her chin thoughtfully. "Nobody's seen her for a long time. I didn't know she even made it through all the trouble with DoDO."

"All I remember about her is she's one strange bird. I only saw her once, I think. Skulking around her own house.

"She seems nice, though." Paige had warmth in her voice.

She'd always had a soft spot for little old ladies.

Alma had broken her. "Sure. Nice." Dexx wasn't so sure about the woman.

"So, what was so important over here? A juicy mouse?" Paige teased him with a gentle poke in the ribs.

What? Oh. Right. "Uh…" He took in a deep breath, not wanting to admit it out loud. "Thought I saw Rainbow."

"Oh." Paige's expression turned sad as she scanned the area. "I miss her too. But when you look for her everywhere, it only makes it hurt longer."

"I'm not trying to. I just see her." He didn't know what to say.

Hattie would know if he did. *Do I see her on purpose? Or is it in my head?*

I do not know. You might be seeing prey where only trees stand.

Was he starting to get better at understanding her cryptic-ness? *I don't think so. But I'll keep my camera handy.*

That wasn't the first time he'd seen Rainbow. The first time had been just after they'd buried her on the property.

She'd never really spoken about her family, and the contact information she'd left was fake. He should investigate, but if she hadn't wanted anyone to know, that was her decision.

Paige had agreed immediately when he'd said he'd wanted Rainbow buried next to Alma and Boot. They both understood that Rainbow had been a part of their pack, their family.

A pair of familiar faces split from the crowd as they made their way back.

Dexx put out a hand, happy to see those tufted ears over the manly manbun. "Lynx. How are ya? Cyn, nice to see you again."

Lynx took his hand, and they shook. He was a good guy, and way too brave for his own good. He'd stayed with Cyn under his own will even though she was…uh, high strung. She was paranormal, but she wasn't anything like Dexx had ever dealt with. She was a generator. Sort of like a power source for paranormals, and those two seemed to work together quite nicely. Somehow.

"I'm doing well," the man-cat said. Bastet had trapped him in the form of a cat for several centuries, and when he'd reclaimed his human body, the ears had remained. "I'm still learning to deal with such a different world than the one I knew. It has been a struggle, but we are getting by."

His formal speech reminded Dexx that English wasn't his first language, but it was pretty good. Probably better than his own.

Cyn didn't say much. Dexx had scared her in the Time Before, and Paige basically sent her parents to the shifter plane forever. Not that the parents had a hard time about it, but Cyn sure did.

Paige took Lynx's hand when he offered it. "I just want to thank you again for staying. You don't know how much I think *every* one of us is necessary."

Lynx nodded in total agreement.

Cyn stood there, mostly impassive. Her scent said she wanted to be elsewhere. But her stance was closer to interest. Impassive interest, but not impatient.

Dexx studied her as she waited for Lynx and Paige to get through the politicking.

She held Lynx's hand at the wrist, gently. A finger tapped as she looked at Paige. A signal?

Lynx's smile broadened. "—really did not think they'd like my skills, as limited as they are, but I will take it." He turned to Dexx. "I saw the peace talks. The news people are flaying you over the results. I do not believe any of it, but they had a good angle when you attacked that priest."

"*That was self-defense.* He was casting a spell. I just drew faster than he did." Dexx'd lost count of how many times he'd tried to get his story out. He hadn't shot first. Bussemi and his henchmen had, and then Mario had shown up.

"Do you think he is dead? The priest, I mean."

"I know what you meant. I hope so, but I know the guy. He's probably back in the shadows pulling strings. I exposed him early, and that was a perfect excuse for him to get back under cover."

Cyn's scent sharpened to barely contained fidgeting, but her tap stopped as she pressed a nail into Lynx's arm. A tell?

"So," Lynx continued, oblivious, "you think he is alive?"

"Unless I see a cooling corpse in front of me, I'm going to assume he's not dead." He couldn't really be alive, but he could be far from death.

"I'm sure you are overacting. But I am glad you are back."

Cyn's finger dug a little harder into Lynx's arm.

Yeah. A tell. It was time to save the poor man. "Maybe. Only time will tell. Hey, why don't you go get something to eat? There's a plate of the best bear claws I've ever had."

Cyn uncoiled her fingers from Lynx. His face lost the tiniest bit of tension around the eyes. "I brought those."

Of course she had. Nobody had the baking touch like she did. "Well, they're the best thing out there."

"Oh, well, thanks." She relaxed a bit, and her scent lost the sharp urge to be away.

Dexx put his arm around Paige's waist. "No problem. Go have some fun."

Lynx led them away.

"She's so strange." Dexx shook his head.

"Cut her some slack." But Paige's expression said she agreed. "Her parents are dead and not...dead."

"Yeah, I know. But you protected the town and *they* volunteered. She shouldn't be so snippy." Maybe she needed to see a therapist and get medication. He wasn't downplaying either. He just knew that sometimes, both of those things helped. Hell, sometimes, he wondered if *he* needed therapy. Paige probably did, too, with all the shit they'd lived through. They'd need buckets of drugs if they survived what was coming next.

Or just really long vacations. He wasn't sure which. Like, entire lifetimes of vacations? On beaches? All over the world?

Dexx walked them slowly back to the party.

Reece Staats, Paige's grandfather, appeared in front of them. "Congratulations, you two. I'm happy you have each other." He reached his arms out for a hug.

Paige hesitated for just a moment and then stepped in. She was stiff and awkward, but Reece seemed happy to have any connection to Alma, his lost love. He had reconnected with Alma for a short time after most of a lifetime apart. There *had* to be a story there.

"Reece, how long are you back for?" Dexx didn't mind the old man. He was actually not hard to get along with. He'd saved Paige once. So, he had hidden his past with Alma and the fact that he was Paige's grandfather. So what? To be fair, *she* had hidden her past just as much as he had.

"I can't stay long," the retired priest said, "but when I heard, I came to see you two get married. The world needs more happiness."

Yeah. They really hadn't sent invitations. They'd managed to rig up the entire ceremony in the blink of an empty moment and had just hoped everyone who wanted to join them could. But Reece wasn't wrong.

However, as a priest, it was possible Dexx could get a little information as well. "Have you heard of a Cardinal Bussemi?"

"Can't say that I know him. Should I?" He broke away from Paige and held his arms out for Dexx.

Well, if Paige could, he could too. He hugged the old man with vigor. This whole having-a-family thing was something Dexx was *still* getting used to. "I would be a bit surprised if you did, but you might have heard of him. Just checking. Come on, let's party."

Reece didn't hesitate. He followed them back and mingled with the rest of the Whiskeys. Tyler and Leah probably liked him the best of everyone. Leslie held a chip on her shoulder because he'd hidden the fact that he was *her* grandfather too. Only a small one, though. Paige had a gift for holding grudges the longest.

She stopped at the table of food and picked at a few of the finger food plates, exclaiming at each. "Ooh, these are so good." She spoke through a mouthful of the bear claws Cyn had brought.

They really were, and that made it easy for Dexx to stroke Cyn's ego.

They were interrupted by a mic and a moment of feedback. Tyler stood in the sparring square facing everyone.

"Ahem. This thing on?" He tapped on the microphone in his hand. Where had *that* come from? "Okay everyone, can I have your attention?"

Yes, it seemed he could, and people faced him, clearly curious.

"How are you all doing tonight, um, this afternoon?"

Dexx chuckled. That kid looked so uncomfortable up there.

"Okay. So, I'll be your entertainment for a while. As you know, we're here for a wedding, and I heard somewhere in the past that there used to be a thing called *wedding singers*."

Oh, shit. Dexx's heart fell. Who told Tyler about that? He was a good kid with a big heart, but he also had a tendency to destroy everything in his general vicinity. With his voice.

"So, I looked up some songs you all grew up with. I got a good one. Can I ask Uncle Dexx and Aunt Paige to take the floor for their first dance?"

Dexx couldn't move. A dance? Stick a demon in front of him, and he'd have several ideas what to do. A dance wasn't high on his list of activities.

"Come on! Don't be shy. Help them up there, folks." Tyler's smile grew as he waved Dexx and Paige up to the floor.

A slow cheer rose up and, in seconds, they had no choice.

Paige dragged him through the chairs to the obstacle course, to the sparring ring that was now a dance floor.

Dexx preferred the sparring ring.

Damn. Double damn. Where was the earth-shattering comet when it could really be useful?

Okay. He could dance if he needed to. He could even enjoy it. But Tyler didn't have a singing voice, and had never shown any interest in singing, outside of blowing things up. But that wasn't singing.

It looked like Paige had more interest in the dance. "Give him a chance."

Dexx spoke through a smile. A forced one. "This can only end in disaster. You know that, right?

Paige took them to the middle of the ring dance floor. She was way calmer. Her scent wasn't even slightly worried. "I think it's cute."

"Help us to an early grave? He blows stuff up." With too little effort. That was his superpower.

Paige placed Dexx's hand on her hip and held the other one in hers. "Come on. It's time to taroom tarah."

What? What the hell did that mean?

Tyler started to hum. The tune *was* familiar. Although a bit before Dexx's time.

Images of Dexx's youth ran through his head.

Hattie stretched in his mind and happy-pawed.

Then Tyler sang, *"Love, love, love. Love, love, love. There's nothing…"* The Beatles tune flowed out and the world shrank to just Dexx and Paige.

He moved with her. He didn't think, he didn't doubt. He danced in perfect time with the woman of his heart, and his memories raced with all the times they'd spent together. All the good times swam on the top, with the less-than-good times somewhere underneath.

Before he realized it, the song was over, and the entire wedding party was applauding.

Wow, that boy could *sing*. Sure, he was born a bard, but he'd *never* used his voice like that before. Not around Dexx anyway.

"You knew about this, didn't you?" Dexx wrinkled his brow at Paige.

"Yeah. I heard him one day. He and Mandy and Leah were hiding in their room and learning songs. I have to admit, I liked his voice when he was practicing, but now, he's really grown."

No shit, he'd grown. That was talent on a Sinatra level.

"Now, I'd like to invite everyone to join. Partners and singles, let's have a good time." Tyler smiled large and music played from somewhere. This was a lot more recent and dancy.

"Can't touch this…"

Tyler went through an entire set of songs, some with music, a few without, but every single one had them dancing. Perfectly. No white boy twitching or silly jerky movements. Real dancing.

Tyler had a future.

When Tyler finally let them leave the dance floor, Dexx's feet felt used but not pained.

Paige laughed with Dexx as soon as the last song ended, happy to be together and sharing the day with the town. Even Reece and Leslie had good words to share.

Dexx sat Paige at a table and got a pair of drinks. Bobby and the twins were followed by Leah, all tired and happy from the day.

They shared hugs, but Leah held on to Dexx for a long time. "I love you, Dad," she said after a while.

"I love you too, Leah." He wouldn't get over the swell of emotion that filled him when she called him dad. He wasn't hers by blood, but he'd claimed her with his soul and he wasn't letting her go.

Dexx had to admit it. The wedding was awesome, so much better than the boring ones. Which, now that he thought about it, he hadn't *seen* any except in movies. They were just boring segues into disasters and action sequences.

"I suppose I could have a worse name than Whiskey." Dexx sat back in his chair.

"Are you saying—"

Dexx held up a hand. "No promises or anything, but maybe it wouldn't be too bad."

Paige raised an eyebrow, trying hard to pinch off a wild grin, her brown eyes dancing in delight. "Well, maybe I should work to get that thought closer."

He liked where this was going. "I think you should."

Paige's assistant walked up and waited patiently.

An *assistant*. But as far as those went, Ishmail was pretty good. He was confident, knew how to take control of a situation, and helped keep Paige in control. That's what Dexx really cared about. With the other one, as nice as she was, Paige had been overwhelmed. But when this assistant walked into a conversation with *that* look on his face, Dexx knew something wasn't right.

"We have news. Nevada just announced they're having talks with the Federalist States."

3

Dexx lay awake in bed. He listened to Paige breathing slow and even, random sleep twitches punctuating her sleep.

If Nevada left the Western States—ParaWest— the Federalist States or whatever they were calling themselves would have a major toehold deep in paranormal territory. There hadn't been a major skirmish for a couple of weeks, which had been one of the many reasons he and Paige had decided *now* was the time to get married. So yay for that, but had things gone quiet so Walton could work some plan to get states back?

Double dammit. This was his *wedding* day. Why was he awake and thinking about paras and normies and not about Pea and her wonderful—

Hattie stretched in his mind, her tone urgent. *Cub. Come.*

Is something wrong? Dexx was already on his way through the tunnels in his mind that separated his world from hers. What could be going on *there*, too? Bussemi hadn't really found a way in, not since Dexx had broken the ward, so what could it be?

He formed the black space, added a tree and light and grass and...he stood as the great cat on a high bluff watching animals on the low plain.

What's up? Hattie wasn't one for hysterics and she sounded plenty upset.

Hattie sat them down, still watching the grazing spirits far below. A few wolves wound their way around in the distance, stalking.

Is that what I'm here for? The wolves? Hattie could take care of those without his help.

Those are shifters doing what they did in life. All will be well.

Dexx took an internal breath. *Then why am I here? You made me think things were about to collapse.*

Those are not why I called. Hattie was holding something back.

She never did that. *Start talking, fat cat. Why am I here and not in bed?*

Mah'se has learned of your friend. The sheneshae you brought with you.

Sheneshae? Oh, right. Rusalka. *You mean Rainbow? How is he just now learning about her? And why would he care?*

She impressed him with her devotion. To you and to him. When we were pushed from the demon's realm, he had plans to bond with her.

Whoa. Mah'se had been bonded only once before and that had been against his will to the lizard wizard who'd broken the Russian lady's stick. From all Dexx could glean, Mah'se wouldn't bond with anyone again ever. He was too much into being a guardian of the spirits around the plains than to be a shifter in the human world. *Well, I'm sorry to hear that. What are we supposed to do?*

Hattie rested her head on her paws and focused on the wolves in the distance. They should have been too far away to see clearly, but this place worked in ways the real world didn't.

A shadow of movement alerted the wolf spirit and it paused in its stalk. An instant later, and the wolf was flying through the air, massive antlers helping lift the wolf higher.

The wolf fell to the earth, and Mah'se appeared above it raising his hooves to stomp the wolf.

Okay. Dexx knew that Mah'se was a protector and all, but this seemed...severe. *Will the wolf die here? In this world, this life, I mean.*

Normally, no. But Mah'se has not been himself since he learned of her death.

Shit.

Out on the plains, the wolf landed hard, and moved barely ahead of the stomping. If Mah'se had been a human, he would have been out of control, with pure hate driving him on. There wasn't any coordination in Mah'se's movements. He just pounded the ground willy-nilly, with no clear plan of attack.

I don't get it. Does he want *to bond or not?*

Hattie pushed some irritation through the bond. Apparently, he'd missed something obvious and vital. *The first bond for a spirit is special. The spirit is in a vulnerable place, and if they do not fulfill the bond promise, it can hurt them.*

Oh. At least Dexx understood that. Hattie described a sneeze that built up and disappeared at the last second. Those were uncomfortable. But were they worth a killing rage? *So, what would you like to do?*

What *should* they do? This wasn't the human world where cops could be called and order reestablished. Or was it? *Come on. Let's go talk him off the cliff.*

Hattie rose and took a step. They slipped through space and her next step put them within feet of Mah'se and the wolf.

Hattie bounded forward and rammed Mah'se with her shoulder.

That hurt a lot. But Mah'se stumbled away.

The grey wolf took one look at Hattie and fled, running, but wounded.

Mah'se rounded on Hattie and Dexx. *How dare you step between me and my work?*

What the hell, man? Dexx blurted out before Hattie had a chance. *You're out of control.*

I am what I always have been. Mah'se lowered his head and eyed them with furious eyes.

Look, we can deescalate, or we can fight. Your choice, but I want to remind you we're not a wolf. They weren't a wolf, but Mah'se wasn't either. If he chose to fight, it could be a close thing.

Leave. Leave now.

Not until we talk. Rainbow was a special person, yeah. I miss her, too. There's only a few things I wouldn't do to get her back.

You know nothing of us. You never tried. You are always about you, and never what someone else might think. Or feel.

Mah'se had a point, maybe even a good one, but Dexx was here, making up for lost time. *I know more than you admit to.* He hoped.

How does a spirit choose a bond? Mah'se took a step forward head low and threatening.

Damn. That was a good question and one Dexx never thought of asking Hattie, but he *did* know how *they* were bonded. *You look for force of will. Dedication to self and mate. At least in adults. Babies must have something in the womb you look for.*

Not good enough. Leave here and never come back. Hat'ai, you will never let him come back.

Dexx'd met many people and things that had an issue with him. That was fine. But telling him he wasn't going to do a thing was one way to light his fire to *do* that thing. *Sorry, bub. You don't get to tell me what I can and can't do.* Dexx lunged at Mah'se.

Dexx's eyes shot open with a sharp intake of breath and

he stared up at the bedroom ceiling, listening to Paige breathe. *What happened? You shoved me out.* Did Hattie knock some sense into Mah'se or what? Things were far from over between them. *Is everything okay there?*

Mah'se has been satisfied.

Why in the nine hells did you call me there and then push me out?

You sharpen his claws well. He will recover.

So Dexx was a claw post for a person with hooves? That didn't sit well with him. Like, not at all.

"I don't understand," Brack said in a surly tone. "What am I looking at?"

Zoe took in a deep breath, trying to remember that while the dragon man was...helpful at times, he was also a mild moron. "It's a virus. Of sorts."

Brack pulled away from the microscope, the bright sunlight streaming in through the bay of windows high-lighting the flecks of green in his blue eyes. "Yeah. And you've already developed a cure for that."

She wanted to wrap her fingers around his beefy neck. "No. I created a Band-Aid for the last one. This—" She stopped and jabbed her fingers at the scope. "This is new. The last one was amoeba based and easy to target."

He tipped his head to the side with an expression that said he was working through it.

"This isn't. All of my research, all of my development so far is..." Zoe pressed her fingertips to her forehead and then exploded them away in frustration. "I'm starting over from scratch."

"But you still have the counteragent for the other stuff."

Why was he so dense? "Yes! Oh my God, would you listen? This is something *new*. Who is this guy? How does he work so effing fast?" Zoe wanted to scream curses at the ceiling, but knew that her mom would frown at her from heaven, or throw her shoe or...something.

"Guy?" Brack looked confused.

Zoe sagged where she stood. "Pip, tell me you're listening."

Brack rolled his blue-green eyes and then dug the listening device out of his ear and handed it to Zoe. "Traitor."

Pip was his hacker assistant and probably the *only* reason he was able to do half as well as he did. Zoe put the earbud into her ear, still amazed at how some of this stuff even worked any more.

"...if you would just wait," a sassy female said on the other end.

Zoe had met Pip once. She liked to stay in her apartment and *really* didn't like to come out. She also wasn't super-fond of wearing clothes. "Hey, Pip."

"Hey, Zo. I'm totally getting you one of these so you and I can be in communication. Love our man, but..."

Zoe chuckled and made sure the earbud didn't fall out. "I'm scared, Pip. I can target the stuff he sends us, but a lot of people are going to die first."

"Die? I thought the last one just made it hard to shift and stuff."

"This one's different." Zoe would only know how bad it was after the victims started coming in. So far, she had one. One victim. Deceased. "I'll deal with this new virus—"

"Until Lex Luthor finds another for you."

That felt severely on par. "—and you and Brack find this guy and stop him." Fear ran through Zoe faster than a brain-eating amoeba. "Can you?"

The loud spattering of clacking keys filled the space. "Yeah. You got it. Now, give the earpiece back to our man before he feels abused. I'll have a new one couriered over to you pronto."

Zoe felt a little relieved. She didn't *quite* know how she, Pip, and Brack would be able to take down an evil bioengineering mastermind, but she also knew that they'd faced their own issues together. They'd find a way through this one.

As long as they didn't die first.

Dexx got up the next morning and made Paige coffee, not sure if they were on a honeymoon or not. It didn't seem like the right time, but...

Well, she hadn't gotten maternity leave and it didn't look like they were getting a break to enjoy their nuptials either. Wars sucked.

"Why are you two out of bed?" Leslie stepped into the kitchen from the hallway. Her hair hadn't been brushed yet, and she wore a flannel robe long enough to cover her ankles. "You should be up there completely twisted up and trying new things." Her grin was the oddest mix of forced and genuine. She liked her coffee, too.

"Just got done with our second session of the morning." He didn't want to disappoint his sister-in-law. "Had to give her a minute to get things reset." Dexx grinned back at her.

The look Leslie gave him said she knew better. "Robin tells me things. You two haven't been up for more than five minutes." She poured a cup for herself, and just like Paige, sipped and savored the first burst of bitterness over her tongue.

Ishmail stood nearby trying to get Paige's attention.

"You going to answer him?" Leslie eyed Paige with a raised eyebrow.

"No." Paige's voice was filled with indignation. "I'm going to enjoy as much honeymoon as I can."

Dexx jerked back. "We're on a honeymoon? When were you going to tell me?"

"When she's tired of her husband." Leslie shook her head. "Too easy."

Dexx sent her a churlish glare. "You should see what he needs. We knew we wouldn't have a ton of free time."

Paige pressed her lips together and got up, walking to her assistant.

The conversation was brief. When she came back, she had a hot frown on her face.

Leslie set her cup down, concern crashing over her face. "What's wrong, Pea?"

"They didn't just go back. The Federalists *took* Nevada. They invaded. The governor agreed to go back."

"So, we going to go bust some heads?" Dexx could use some quality doing-what-he-did-best time. Mah'se still had him itching to hurt something.

Paige shook her head tightly. "Escort paranormals out before they're jailed and lost."

"DoDO helping the feds?" Dexx could really let go if that was the case. They *knew* what they were doing and were foreigners in an invasion. No bad feelings when they didn't go home alive.

Paige shook her head, her dark eyes narrowed. "I'm going to help. You stay here."

"What—why? I'm the best equipped to handle DoDO, or anything else out there." He was, too. And he wanted the chance to kick more DoDO ass.

"Because I smell a trap." Paige brown eyes locked on Dexx's. "I would agree you're the best to go, but if they're tapping the ley lines again, *I'm* the best choice to go."

"Pea," Dexx took a breath to calm himself. "If this *is* a

trap, you should be the *last* to go. They want you and they're baiting you. Please don't be the last to see it." He couldn't lose Paige again. Not after the long slog back. Not that.

"I don't think either of you should be going." Leslie stomped over and slammed her coffee mug down on the table. "None of us. Let the professionals do their thing and keep us out of it."

That wasn't like Leslie. Was she really okay after her coma? She kept saying she was, but little things like this spoke to something different.

"We *are* the professionals, Les." Paige spun her cup on the table.

Reece walked into the dining room from someplace else. "I think you'll *all* be needed before this is over."

Leslie bared teeth. "Why are you here?"

Paige studied their grandfather. "I don't remember saying you could stay."

"*I* let him stay." Dexx sighed, wanting to roll his eyes, but refraining. "You guys are going to have to hammer this out sometime. I suggest now is a good time. *I'm* going to get the paras out, and if you have a problem with that, too bad."

Both women glared at him.

Dexx stood. "Um. Where do I go?"

"Nowhere." Paige stood. "I'm going, and you aren't."

Leslie stood. "*Nobody* is going. And that's final. And I'm pissed that you let Reece stay here without asking me."

"Strange, I thought I thought I was an adult with adult decision-making rights in a house we *share*." Dexx let Hattie color his eyes.

Leslie's eyes grew orange, Robin coming out in her features. Her face grew sharper, and she broadened in the chest, stretching her robe to the point of ripping.

Dexx rarely had to push Robin and Leslie anymore. But he let her have the alpha push.

Leslie had a strong will to start with and Robin made her way harder, but with Hattie, he shoved them into submission. "Reece is part of the family and you two"—he pointed to Paige and Leslie one at a time—"are going to have to come to terms that *Alma* didn't tell you about him way before *he* didn't tell you about him. Am *I* clear?"

The two women didn't respond quickly, but they didn't fight him.

He must have hit a nerve. "Reece, you stay here until you three understand *why* you and Alma kept things under wraps."

A doorway opened and Derrick Blackman stepped out, his trench coat and rings in place. He looked to the four people standing around the table as he closed the portal and opened another. "Bad time?"

Paige turned away from Dexx to walk to the doorway. She stopped and turned back to Dexx. "I love you, and I'll be back as soon as I can." She led Derrick back through the doorway, and then it closed.

Dexx turned to the former priest. "You stay here until things get resolved. Leslie, you want to go kick DoDO's ass?"

She swiveled between Dexx and her grandfather. "Right now, yes. Yes, I do."

"Good. Where's Leah?"

4

Tyler blinked his eyes open.

The room didn't have light, and the floor was hard and cold. He rolled to his side, easing the pain from sleeping on the floor.

This wasn't Mandy's room and this wasn't the floor of the baby room. Fear set in.

Where was he? Also, it was creepily quiet. Where was everyone else?

He sat up and felt around. More smooth, hard, *cold* floor. Concrete.

Should he call out for Mandy or Leah, or should he stay quiet? What if they were just as scared and didn't want to let whoever had them to know they were awake?

The night was mostly a blur. There'd been a party. He'd done a super job with the singing, which wasn't a big surprise. And then…nothing. He should have remembered going to bed. Eating his weight in cake. Stuff. He should have remembered…stuff. But he didn't. He barely recalled maybe seeing a DoDO uniform, but the details were super sketchy.

Screw it. He whispered low, "Hey, guys. You here?" Who else could be in here?

"Good, kid. You're awake." The voice sounded older, but not evil. Evil would sound...more evil, right? "Uh, yeah." What did this guy want? "Where am I?"

"I know what your power is, and if you try it on me, I'll have to hurt you. Do you understand?"

No. No Tyler didn't, but he had to be patient. That's something his dad would say. "Okay." He blinked, trying to get shapes out of the bright light.

His power didn't need to be heard to work, not always, but it certainly did help.

"Tell me how your wards work."

The wards? Tyler had a good idea how they worked, but they were boring *and* that was his mom's and Aunt Paige's thing, which made them boring-er. "I don't know."

"Are you sure? Have you never *helped* with them, put your power into them?" The man didn't sound angry, but he had a push in his speech.

That felt familiar, like when his mom told him to do the dishes. Even when he didn't want to. But he quietly resisted, like when he had to clean his room. "I...have." Why wasn't the guy turning on any lights? This sitting-in-the-dark thing was getting old. "But that doesn't mean much, you know. I'm a kid."

"Right, well. Before we get much further into this, you should know that if you tell us what we want, we'll let you go. All you have to do is answer our questions. Then, we let you go. Like you were at a sleepover. You have those, right?"

What did this guy think he was? Eight? Yeah, Tyler knew what sleepovers were. He watched TV, too. Well, before that was shut off. So, Tyler knew this was the way the bad guys got answers without torture. With the light and the promises and all that stuff.

So, Mr. Dude didn't want him using his powers. Okay. It was time to see how creative Tyler could get with them. "Oh, sure. Is that what you want? To have an overnight with us? I can ask. But I'm pretty sure the answer is no." He wove some power in his words. He had to make the man think he was just a kid. Not a smart one.

The man made a noise to interrupt.

Tyler kept on. "She didn't like it when I hid in the clothes rack at the store, and this is kind of like that. I didn't get *any* candy. She was pretty mad." Where the heck had that even come from? Okay. There was babbling and then there was just sheer *babble*.

"If—"

Tyler cut him off again. He had to keep talking, trickling ever more power into his words. Make the man think he had control, and *if* he could tell if he was using his power, he had to start so low, *nobody* could tell.

The trick had worked on Dexx and his mom a few times, anyway. They knew how to see through him now. This guy, though? "But I suppose if you met her and asked what you wanted, I bet we could get you one of the cabins. I think we have one you could use. Wait. Who are you? Because they wouldn't like it if you were a bad guy."

Slow, incremental increase in bardic power while speaking wasn't as easy as just singing, but it was his *voice* that mattered.

"Look, kid—"

"I mean, I think you could be legit? It's kind of weird being in here all alone with you. How do I know you're a good person? I've had some classes at school, but you *sound* okay."

"Can you stop for—"

He didn't have enough power out there yet. It was hard just to come up with poop on notice, but he had experience.

People thought he and Toby were only excited about blowing things up, and that *was* fun, but they practiced other stuff too.

"It's just that I can't pull any strings for you if I don't know you. Oh, hey. If you *really* wanted to stay with us, you could talk to my Uncle Nick. He has a boyfriend, Mark, and if you stayed, it would just be an adult sleepover."

Oh, inspiration but of what kind? Nice. Just keep the man listening.

"When I say adult, I mean just older, not you know, *adult*. I've had sex ed, and I know some things, but not all of it, you know. So just adults having other adults sleeping over."

"Stop—"

"But that's weird, now that I think about it." Tyler had enough power out now he could try to trance the man, but he needed enough to be sure. "But I suppose it would be fine if you brought all your own clothes, like if you were at a hotel. That wouldn't be so weird. Or if you paid them to sleep over. Have you ever paid for a sleepover? My uncle Dexx—oh hey, my uncle Dexx just married my aunt, so I guess he's *really* my uncle now—but anyway, my uncle Dexx is a police officer. He has people sleep over in the jail. I bet you could sleep over there—"

A sudden sound like a chair scraping against the floor and cloth rustling gave Tyler his cue. He snapped the power in place but kept it slack. "No, don't hurt me. Ow, ow, ow, ow." Keep him off guard, make him feel sorry first. Strong emotions were easy to hide things in.

"Shut the hell up. Listen. Speak when spoken to. Answer my damn questions and we'll let you go. Get me?"

"Sure, sure, sure." Now that he'd charged the room, it was time to figure out how to get this guy to do what Tyler wanted him to. Quinn had taught him that nobody was immune. Nobody. So, he released a little of his gift to soften the guy up. "Just don't hurt me. I'm only a kid. You can't expect me to know it all. I don't do that stuff anyway. I just learned how to lift rocks. Little ones. I'm not as good as my mom or Aunt Paige. Don't hurt me." Good. The room was saturated.

Mr. Covey had taught them about saturation in school. It meant that no more of a substance could be absorbed into something else. And the room didn't want to hold more magick.

"Could we have some lights, at least?" Tyler pushed his intent at the guy who had obviously not wanted the lights on in the first place. Try something simple, then work from there. And keep the trickle going, just in case. "I'm helping, really. I want to go home."

The lights kicked on, and the room was a surprise. It was long and white, with five people standing around a sixth who had just stood from his chair.

The people were all dressed in the DoDO black tactical gear.

The DoDO agents looked at themselves in surprise, and he saw the room on the other side of a mirror behind the DoDO agents explode with activity.

Tyler couldn't wait. They were going to attack. He didn't need to work up to the right frequency, not anymore.

He screamed out destructive force. He used it all.

The walls halfway between him and the interrogator shattered, the desk shoved backwards disintegrating, and the people...

Well, they didn't stand a chance.

He'd knocked a demon out and destroyed part of a building once. Since then, he'd learned control.

He tried not to look at the mess. The room had an exit now. Many of them.

Time to go home.

A portal opened in the room between the back door and the kitchen.

The kids, all of them—Tyler carrying Kamden—stepped out. Leah was last, with Mandy and Ember filling the door with fire so hot the room heated instantly.

Leah slammed the door closed.

Leslie stood up, her chair screeching. "What the hell?"

Rai turned to her and just frowned, her mouth slack.

Kate shrugged and went to the kitchen, grabbing a cookie.

Leah ran to Dexx and hugged him. "Dad."

Mandy clenched her still fiery fists.

Ember shook out his hands, the fire disappearing. "I'm starving. Eggs?"

As far as entrances went, this one was almost kinda normal. Except for how scared Leah was. Tyler set his brother down and went to his dad and fell into a big hug.

That wasn't normal. "What happened?" Something was off here in a big way. Dexx needed to go after Paige, who was in trouble, but it looked like the kids were *more* in need of him.

Tyler broke away from Tru. "DoDO."

"What?"

Leslie held up a hand. "When?"

"I don't know how." Tyler went to the kitchen and grabbed a glass of water, chugging it back. "I totally remember nothing, but I broke out and found Leah."

"What?" Rai demanded around a mouthful of sandwich. "*You* did?"

"Whatever. *We* did. Happy now? Then, we escaped." Tyler's smile almost reached his ears, but something lurked right behind his brown eyes.

The look was too familiar. Tyler had seen something

41

adult, something that would change him forever. That pissed Dexx off something fierce. However, none of this was making any sense. "You're saying that—"

"DoDO kidnapped you," Leslie finished for him, her voice rising.

Anger leapt in Dexx's chest. It was *one thing* to go after adults in a war, but to go after the kids? And *how* had DoDO even gotten through the wards? He needed answers and to put a hurt down on these guys. "Open a doorway for me. I'm going to let them know you're off limits."

Leslie turned angry eyes to him. She was the protective mother, shielding her kids from the outside.

Dexx was the sword, *killing* things that might go after them.

Leah pushed away from Dexx, wiping her eyes. "Mom would say no. But I want to go with you and do whatever you do." Her face was a mix of fear and anger and splotchy mascara.

She had *makeup* on? He could understand wanting some revenge. But *makeup?*

"No," Leslie growled.

"Yes," Dexx said at the same time.

Leslie turned to face Dexx down, an enraged mama griffin. "You have *no right* taking her back there to get hurt or killed. *I* won't allow it."

Dexx let the anger boil in him. Someone had targeted his *kids*. Again. This was going to stop. "I don't care *what* you think. They go after us, *we* get back at them. If they go after the *kids,* I say we give them a chance to show the assholes what it means. You want your kids to stay, fine. They aren't mine. If Leah wants to go, I'm gonna let her. She can't stay a kid forever."

Dexx's stomach fell as he listened to his own words. He knew someday they'd have to grow up, but this felt too soon.

They should have a few years of being innocent and *kids*. Not going into adult fights.

But he hadn't been much older than Leah when he'd tracked his first demon down.

The world was harsh, and his children had the misfortune of being Whiskeys. They *needed* to have the choice to be who they wanted.

"Dad." Rai looked at him like he'd lost his mind.

Was Dexx doing the right thing here? The rage inside him said yes. "Little Leah, you have to stay close." He was preparing her for survival. All of them. "Do what I say."

She nodded.

Leslie's eyes went orange. "I can't let you do this."

Tyler took a step toward Dexx. "I want to go, too."

Flames flared in Leslie's eyes. "Absolutely not. I forbid it."

Rai pointed at Leslie. "You weren't there. *We were.* Tyler's got this. They had *nothing* that would touch him. No magick anywhere. Because the people who could use it just...forgot how."

Leslie turned her eyes to Tyler, and the magick retracted but tears fell. "No. Not my baby."

Mandy hugged her mom. "I think we *all* have to go. Mom. We'll be okay if *you* go with us. You and Dad."

Tru shook his head. "I can't. I'm just a mundane. I don't think *anyone* needs to go. Hunker down here and protect ourselves."

"They wouldn't be expecting it," Mandy said, looking up at Dexx.

He tipped his head sideways. "In all the times we've gone to war or fought *anything,* has that ever worked?" Tru was a good man. Really he was. If only he had a shifter spirit. He could *really* be a part of what they experienced.

Tru deflated. "Never. So, what should I be doing?"

Kammy barreled into his dad. "Carry me."

Tru stooped to pick up his not-so-small son.

Time to figure out what the right thing to do was. As much as he wanted to do otherwise, Paige could and would take care of herself, but DoDO and Walton both needed to learn they couldn't target kids and get away with it. He also needed to give those kids more fighting experience outside of the obstacle course. This war was getting way too real way too fast and he and everyone else wouldn't necessarily be around to protect them forever. "They need to know this isn't okay."

Leslie didn't lose any of her fierce look. "Fine. I'll hold *you* responsible for anything that happens."

"Fair enough." That was the job of the alpha. *We got this, fat cat?* Leslie wasn't wrong to be scared. DoDO wasn't a joke, and they *liked* killing paras.

Cubs have to learn to hunt. You can't hunt for them forever. For all her bluster, Hattie allowed a thread of nervousness slither through the bond. There never was a guarantee that everyone would come home.

He knew that better than most.

Dexx loaded up on guns and stood ready in the living room.

Kate hadn't gone anywhere, but she'd come up with a black cloak.

"You don't have to go." Besides, she probably hadn't told Nick or Mark, and they'd be sick with worry.

"They killed my people. I have the right." She set her face to unreadable passiveness. Her scent was as scared as any of them.

Dexx began to have second thoughts. Would he be leading them into a trap, or worse? They were *kids* going into *battle*.

Okay. Time to call off the raid. "Hey guys, I don't—"

Leah stood in front of him, her face determined. "We go, or I raise the dead *here*."

Zombies.

Oh fuck. He hoped he made the right choice to let them go.

The Whiskey clan was ready. Nervous, but ready.

"Let's go."

Emma rubbed her eye, tired as hell of this argument. She and her pack had been debating for the past several weeks whether or not to stay. Mason was all for it. His parents were ready to find somewhere safer. She couldn't blame them. They were old rats who didn't want to live in a war zone.

Juliet and Brett, however, couldn't make up their damned minds. Most of the pack *debate* was with these two as they flipped from one side to the other.

A decision needed to be made and, as the alpha, that fell on her. "We're leaving."

The heated argument stopped, leaving silence to fill the double-wide trailer as everyone turned to her.

Mason shook his head, pushing up his blacked-rimmed glasses. "You can't be serious."

"I can." Emma was so tired. They'd been trying to make a go of things here in Troutdale for a couple of years now and it just wasn't working. A lot of that had to do with the fact that every time they got their bearings, another war would crop up. She met Juliet's blue gaze from across the small kitchen. "Canada is safe?"

"Mostly." The polar bear shifter shrugged, her pale blonde hair giving her a halo effect in the glow of the sun behind her. "Getting across the border might be a bit tricky."

Did they really have any better options? "Can you arrange it?"

Juliet pushed away from the cheap laminate counter and unfurled her arms. "Yes. I'll see what I can do." She gestured to Brett. "You want to find a vehicle?"

Emma let them deal with the details. She held up a hand to stop Mason as he rose to speak his mind. Again.

He wanted to fight and die for Paige's cause. That was all well and good, but Emma wasn't willing for all that. The loss of her three stillborn children lay heavily on her heart. She couldn't lose one of her clan. They might be a ragtag group that didn't make sense, and they weren't a strong pack, but she was still invested in each of them.

She needed to talk to her brother again though, to see if she could get him to join *her* clan instead of Dexx's.

So, Emma left Mason to stew and shifted into bear form to visit her brother a few miles away.

He and Ripley had been living over the bar, but after the ghost attack, they'd moved to the Whiskey lands. She dropped her travel bag at the base of the tree—something she'd learned from her porcupine mate—and climbed the trunk to her brother's treehouse.

Joe greeted her with a smile and hugged her before she'd fully transitioned to human again. "Hey, sis." He pulled away, his dark eyes staring deep into hers with a shadow of sadness. "You made your decision, then."

She nodded. "It's not too late. You and Rip could join us."

He shook his head and bowed it. "Emma." He clamped his lips closed and walked away to one of the chairs in the living room, though he didn't sit. "We can't just leave when Dexx needs us most."

"He's sending you into battles like you're toys."

"But we're not," Joe said forcefully, spinning on her. "Can't you see that? He cares for us."

46

"Does he, though?" It irritated Emma to no end that Dexx could be so cavalier about the safety of his pack. "Really? Or does he just care about his wife and kids?"

Joe snorted and looked away, balling one hand into a fist. "If you just joined us, you'd understand."

That wasn't likely to happen. "I'm keeping my clan safe."

"Right." Joe jutted his chin forward as he released a gravelly chuckle. "Whatever you gotta tell yourself to sleep at night."

Emma didn't want to leave like this. This might be the last time she saw her brother. "I love you," she said quietly.

"Yeah." He nodded, then swallowed. "Love you back."

She knew—she *knew*—he would die in this war effort, but only because when disaster hit, Dexx and his entire pack ran toward the danger, not away from it. That didn't make them heroes.

It just made them more likely to die faster.

And Emma wasn't going to let *her* pack die in a war they couldn't win.

5

I t couldn't be this easy. They weren't this lucky.

After Dexx had disappeared for whatever reason, they'd gotten reports of clumps of people fleeing Arizona, Utah, and New Mexico, which were all in conversations with Walton about returning to the Federalist States. Walton kept calling it the United States, but what he had power of wasn't the United States of America anymore. Paige still hadn't figured out what *she* was going to call his country, but the Federalist States seemed to fit the best. Though, everyone seemed to have their own name for each of the new countries, which wasn't helping anything at all.

Aside from those three states, there were also rumblings from Southern California, with pockets of people fleeing men calling themselves wolves fighting the coyotes who were bringing the refugees in from Mexico—*and* the paranormals fleeing persecution.

It seemed weird that humans were using animal terms to describe themselves when they were hunting shifters. But what did Paige know?

There were other reports in Kansas, Nebraska, and Oklahoma of people being tagged for being thought to have paranormal abilities. It was like a roaming witch trial. There were rumors that shortly afterward, the tagged people would then disappear.

General Saul was in charge of deployment to each of these regions and she was trying to be as strategic as possible, using her resources frugally. They couldn't help others at the risk of their own country.

There were a lot of Blackman witches, to be sure. Those people multiplied. A lot. And *their* door magick gift seemed to travel down the family line better than even the Eastwood blood magick, which was neat and weird. But not everyone were exceptional door witches, Paige being one of those, and they weren't all old enough to go on dangerous missions.

General Saul had also specifically stated that in the most severe cases, she wanted *her* soldiers to go into the battlefront because *they* were trained. She wasn't yet used to the paranormal forces like Dexx and his pack, and with the fact that they were now fighting on their own soil, it was imperative that things go smoothly.

Which was okay because Paige had no idea where Dexx even was.

Doe's pack exodus was going well. They were traveling on foot so they wouldn't drive up to any of the many blockades both in-state and along the borders, but the regional pack had been shielded from detection by a rather large storm.

And that storm was now gone, meaning, they needed a witch capable of keeping it over them to help them remain undetected by satellite for a few more miles.

There were no other witches capable of doing that. For all that the Blackmans could do doors and the Eastwoods could do crazy blood magick, Paige was the only one of the witches they had who could summon storms.

Well, aside from Rai, and she wasn't going into battle. So,

Paige had volunteered for the solo mission. General Saul had been absolutely against it until she realized she didn't have any other door witches to send to just transport them to Troutdale quickly. With this many shifters, the door witch would be in enemy territory for potentially hours, and they were ParaWest's greatest asset. Paige also reminded the general that she'd be surrounded by a pretty powerful alpha and thousands of shifters if things got a little hairier than she could afford.

If things got dire, the *face* of the revolution could call for a door or make one, maybe, for herself, and get the flock out of there.

Would she? Paige didn't know. But, in theory, she could.

All they had to do was to get through the last few miles of Nevada, into Northern California, and then they would be in the clear. There were buses waiting to take them to Troutdale.

Easy.

"I still don't like this," Derrick said as he closed the portal behind him.

"Noted. Again." They'd discussed *all* the other available options and this one wasn't...as reckless as it might seem.

"You should be staying behind." He flicked his trench coat. "Like General Saul recommended." His coat was ridiculous out here in the Nevada heat, but Derrick had infused it with protective and defensive magick that had saved his life more than once.

"We didn't have that luxury this time."

"So you say."

Paige reached for the air, spinning it up into a gusty wind and then reached for water, beginning the process of the storm. She told them both what she needed, pushing her with her emotions, letting both elements know what was at stake.

They rose with force, answering her call.

Derrick shook his head. "I'm going to stay."

"And risk falling into enemy hands?"

He raised an eyebrow.

She saw what he'd done there. "Without me, you guys will be fine. But you're a weapon we can't afford to lose." Technically, neither was she and, yeah, maybe this was a little dumb. But she'd literally been in worse just months ago. "I'll be fine," Paige said, seeing Doe appear through the trees not far away as the winds continued to rise.

"You better be."

Paige smiled at her brother. "This is a milk run. The California border is just a few miles that way. Easy-peasy. By the time you're done, you'll be bringing me home safe and sound."

He snorted. "Make sure that's the case."

Paige shot him a grin she didn't really feel and watched him cut open a door and step through. She turned to Doe as the storm built above them. She met the alpha halfway, stepping around scrub bushes and pine trees. "Trip going smoothly?"

"We're a little wet," Doe said as sprinkles of rain pelted them. "But other than that, we'll be okay."

Paige fell into step beside the alpha, missing her shifter spirit who would have made it easier to sluff off the cold effects of the rain. Her rain jacket would just have to do. "No patrols?"

"A few." Doe rearranged the backpack of a young man beside her and then gestured to another man. "But we found a way around them."

"Good." Paige pointed in the general direction they were headed. "Just a few more miles and you're safe."

"This was really unnecessary," Doe said, shaking her head. "You really didn't have to do this. We're fine."

Paige didn't really believe that. She was actually more than a little surprised that Doe's pack had made it this far unmolested. "Better safe than sorry."

Doe shook her head and chuckled. "Yeah, I guess—"

The sound of gunfire ripped through the air and three people shouted and stumbled to the ground.

Doe's eyes gleamed as she bared her teeth. "We're under attack."

Paige called on her magick, releasing her witch hands, searching for her target as shifters swarmed around her and Doe, shielding them.

All they needed was a few more miles.

And after Lawrence, Paige was really ready for just about anything.

She hoped.

———

Dexx stepped through the doorway first.

Mandy followed him in and laid down a burst of cover fire. Sheets of cover fire.

But as Dexx, Leslie, Tru, and the rest of the kids stepped into the room, they were greeted by no one except those who hadn't survived the escape.

"Look at me." Dexx turned to the kids. "These guys are the enemy. Remember that." Dexx stood up and addressed the rest of the kids. And Tru. "These aren't people, they're animals. And worse. *This* is proactive self-defense. So, anything out there that isn't us, *cannot* make it out of here." It hit Dexx in that moment, the line he was crossing. "Am I clear?"

Bobby, Rai, Ember, and Tyler looked ready. Tru not so much, and Leslie had dark eyes for everyone.

Leah and Mandy looked like they were ready to bolt. Kate looked just kind of bored.

"Leslie, you take Tru and your kids that way. Tyler, destroy. I'll take mine this way." He pointed to the hall with a corpse laying in the doorway.

Kate looked between the two groups.

"With me," Leslie said.

At the same time Dexx cuffed the elven girl behind the neck and brought her along. "Kammy, keep us in touch."

Leah set her jaw and put an arm up, palm out.

Inky black tendrils flowed from Leah and touched the bodies sprawled through the room. They twitched once and lay still.

Good, because the thing Dexx had a problem with was zombies. Those things were just so unnatural. Vampires were a close second, except maybe a rusalka in full rusalka mode, but zombies took the cake. His stomach roiled but settled when the corpses did.

Then arms and legs moved to push themselves up.

Dammit. Dexx had to look away. *Oh, that's so gross.*

This is your hunt, cub. You brought the hunters, and they use their teeth in their own ways.

Yeah, but does it have to be...dead bodies? Dexx heard the whine in his own sending.

Hunt, cub.

Dexx's lips pulled back in disgust, but he put on a brave face when Leah turned around.

She was looking for approval. Shit. Right. "Good job. Are they in front or behind?"

"I, uh...I don't know."

Dexx looked back to Leslie, but the other Whiskeys were already gone. "Behind. We'll pick up more, and you can send those ahead of us."

She smiled way bigger than he could have.

No matter what he thought of zombies, Leah was one hell of a kid.

"Rai, can you clear the halls, please?"

"Yes, Dad. Yes, I can." Rai walked *right by* a zombie without a glance and stretched one hand out in both directions down the hall.

The room trembled with the concussive blast of wrist-thick lightning. Glass shattered and walls scorched where the lightning touched...well, *anything*.

Kammy, you on? Hopefully, they could work on a private PA system. Or like the comms DoDO used.

Yes. Mom says to hurry up.

Dexx couldn't argue with that. The longer they took to completely destroy whichever installation this was, the more chance DoDO had to regroup and put together an adequate response.

Which...was none at all.

That didn't seem strange, did it? Dexx stepped to the doorway and signaled for Rai to stop.

The lightning danced over walls and windows for a few extra seconds. "Is that clear enough?"

"You bet, kid." So, why hadn't there been a team there to greet them? *Kam, are you guys meeting any resistance?*

No, the kid answered. *Mom says it's empty.*

That made destroying this place easier, but what were these guys planning? They *had* to be planning *something*. "I want you guys to stay behind me. Leah has her—" Dexx took a deep breath, "—her magick behind us." Come *on*. He had to show a bit of backbone in front of the zombies.

Dang. They could shift into *anything*. "No wait. I have a better idea." And maybe keep them safe at the same time. "You two, shift into flies or something. Bring back intel. Leah, put as many of your help behind us."

Dexx shifted and got down for Leah to climb up.

Rai and Ember shifted.

One chose a mosquito and the other one turned into a honeybee.

As long as they stayed mostly invisible, he could handle that. He saw them as two sparks of magick, as they zipped down the hallway to an intersection and split.

Something was going on here and Dexx was going to find out what exactly that was.

So, being back home was fun. Like, buckets of it. No, not really.

After Veronica, I really thought Mama Gee would at least want to say goodbye or something.

Nope. She'd just sent me my stuff in several boxes via a door witch.

This was probably the *easiest* move to Alaska ever. I'm just saying. *Moving* to Alaska was a trial. If you could survive that, you *might* be able to survive living here. Maybe.

But I'd been here for, I don't know, a couple of weeks—months. It'd been months, and I was already tired of the pioneer woman spirit and needed just to *make it*.

"Hey," I called, ringing the bell for service at the counter. "Is anyone here?"

Fox and I were out running errands because his truck was working. My car wasn't and Evie's was in use. Bella was at work, so she was using hers, and Gertie's was off limits. So, I'd had him stop by the local car parts store on our way back to the house and was waiting to be served.

This was like the third time that day I'd had to beg to be *seen*.

It hit me in that moment that it'd been the *third* time that day. The...third time. And each of the other times, they'd talked to Fox, giving him the answers to my questions. Once at Lowes and again at Home Depot.

Glaring, I stomped into the frigid snowy parking lot and got Fox's attention.

He looked up in surprise like he was pretending he *hadn't* been about to take a nap. Frowning, he stepped out of the truck. "Everything okay?"

"No." This was really irritating. "I think I need my man to come speak for me. Again."

"What?" His face twisted in disbelief and he shook his head. "I'm sure that's not the case."

No. I was beginning to think it really was.

Sure enough, he walked in and three men appeared from the parts area behind the counter. One of them smiled at Fox and asked, "How can I help you?"

This was stupid.

"She needs a part for her car."

"Ah," the man said as if Fox had brought in his kid and this was some kind of a treat. "What vehicle?"

He still wasn't talking to *me*.

Fox just shrugged. "I don't know. It's her car."

"I need an ignition cylinder for a sixty-six Pontiac Le Mans. It's basically a Tempest, so if you need to look it up that way, do it. It may come up under a GTO because that's the more popular package, but I think in those days GM pretty much did things all the same. You might be able to punch in any old GM from sixty-six, but hey, *you've* got control of the computer.

The man looked back and forth from me to Fox, and then his eyes twitched. "You sure?"

Why was he *still* talking to *Fox*? "Yes, I'm sure." I'd built the damned car.

He looked it up under the vehicle with the information I'd given him and presto. The man's head jerked back in surprise. "We have one in stock." His eyes were wide with shock as he quickly disappeared between the parts shelves.

Lemon was the baby I'd pulled from a junkyard in high school and had built up with Aunt Gertie's help. I'd given my car a personality too, much like Whomper. I'd regretted it a few times, but only a few.

Like when I couldn't get him to start. Guess where I'd put his personality. No. Guess. Yup. You got it. In the ignition. I'd wanted to start him when I was inside on cold days and that worked great. But the key was worn and tired and...just needed to be recut. Seriously. That's all it needed.

But after spending days calling men about a key, I'd been told that none of them could make time to do it because *they* had businesses to run, which...yeah. I got that. We were in the middle of a war and a lot of businesses were shutting down. That was a thing.

But I was trying to *give them business*.

So, I'd decided to just replace the whole damned cylinder because, let's face it, if the key was tired, the cylinder probably was too. I'd have to replace Lemon's personality spell and maybe add on to it. I didn't know. I mean, Lemon was more than just a broom. He could use something more than just an on button.

"Huh." The man returned and finally looked me in the eye. "It's a bit dusty, but we had one. Sometimes the computer's wrong." He blew off the box with a puff of dust flying.

One small step for womankind.

I got my part, but he let me know about the return policy. "We get that a lot, people trying different things out." He shrugged with a smile at Fox. "It's a learning experience."

"Be blessed," I said, taking my ignition and receipt from him and stomping into the snow and ice.

Fox got in and just sat there as if afraid to move. "I'm sorry."

Sorry? He'd been supportive. "If this is going to be my every day, this is going to get real old real fast." And it had been so far.

I'd called to get our internet to go faster. Yeah, okay. I understood we were in the middle of a war and things were going weird and we really didn't know if we were going to have working internet from one day to the next. So, you know, typical Alaska living.

But they'd asked me if my husband could get on the line.

We didn't even have a man *in* our home.

I wanted to move down south so bad, especially thanks to the third *week* of double negative weather—sorry. *Below-zero* weather. I knew—I *knew* we were in for another three months of this shit. At least.

Why?

Because this was f'ing *Alaska*. That's why.

I just didn't remember it being so damned sexist.

Maybe this was because of the war? I didn't know.

If it wasn't for the fact that things were getting better with Charlie and Evie and Gertie, I'd be leaving.

Fox sighed and gripped the steering wheel. "Want to grab a bite to eat?"

We really couldn't. With the supply chain down to a trickle, a lot of the restaurants had been forced to close. I'd have thought the fast-food chains would be the last.

Nope. They'd been the first. The smaller restaurants, those ma-and-pop ones, had fought to stay open longer because they at least had local connections to meat and produce.

But even that was curtailed thanks to the fact that it was *February* in *Alaska*.

We could go to Fred Meyers because it was one of the few stores on the delivery list Paige had been able to negotiate being restocked with the help of the door witches.

This whole damned thing was a mess. Living up here when business was good and things were normal was one thing. When supplies were short and people didn't even have money?

Fox went eerily still.

I didn't know what was going on. I also didn't know how his magick worked, so I gave him a minute. "What's up?"

He shook himself out of it and then looked over at me. "I've gotta go. Can you get a ride?"

Not really. "Sure. Just drop me off at Freddie's."

He started the truck and gave me a look of apology. "I'm sorry."

Yeah, yeah.

Being back home was not nearly as nice and convenient as I'd hoped.

But at least I was reforging connections with my family. That had to count for something. Right?

Something was off.

The place looked like an office building with the dropped ceiling grid and the cubicles. But it was...empty. There were a lot of desks.

No one was at them.

Where had they all gone? What was the place? A research facility? Why would it be abandoned?

Kate, Bobby, and Leah started looking around, searching through the paperwork. The zombies were standing guard, which made things easier.

Dexx sniffed the air. It didn't feel like a trap, really, but it definitely felt...off.

"Hey, Dad," Ember called from up ahead. "You gotta come see this."

Dexx walked farther up the hall and found both the twins in human form. Ember flagged him down and disappeared back into an office as Rai paused and then stepped into another.

"What are you guys doing?" Dexx asked. "I thought you were scouting."

"The coast is clear," Rai said from the office on Dexx's right.

"Yeah," Ember said to Dexx's left. "You gotta see this. I don't think this is DoDO."

Was this something Walton was doing?

On the wall of the office was a circular plaque with a spread-winged eagle and a shield in front of it. Department of Homeland Security was written around the edge.

"Fuck." The ramifications of this swatted at Dexx's head. "Had to be here. They couldn't take you to a black ops, but a regular office building." Looked like the U.S. government had declared war on the Whiskeys personally. That was stupid.

But if that was the case, then where was everyone?

Kammy.

Yeah, the toddler said, but he sounded distracted.

Have you run into anything?

Not really.

Okay. Well, if Walton was declaring personal war on the Whiskeys and the building was basically empty anyway...

Then maybe it was empty because they knew Dexx would be back after discovering they'd taken his kids? And they were scared?

But did that make sense?

It was a stroke to his ego, sure, but no. That didn't make sense. This building could hold hundreds of people, soldiers with guns. They could easily outnumber him. Something else was going on here. But what?

Leslie appeared around the corner, followed by her family. "This place is empty. It's time to leave."

Dexx agreed.

"I got stuff," Ember said, his arms full of papers. "Don't know if it's good, but it's stuff."

That kid had a lot to learn about information gathering, but something tickled at the back of Dexx's neck. Like... "Yeah. Open the door."

Leah concentrated. "I...I'm having trouble. Something is trying to get in the way."

Oh shit. This wasn't good. "DoDO?"

"No, it feels..."

Bobby's eyes glowed gold and he clamped down on Dexx's hand. "Fire."

Dexx didn't know what that meant, but he knew it couldn't be good. "Lee?"

The doorway opened up, but wavered unsteadily. "Go," she shouted. "Hurry."

Dexx pushed Tru and the rest of the kids through, leaving Leslie and him last.

Leah stumbled through as the building jumped, and let the door fade as a concussive sound started at the far end of the hallway, filling with angry fire pushing furnace air in front of it.

"Did we win?" Tyler let a slow smile spread across his face.

Dexx looked around to the family. Everyone was accounted for. "Yes?" But why hadn't that felt like a win?

"Woohoo!" Tyler cheered with a punch in the air.

"Yes, very well done." Merry Eastwood lounged in a chair with a glass of wine. "You're as stupid as they are. Congratulations."

6

L eslie stalked toward Merry. "Get out of my house."
Her eyes burned with orange intensity that bled out
to light her body with a soft orange glow.

"Oh, please. Do calm down," Merry said with no real
concern. She was one hell of an actor. Her scent and her
ready magick said she was terrified of Leslie.

Most smart people were.

"The one person you want here most right now is me."

Somehow Dexx doubted that. "Then you should probably
start talking fast. Had a rough night."

"I know. Your exploits are all over the news. Or they will
be. I assume it *was* you who attacked the federal building in
Pennsylvania?"

Had that whole thing been a set up to allow Walton to
proceed with war? Dexx knew that Paige had been incredibly careful with what she was willing to do, the lengths
she was willing to go to in defending herself and the people
she was now representing. "Who said we even left
the house?"

Merry snorted in surprise. "You might fool the sheriff

with that one, but not me. The entire house was empty and cold until you walked through your portal."

Leslie crossed her arms. "Well, you're half right." Her Texan accent thickened when she was angry, and she had her full drawl on.

"Disappointing. You've been taking lessons from Dexx, I see."

This was getting old. "What are you here for, Merry? Make it quick, then hit the road."

She pressed her lips together. "We have a situation and an opportunity, now that Walton is sure to officially declare the war."

"Shouldn't you be discussing this with Paige?"

"I am waiting for her."

That made no sense. "She's in her office."

"I assure you, she is not."

Hold on. "How did you even hear about what we—"

Paige's assistant or secretary or whatever, Ishmail, poked his head around the door. "Uh, I need to let you know we have a slight situation."

Leslie threw up her hands and headed toward the back of the kitchen.

"But please be assured we have options." The rest of Ishmail's body followed his head in.

Behind him, Dexx felt annoyance rise in Merry.

"What's bad, and exactly what options?" What was going on?

"If you people had *listened* to me, we could have mitigated this." Merry let some of her tone color her words.

Dexx spun on Merry. He very carefully kept his tone even, but his voice still slipped close to a growl. "What did you do?"

Merry's scent spiked, fearful, but she remained cool on the outside. "*I* did *nothing*. If *you* had stayed here, we could have done something more effective. But you decided to avenge your children, who are all perfectly safe."

Was it just him, or did she know an awful lot about what had *just* happened? "Explain."

Tru shooed Kammy toward the stairs and his room. "Yeah. I need a few answers. Like, how do you know what we were up to?"

She shrugged. "I have friends in all sorts of places, gentlemen. I hear things."

"Shut it, Merry." Dexx turned back to Ishmail, realizing they weren't going to get a straight answer out of her. "What's going on?"

Ishmail took a deep breath. He obviously didn't want to go into it. "Okay. So, we have someone claiming to have taken Paige prisoner."

"*How?*" Leslie practically flew back into the living room, going into full interrogation mode. Kids everywhere made up whatever would keep them safest when they heard that tone.

Luckily, Ishmail was made of sterner stuff. "I don't know. As far as information goes, we're still learning. But what we *do* have is—"

Dexx felt Leslie's griffin pushing forward. She wasn't putting up much of a fight.

He pushed them both back and settled them a bit. If things went further downhill, he'd let them both go.

"We don't know much more than that." Ishmail looked pointedly at Merry, his dark eyes narrowed.

"You're going to trade McCormick for her."

No. They weren't.

Ishmail shrugged and looked like he hadn't wanted that information to be revealed just yet.

"I didn't realize we still had him."

"Of course you do," Merry said. "You couldn't just let him go after you told him all your grand plans, now could you?"

But they could now? Dexx turned to Ishmail confused.

Merry turned her eyes back to Dexx. Her scent moved to quiet confidence, but her spells were still ready. "We can't release him or trade him. Not yet. He knows too much and he's proven he's loyal to Walton."

No, the man had proven he was loyal to his country, something Dexx couldn't fault the man for. He was just upset they still had him and he hadn't known about it. "I'm sorry. Were you *asked*?" Dexx tilted his head a fraction and waited.

"I *need* to be consulted. On *everything.*"

Wow. Really? "Who voted you grandmaster rebel leader?" Because *he* didn't trust her. He had *never* trusted her.

"You should. Look at you. Your kids are kidnapped after you take time to get married, you leave on a revenge tour, and then your *brand-new wife* is taken prisoner." Merry raised her chin to look down her nose at him. "If you had to go through me as I've offered many times before, none of this would have happened."

Was this something she'd offered before? And if Merry was making a stand now, that meant Paige had told her no multiple times before.

Also...if Merry *knew* about the kids being kidnapped *and* that Dexx had gone on a *revenge tour*, it meant that she might have been the one to help kidnap the kids while inside the protections of the strongest wards imaginable.

Too many things were starting to add up, and it wasn't looking good for the woman who needed to be behind bars in the first place.

"As it stands, I can help. This isn't the worst thing you've ever done, but now that the world is in such a precarious position, I would strongly advise you not be as reckless in the future."

Dexx turned his back on Merry. If he had to look at her for another five seconds, he'd be looking at two of her. A top half and a bottom half. "So, we have a bargaining chip." Why hadn't he been told about that? When had they started taking prisoners? He put his fear in a little corner in the back of his head. Walton was using DoDO. They knew that because Dawn Flynn had started that. What was it with Paige and teaming up with the enemy like it was nothing, like all things could be forgiven? "How long will it take to get her out?"

Ishmail shook his head. "I can't say for sure, but—"

"What he's trying to say is," Merry interrupted, bringing herself into the lopsided circle, "that there's negotiations involved."

Leslie clenched her jaw but managed to talk through her teeth. "And what do you propose to negotiate with?"

"We wait. Make them come to us. It gives us the upper hand." Merry's scent turned to confidence.

Dexx didn't like that, nor did he like the fact that Merry was taking control of the situation that she was entirely too intimate with. "What are the chances of that actually working?" Dexx pointedly stopped looking at Merry. When she was confident, he had to look for the hook.

"It's a plausible form of negotiating." He nodded, but hesitated. "One I don't necessarily agree with. It might work, but I think they want Paige to be discredited. Take the morale out of ParaWest and the South."

"Sounds about right." Leslie traded her scowl for thinking face. "Walton isn't very forgiving when it comes to our kind. Or *us* in particular."

Merry almost hissed her breath. "He's *not* that kind of politician. He wants to control the country. What he'll do is lord her around a bit and convince everyone to stop these games."

Dexx slowly turned to Merry, making it clear he stood on

the razor edge of shifting. "You think this is just a game? Paige is just a piece? Are you a player or a piece?"

"No. I don't think it's a game, but we have to treat it like one." Merry lost her confident smile and her face slipped. "I'm the same as you are. Trapped and threatened. Just like you." Her smell didn't match, though. She *had* to be up to something.

An alpha approached the front door. Hattie took note but didn't push at Dexx. She knew that she could be a higher alpha.

"Leah, would you get the door?"

Leah looked at the door, then Dexx, confused, then left as someone knocked.

Chuck Deluca followed her into the living room, a look of surprise on his Greek-featured face. "I came with news, but I see you already have it."

"We might. Whuchyou got, we'll compare notes." Too many romcoms had left too much of an impression on Dexx.

Chuck passed a significant look to Merry, and then narrowed his blue eyes up at Dexx.

"Just tell us. Merry's in it up to her eyes, too." But she wasn't telling everything.

The regional high alpha nodded. "Paige was helping Doe lead refugees from Nevada."

"Why would she do that?" Dexx demanded.

"The risk was minimal. They didn't reach the rendezvous spot on time. We know there's new technology that dampens para abilities and we think it's being used. Paige..." Chuck looked uncomfortable. "...might be in trouble."

Dexx turned to Ishmail and sighed. "We need to know if she's been captured, or if they're still fighting and just missed the window. A lot of things could have gone wrong." He didn't want to mention Merry or even acknowledge her.

"And we can't be holding McCormick against his will. Dammit. Let's find a way to get him out of here."

Ishmail nodded and left.

Merry smiled helpfully. "I'll contact my—"

"You'll sit on your thumbs," Dexx growled, pointing for her to take a seat in one of their chairs. "Don't even twitch."

He didn't know what the hell was going on, but he was going to get to the bottom of it one way or another.

Paige couldn't get a clear picture of their attackers as everyone ran for cover. It didn't seem that there was a lot of shooters though. Something wasn't quite right about this. It wasn't strategic, not like DoDO could be. There were too gratuitous with their use of portals or magick. This was just bullets.

But what better way to take out people with magick than with none at all?

"We need scouts," Paige said to Doe as they hid behind a boulder.

Someone else was taking care of the wounded.

Thunder rumbled overhead as the rain began to pour.

Doe looked up at Paige with a confused frown. "We can't shift."

"What do you mean?" They couldn't shift? This *had* to be DoDO somehow, but how? "Can you still communicate with your spirit?"

Doe nodded.

The man beside her shook his head.

Interesting.

Another volley of gunfire filled the air.

"Okay, see if *you* can," Paige said to Doe.

The alpha shook her head, but started disrobing. "If they

can't—" Her shift was easy and within moments, a large wolf stood where Doe had been moments before.

"You were saying?" Paige turned her attention forward. "Tell me what we're looking at."

The wolf said nothing more, running off to the side to circle around.

Paige already knew that magick wasn't a great defense against bullets, but she'd also survived Lawrence by using magick. She just had to get creative.

Last time, she'd sent the agents to hell. The demon queen Mavofne hadn't appreciated that, but if it had worked the one time...

Paige edged closer, trying to get a look at their attackers to see how many she needed to corral through the doors.

But these guys wore camouflage, not the normal DoDO black.

Was it possible that these guys were just locals trying to hunt them down?

Well, crap. Did that mean she *couldn't* send them to hell if that was their only choice?

No. To hell with that, no. They were shooting at her. She could kill them with air, water, earth, or fire. Or she could send them to hell. Those were the skills she had.

So, she started with air since fire really had been a bad idea in Lawrence. It'd seemed a bit like overkill watching the replay, though at the time, the only thing she'd felt was that it had been necessary to not die.

A few shouts told her that the wind wasn't appreciated, so she kept it up, swirling it around the area the gunfire seemed to be coming from. She'd only been able to see two of them.

Doe came running back in wolf form and shifted into human, crouching next to Paige naked. "There are only fifteen of them. They're heavily armed, and two of them are only boys. They're not professional."

Militiamen, then? But how had they gotten their hands on a device that could keep shifters from shifting? "Stay here." Paige whipped up some water to add to the wind she was throwing at the men and crept away from the boulder.

Doe stopped her and shook her head. "You can't do this."

"*This* is the whole reason *I* came. Who else can?"

Doe shook her head again, but she let go of Paige's arm.

Released, she made her way up the hill, staying behind cover. She saw where the weapons were, stashed in the back of an old body style red Ford truck.

She called on the earth to open up and swallow it.

A few of the men yelled out, running toward it, spraying the air with bullets on their way to…

Fight the soil for their truck back? She didn't think so.

The earth also opened up, grabbing on to their ankles and holding them in place.

Paige waited until they were out of ammunition, which took a while. Their truck might be gone, but they were wearing enough ammunition and guns to outfit a small army. Or only a few militiamen.

With most of the men contained within the force of the earth, she relaxed the air and wind pummeling them and stepped out from behind her hiding tree.

The man in front dropped his rifle to hang from his body sling and pulled out a knife, but his feet were still sucked into the soil. It wasn't like she was going to accidentally get stupid enough to get close to that. He could try throwing it, she guessed.

She didn't want to tempt fate though, so she hit him with a fist of wind, knocking the knife out of his hand.

He looked up at her and glared. "Get off our lands, witch!"

Clever. "That's what we're doing. Just let us by and we won't bother you again."

"You're trespassing," one of the two boys spat. "We can do whatever we want to you for trespassing."

"This isn't Montana, kid," Paige told him. "Castle law only affects your home or your car, not your land." She actually didn't know what the gun law was in that state or if any of those laws even mattered anymore. "We're just passing by."

"You're a bunch of freaks," the lead guy said angrily. "You shouldn't even be allowed to live."

"You're as illegal as they come, freak!" another shouted.

Well, they were being subdued, so Paige gestured to Doe to start moving her people forward.

There was movement in the trees behind her, so she assumed they'd continued their march.

"Are you working with anyone?" Paige asked the leader.

He just stared up at her from under the bill of his camouflage baseball cap. "I don't have to tell you nothing."

That's right. He really didn't.

But she didn't have to restrain the earth from wanting to reclaim his body either. Not that the earth really cared, but...

He slipped a few more inches into the ground as if he was in quicksand.

He let out a shriek and the others yelled out for her to stop.

She shrugged. "Are you working with anyone?"

He glared.

She smiled and invited the earth to take the group just a little closer to her bosom.

"Fine!" The man put his hands on the ground as if that would stop him. He was in over his knees. "There was a man. Came by and said we might need to use this box, that it'd keep your kind from infecting our lands."

"Where's the box?"

"I ain't—" He stopped when he went into the earth up to his hips. "Hot dammit! Stop! It's back there." He waved his hand in a general direction behind them. "By that tree."

Paige gestured for someone to go check it out and heard footsteps trekking through the forest floor.

"You will never get away with what you're doing," the leader snarled.

She was sure. "Did you find it?" she called. "Should be a black box."

"Yeah," a male voice called back. "Found it."

"Well, turn it off, grab it, and let's go!"

Doe stepped up next to her fully dressed. "What do you intend to do with them?"

Paige shook her head. "Nothing. When we've passed, they can dig themselves out and go home."

"That's more than they would give us."

"Agreed." Paige met the leader's gaze. "But we can't allow ourselves to be the animals they are."

"We're not animals." He looked at Paige in disgust. "You are."

"We weren't the ones shooting at children," Doe said hotly, her eyes lit with an inner fire.

He pulled an ugly face. "I just see mongrels that need to be taken out before they turn."

Doe clenched her fists, ready to strike out.

Paige took the alpha's shoulders and propelled her forward. "Lead your people to safety."

Doe shook her head.

"Go," Paige said tightly.

They'd miss their rendezvous window, but at least they were all relatively safe. She just had to make sure these yahoos didn't do something else stupid. She let the air out of every tire on the old truck.

And when she got home, she was taking a long bubble bath.

But not before she got that device into someone's hands to study. They needed a defense against it and fast.

DoDO knew how to take away the greatest paranormal strength. Without that, Paige's growing force wouldn't amount to much. And that was something they couldn't afford.

7

B y noon, Dexx was shown proof that DoDO had Paige and an exchange deal was made. By mid-afternoon, Dexx drove the donated black Suburban to the rendezvous where they'd get Paige and release McCormick. Walton was pretty keen on getting him back, which Dexx understood. He just didn't understand why Paige had allowed them to keep him detained for so long. It'd been months since General Saul had come on board.

The general was in the back, but so far had been closed mouthed. McCormick had a knack for taking it all in and being even-keeled through it all.

Maybe it was because McCormick's kidnapping experience was nicer than Dexx's had been. "Remember, if your guys do anything bad to Paige, you go, too."

"I understand. This isn't my first rodeo, son," McCormick said like a true soldier.

Dexx *hated* when they did that. "I'm not your son, pops. Look, as far as I'm concerned all of you can go rot on your piles of high-power politicians."

"I didn't mean to insult you." McCormick held a hand up,

gently surrendering. "There are plenty of factions in the States. Just because I'm with the government I swore my allegiance to doesn't mean I agree with everything they do."

"It's a bunch of bullshit. People are people. And remember, *you* shot first. We're here because you went all herd mentality and stampeded."

McCormick sighed heavily. "Mistakes were made. I do not and will not speak for them."

"I was always fine with 'you do you.' You tell your people to stay the fuck away from us, and things will stay fine. Invade another state, and we're gonna brawl."

"I understand."

That seemed to be the end of the conversation.

They pulled onto the tarmac of a small airport at the edge of the disputed lands in Nebraska. A plane sat alone on the runway.

A train of military personnel drove in from the far side and parked in an obvious display of overt force.

A bad feeling settled in his stomach.

You ready if they try anything? Hattie was always ready, but he liked to hear her, and know she was close.

I am. Hattie didn't feel like talking. She was amped to get Paige back too.

The train kept coming and seemed to have no end. But finally, they did in a semi-circle around and behind the little charter jet.

Dexx got out and opened the door for the general. They stood together for the exchange.

The door on the jet popped open and two suits in dark sunglasses came out and stood on either side of the steps.

A man stepped out of the plane and adjusted his tie, taking the first step off the plane.

A portal opened and Paige stepped through, followed by Derrick, who closed it behind him. She frowned and headed toward Dexx, her hand extended on either side of her, her magick on hand.

What the hell? "They didn't fucking have her?"

McCormick raised his eyebrows and then frowned but said nothing.

"What the hell is going on here?" Paige demanded when she got within hearing distance.

The man who had been debarking from the plane paused, but then continued, walking a little slower as he assessed the situation.

Dexx had no fucking clue. "They said they had you."

"Well, they didn't. McCormick," she said with a nod to the general.

He nodded back.

"You didn't tell me we were keeping prisoners," Dexx said under his breath.

She shrugged apologetically. "What was I supposed to do? He has sensitive information."

Why didn't she seem more apologetic? "So...are we giving him back?"

If the Federalists had any tricks, their window was rapidly closing.

As things stood, the million-man army had arrived all dressed up in gear and swinging big guns around. They actually looked pretty cool. But the swarm of suits looked like bags of dicks waiting for their douche.

Paige shook her head.

The man from the plane stopped halfway.

Paige crossed her arms over her chest and looked at him.

He gave a cool look, glanced at all the men around them, and continued forward. "You will hand over McCormick."

"Hmm," Dexx said, watching his wife like he didn't know her. "Will we?"

"You will."

"I don't think so," Paige said.

The man smiled and gestured with one hand.

Two men brought in a big black box and it down on the tarmac. It glowed red underneath and gave off a soft hum.

Paige hid her yawn behind her hand and then smiled at the man with the tie. "We kinda already met that thing once. We've got one, actually. We're tearing it apart as we speak."

"But you can't shift."

She gave him a scared look and the wind whipped around them. "I think you'll find I don't need to. I'm kinda scary on my own."

Dexx didn't want to be outdone. He allowed Hattie to move forward a little and growled low.

The man's eyes grew wide in alarm.

The military guys snapped up their guns, but nobody fired.

Dexx tensed, searching for the best place to attack first if they so much as twitched out of line.

McCormick turned to her and sighed. "Let me go."

She didn't move.

"I have a family."

"So do we," Dexx said, Hattie still in his throat.

The man just looked at them both and nodded. He then turned his back to the man in the tie and faced Paige and Dexx. "I'm loyal to my country."

Dexx took a step forward. "It's time you start figuring out what that means. You're on the wrong side."

McCormick shook his head.

Paige tipped her head to the side and looked at the man in the tie before turning her attention back to McCormick. "I was going to let you go soon anyway. I can't have you telling them our secrets."

"My *loyalty*," he said carefully, "is to my *country*."

She nodded in understanding.

Dexx didn't. "Are you going to rat us out or not?"

Paige took in a deep breath and announced to the douche bags in the suits, "You have five minutes to be outside the boundaries or you will be taken as prisoners of war, okey dokey? Have a lovely day."

Dexx didn't understand why they had kept McCormick as a prisoner for so long only to give him back so quickly. But if everyone had five minutes to clear out, that meant they needed to as well. "Come on, babe. Get in the car. It's warmer in there."

The general gathered the man in the tie, and they walked to the plane. The engines whined to life before the stairs were raised and the door was closed.

Soldiers filed into troop carriers and drove away as fast as the things would move them.

Dexx opened the rear door for her and closed it after she got in.

Derrick let himself into the back seat.

Dexx got in on the other side and sat next to her. "So, before we go any further here, I just want to say I'm over the top with you being home. I don't have a word for it, but you being back is…way good."

"I wasn't…gone." Paige shook her head.

"You, um… You look pretty pissed off." Everything about her said she was way past that. Her scent, her body language, the magick that peeked out randomly.

She shook her head. "I don't understand what happened while I was gone. But we need to get out of here. So, let's go home."

Derrick opened a portal for the Dexx to drive through that cut down on a lot of drive time between Nebraska and Trout-dale and he didn't stick around long when Dexx pulled up in front of the Whiskey house. Paige waited until they were walking up the steps before asking for the full story.

He gave it as quickly as he could.

"Merry was behind this," Dexx said. "But why?"

Paige narrowed her eyes in thought. "To get McCormick back to Walton?"

"Because she's going to get something out of Walton?"

"He's not going to get anything out of McCormick." She sounded pretty sure of that.

But how? "Of course he's going to—"

"Didn't you hear him, babe?" Paige watched as the old police cruiser Red Star had inherited from Sheriff Tuck rolled up the driveway. "He's loyal to his country, not the people running it."

Dexx didn't think that was going to hold McCormick's tongue. "I hope you're right."

"Me, too."

Frey sat in the passenger seat, but was the car driving itself?

No, the top of a head bobbled just above the steering wheel. It looked like Joel the goblin had somehow talked her into letting him drive.

The car stopped and Frey's door popped open, but Joel made furious movements from the driver's seat and the door closed again.

Joel leapt out and ran around the car to open the door for Frey.

She got out with a tight smile and walked toward Dexx, Joel to her side and a half step back. That was new.

"We've been in contact with Hawaii and Alaska," Frey said, shaking her head as if wondering why she was there sharing the message. "And they intend on joining the Confederate States."

"Fuck," Paige groaned.

"They're going to break with us?" That *was* news. Para-West was in a precarious spot with so many states jumping ship. Dexx didn't even understand the political plays of power, but he knew things were looking grim for their plight.

"Why would they do *that*? The Southern states don't like paras much more than the Federalists."

"Military backing," Paige grumbled and shook her head. "We've got to find a way to support them, or everyone will be leaving before this can get started." She sighed and headed toward the office.

Dexx stopped her. "There's a whole house of people who thought you'd been taken hostage. You should go let them know you're safe."

"I was never in trouble."

"We didn't know that."

She rolled her eyes and disappeared into the house.

"So," Dexx asked, "Why are you here?"

Frey crossed her arms and hid her significant look at Joel.

Dexx looked at Frey, then Joel. Oh. Oh!

"Gotcha. Okay, thanks for the info. You guys want to come in?"

"No, I've got to get back. Scout's taking over in about an hour, and I want to get the turnover sheets in order."

"Shouldn't be a problem, boss lady." Joel tilted his head up to Frey. "You always do the best job. Really don't even need to. *I* can do them for you."

Dang. Frey had her very own goblin. "Glad to see some stability in the shop. Did anyone hear from Michelle today?"

Michelle had gone back to her grove after the trip into the Time Before and hadn't been seen by anyone since.

"No word. We may be looking for a new detective." Frey pressed her lips together. She didn't want another person on the force. She'd told Dexx several times since the new team had joined, but the rifts were mostly gone. Scout and Frey weren't quite *friends*, but they weren't adversaries anymore and that was a step in the right direction.

"She'll come back when she's ready. Just keep her desk warm." Dexx wouldn't kick her off the force. If they all died of old age and Michelle went back a year after, the job would still be open for her. She'd risked a lot to get Dexx back. And he'd do the same for her.

"Can do. I have to ask, though." Frey frowned and lifted her chin. "Is it bad?"

The whole world seemed to be bad. On fire or worse. "It's bad enough."

"Think we'll win?" That was a strange question from Frey.

Joel rolled his shoulders like he was limbering up to box. "Of course we'll win, boss lady. Nobody can outfight you. I don't think even the captain could. Not with your—"

Ew. The little guy was pouring it on kind of thick. "Good call. Just keep that attitude. Should be easy."

Frey turned to the cruiser, took two steps, with Joel right on her heels, then spun back to Dexx. "Almost forgot."

Joel stopped in his tracks, way inside Frey's bubble.

Frey glared at him, and then pushed him aside. "Texas just invaded Oklahoma. We don't know how they're doing, yet."

"Dammit, you could have led with that."

"Too much shit falling around our ears for me to keep up with it all. But Texas is going for more ground. I hope they do well. The less the Federalists have, the better."

Sure, unless they got desperate. Then the Federalists might do something *really* stupid. "Let's hope they take the heat from us for a while."

Frey pursed her lips and nodded. "Let's hope. You're out for the rest of the day, right? See your tomorrow."

Dexx turned back to the house and remembered he had a honeymoon he hadn't yet gotten to enjoy.

———

Frey sat at her desk finishing the turnover notes for Scout. The harpy wasn't a bad person, not really.

At least Frey could relate to her story. Always passed over by men who had less experience or had friends in management or higher rank. Scout was actually pretty good as a detective and police officer. Just like Frey, and they both were ambitious enough to let it get them into trouble. Not that Frey would admit that out loud.

Joel had taken over Rainbow's desk after she'd died. So, he had the first desk that people would walk by through the bullpen. Paige had altered the growth around the desk to be more to Joel's liking. His preference was cactuses and weed plants. The stuff that didn't die easily.

So, his desk looked more like an abandoned yard than a workstation.

Frey liked ferns and mosses herself.

She moved her stack of papers to the corner of her desk and sat back. She'd come a long way, and eventually she would have the department, Scout or no. She had the seniority, and she'd fight for the top spot when it came her turn.

The phone rang.

Frey stared at it like it was possessed. That thing hadn't worked for months. It rang again and she snapped the headset to her ear. "Red Star, this is Frey Van Sant."

"Dexx Colt." The voice was an older male, with an accent she recognized instantly. "Bring him to me." This was the bastard who had experimented on her and Tarik.

"No, you son of a bitch. Where are you?"

"I remember you. We had a connection."

"Yeah, we did. Where are you?" She could slice that head off as easily as any others. She'd be in line for that promotion within a flat second.

"Follow your heart. I know you want to come back to me."

"Sure. Just tell me where and when."

Joel gave her a screwed-up look of confusion. "Who is that?" he whispered.

Frey made shooing motions.

"You might work to bring Dexx out. I am at the edge of your wards. They mean little, but I could not break them without someone feeling it."

"Sure, pal. Edge of the wards. That's a lot of—" Frey felt something. A pull, a yearning.

She took a hold of the pull and crushed the part that *yearned*. She gripped the rest and used it as a tether.

She hung up. "You stay here. Tell Scout I'm on a call. Do *not* follow me. Understood?"

"Your secret's safe with me. You can tell me anything and I would take it to my grave. Scout's honor."

"Scout? No, never mind. Just stay here."

"Sure. I got your back. Front, too, if you want." Joel smiled, his lip pulling up from his tooth.

"I got the car. I'll be back." She left Joel in the bullpen waiting for the next shift to arrive.

Turned out, she didn't have to really let the tug bring her to that son of a bitch.

He was right where DoDO liked to turn people away from the city.

The old man stood in red robes, hunched over and looking like a grandfather. Just a kindly old man.

Frey parked inside the wards and got out. "You're in the wrong place. But since you're here, I suppose I'll just take out the trash."

The old man chuckled. "Are you sure you would not like to join me again? The power I could show you is great."

"Nope. Fool me once, shame on you. Fool me twice…"

"Then, I see it's shame on you." The old man tore and shifted, screams of pain and torment echoed off the embankment.

In a few seconds the demon stood, fire dancing along his mane and horns and lightning dancing from his eyes.

Bahlrok.

This demon was the only one she ever remembered getting away from her, the only one she'd decided to kill that had remained standing. She pulled her sword from the dimension sheath and readied herself.

"You are brave, but in the end not good enough." The demon held his hand out palm up. A swirling black and red ball of liquid malevolence glowed in his hand.

Frey took a step forward and began the opening move from ready stance.

She began the backward sweep as the Bussemi-demon brought his arm back to hurl the ball.

"*Stop.*" The earth reverberated with the sound.

Frey froze in place.

The balhrok stopped moving. "*You.*" He spat the word but didn't move.

This is not yet your time. The air turned a golden color as a figure floated into view. A woman that looked very familiar, but she couldn't place her. *This is not your time and you will stop hostilities.*

Frey couldn't move yet, but the woman had floated perfectly into view.

"This *is* my time, my world, and you don't belong here anymore." The bahlrok snarled and shook, but he still didn't move.

Yet you will cease. You will move on until your time. The woman turned to Frey. *This is not your fight. You will go and will not seek this battle again.*

She couldn't move. "I choose this fight. Don't stop me or I'll come for you, too."

You will not seek me out. The woman turned to the demon. *Be gone until the right time.* She raised a hand and the Bussemi-demon vanished.

Frey was released and she could move. "What the hell? I could have taken him."

You would not have survived the encounter.

Fuck! Frey remembered where she remembered the woman from. That was Rainbow's ex-girlfriend, Molly. "I know you. Why would you stop me? Didn't she mean anything to you?"

None know me. I serve. With a flash, the woman disappeared. And so did the rest of the roadway.

Somehow she'd been transported back to the precinct with the car in its parking spot.

Scout stopped halfway in the door and stopped at Frey's sudden appearance. "Frey? What the hell?"

"Helvete!"

8

Dexx eyed Frey for the thousandth time. She had seen *Molly Hammond* send Bussemi away like undercooked fish? "Molly Hammond. Cute. Blonde. Interested in girls. An FBI agent? We're on the same page here, right?"

"Yes, Dexx. For a hundred and twenty-three times, *yes*. Molly Hammond, who you haven't seen in the four months since Rainbow died. *That* Molly Hammond."

Damn. Dexx tapped his lip with a finger. "You say she said she *served*?" She'd said something very similar another time. When he'd first met her. He had just as many questions about it then as he did now.

"Call up the office. Get her down here."

Turned out getting an agent from the FBI, and the one agent they were looking for, wasn't that easy now that the FBI was about as broken as the rest of the country was.

First, they had to get the office to answer a call. After that, the agent they requested to talk to had to answer, then be convinced to come down to the station.

But in the end...

Molly stood in the bullpen, her arms crossed, with her partner hanging back a bit. "Captain Colt-Whiskey. I thought my refusal to talk would have been enough for you. Rainbow said you weren't all that bright."

"She wha—? No, she didn't."

"How would you know? You never treated her like a real person. Not like a real law enforcement officer, anyway."

Damn. She let go with both barrels.

"I didn't ask you to come down to talk about old friends and regrets." At least not in front of everyone else. "If you would like to talk in the office?"

"No. What you have to say to me you can say right here."

Really? Okay. "How did you get Bussemi to stop his rampage?"

Molly's face lost the scowl. "In your office, then." She walked right passed him into his office.

Oh. So now she wanted to talk in the office. Dexx shut the door gently when he entered.

She started as soon as the door shut. "I don't know who you've been talking to, but whatever they said was wrong."

Sounded maybe like it was *exactly* as he was told. "So maybe you'd like to set the record straight?" He raised his eyebrows in question. In his years, he'd never gotten a woman to talk when she didn't want to. And Molly looked like all she wanted was to get Dexx to never talk about what he'd heard.

"I don't know who you talked to. But it's not—"

"Not what? What I think? Are you saying you *didn't* stop Cardinal Bussemi and Frey from fighting? You *didn't* teleport Frey *and* the cruiser back here and then disappear? What part do I have wrong? I'll be happy to set my source right."

Molly worked her mouth for a few moments, then she let her breath out. "I—your source isn't wrong. And *nobody* knows. Not even my parents. Bow knew as much as anyone ever has, and that's not much."

This sounded promising. "All I want to know is if you can stop a bahlrok, why didn't you do that before? Or Sven? Hell, you could have stopped *this* whole war before it started. Hell, if you can stop him, you could be the leader of this movement."

"And here's what *everyone* says. Do this. Do that. All that power and you just let us...fill in the blank." She shrugged and pressed her lips together. "I don't know who or *what* I serve. I don't even know when I *am* serving. Vague images are what I'm left with. Time stops for me. I don't know what I do, generally, or the power I have. I have a few eyewitness accounts of things I've done. That's it. So, when I say I can't help you, or *anyone*, I mean it."

"You don't even know what kind of para you are?"

She looked disgusted. "No."

"And nobody knows you are one?" That put her in a very exclusive club.

"Nobody who can get me in trouble." She gestured around her, vexed. "Though, now I'll have some explaining to do."

"Are there more of you?"

"I don't know. I don't know what I am."

Hell of a thing to be. No control of your own body. No control of when or if that control would be relinquished. And the worst part was being a part of a thing so powerful? It needed a human host. Better her than him. Hattie was enough. Plenty.

But he needed away to *stop* Bussemi. For good.

Dexx had to be delicate with his question. Maybe. "Is there any way to get in touch with your...benefactor?"

"None that I know of, but if you'd like to show me how, I'm all ears."

Okay. Not delicate enough. "Yeah. I just want to know what you are. Seems to be such a waste of an ally—"

"*You* don't know anything about it. What it is, or *who*. I could be serving a demon a thousand more times more powerful than *Satan*. You ever think about that?"

Dexx rubbed his face to hide his grin. "No. I haven't." Dexx put his serious face back on but rode the edge of laughter. A thousand times more powerful than Satan. That was funny.

"Is that all you wanted to talk about?"

He *wanted* a solution. "I think so."

"Here I was worried that you wanted to talk about, oh, I don't know, how you let Rainbow die."

His humor left. Dexx didn't have magick anymore. He stood straight, and Hattie slipped past his hold. Or maybe he just didn't want to hold her back. "When you've walked a mile in my shoes, I'll let you ask that. If you want to go toe to toe with me and see if the guy you *serve* saves you, keep on pushing."

"Forget it. What would you know anyway? Did you even care? She looked up to you like the sun rose and set with you. I thought I had to compete with you for her and she didn't even swing your way. How am I supposed to feel about that?"

Dexx felt like shit. Even without Molly digging at him.

She obviously had unresolved feelings.

"I never got to say goodbye. Never had the chance to see if we had something real. So, what would you know?"

"I knew she was my friend and I'd almost burn the world to get her back. I knew that she was special, and the world is a little darker without her in it. That's what I know."

Molly's eyes filled with tears, but she hardened her face. "Don't call me again." She walked out and gathered her partner up without slowing down.

Damn. He probably could have handled that better. "Sorry, Bow. I tried to keep you clear." Really, he had tried.

He sat down hard in his office chair. How many more ways could the day fuck up?

There was a soft knock on the door.

He'd *had* to ask. He really didn't want company. At all.

"Busy." He called out through the door. "Go away."

The knock came again, and it opened before he had a chance to answer.

Frey pushed the door open, then half closed it behind her. "Someone's here to see you."

"Can they leave a message? I don't want to talk to anyone else today." He made shooing motions at the door. He could *actually* do some paperwork.

"She says you want to talk to her." Frey raised half her lip in semi-confusion.

"If it's not Paige, then probably not." But if it was Merry freakin' Eastwood, he could take some aggression out on her.

"She seemed...insistent." Frey twitched a look to the other side of the door.

"Can I get some peace, I—"

The door opened and the tiny old Russian lady came tottering in. Annelle Rovoski. "Mr. Vhiskey, I think it is time we talked." Her accent had Russian hints. The accent was pretty cool. Soft and confident and...old.

"It's *not* Whiskey. Who told you it was?"

"Nobody. I just assumed..."

Why would anyone assume that? Wasn't he the husband? "Well, you know what assuming does. Now, why are you here, outside of insulting me?" This had better not be a cat up a tree, or a tear in the bottom of her change purse and she couldn't get the coins out or something else just as stupid.

"I believe we have someone in common. You knew her as Rainbow."

Well, *that* wasn't a faulty change purse mystery. He was glad he was already sitting. "You knew her? Rainbow?"

"I did. But not by that name. You see, she vas my grand-daughter."

Uh. He wasn't a geneticist or anything, but this lady was Russian and...well, Russian. Rainbow had been...not. "Are you—are you sure? She never said she had any living relatives." The most she'd ever talked about had been her grandmother, and she hadn't gone into detail.

"She vas indeed my family. Annika vas a lovely girl."

"When was the last time you saw her?" Dexx's head was in a tailspin.

"I last saw her just before she disappeared and became a fugitive."

"Whoa, hold on. There's a lot to unpack there. She wasn't a fugitive, and she didn't disappear. She—" What could he say that didn't make him look like he was directly responsible for her death? "She was one of my best friends. I respected the hell out of her."

"As did I. *E na staroohu bivayet prarookah.* Even a grandma can make mistakes."

"Sure. I do two wrong things before I get out of bed to keep the count right."

"You know Russian proverbs?" Annelle tilted her head to the side.

"No, but I've known people that talk in riddles. I picked it up."

"You have a talent."

Dexx tapped his thumb against his desk. "Look, I'd like to trade old wisdom all day, but is there something you want-ed?" Two talks about Bow in one day? He was going to need a beer or six when he got home.

"Just that I offer my services. Annika always spoke fondly of you."

She did? Damn, he wished he could have her around just to talk to. She had the dual quality of exasperating him while amusing him.

But there was something about this old woman that... He didn't know. She just made him feel like there was more going on behind her old looks than met the eye. "What services would those be?" Could she possibly cook as well as Alma?

"Are you sure you knew little Annika? Are you aware she had powers?"

"I *was* aware. Were *you* aware she knew what she was but was ashamed of it?"

Annelle blinked several times before she answered. "I vas suspicious. She left home very young, and—"

"So, what exactly did you want to offer?" Dexx needed those beers *now*.

"I am vealthy as you see things. And I am a rusalka. I can be of use to you."

"You're not going to fight. DoDO might seem like a bunch of pushovers, but they really aren't. Thanks, but no thanks." He really didn't want to be responsible for *two* of Rainbow's family's deaths.

Annelle Rovoski held her hand out, palm up. Water drew out of the air and pooled in a blobby bubble above her palm.

"Shit." He widened his eyes in surprise. Rainbow had excellent control over the water, but not like this.

"I am not so feeble as I look, yes? But I am not young like I used to be. I vish to fight. Vith the loss of two states from the Vestern pact, I vould say you need all the force you can muster. Am I close?"

She wasn't wrong. "Look. It doesn't matter what I want or need. I cannot and will not put you in harm's way. Sorry." He wasn't sending another woman to her death.

"You drive a hard bargain. I vill call on you tonight. I

believe your family likes to entertain, do they not? I vill come and ve vill meet. Then after the night is over, I vill ask again, and if you refuse, I vill...not ask again."

"No, I'm not going to—"

Annelle's features changed. She went from old and wrinkly to old, wrinkly, and dead. Her silver-white hair darkened a touch and went lank and slimy. Her eyes darkened past the eye sockets and her mouth went black. "Entertain me for dinner tonight."

Dexx felt his head nod. "Yeah. Dinner." His voice sounded slow and sleepy. Damned rusalkas, he was going to—

"Thanks so much for coming to dinner." Dexx greeted Annelle Rovoski at the door to the Whiskey house in the cold February breeze. "Pea, we have a dinner guest," he called over his shoulder.

Wait. What the hell had just happened?

Paige walked out of the kitchen wiping her hands on a towel. "Dinner guest? I didn't know we were having anyone over."

"I told you...didn't I?" Dexx scrunched up his brows. He didn't even remember coming home.

"Mrs. Vhiskey." Annelle held her hand out for Paige. But not the normal shake. She held her hand out like she was royalty waiting for her rings to be kissed.

Paige took the dead-fish handshake in style and gripped her fingers lightly. "So glad you could join us, even if Dexx didn't let me know." She passed a glance at him that promised words later.

His vision wavered as the old woman passed him. A hazy memory passed in front his eyes, telling an old woman to go home and stay there while others did the fighting.

Fucking rusalkas.

Dexx passed a thought to Hattie. *Didn't think to* warn *me? That I'd been bamboozled by* another *rusalka?*

I was not aware of trickery. Hattie seemed curious.

Well, keep your eyes and ears open. I smell a rat.

The old woman didn't eat very much. But she told interesting stories, entertaining the kids.

They all showed her tricks and demonstrations. Dexx and Paige let their kids at least put on a good show. Leslie and Tru seemed to be focused on a disagreement brewing between the two of them. Tyler couldn't be stopped and he put on a *spectacular* show of singing and voice acting with different characters and a real plot. It was half romance and half coming-of-age story, but he did it well.

Finally, Annelle rose from her spot at the table. "I must leave soon, but have you thought over my request?"

Dexx looked up at her. "What request?"

"My dear, are you losing touch with reality so soon? My request to help in the fight against oppression and tyranny. Ve vould *never* have put up with it in the old country as long as you have here."

"Um, didn't I already say no?" He was sure he had. It felt right.

"You said to come to dinner. And ve'd talk it over then."

Nah. He wouldn't do that. Would he? "Well, it's not up to me. I'm just the police captain, and not much for fighting."

Annelle narrowed her gaze at him. "Somehow I don't believe you." She turned to Paige. "If I give you an important piece of information, vill you allow me to fight in the war?"

Paige sighed heavily and looked over at Dexx like he was losing it. "It would have to be a big piece that we didn't already know. And then we'd have to discuss it. So, what do you got?"

"The Federalist government is invading Kansas. And the elves are fighting alone."

Okay. Look. I get that I can get pretty uppity and frustrated about some...petty stuff. Like the fact that my entire wardrobe was absolutely useless in Alaska. Right? Like, all the clothes I loved to wear? Couldn't, unless I enjoyed freezing to death. There was no sense in wearing makeup or doing my hair or wearing fun clothes.

But that new ignition switch worked just like I thought it would. And all I'd really needed was a key.

And I realize that the two things didn't go together logically for anyone else, but for me, they did. They were two very good reasons why I didn't want to be in Alaska. Leaving the first time had been one of the best things I'd ever done.

I was serious about leaving, about going back to the Lower Forty-Eight, or whatever they were going to be called now. I mean, I had no idea.

I was, however, more than a little surprised to see myself at Charlie's door, knocking to be let in.

"Yeah," she called from the floor at the foot of the loft bed.

I tiptoed in like I was disturbing her sacred space. I mean, I kinda was. This was her safe space, her bedroom.

She was sprawled out on a couch of pillows watching something on her laptop. She looked up with a smile. "Hey, Wy. What's up?"

"I, um—" Had no idea what I was doing there.

She blinked and then took out her headphones. "Yeah?"

"Would you come south with me?" I blurted out.

She recoiled and shook herself. "What?"

I had *no idea*. "I, um..." I frowned, not sure what I was even saying. Or thinking. "Living here is stupid hard."

"Uh, okay?"

"And I was thinking that after all this is done and blown over that maybe you and I could start over somewhere."

"Like where?" she asked, taking her headphones off completely and scooting up to a sitting position.

I had thought *none* of this through. "I don't know. Oregon? It's kinda like here, only nicer because there are stores there."

"There are stores here."

"You…" It was obvious this poor girl had never left the state. "…have no idea. And there's…" Shoot. What else. "Schools?"

"We have those here."

And they did. I was losing this. "Opportunities." I closed my eyes and shook my head, realizing what was really getting to me. "If you stay here, you'll be someone's wife making someone's babies. That's…all that's offered for us here."

"No, it's not."

"Yeah. It is." I closed my eyes and replayed all the names of all the people I'd gone to school with. The girls were all married, some several times, with several kids, and very few had jobs, much less careers.

"Evie and Bella aren't."

"Evie and Bella are the exceptions," I said clearly. "They're not the rule. Like, you don't even understand the programming going on right now. The—how many times are you completely looked over? In public?"

Charlie shook her head and looked away with a sigh. "Wy." She released a frustrated breath. "You walk around with this everyone-owes-me vibe. Everyone says it. I've noticed it too. Like, no one wants to deal with that. I'll be fine. I've *got* a plan. I'm *going* to succeed and I'm *not* running away from home."

A belch escaped me, ripping through the room.

"Nice," she said, dismissing me. "Run away if you have to, because that's what you do. But that's not me."

I walked out of her room feeling defeated when I hadn't even had a purpose entering it. She was right on one hand.

But I was right on the other. She didn't understand how much *easier* it was in other parts of the country.

I stopped at the door to my room and rubbed my eyebrow. How much did I care, though, and how far was I willing to take this?

I didn't know. And that scared the crap out of me. I was starting to care a crap-ton for a kid who didn't even want me to exist.

Yet.

She didn't want me to exist in her lift...*yet*. I could change that.

9

Dexx's first reaction was to do something bad to the Russian woman. Like remove a limb or separate her head from her body. The entire sequence ran through his mind in stunning detail. Instead, he carefully lowered his eyes to the table, seething.

"Why wouldn't you lead with that?" Paige rose from the table. "How long?"

Annelle brought a finger to her lips, making a show of thinking it over. "Four days. Maybe five. No more than that, I think. Neither side is doing very well, but the elves are hanging in there."

Paige had told Dexx about the elven queen, and he'd even met her a few months back. She didn't really like humans that much, but she'd treated Paige with at least a little respect.

Dexx didn't like this. "What game are you playing? Why wouldn't you tell us since we *clearly didn't know*?"

"I told you. I vant to fight with you. I vould have explained it all already if you had only let me fight. Annika never had this problem vith you, did she?"

Paige stopped mid-retort. "Annika? Who's Annika?"

Damn. It. He'd forgotten completely, and therefore had never told Paige. "Rainbow. Sorry, Pea. She hit me with a whammy and I forgot all about it until now." Now, he *really* wanted to throttle the old woman. "This is Rainbow's grandmother. She came into the station today, asking to be put in the fight. I told her no. Then she hit me with the rusalka-flashy-thingy." The *Men in Black* had a more technical name for it, but Dexx's head had a different train running.

"She's not fighting."

"That's what I said."

"Okay." Paige turned away from him as Ishmail came up to them.

Leslie stood and began to gather kids up.

Tyler in particular began protesting, but Leslie shot him the *mom* look and he quieted.

Dexx regarded Annelle as he spoke to Hattie. *Can we trust her, do you think?*

Hattie gave an impression of a shrug. *As much as we can trust any para or rusalka.*

Well, *that* didn't inspire any confidence. On the one hand, paras should be united in their common defense against a clear aggressor. But then they had people like Merry Eastwood, Mario Kester, and Cardinal Bussemi. And like Molly Hammond. At least Annelle Rovoski wanted to fight.

"My Annika knew you vell?" She smiled at Dexx.

He looked away fast but kept her on the edge of his vision. *No need to let her flashy-thing us again.*

Hattie shook her head. *Her kind does not need to see your eyes to work her magick.*

Maybe. But every time he'd been hit by one, they'd been looking right at him.

"As well as anyone did, I suppose." Except for maybe

Molly. But they hadn't been together for long. "She didn't talk about you much. Why is that, do you think?"

"Little Annika was a troubled girl. She...resisted her heritage."

"I'll say. So ashamed of it, it nearly got us killed."

Paige turned, rubbing her head as she shook her head. "Congratulations. You get to fight. You're on the front lines with us."

The old rusalka smiled.

Annelle walked through the hole in the air the Blackman boy tore through space. If she had been able to tear space, she might never have left the motherland.

The night was full dark, and bitter cold to those who felt it. She felt the closeness to the mother currents.

Dexx Colt and his family fanned out, looking for safety. Out in the dark, softly glowing lights marked humans, warm and ready to be harvested.

Annelle felt one of the younglings slip through the hole just before it closed. That boy might not make it.

Bodies from both sides littered the plain between trenches.

A fast-moving *whoosh* sound drew her attention. She pulled strength from the currents and let the explosion of fire, frozen dirt, and metal shards flow around her.

She heard the people behind her shouting for her to get down.

She hadn't walked the world for hundreds of years and not learned a few things, especially about war.

She sent her aura out, calling to the warm dots in her vision.

The dots moved, slowly at first, then with growing speed.

Soldiers, even para soldiers, were only humans. And humans were hers to call forward. And kill.

The water around her and in the air answered her call. It was ice, but that worked as well as the liquid kind, and soon the blue dots winked out, their lives extinguished.

It was easy, too easy. With the ease came satisfaction. She had never been *invited* to kill so many, all at once. There'd been other wars, battles, and disputes, but even then, she had to take some care not to take too many at once. This time she killed as many as her area of effect covered.

Too soon for her, none of the humans lived. For a moment, she considered carrying on and killing the para forces, but they might pull out a trick and stop her somehow. And for right now they were more useful alive.

The Dexx Colt boy was another matter. She wanted him alive to suffer. Annika left her entire life behind for that para.

She had never fully accepted who she was, but after she joined the local police force, she left even more of her heritage behind. And Colt was to blame.

Her anger slipped and she sent a massive plume of magick calling more humans. The first reached her and at her touch she stole their life force. She took a step forward, and then another, until she left a steady stream of the dead behind her like breadcrumbs.

The Colt boy could wait.

A single human could sustain her for a while, but dozens, or soon to be hundreds? Well, that would be a treat for the ages.

But not as much as the Colt boy would be. He was going to be the centerpiece of her collection. The rest of his family would make excellent supporting exhibits. But the Colt boy? Oh, yes. His days were numbered.

She ignored the sounds coming from the cowering paras, concentrating instead on the humans out on the battlefield.

She let herself go, flowing with the currents and calling to the walking dead humans. Her vision shrank to pinpoints, concentrating on the next in line.

On and on they came, sacrificing their lifeforce to the old rusalka. The feel of the dying humans left her giddy. When had been the last time she had felt light with amusement and laughter?

Her first kill.

He'd been an ex-lover currying favor with the local landowners. He'd slipped into her bed, and soon after slipped into her father's holdings. He had left when he'd gotten what he wanted.

Other daughters had suffered as she had.

She'd made it her mission to track him down and make him suffer as she had.

She'd almost failed. Through sheer cunning, she'd lured him out to a bog. Before she could kill him in the trap she'd set, he'd figured out her plan and had thrown her into the water to drown her.

She'd cried for mercy, had begged for help, and it had seemed none would come.

Then the mother currents had arrived, had taken her and comforted and made her strong. The currents had made her more than the equal of the man killing her. Or *had* killed her. The memories of the seconds between her silent pleading and the power granted by the mother were...indistinct.

She had killed her man, and it had left her feeling...good. Happy. Euphoric in a way that matched the soldiers falling in front of her.

Noises increased in intensity, but she ignored them. She stood far above other mortals in power, strength, and—

The ground met her with force. Her old bones might need binding or set.

A face filled her vision. The Colt boy. He was saying something. Why was she on the ground?

"—hey. You read?"

He looked concerned. Why would he be— Sounds crashed into her. Explosions and screams. "Vhat have you done?" Annelle reached for the boy with her power, but she couldn't touch him. There was a nothing, a blankness standing between her and her power. "Vhat is the meaning—"

The Colt boy sliced his hand in the air in front of her. "Shut it. Can you stand? Or better, can you run?"

Could she? She tried to bat him away. Her arm didn't work. Her legs didn't respond either. "I am damaged."

The Colt boy scooped her up and carried her away from the softly rising steam of...a small crater.

The walk took far longer than she remembered. "Where are you taking me?"

"We have to retreat. They got the dampers online and we can't use most of our magick. That includes you."

"I am fit. Unhand me, you peasant."

"Much as I'd like to watch you on the struggle bus, I can't let that happen. Me and the currents got an agreement of sorts—"

A whooshing sound came from a distance, but the noise became a shriek, and the Colt boy bent to the ground and covered her with his body.

The explosion was near-deafening and left a ringing in her ears. Frozen dirt rained down on them bare seconds later.

"We need to get out of here. That means you're coming with us." The Colt boy lifted her without so much as acknowledging her added weight and ran on.

Very slowly, by the time the boy stopped, she had regained enough control of her body to find out that nothing was permanently broken.

The boy set her down on the ground feet first and helped her to stand on her own.

"So, like, what's the deal? What are ya doing going all halfcocked out there?" He shook his head. "You got a death wish or something?" The boy's eyes glowed green in the sparse light of the night.

Annelle did not know why he was so concerned. "I had the ruffians under control, young man."

"If under control, you mean they were about to drop a bunch of bombs on you, then, yeah, I could probably agree. But if you *really* wanted to help, maybe you could use your rusalka powers and see if you can locate the dampers."

"Vhat are dampers?" Annelle didn't like the slang that came from the youth of the day.

"The things keeping us from using our gifts? You know, I *just* told you about them?" He had a deep scowl on his face.

"Perhaps you did, but I still do not know vhat are dampers. You use the same vord to define the thing I do not know. It is not helpful."

"It's the things keeping you from going all swamp witch on 'em."

A memory tugged at her. Swamp witch. She'd known of one a long time ago. "I do not know vhat you mean."

"I see the resemblance, now. Okay. What I need you to do is to see if you have enough magick wrapped up in your bony body to tell me where the source of the drain is."

"Dexx, she's had a rough day." The boy's new wife rested a hand on his shoulder.

The impertinent boy snapped his mouth closed. He did not know who he dealt with.

Annelle gathered the power of the currents and...the currents resisted her call. The mother *never* did that. Not even when she was first learning how to use them. They had *always* answered. "The current mother. She does not answer."

"Fits pretty well with dampers, I'd say. Now, can you feel how far away the edge is, or not?"

"I...I cannot." The admission felt like admitting defeat.

"Then we have to keep moving. Keep them far enough back that normal munitions are mostly ineffective. Pea, it feels like they're using magick. A form of it anyway."

"How can they be using magick to dampen magick?" she asked. "First, dampening the shift and now this? We're sitting ducks."

Annelle let that register. Someone was affecting *her* ability to perform magick? A rusalka of her supreme power? That was ridiculous.

"I wasn't on the R&D team," the Colt boy said. "I couldn't tell ya. What I do know is we have to keep moving before they get a good lock on us. Are the elves ready?"

It took a moment for Annelle to remember why they'd come in the first place. *They* weren't after the delicious morsels of human death energy. They were here to *save* lives.

For later.

"They already have the wounded loaded up and are on the way," Colt's witch said. "We'll stay back and give them more time."

The boy turned to Annelle. "You have to go, too. There's no way I can hold them all back all by myself."

"Did you not tell me magick is useless?" Had they realized who she was? No, those plans were buried deep. But if this was a ruse of their making, it was elaborate.

He shook his head as if he was tired of playing her games. "Somehow," he said to his wife, ignoring Annelle, "a powerful alpha can keep their shift. I want you to get out of here. Get out now, and I'll be back as soon as I can."

"Dexx, wait!" the Whiskey witch called after her husband.

He turned around. "Yeah? I'm sort of—" He cut off as she grabbed him and kissed him on the mouth. Their arms encircled each other, and they stayed together for a long time.

When they broke apart, he smiled. It defined him in her eyes. Overconfident and pushy to the point of bullying.

Annelle imagined little Annika in front of the boy. He'd broken her granddaughter and he pushed against his new wife.

"I'm coming back. Make sure you get them all out safe." He smiled again, and surprisingly the woman smiled back. He turned to the darkness again and his smile faded. "Run, Pea. Run now. Shit, they have zombies. *Run.*"

10

Dexx shifted before he'd taken two steps.

The zombies turned and charged toward Dexx.

Ever since the Whiskeys had moved to Trout-dale, there had been reports of shifters going missing who had never been recovered. He and his team had gone in search of them, had opened files, but there had been zero leads, so nothing to follow.

He'd just found the two years' worth of missing people.

They were dead, and trying to make him dead, too.

Wolves, foxes, coyotes, different deer, and other shifters were blacker than the countryside in his vision. No heat signatures at all.

Damn. Leah could probably have dealt with all of them with a thought.

Get ready, girl, he told Hattie, not sure she'd have any posi-tive effect on zombies. *This is going to be a bumpy ride.* Dexx scrunched up, ready to jump past the leading edge of zombie shifters.

A few of them ran by him, looking to get to the other living beings, but more than a few zeroed in on Dexx. He leapt over the vanguard and into the thickest of the rushing zombie horde. He crushed a small wolf and rounded on a lion. The thing didn't stand a chance. He broke its neck with one swipe, and it crumpled, dead again. Hopefully, the para had peace now.

Hattie snarled as they worked their way through the horde. The zombies moved eerily quietly. The only sound they made was a collective rumble of feet tramping the ground.

He hoped he'd given the others enough lead time to get away. Paige with her magick was their biggest weapon, and that was gone.

A bear reared up, pulling back a massive paw to swipe at Dexx.

The great cat ducked the swipe and jammed his shoulder into the bear. It fell over backward into a pair of rabbit shifters.

Rabbit shifters? Really?

A pack of wolves attacked as he turned from the bear, hitting Dexx as a unit, two from each side and three in a frontal assault.

The two on his left jumped at Dexx. He didn't have time to duck or dodge as they landed on him with teeth digging in.

Hattie flung them off and met the three in front of her. The pain of the wolves' teeth lingered, heat spreading from the bites.

Shit. Was he infected? How long did he have? How did this work in real life?

Didn't matter, he needed more dead than undead.

Hattie rushed the wolves while he was distracted, catching one and crushing important bits like spines. The others soon followed in a second death, and more shifters after that.

The press of the zombie horde became a wall of undead flesh that inexorably moved forward, pushing him back.

As good as he and Hattie were in a fight, he was taking on wounds, and every single one of them started off as a ring of heat and then spread, growing hotter the more time that passed. They were being overrun.

How much time *had* passed? The frozen ground became littered with the bodies of the undead dead, and in the distance the regular dead.

Dexx risked a glance up and saw...he didn't have a chance. He'd killed dozens, maybe hundreds, and there were hundreds, maybe thousands more. His wounds were heating up and if they continued on the way they were, he would have minutes left.

He hoped Paige and the elves had the time they needed to get away. They should have brought Leah.

No. Her magick wouldn't work with the dampers running.

Where were the dampers, anyway? Maybe if they destroyed those, then Paige could put the whammy on them. Again.

How had DoDO altered them to run on magick while dampening magick?

How much time would it really take to finish Jackie if he got out of this alive?

Dexx was slowing down. He took more hits than he gave out. A circle of zombie shifters had him swirling and defensive. The end would be soon. Hopefully, Paige could take him out before he could do too much damage as a zombie. Hopefully, it would be Paige.

Would he come back as a shifter or a zombie with the *kadu*. Would Bussemi destroy him in the next lifetime too?

White wings flashed overhead.

He took two more bites when he risked a glance upward.

The creature speared out of the sky and lifted zombies from the ground, dropping them back into the ranks.

Dexx fought on.

The circle around Dexx widened, and the winged creature came back, thudding to the ground. Dexx's vision was blurred and he had no idea what he was looking at. Roxxie?

The circle widened further, as the zombies hesitated.

That's when he saw who the winged creature was. Standing before him in rare form was Robin, Leslie's griffin. A golden eye traced with lightning eyed him. *Looks like you could use some assistance.* Leslie's voice came through loud and clear.

I've been infected. You have to kill me before it takes me over and you have a real problem zombie formerly known as Dexx.

Leslie-griffin stomped a foot and clawed the ground. *Don't be silly. You can't be infected as a shifter.*

Then explain why we're fighting zombie shifters right now.

This is a spell or something. I don't know. But...trust me. You're going to be fine.

The first of the zombies rushed forward.

Dexx didn't move appreciably faster, but he fought on. If he couldn't be turned into a zombie—but how would Leslie *know* that?—then exactly why in the nine hells was he on fire and so tired?

He didn't have much fight left in him. The tide of zombies rolled forward, pushing them back, and even Leslie who could fly didn't have a lot of power to keep them back. Dexx was spent, with nothing left in the tank. He just needed to sleep for a day...or a year.

The closest zombie fell over backwards, arrows sticking from his eyes and throat.

Dexx barely felt the ground bounce into him.

Cardinal Bussemi beat at his prison walls of is his mind. When the bahlrok was in control, the all-mighty, all-powerful Bussemi was nothing more than a flea in his body.

That only angered him more.

The beast looked through the scrying hole he'd cast from air and Bussemi pushed forward to see what the demon saw. The latest reincarnation of his brother fought undead paras. Soon he would lose against the sheer numbers. The beast used *his* hand to caress the *kadu* that hung from his neck. The magick resonance rippled through his hand and up his arm.

This wasn't the life he'd bargained for, but it gave him access to *so much power*. Only one thing mattered to Bussemi: destroying his brother for what he had done.

Bussemi relaxed his push to take over the body and watched the scry. The griffin landed near him. How he'd managed to tame it was beyond reason.

The foot soldiers fell by the dozens, which sent a thrill of excitement through Bussemi in spite of himself. Bussemi didn't have an unlimited number of men at his disposal, but he certainly had enough to take out the cat and this twisted version of his reincarnated brother. Soon, even the griffin would fall under their pressing weight.

Watching the two falter under the overwhelming onslaught filled Bussemi with pleasure even in the confines of his mind. Dexx would be dead soon, and his offspring were soon to follow. The two held creatures of barely fathomable power, and were killing the children. They had less than a year before they were dead.

They had an effective weapon against the paras, except for a few, something they would not be able to negate.

And Dexx suspected nothing.

The big cat wavered. The dead paras closed in.

Dexx would soon be back in his *kadu* and then...then it would be over.

Dexx would lose. And Bussemi would win, after all this time.

Get ready, Bussemi told the demon controlling their body. *I want his body before it loses too much to the veil, and before they suspect.* Bussemi would have salivated if he had control of his mouth. He'd waited so long.

Do not seek to tell me what to do, mortal. I know our deal, and I know how best to end it. The demon growled and jerked Bussemi's head to the side.

Of course. How infuriating to be so close to so much power and be unable to wield a trickle. *It has been a long time. I am anxious to serve, and my brother had been powerful. I do not want to lose any more than necessary.*

You will get what I give you, and you will not complain.

Of course. Bussemi could have struck something. *Anything* nearby. This was *his* body, and although the deal had been to share, over the years the bahlrok had taken many more years to relinquish control than it had in those first ones. It should have been a partnership.

The cat fell, and the undead followed quickly.

Let's be gone. We need to claim the body quickly.

Zoe shook the envelope, dumping the small black earpiece into the palm of her hand. Pip. Smiling, she put it in her ear and turned it on.

"Ah," Pip answered cheerfully. "You got my package."

"Yeah." Zoe turned her attention back to her computer. "Tell me you know where this guy is and how to stop him."

"Well, no. He's still a *bit* of a mystery, but I do have it limited to like a hundred or so people. Less than that, but yeah. I'm getting closer. No, that is not why I sent you the comm. You're at your computer. Great. I'm sending you—"

Zoe's cursor moved. She grabbed the mouse and tried to move it back.

"Would you stop that? It's me."

"That's not cool." Zoe didn't know how she felt about Pip's ability to hack into her computer and just take control.

"Seriously, it's fine. I don't want to spend the next hour telling how you to find the file I just sent you." Pip pulled up a file management window.

"I take it that's a conversation you and Brack have?"

"He's like an old man."

Well, he was a dragon and from what Zoe had learned, for all intents and purposes, he *was* old.

A series of reports opened on her screen.

"What am I looking at?" They looked familiar in the sense that they were whitepaper reports, but they were moving too fast for her to really read any of them.

"This one first," Pip said, pulling up a series of graphs in a multi-page report. "Look at these levels."

The graphs were talking about contamination in water tables and water sources. But this wasn't new information. Even water that came from water treatment facilities had high contaminants. "Is there something in particular?"

"I'd say."

The cursor stopped moving, so Zoe assumed she had control for a bit.

"You said something that got me to thinking. How would they be able to keep it in the water?"

Zoe zoomed in to read the reports, scanning through to find anything that popped out at her. "Various ways."

"Yeah, right? But then I remembered you saying how this guy was supersmart and how you were working to stop the spread of that brain-eating amoeba thing that was targeting shifters and stuff. Gross, right? Exactly. So, then I got to thinking, maybe they're linked."

That was a bizarre leap of logic that didn't make...any sense. "No one would make—"

"And then," Pip said, plowing on, "I thought, 'Hey! If I was trying to infect a bunch of computers, how would I do that?' That was easy because I've already designed that and—yeah, well, enough about that. But! So! I was thinking and look at this."

The screen flashed again and another report came up.

This one definitely caught Zoe's attention. It was a report of the different bacteria and amoeba showing up in the water at different areas. The *Naegleria fowleri* amoeba was showing up in high abundance in a lot of places. "No."

"Right?"

"No." Pip didn't understand. "This is a very fragile amoeba."

"That eats brains. And there's a strain that only like shifter brains. I couldn't find a report for that."

It was unlikely to *be* in a mundane report because as far as Zoe was aware, no one outside the paranormal regions even knew about it. "It can't survive in most water sources." As far as things went, it didn't have the ability to survive.

"Yeah, well, that's what I thought was so freaking interesting, because this one is surviving. A lot of places. And..." Another report popped up. "...humans aren't being affected at all."

Zoe read the report, her heart hammering in her chest. Someone had both found a cure and a way to make this particular amoeba worse. How was that even possible? "Pip," she whispered. "We're in trouble."

Dexx awoke to an eye the size of a dinner plate inspecting him.

He flailed, trying to get away.

"Dexx," Paige asked behind him, "are you okay?"

"Step away from me, peasant." He waved his hand, shooing away the eye. He knew it was Robin, but dang, that griffin didn't understand the need for personal space.

The giant eye moved back and resolved into a large bird with taloned front feet. The bird reshaped and became Leslie. "Yeah, he's fine. Told you. The *venom* and the infection you were so worried about was nothing."

That hadn't *felt* like nothing. "I assure you it was something." Dexx sat up and rubbed his head. Long dark hair ran through his fingers. Longer than normal hair. "How long was I out?"

"An hour." Paige knelt next to him.

"Zombies. Those were really zombies."

"Yeah. I know. Are you sure you're fine? I've never seen you get that tired so quickly." She rested her hand on his shoulder.

He'd already told them he wasn't. "Yeah, sure." Because Leslie was adamant that he was. "It must have been the zombies and their perfectly innocent bites, I'm sure. I'm just tired." He looked around the dark night. "Where are we?"

"So, an amazing thing happened." Paige turned her gaze up and around. "A caravan of truckers sent by General Penn who had connections with some generals nearby who knew a few people in the area who all collaborated to come save our bacon. They picked us up. We lost a few, but the majority is safe for now."

"So, what happened to all the zombies?"

Paige shrugged and gestured wildly with her hand. "They...stopped. Right after you passed out and the elves began their attack, it was like they lost the magick holding them together."

"Why didn't thing suppressing your magick affect them?"

She shook her head. "The dampening field is still there. We bought ourselves some time with the trucks, but we have to be a lot farther along to get away from the area of effect. But for a few minutes, we had limited use of our gifts."

"I see." Dexx sat up to see the trailers lined up on both sides of the road and people milling back and forth between them. Someone had lit a fire with shrubbery and broken sticks. Several other fires dotted the safe zone.

He rose, his joints complaining. "I feel rigor setting in."

"It was probably the truck ride. You didn't shift until a few minutes ago." Paige sighed, looking out across the area. Through the smiles and reassuring touches, she was worried. "I've got to be smarter."

He wasn't going to argue with her. That attack felt like they'd been played.

Paige stood, taking a step toward her sister. "How is your magick working?"

"How the hell should I know?" Leslie's accent deepened with each word. "You're the expert. Why don't you tell me?"

"I don't...it's just that it's weird. Dexx keeps his shifts, and somehow you do too, and now your magick is poking out. I don't like it. Is their dampening field working or did they turn it down, or... I don't know." Paige ran her fingers through her hair.

"Could be they have a weakness for big birds and cats."

"You trying to be funny, Dexx?"

"No, trying to be helpful. Put a positive spin on things."

"Go spin yourself." Leslie didn't growl, but...maybe she did.

"Dexx?" Paige placed herself between Leslie and him. "Can we talk for a minute?"

"Sure. What would you like to discuss?" Dexx let her pull him away from the rest of the elves and her sister, who were all milling around the rather full truck stop. The parking lot lights lit up the night and an autumn wind blew, ruffling his hair. How long were they planning on staying there? They sooner they were all back where magick worked, the better he'd feel.

"I've been thinking about something. A couple things."

"That sounds like a common ailment." And serious.

"That was lame, Dexx. Even for you."

Dexx nodded but didn't say anything.

"How do you have your shift? We're in a magick dampening field right now, so why do you and Leslie have your shift?"

"I...don't know." She was angling toward something. Something she didn't want to talk about. "What are you asking?"

"Doe had her shift too. I think a powerful shifter keeps their shift. If that's true, then maybe Chuck would, too. Leslie has her magick, or at least some. But I don't. Not even a scry bubble."

Dexx clamped his lips shut waiting for her to go on.

"Now what if the powerful shifters keep their shift because they have powerful shifter spirits in their pack?"

"So?"

She raked her top lip with her teeth. "I can't help but think I could do more. More than walking back to the rest of the world. I *know* these people. I spent some time on the inside, and I got some great insight to how they work."

Dexx shrugged. "Yeah. I'm sure you did. How do you propose to get more power? You aren't going to try to suck the juice from shifter souls are you?"

Paige smiled, but it was the life-saving kind where she held her mouth closed so nobody died. "No, I want you to bite me."

11

He wanted to feel the excitement that flared inside him. "That's great—"

No, cub. Hattie's soft voice cut him off as she pushed forward. *She might not survive.*

But she was chosen before.

Not through a bite, Hattie said carefully as if was walking through a field of landmines. *Also, there is the fact that Cawli died serving and protecting her. That is not something the ancients will forgive lightly.*

Paige frowned at him.

He held up a finger to buy himself some time. *So, what does that mean?*

It means that this should be thought through carefully because the consequences could be quite severe.

He looked at Paige. "Okay. Why do you want the bite? I thought you had been concerned with being too powerful."

"I had been," she said. "But look at this situation. Every single time we come up with a new solution, they find something else. We can't afford for me to be at less than full power."

He could understand that. "But there's also the fact that maybe General Saul is right. Maybe you shouldn't be out in the field."

She shook her head. "When we're under intense fire, you honestly think I'm just going to sit around and watch? No. If I'm needed, I'm going to help where and when I can. The end."

Dexx pushed Paige away. He understood that this situation sucked, but was it really this bad? *How concerned should I be?*

Hattie was quiet for a moment. *The ancients did not approve of Cawli choosing Paige.*

Damn. Dexx slashed at the air between them. "No way. No. You can't go around making proclamations and just think you're going to be more powerful than the next guy because you *think* you want it." Because…because this, ultimately, was bigger than just having his mate officially back in his pack with him, which would make him feel better. If he stepped outside of himself for a minute, he realized that what they were fighting against was this very thing in the first place. Well, not really. Yeah, actually. Kinda. Power plays. They needed to get out of that whole cycle.

"Dexx, that's even more stupid than your usual."

"No. I think you're power-hungry."

She stared at him like he'd lost his mind, then got up and took a step back, leaning against the tire of the eighteen-wheeler. "Think about it. We *need* the extra firepower here. If I had my shift, I could help. Probably."

"You don't know that."

"No, but they keep building bigger weapons against us and we need the ability to rise to that."

"You want *more* than you have, and you wonder why they keep building bigger weapons? You fight against the government for grabbing power, yet you do the same thing, but it's okay for you because you're Paige freakin' Whiskey?" Dexx spun away from her, wondering where that particular pulse of anger had come from.

What was he talking about? Wasn't he always the one who wanted more power out of that car he doted on so much? But when it was government, that was different. And truth be told, he was still struggling pretty hard with the fact that the woman he loved was becoming the thing he hated most.

"Dexx, please. You *know* I'm right. I don't *want* more power, but if we want a life, a *free* life, you know this is the best way. Sure, I'll have more power, but you *have* to see it's the best way to help. The best way for *all* of us."

Listening to that case right there? He didn't even *need* the potential threat of her not surviving the bite to lord over his head. He didn't *want* her to have the extra power. "All I am to you is just a means for more? We fought. Together, we fought against demons, but you think everything will be grand when you become a thousand times more powerful than their head guy? Isn't that a lot like Merry Eastwood?"

"No, I—" She stopped herself and blinked, a pained frown on her face.

Dexx pressed his advantage. "How many times has Merry Eastwood defended herself the very same way? Just a little more so she can remain relevant. Just a little more so her competition can't compete. The Blackmans might want a new leader. You want to co-opt *them* now?"

Paige rubbed her eye and then shook her head. "Are you okay? What happened out there?"

Was *Dexx* okay? Who was she anymore? "You can't take on the world by yourself. That's why you have us. That why you have *me*."

Dexx just had to make sure he didn't lose the version of Paige he loved most in this war.

Paige didn't want to admit how close to the bone Dexx had cut. She'd honestly thought he'd be happy about her wanting the bite. Not that they'd done a lot of pack things together, because she'd always been busy, but...

The *way* he'd told her no had been a massive blow to her ego.

"You're having a tough night of it." Leslie hit her in the shoulder and sank down on the bench seat. "What's going on?"

Paige shook her head. "How much longer are we going to stay here?"

Leslie shrugged. "There's a storm overhead. I'm tryin' to see if I can get it moving with us. You're better at that than me."

And she was completely useless right then.

"What's eating at you?"

"You mean besides the fact that we just got our butts handed to us?"

Leslie shrugged and nodded. "Yeah. Sure."

This wasn't a *yeah, sure* moment. Paige had done things the way she'd *always* done things. She and Dexx had handled this latest elf extraction like they always had, guns blazing, powers at the ready. That'd always worked.

But not this time.

"Walton is too powerful."

Leslie snorted. "Sure. That guy is too powerful for you."

"As a human?" Paige hated to admit it. "Yeah. Take away my witch abilities and I'm..." She *hated* just being human, just being a witch. Magick wasn't even her strong suit. She played with elements, sure. That was a thing. But... "Dexx said no to the bite."

"What?" Leslie frowned at Paige. "I didn't realize you were thinking about it."

"Yeah, well, I was."

Leslie winced and pulled a long face, clasping her hands together and squeezing them between her knees. "Are ya sure you wanna do that?"

"Yeah."

"Okay."

What was this? "Why are you against this too?"

"I'm not." Leslie shrugged and sat up. "I just... You know, Cawli kinda died on your watch. Do you really think the animal spirits are gonna be open to this?"

Why wouldn't they?

Leslie snorted and shook her head. "Pea, how many shifters do you know who have survived their spirit animal?"

None that Paige could think of.

"Exactly. So, what makes you think they're going to want you to join their ranks again?"

"I didn't want him to die. I didn't ask him to sacrifice himself for us."

Leslie shoved her tongue in her cheek and looked around as she nodded.

But that was a thought Paige hadn't quite worked all the way through yet. "You think it's a bad idea."

"Why do you even want the bite in the first place?"

"To win. Look at us, Les. We're stranded in the middle of nowhere with no reinforcements. If they find us—"

"Those drones they're using are getting closer to us. There are only so many of those I can destroy before they know exactly where we are."

Right. "Exactly. When they find us, we have no way of fighting back. We can't allow ourselves to be this weak."

"Paige." Leslie bit her lips and frowned.

Paige knew that look. It meant that her sister was about

to say something she was pretty sure would garner a response.

"You're the leader of this movement, right?"

Against her will. "Yes."

"Then, maybe you should do what other leaders do and not be in the middle of the fighting."

"No." How was that going to work? Paige couldn't *ask* others to do something she refused to.

"Okay, well." Leslie got up and dusted herself off. "Think about it." She sighed and flopped her hands to her sides. "Or don't."

Paige rolled her eyes and got up. "You and Dexx should do some scouting runs. It looks like that storm is going to head in the right direction."

Leslie looked up to the sky and nodded.

At least it wasn't raining currently. Paige hadn't brought a rain jacket this time.

Turning away, Leslie stepped onto the bench, preparing launch herself into the sky.

"And Les?"

She paused and looked back. "Yeah."

"I heard you."

Leslie nodded, tipping her head from side to side as she did. "Okay. Love you." She leapt into the air and shifted into an eagle.

"Love you too," Paige said quietly. She didn't like it when the two people she trusted the most teamed up against her.

She knew *they thought* they were right.

But they weren't. She'd have to find a way to get that bite, sooner rather than later. She couldn't be the leader who stayed behind. Her people were fighting a war where their brute strength and magickal flexibility was the only way they were going to win.

She couldn't risk losing any of her people because she was

too weak to stand up for them. That wasn't a legacy she was willing to leave behind.

Paige Whiskey was the woman who fought with everything she had in her.

And that was the woman her people needed.

Chuck Deluca had a stack of approvals in front of him. The amount of commerce that still poured in through the blockade was enormous. And he was still in the business of business, playing against the Eastwoods.

The next stack of papers were shipments from former drug smugglers who were now smuggling legit contraband, like milk and cheese. They also required a cash payment at the docks. With a quick flip through the papers, he gathered them up in a neat stack and stood.

"Grant? Come in here, please."

After a few seconds, Grant opened the door and stepped in. "Sir?"

"Gather a detail. We are going to the docks." As the highest-ranking member of the shifter packs in the west, he'd been appointed the general of the para fighting forces.

Grant only turned around to get people because this was just the new protocol with the way their lives had been turned upside down.

Chuck flexed his hand, extending his fingers and holding them outstretched for a few seconds. Ever since that witch, McCree, from Australia had stolen his power, his hand had ached. It didn't tell the weather, or stress, or anything useful that he could tell. It just ached until he stretched it.

Since then, alphas moved in pairs as often as they could, always on alert when they did.

Grant walked in, pulling on his coat. It wasn't especially

cold out, but the coat hid the gun under his arm. "We're ready."

They met four others in the parking lot. None of them were alphas except Chuck and Grant, but none were weak either. There were two for each vehicle, all ready for action.

Too bad he couldn't convince Dexx to be on permanent detail. Dexx would have more influence in the region and would probably have a larger pack. If he really applied himself, he could take the region from Chuck and Faith, giving them a chance to retire gracefully. But every time it had been offered to Dexx, he'd turned it down flat.

One day, Chuck was going to offer and Dexx would be unable to turn him down. Chuck *was* going to retire and spend some quality time with his family, especially his kids who were all growing up much too fast.

"Let's go. You know the drill."

Nobody answered. None of them needed to.

The drive to the docks wasn't long, not anymore, but that didn't matter.

Buildings flashed past, and Chuck lost himself in his thoughts until the caravan parked in front of warehouses flanked by stacks of shipping containers.

This shipment was supposed to be special. People.

But not just any people. Paras fleeing Walton's states and ready to join the Paranormal Western States. They were fighters and were ready to keep the free people free. President Walton was marshalling his forces, so the West had to work in kind.

The smuggler captain met him at the warehouse and showed the packed in.

The warehouse held stacks of containers from ships coming in and out, and also, had a large open area, with a thousand or so paras milling in a cordoned-off area. Forklifts and tugs towed containers nearly constantly.

A few weren't milling. They stood with purpose.

A man and twenty or so didn't appear like to be displaced like the rest. The man wasn't the regular sort of para that flocked to the free states. He was a tall, dark-haired man, with his hands folded on a cane. It might just be a walking stick, however. He wore a suit that looked equally expensive as Chuck's. Who under the stars had the smuggler carried to their shore?

The man nodded once as though he knew Chuck. The man was familiar, but he was positive they'd never met before.

As Chuck studied the man, the barrier opened. He stepped forward and was followed by several others.

The barrier closed again after the last of his entourage left the waiting area. They crossed the space and the man stopped in front of Chuck.

Harfor pushed to shift and attack.

Chuck calmed the wolf with his alpha will. They'd been past that kind of adolescent posturing for years. *What's wrong? Be calm.*

The man has the flavor of the spirit thief.

This was not possible. "McCree?"

The older man tipped his head as if congratulating Chuck on a job well done.

"We need to talk." Chuck put some alpha will into a push.

McCree smiled. "G'day. Are you the one they call Dexx Colt?"

"No. I'm the one they call the regional high alpha."

"Well, then you *might* be the person to talk to."

Chuck liked to think he wasn't the kind of alpha who allowed small men under his skin, but this man was getting under his skin.

"Unless you were sent by someone else. In that case, I

would need to speak to your boss. I don't really deal well with underlings."

The men behind him chuckled.

Chuck wasn't going to waste his time. He turned to the person manning the dock. "You can send this one back."

McCree's interest was piqued. "I'm looking to help send the East Coasters back to their side of the continent."

So, this witch was helping Walton? "You and your twelve men."

Harfor buzzed with the need to get his teeth into the man.

"Nah, this is just the beginnin'. I left my secret weapon in a secret place."

Chuck shook his head and gestured for the man to be taken away.

"You know what we're capable of. You will want my help."

The man was offering his help?

"I see you're confused. Let me help with that. I'm currently rustling your enemies out of your camp."

Chuck bristled. They hadn't come up with a plan for those who wanted to flee back to the Eastern states. Unlike Walton, they weren't actively trying to keep people trapped, either.

"I plan to contribute in other ways as well, but I won't help for free." McCree's hand rubbed over the other one.

Chuck was out of patience. "You do not get any higher than me. Not here." He was ready to be done with the man.

"Unless *I'm* around." Merry Eastwood crossed her arms and cocked a hip. "Then you talk to me."

12

Dexx walked along as the sabertoothed cat down the road with the refugee elves, ready for whatever might be thrown at them and still seething a little from Paige's request and the fact that she might not be as safe as he wanted her to be.

Leslie didn't have a lot of her magick, but she had managed to keep the storm over them, shielding them from satellite view, which helped to keep the military away.

For the most part.

They'd been sending in drones. She'd killed thirty or forty of them. The odds just weren't in their mechanical favor, so the people operating the had pulled back and followed, just on the edge of Dexx and Hattie's enhanced vision, though several more were being lost to random bursts of wind. Yeah.

"...you know I'm right." Paige said, walking beside him.

The convoy had been forced to leave in order to maintain their freedom to ride the highway, the power of commerce pushing allowances that normal citizens weren't allowed to experience. These truckers were the way the rest of the states were keeping their stores stocked because *they* didn't have door witches.

Though, Dexx was sure that Paranormal West or Para-West or whatever they were calling themselves were *also* using trucks and truck drivers within the boundaries of their own country. It was just crossing the new borders that was an issue.

Dexx wished not for the first time that they had another ride. They still had miles to go and a lot could still go wrong.

"I *am* asking for more power, but only to defend ourselves." She gestured around them. "It's only us out here trying to keep everything and every*one* safe. Even you have to see the merit, don't you?"

Dexx had let Hattie control their body for the last hour, maybe more while he rummaged around in his brain for fun things to look at. Cars, kids, old fights and recent ones. Bussemi took up a lot of space in his idle thoughts.

If Bussemi wasn't a threat, he wouldn't even consider it. But he was and he had no idea how they were going to defeat him. They had to find a way this lifetime. He didn't want to die knowing he'd just have to do this all over again next time.

Hattie gave Paige a noncommittal noise and kept walking. At least Dexx knew it was noncommittal.

Paige took the opportunity to keep up her argument.

Hattie jolted in her step, and in between strides, they were no longer in the real world. The plain stretched out in front of them, animals missing from their traditional feeding grounds. The earth was cold, with small snow drifts tucked at the bases of clumps of grass.

What the hell are we doing here? This was a hell of a time to check out. *Are we going to fall down in the real world? And why in the* hell *is it snowy here?*

Hattie sent him a reassuring pat on the head. *We will be fine. This place does what it will do.*

Yeah, I get that, but it hasn't snowed here ever *since we've been together. I'm glad it's you out there. But really, why are we here?*

Mah'se. He felt the thread of concern rippling along those words. *He's still in pain. The shock of the first bonding is big.*

Wait. First bonding?

With Rainbow. I'm sure I mentioned it.

Maybe, but Dexx hadn't realized they'd bonded. *So, they made it official? Rainbow was bitten and was going through the transition?* Where had Dexx been through all of that?

No, cub. Hattie shook the snow off her coat and padded forward. *They had only just begun, but the dance of bonding is an intricate and delicate one.*

Apparently, if it started before the bite.

Was that...something he'd have to consider if he was entertaining Paige's request?

Sometimes when a bond is chosen on the unborn, the child dies. With a first bond that doesn't make the spirit goes mad. You should know this already, cub. But Mah'se had chosen a grown bond mate, and one with strength.

Dexx had only seen them sit together and talk.

Mah'se will not recover until he has a bond to replace her.

Really? This wasn't making a ton of sense to Dexx because he hadn't really *seen* the two of them strike that chord. There'd been one bite. *What happens if he doesn't get that?*

He will start killing the spirits he's sworn to protect.

That...wasn't good. *So, he needs a host to bond to so he doesn't become a serial killer?*

Yes. The cliff sat on their left and the wind blew up the side, curling snow at the top and ruffling Hattie's thick fur.

Mah'se needed a host and Paige needed a spirit. Hmm. *Okay. So, we're here. Now what?*

The outline of a plan formed. No. Not a plan. A solution to a problem. Paige wanted a spirit animal to shift again, and no one of them wanted to bond to a spirit killer. There was a spirit that needed a home, or he would go insane and become a killer of spirits himself. Well, maybe not a killer, but the wolf they saved the last time might disagree.

Hey, fat cat, I got an idea—

The ground trembled with the thudding of hooves. Mah'se came crashing toward them, his antlers down and ready to gore whatever they touched.

Hey, bud. Calm down. We're here to help.

Mah'se pounded the ground harder.

Hattie squared off with the ancient, her own head lowered, and gathered her haunches beneath her.

We're taking him on? Is that a good idea? I mean I'm sure we'd win— Dexx's thought was lost as Hattie jumped forward and over the reckless charge of the ancient elk.

He lifted his massive rack as she sailed over, but Hattie had already gone past. She grabbed the frozen ground with her extended claws and turned before Mah'se pulled his head around for another attack.

Hattie leapt forward, her weight pulling them at an odd angle. She missed Mah'se's greatest mass, but still managed to snag the elk along the thick fur along his neck, pulling him off balance.

He flailed his head as she went over, her claws embedded and dragging him along and finally down to the ground.

Hattie didn't waste any time scrambling over Mah'se, trapping him with her body as she clamped her mouth over his nose, and leaning on her foreleg, cutting the circulation to his brain.

He struggled at first, almost throwing them off, but Hattie held on, shifting with Mah'se to keep him pinned and losing strength.

The kicks became feeble and soon stopped all together.

Are you planning on killing him? He's not moving. You sure you have to kill him? Dexx saw his perfect solution dying on the frozen ground of the Time Before.

Hattie didn't respond, she just lay there, her mouth clamped down and her leg stopping circulation.

Come on, girl. let's ask if he'd like to join another bond. I'm sure Pea'd love to have him. She's a dog person, and he's like a dog, sort of.

Hattie didn't relent.

Mah'se relaxed.

After a few seconds, Hattie opened her mouth and let Mah'se's muzzle drop out, and she lifted her leg from his neck.

He is not dead. But he will sleep. Foolish cub, you want to reason with the unreasonable. Mah'se loses what he is, what he was. He becomes sick without the bond. After a time, he may never recover from the strain.

All the more reason we find him someone ready to take him on right now. Paige is ready, right now. *Is there some way we can push him in or force him or something?*

Hattie shook her head at Dexx. Something internal that felt more like he hadn't gotten the concept.

You would force him into a bond he didn't want? Hasn't that very thing been done to him before?

Oh. That. *Well, yeah. But this would be for good. For* his *good and not the whims of a power-hungry witch.*

Did you not suggest that your witch was hungry for more power? You cannot free one by enslaving another. Would you be a puppet for the one who has hunted you through your lifetimes? He sees you as a thing he can trap or force into his own pack. This is what you want for Mah'se?

Wow. That was well-reasoned for Hattie. Also, it had the effect of making him feel lower than whale shit. He'd never been in the position of being embarrassed by Hattie. Coerced, cajoled, directly opposed, and a host of other things, but never embarrassed by her. His cheeks would have gone hot, but without his body, he just felt bad. *Point taken. I'm sorry, I just thought things had a perfect fix. Mah'se needs a home. Pea needs a companion. Well, she* wants *a companion.*

Do you not worry she craves power? Do you not think that is a growing darkness?

Dexx had thought Paige'd been dark for other reasons over the years and she'd proven him wrong each time. *She's the demon summoner, remember?*

Hattie snorted. *That is not the same thing.*

It's not different either. I thought she'd go dark side then and she didn't. She was even possessed by a demon once, and came out. Is she great all the time? No. Especially when she's giving me pep talks that just make me want to go back to bed. But…she's a good person, cat. And you know this.

Hattie was thoughtful as she watched the now-sleeping elk.

Is Mah'se more powerful than Cawli?

Cawli was special, Hattie said carefully. *We will feel his loss for a long time. We may never be what we once were without him. Mah'se is different, but he is not weak. To compare the two would be to compare two very different things. One mountain may be the tallest, but the plains cat runs the fastest. They are not the same.*

Gotcha. He didn't understand how they were comparing mountains to cats, but… *I guess what I need to know is if they would be a good pairing.* Dexx was a shmuck. Why would he do the very same things he hated Bussemi and DoDO and the Federalists for doing?

Because it was *him* doing the forcing, and his intent was somehow purer than theirs? He was willing to bet that's exactly what Walton was telling himself. *I don't want to force anyone to do anything.* He'd always been the guy pushing for freedom, and the ability to choose for himself. Dammit. Was responsibility always this hard?

The wind whipped at Mah'se's coat, dropping needles of icy snow in the hollows behind him.

So, what do we do? Dexx was willing to take the back seat on this one. Especially after the flub on the whole let's-make-him-do-what-we-want episode.

We wait. Hattie dropped her butt to the ground and surveyed the plains below the bluff. Truly, the land was sere, frozen and abandoned.

How long are we supposed to do that, and what happens when he wakes up with a smashing headache and wants our blood?

We will deal with that if it happens.

Ugh. Dexx sent a facepalm to Hattie. They always waited to see what happened and reacted to that. They never set up anything to make the bad stuff stay away through preparation.

Shit. Did he sound like Paige?

Hattie sat next to Mah'se, as still as he was. In a few minutes, the wind stopped howling and the snow stopped stinging.

Mah'se's chest rose once in a deep breath, and he let it go, almost snorting.

Still Hattie sat, not moving.

I have told you I don't want you around. Go away. Mah'se sounded tired, but still angry and ready to commit to more violence.

You have, Hattie said calmly. *But I will not let my friend kill himself by not taking another bond.*

My bond died before it was complete. You have never had to go through this pain.

Hattie nodded, but Mah'se couldn't see it. *This is true. But my bond was one of the first. We did not know how. The two could have been the same. But I went ahead with it.*

Mah'se made a noise that sounded close to a growl.

Dexx opened his phantom mouth to say something, but

didn't follow through. He pitied the elk. How would he have felt if Paige had miscarried their children? Still, he didn't say anything.

Mah'se lay on the ground, just breathing. After a minute, he picked his head up. *You have not helped me. Once I leave here, you will be my enemy once more.*

And I will take care of you again. I have hope where you do not. There is a bond without a spirit. She hurts the same way you do.

How is there a bond and no spirit?

Cawli's.

That bond is cursed. None will go near her. She came to the doorway and swayed a few. I saw her, and she was not strong enough. Cawli was a fool.

Was he talking about Paige? She told him about the spirit lake when she had been on trial of sorts. She'd met the spirit...*conclave?* They'd talked to her and had decided she was worth the risk. But Mah'se didn't?

You will leave now. Or I will. But if I leave first, I will fight you.

Hattie dropped her head sadly and let out a breath in a huff. *I will leave. And I will come back. If the best prey is too fast for you, then look to the second fastest. Then the next. There will be one you can catch.*

And there it was. Hattie spoke in riddles way too often. The bright spot was that she did it to the ancient, instead of Dexx.

The grey spot on the silver lining was that it was too easy for him. If Mah'se couldn't have the bond he wanted, he should look for the bond he could take. Damned cat, that actually made a lot of sense.

Hattie let the plains and the bluff fade away. The scene changed to the perfect picnic tree under the perfect night sky above.

What are we doing here? She'd never *ever* brought him back to the tree after they'd been in the Time Before.

I want time with my bond. To just be together without inter-ruption.

But…we're walking. *Aren't we?*

Yes. Hattie…shifted. But it wasn't the regular shift. More like she *moved away from* Dexx and after a few moments, Dexx stood in front of the great cat.

"Wait." Dexx looked at his hands and body. "What are you doing? We can't be apart. I don't *want* to be. You're not —" Dexx paused and swallowed hard. "Dumping me, are you?"

Hattie stood and rubbed her head along his, from nose to past her jaw. *Never. I just know how special we are. I wanted to see my bond mate.*

Oh. Dexx raised his arms and hugged the great cat.

She raised a paw and pulled him to her and hugged him back.

He realized that one day, they would die and would not make it back. He didn't want to know when that day would come.

Hattie's paw touched the pavement silently and smoothly as her last step. How long had they stood there in the space between the two realities without moving? Dexx had no idea, but very little time had passed in the real world.

Leslie's hawk form flew ahead, soon becoming a dot and then too far away for even him to see.

After a minute or so, she came back, streaking hard for the ground. She flared her wings at the last possible moment and slowed to a run and she shifted, still running. She franti-cally motioned for Paige. "We have to hurry. The edge of the dampers is up there."

"You found them?" Paige asked, jogging toward her sister. "Where are they?"

"I didn't see the boxes," Leslie said, turning to walk briskly the way she'd come. "I found the edge of the effects. Maybe a few miles up the road. We can open doorways and get everyone out of danger."

Paige looked behind them to the following parade of elven families. "Can you fly me there? Maybe I can do something to stop them from chasing us back to Troutdale."

Leslie curled her lip. "No."

Paige grunted and walked beside her sister. "We have to be smart about this. What can you do? What *should* we do?"

Dexx shifted *with his clothes on*. "We have to stop our escort and take the dampers offline. Those are our two priorities. The next would to be to get to a safe place where they can't follow. Get behind our wards."

Leslie pressed her lips together. "That's more of an outcome, and not a plan. So, when you have a plan, please jump in."

Dexx felt the urge to push her with alpha will but decided against it. He shouldn't use that as a first course of action. "It's possible," Paige said, "that they're going to attack us as we're crossing that border. That they'll be expecting us."

"They have a greater chance of winning against us here. Why wait until we're at our full strength?"

She shook her head. "This whole mission has felt like one test after another."

Dexx had to agree with that. "Is there a way you can get a ward up once we're on the other side?"

Paige tapped her lip. "I've been wondering if I can make something less temporary."

Dexx shook his head. "No, just something to protect us while we're shuttling people through the doorway. I have to call in because we're going to be sitting ducks."

"Agreed. Let me see what I can do."

He, Paige, and Leslie picked up the pace, moving toward the edge of the boundary as quickly as possible. Leslie took to the air to see if there were any traps ahead.

Paige stopped, her hand out. "Do you feel that?"

There was a noticeable shift in the air, a difference in the feel.

"Is this the edge of the force field?" Dexx asked, scouting the area, looking for an ambush.

"Yeah." She wasn't focused on their conversation though. She was looking at the ground and gathering magick. It seemed to leap from the ground to her.

Dexx wasn't going to pretend he understood anything about the magick he had for so short a time. "Did the devices...stop here?"

She nodded, narrowing her eyes as she searched the landscape for more.

An older elven male stopped beside them. "Are we okay?"

Dexx shook his head and shrugged. "I don't know. Be vigilant."

The elf nodded and continued forward, the small flood of people following him.

Paige took in a deep breath and pulled earth magick. "I hope he understands warnings." She drew her magick inward and let it explode north and south.

Magickal force popped from the earth and rose with a crackling energy, flowing from the ground and bounding in the air out of sight.

The elves stopped.

The earth rumbled and shook, then ripped in a jagged line following the bouncing ball of earth magick.

Dexx and the elves worked hard to stay upright, but Paige stood rooted to the spot, her hands and eyes lit with earth magick.

The ground kept ripping and spreading until the gap had grown to fifty feet wide, and maybe as deep.

The earth quieted then finally stilled, little avalanches of dirt still tumbling down the bank.

Paige pulled the magick back and abruptly fell to her knees, breathing hard.

Nothing was going to cross it without help.

Dexx looked down at Paige and put a hand to her shoulder. "Are we good?"

She shrugged and reached out to touch the ground, then she pulled away, blinking. "Come on. Quickly. This'll protect us until we're gone."

Win for their team, but...

Dexx still didn't have an answer for what he was supposed to do about Paige and Mah'se. As the last elf crossed, Paige stepped through the boundary she'd created and a military force appeared on the Kansas side, rolling in with tanks and armored vehicles. A flight of five helicopters flew over.

A cold expression filtered over Paige's face as she patted down the knees of her jeans. Dust flew from the fabric. "I hate them for what they made me do."

"Yeah. Let's go. The dust settled as everyone stood stunned.

They now had a border of sorts, at least in this stretch.

The united was now divided.

13

"They're calling it an attack," Lovejoy said as she walked through the front door to the Whiskey house a few hours later.

Dexx knew she was talking about the canyon. It was the only thing anyone had mentioned since they'd made it back. Was it overkill? Had Paige gone too far this time? Dexx didn't even know what his thoughts were on this on, but, you know, if he wasn't married to Paige, he might think she'd gone a little too far this time.

Come on. She'd made a *canyon* to separate Colorado and Kansas.

"Attack, my ass. They attacked *us* and moved their border *way* west," Leslie growled on her way to the kitchen.

"They're just spinning it so they can maintain their hold on the people." Dawn didn't close the door behind her as she followed Lovejoy, which meant more people were probably coming. "Most wouldn't really fear us, except the government is whipping up the fearmongering, and then when the people are really in a frenzy, they step forward and offer to keep them safe by targeting and killing people different than them. It's an old practice, but it's effective."

Dexx connected the dots easily. Blame a segment of society for problems and publicly create a problem. Then do something about the *different* people. Instant support. Good ol' Adolf and his cronies back at it. The difference this time was that the persecuted had teeth.

What Dexx wanted was a week under the sheets. Responsibility pulled at him, though. "Good job, Pea." He still didn't know what he thought about her excessive use of force, but it had kept the military on the other side of the canyon. Even with their helicopters. So, what did Dexx know?

Except that he wasn't sure Paige *needed* any more power.

What kind of crappy husband was he turning out to be? "We have a day or a week to breathe. Too bad for the amber waves of grain, though." He pulled in a deep breath and let it go, trying to talk himself into backing that statement with feeling. "I have to get back to the station and make sure it's not torn down or abandoned. I'll see you tonight."

"Okay." Paige bit her lips instead of coming in for a kiss and frowned. "Don't be too late. We're having chicken strips and tater tots for dinner because I managed to score that on the last delivery."

Dexx half smiled at her. "You bet. Wouldn't miss it." He headed up to their room.

He stripped his clothes off and tossed them to the hamper. Sure, he'd spent quite a bit of time as a sabertoothed cat, but somehow his clothes had taken on the smell of days on the march and zombie battle.

Dressed in country-fresh clothes, he grabbed his keys. Jackie still wasn't finished, and she didn't seem like she ever would be.

Since coming back from his adventures in the Time

Before, he'd used the cracked bowl *shamiyir* as his key holder. As good a use as any for the broken bowl.

The bowl also served as his mysterious crystal-of-ulti-mate-power holder. The amethyst turned out to be a passable nightlight for Paige, too. He didn't need one with Hattie's night vision.

He scooped up the keys and stopped. That crack had almost broken the thing in two, but was now significantly diminished, and the large scorch around the crack was gone.

"What the hell?" Dexx dumped the crystal and other keys out and inspected the bowl. The thing had been a dead keep-sake. Bussemi had probed the rock for its secrets, and had broken it in the process. How in the nine hells was it fixing itself?

He picked the amethyst up and inspected it beside the bowl. Did the crystal look dimmer? From his brief time as a war wizard, he'd discovered that the crystal held more raw potential magick than he could have spit out in a year at full blast. But he'd never been able to open it. Dekskulta had told him it was a weapon against Bussemi, but his evil first-brother had dropped off the earth. Not a peep, not a whisper, not a sighting. He was probably still directing DoDO, but doing it in deep dark.

He stacked the bowl and the crystal back on his dresser. He set the keys off to the side. If something was going on with them, he wanted to know, even if he couldn't *do* anything with them. Knowing, after all, was half the battle.

The house was a beehive of activity with kids and people and more kids as he pulled Paige's car out of the garage.

Jackie shrank as he pulled out and the descending door finally hid her from view. He'd get to her. He would. Maybe. If time allowed. Stupid Cooper McCree for breaking her in the first place.

The station wasn't a burned-out crater. It wasn't a

spider breeding ground either. Scout and Barn had their desks huddled off to a corner and were discussing something.

Rainbow's desk was empty. Good. *Nobody* would get that desk. Feelings still pinged when he saw the empty station.

Michelle's was...*not* empty. She sat at the screen furiously tapping the keys.

Dexx took a few steps toward her. "You back?"

"I am." She sat back from the screen and folded her hands on her lap. "And we need to talk."

"Okay. Am I in trouble?" He wanted to feign worry, but the truth was, a pit formed in his stomach. What had he done wrong, now?

"No, but could we talk in private?" Michelle stood and led the way to his office. She stood at the door and waited for him.

He stopped at the door when he saw Frey and Joel inside. Frey filled out paperwork, and Joel worked on a running commentary of soul-sucking affirmations.

Frey worked, muttering, "Uh-huh."

Joel, the goblin looked up hastily. "Go away. The boss is busy here. She doesn't need—oh sorry, Colt." He stood and waited.

Frey stood, picking up her papers and a pen. "Sorry. We happened across drugs and—never mind." She motioned to Joel. "Wait outside."

The goblin looked like he was about to salute but turned on his heel and zipped between Michelle and Dexx.

Frey shook her head as she rounded the desk. "I had to come in here to spare the bullpen from his rambling. He's a good guy, mostly." Her frown said she wasn't sure why she was saying that out loud.

Dexx raised a brow. He'd never pegged her for an ego boost kind of girl.

"Hey, boss-girl," Joel called from her desk. "Got your chair for ya. I'll grab you some coffee, too."

"Is that...creepy?" Frey asked.

Dexx shook his head.

Michelle nodded. "Definitely. I'd nip that in the butt.

"Good call." Frey half smiled at Dexx and left the room.

He motioned for Michelle to lead and closed the door behind him. "You know what that's about?"

"No," Michelle held her smirk awkwardly, trying to stop the laugh from bubbling up. "But I'm glad it's her, not me."

Dexx let his smile out. "Wow. Well, I guess. Whatcha got for me?"

"Okay, so a quick recap. I'm a dryad, and we can talk through our roots."

"Yeah. This is an *old* review, but anyway." He motioned for her to continue as he took his warmed seat. If she was going that far back, this must be a real left-field talk.

Michelle tipped Joel's chair forward and swept it out, then sat. "And you know we're technologically advanced, right? Like a few years ahead of the latest tech?"

"No. I knew you had pretty good computer skills, but technologically advanced? That's new to me."

"So, we'll start there. Yes. Dryads have an affinity for technology, especially computers and communication tech. Some of the grove have been working on something, and they let me have a prototype. You can't hold it so don't ask. Soon enough everyone will know, though."

This was getting weird. What could the grove be working on that Michelle wanted to play secret agent about it?

"So what is it?"

She pulled a cell phone from her pocket, pressed a button and showed it to him. The home screen lit up, with the time in large numbers, with a background of a tall oak tree.

How do you have a working phone?" His hands itched to touch it.

"Techno-magick. There's more." She hit a button on the surface and a holographic projection of someone's head formed.

The man looked around and he raised a green eyebrow. "You decided to go ahead and do it, huh?"

Michelle rolled her eyes. "We couldn't keep this to ourselves."

The man opened his mouth to say something.

Dexx interrupted him. "How does this work?"

"Dryad communications," the man said.

"Like satellites."

"Yeah, sure."

"No," Michelle said impatiently. "Have you ever noticed that we communicate to one another?"

No. "Yeah."

"We talk through our roots."

That made no sense at all. "Oh, great." How was that better than satellites? Wouldn't talking through dirt slow down or limit the signal strength?

Dexx reached out for the phone, intending to inspect it closer.

Michelle slapped his hand away. "I said you couldn't touch it. So don't."

"Wow, that's cool." But how did it help them if she was the only one with a working phone? "No jokes, that's cool. How soon are others going to get some?"

"We're working on that." Michelle raised her eyes seriously.

"Yeah, but *how quickly* are we going to be seeing these?"

"I really don't know. That's why I'm talking to you."

Uh, okay? "Why?"

"Because you're married to Paige."

That still wasn't making any sense.

"I can't get in to talk to her."

Oh. Well, that made him feel a little cheap. "What do you need?"

"Resources. People." She shrugged. "Anything to help us boost the speed of production."

Paige probably wasn't event even the right one to speak to. Hadn't she handed that off to someone else? "Okay, how about a test? Hold it out on your palm. I won't touch it."

Michelle hesitated, but did as she was asked.

Dexx place his palm flat over the phone and felt for resonances. He couldn't *cast* spells, but he could see them and feel their intent. "Let's see. There's earth and fire in there. A bit of air, and I don't feel any water. Air and fire have the largest totals."

Michelle's eyes went wide. "How did you—"

Dexx held up a finger. "Not done yet. Earth magick is less, but it's there for an anchor. This anchor is a bit different, though, so probably something rooty? It feels like a cross between a deadman and an active safety net, or maybe rolling support. Descriptions are kind of funny. But it's a fine net. There's other stuff in there, but I don't want to be here all day describing a phone. Am I close?"

Michelle folded her fingers over the phone and put it away. "Have you been talking to my people or...or *spying?*"

"Yeah, that sounds like me, but really, do I have *that* kind of time?" Dexx sat back and folded his arms. "This is what happens when you go away for a while. I do shit you wouldn't dream of. Long story short, I can feel magick and what it's doing."

Her mouth worked, but no words came out. "How did you come across this power? Does this have something do with that stone the demon gave you?"

146

"Yes. And no. Anyway, what you have there is very cool. What are you going to do with it?"

Michelle shook her head and shoved the phone in her pocket. "That's what we're trying to figure out."

He grunted.

"You realize what this means, right? A whole new market for devices that power themselves. This is limitless. No batteries to recharge."

Well, that was certainly cool. "Yeah, sure. Now all you need is to invent an EMP gun to cancel out regular tech—" Dexx stopped as things fell into place. The magick dampers the Federalists were using against the paras. They couldn't be straight-up spells *or* tech. It had to be a combination like this phone. "I think your people are way behind the eight ball. The other side already has a network that negates most magick, and shifters."

"What, like the collars?"

"Way bigger than that. And remote. DoDO and the Federalists are dampening magick with *something*. I was able to keep my shift and Leslie did, too. Paige lost all her magickal abilities, though."

"I thought she was able to still summon the storm."

What? When? Then he remembered. "That was with Doe in Nevada. No. I'm talking about when we went to save the elves in Kansas."

"So, two different kinds?"

"Probably developed."

"Huh." She bit her thumbnail in thought.

"You think the grove could make something to combat those?"

Michelle stared at him with big brown eyes. "Paige sent over one of the boxes and they're already looking at that. So, yeah, I'm sure."

"Cool. That made him feel a little better. "Okay. Keep me

posted and I'll figure out who you should really be talking to about this."

"Thank you." She paused, then bit her lips and closed the door behind her as she left.

One step forward.

Walton had thought he'd won big when he'd taken down communications. Dexx would love to be a fly on the wall when he found out that the paranormals had not only a way to call each other, but that their tech was cooler than his.

That didn't make Dexx childish at all.

Merry crossed her arms and set her hip. She wanted her curves to start wearing the man's defenses away. Males were so easy to manipulate. A hint here, a suggestion there. A series of misplaced words and they thought they had the superior intellect. Sure, the regional alpha hadn't trusted her in years, but he had facets to be manipulated that he refused to recognize.

Like how angry he was and all she'd done was step into the room with an air of authority.

McCree lifted his chin. "Ah, Ms. Eastwood. Your description doesn't do you justice," he said with his Australian accent. "I was just wrapping up with the junior squad. You may leave, Luca. My business associate has arrived." The men behind him shuffled and made faint mocking noises.

The alpha bristled, his two bodyguards growing fur that outlined their faces. He held up a hand and they visibly calmed themselves. "I am the only recognized personnel acquisition placement here."

"Really?" Merry let her contempt show with a crooked smile. "I don't recognize you at all. Come, McCree, I believe we have an appointment. I did not expect so many to be with you or I would have arranged transportation." She actually *had* been informed of the rather large contingent, but it wasn't up to her to care for them.

"I'm sure they can handle themselves." He took another step.

The alpha stepped in front of the man. "Do *not* get involved with Merry Eastwood. There's only one way you end up when you do business with her."

"I'm sure your next word will be 'dead,' am I right? We have koalas more fierce than you Yanks. I'll be right fine, and you can deal with the others over there. They seem to be... anxious. G'day, mate." Tom moved the alpha away from him with his cane and walked toward Merry, a false smile plastered to his face.

At least the old witch understood how to wield power. That was something Merry missed.

She turned and headed back to her limo, sketching a rune on the wall of the warehouse on her way out, infusing it with blood magick.

A low growl emanated from the parking lot.

Vampires. They were the easiest to lead. Her magick was like a drug to them and they couldn't get enough of it.

That should keep the shifter alpha busy for quite a while.

She had plans to set in motion and she couldn't afford for him to get involved or to let Paige know of her intentions until she was ready to let Paige know herself.

Tom waited until the door closed on the limo before he spoke again. "So. Tell me again which states I'll be receiving?"

Merry smiled. Let Paige think she was running this revolution.

She was the real power player here.

I finished the last touch on the sigil and studied it to make sure it was right.

"You're sure this is right this time?" Fox said as he took a step away from the square table in the chilly plant room.

"Yes, it's right," I said a bit more testy than I probably should have. I'd thought I'd had it right the last three times and I'd managed to set off the smoke detectors twice and to kill one of Gertie's prized plants. Though, technically, the plant had died because we'd been forced to open the window and it was twenty below outside.

After that, I knew to move the plants to warmer spots.

Fox just shook his head and bit his lips as he looked at me.

Not super-helpful, that one. Releasing a long breath, a charged the sigil.

It flared to life, emitting a violet film between me and Fox that almost looked like an oil slick on pavement. It looked stable enough, so I reached out with my karmic magick to get a feel for the intent. That was the thing with sigil work. Lines and dots and circles could mean just about anything, really. The person creating the sigils was basically making up their own language.

I'd *thought* this sigil would have something to do with attacks, which had been why when I'd set off the smoke alarms, I hadn't been super-surprised.

But this didn't seem like it was doing anything.

Until Fox folded over, his hand going to his throat as he gasped for breath.

The leaves of the plants around him started to brown and curl.

Was this stripping the oxygen out of the room?

I smudged the sigil, breaking the spell and Fox took in great gulps of air.

Well, that'd certainly worked, though not the way I'd thought it would.

However, knowing what this one did would help me to decipher some of Threknal's other spells and sigils.

Gertie walked and surveyed the damage to her plants, ignoring Fox, who was obviously still breathing. "You need to take this out of my room."

I opened my mouth to speak, and then shut it because I'd discovered something in the last week. Plant people in Alaska were like rabid wolves. I'd just done...a lot of damage. "I am...so sorry. If there's anything I can do..."

"Oh, there is." She stepped toward me and daggered me with a look, shoving a finger in my chest. "You're going to get me an albino monstera and then you're going to stay the hell out of my plant room."

I had no idea what that plant even was, but I knew I wouldn't like what I'd find once I did. I just had to be glad that the internet wasn't stable yet. And that we didn't have proper forms of money yet. "Okay. I love you?"

She glared at me and then went to her plants, talking to them as if Fox and I weren't in the room.

Which, you know, by rights, we'd been kicked out, so we shouldn't be anymore.

I gathered Threknal's journal and notes and headed toward the low-ceilinged living room. "Are you okay?" I finally asked Fox.

He glared at me, finally breathing better. "Tell me this helped and that you're making progress on those things."

I nodded. We'd only been working on these for a few months with terrible success.

He sank down at the dining table. "I heard you asked Charlie to leave with you."

Had she told everyone or just one person and that one person was then telling everyone? "I did."

"So, you're not staying?"

I still didn't know. My frustration from the whole car incident had waned, but it hadn't disappeared. The root cause was still alive and flourishing.

"You know," he said, jutting his chin forward as I sat, "you could be the path of change."

"Oh, fuck off." Be the path of change. How many times had I heard that? Not always directed at me, but how many times? "Do you have any idea what that even means?"

"Yeah. As the person who *stayed* instead of fleeing after high school, I do."

"Says the guy."

"Says the black guy in Alaska, thank you." He shook his head and looked at me like I was a disappointment.

Okay. That was valid, but... "It feels like moving a mountain."

"Some days. Sure."

"And I'm not a mountain mover."

Incredulity slammed over his features. "The hell you aren't."

I didn't know. Since coming back home, I found myself falling back into old routines and following along and doing things I wouldn't have done a few months ago. I no longer wore my T-shirts tight, or short skirts, or cute boots. Those were all stupid and ludicrous and didn't make any damned sense anymore. I didn't do my hair. I hadn't worn makeup in months.

I...didn't feel like myself. I was becoming this invisible mouse of a woman. It was like...

It was like Alaska was winning.

Fox dropped his gaze and nodded at the table as if seeing all that on my face.

I mean, maybe he did? People did a lot of talking with their faces and not everyone was dumb to it.

"Find you again, Wy." He got up. "The old you who was a fighter while here, and the new you who's a different kind of fighter."

"I don't belong here, Fox," I said quietly.

"Why not?" he asked. "Because it's hard here? We're in a war, Wy. Things'll get better."

"Really?" I tried to remember when anything was *easy* up here.

"You're soft."

I snorted. "I just don't like celebrating the fact that I have to work this damned hard to barely make it."

He stood and scratched his collarbone before heading toward the kitchen and the front door. "Well, some of us are able to see the beauty in the people we have around us."

The front door slammed, letting me know he was a lot more pissed than he'd shown.

Weeks later, Dexx sat down hard in the chair still a little sore from the vampire fight that had gone long into the night. He cracked the top off the beer and just held the bottle, watching the moisture-laden carbon dioxide waft up the top.

How had *anyone* thought vampires would be good reinforcements to the paras on the docks? They shouldn't be allowed near *any* non-vampire, especially not when blood magick was in play. Hadn't Paige thought that out? Hadn't she been keeping the Eastwoods out of the field for this very reason?

But maybe that was the reason Merry was making such an obvious power move now. Because she wasn't getting a piece of the action.

Here they were, going into battle, and the Blackmans were growing in power and prestige, to the point where they were in negotiation meetings and had an advising office for Paige.

Merry wasn't even invited to the office. She was like a woman scorned.

But...as much as he wanted to blame the Eastwoods— particularly Merry—for the recent vampire attacks that had been going off and on for weeks now, there was no sign of blood magick in the affected areas. Paige had tested too.

Tom McCree ran around Portland as if he owned the place. Well, like Merry had promised him the rule of the city. He was never far from his entourage of thugs.

Dexx tipped the beer back for a couple good glugs. Nice and cold and bitter. Just like a beer was supposed to be.

Paige sat with him, her own ale unopened. He reached over and grabbed the cap. She turned the bottle, her gaze focused somewhere beyond the patio door as the beer closed the distance to her mouth and stayed there until it was empty. Burps came up through her teeth in in little poofs.

"Hard day?" Dexx belatedly tipped his bottle to clink against Paige's empty one.

She grunted, but not to agree or disagree.

Dexx switched the beer in his hands and placed his free one on Paige's thigh. She covered his fingers and squeezed.

There they were, newlyweds, and they couldn't even get up the ambition to take advantage of an empty house.

The house hadn't been empty since they'd moved in the day after it was built. Well, maybe a few times. But still Dexx had his ass firmly planted in the seat and wasn't moving it for a while.

"Merry and McCree are up to something." Paige hadn't pulled her thousand-yard stare back.

"Yeeeup." Dexx answered in a mimic of Bugs Bunny.

"I can't tell what, but they're up to something, and nobody can catch a scent of it. Not even Ollie can pick up on it."

"Yeeeup," Dexx repeated.

"But if they do their jobs, I can't even bring myself to care much."

"Yeeeup." Dexx relaxed further and let his eyelids relax as he squeezed her hand.

Dexx let the silence go on for a minute, then closed his eyes. The darkness was complete. So, he planted a tree in his mind. A big one where two people could lean against it in cool shade.

The tree was a marvel. The bark was just rough enough to grip, and a full canopy umbrellaed over to nearly hide anyone underneath.

Hattie rubbed her head along his, flattening her short whiskers back.

"Hey, kid. You wanna raise some Cain up in here?" His body might be tired, but he still had some restless energy.

Why would you seek out the thornback?

"Because sometimes it's fun to see just how hard you can poke the bear and get away with it."

A paw wrapped around Dexx's front and an imaginary claw caught on his imaginary pants. *This is a dangerous place to find a bear to poke.*

"How dangerous is it when we're bigger than the bear? Come on. I had a really hard day and I want to have some fun while *sitting* in my chair at home."

This is not a place to have *fun. Natural laws are followed here, and those are to be on guard or be killed.*

"Who says we won't be on guard while we're playing? Besides, the particular bear I want to poke is already riled. Unless you want to poke at the djinn, in which case, that's leaning more toward death-wish scale, but I'm still down if you are."

Hattie sat on her haunches and went silent. She couldn't *actually* be contemplating going to the djinn stronghold?

I do not think we should do that just yet. They have a long memory and we...did not leave them happy.

"Yeah, I got that already. How about we just stick to the problem at hand? I thought we could build up Mah'se a bit. I still have some hope that we can get him to take a bond." And if he wanted to take a bond, perhaps Pea could bond him. They could be a good match.

You do know he will not be helpful if you are in the Time Before.

"So, we hit him with the good-cop-bad-cop routine. Works all the time in the real world."

You are incorrect. But there is a chance we can help him. He is my counterpart, and I have known him longer than I have known you.

"Is that a jab at me?"

It is the truth.

"Then let's get this show on the road." Paige would thank him in *all* sorts of ways if he could get her a bond again.

He didn't know if he was totally against her having the

bond, but a large part of him missed feeling her in his pack bond. He missed the closeness, of knowing how she was feeling and doing no matter where she was. He felt disconnected from her, and with all of her duties, they mostly just sat on the couch in exhausted silence when they had a few free moments. They didn't even share the same bed at night because they weren't on the same sleep schedule.

But at least he'd made himself heard and she was thinking about *why* she wanted the power, and knew that people were watching as she claimed more and more *exactly* like Walton.

Power corrupted, and absolute power corrupted absolutely. Just like Bussemi. All the power in the universe and all he wanted was to make this world feel as shitty as he did.

"Hold on a sec." Dexx pulled back from Hattie a little and grabbed both sides of her head and pulled her close. "It occurred to me once or twice that we really haven't spent time together where you *teach* me about this place. We're usually running from something trying to kill us or running to something to kill *it*. Before we mess with Mah'se, how about *I* learn how to use this place and get a few pointers? Could come in handy if we have to go toe to toe with the big guy." The truth was he *liked* the ancient and thought the ancient deserved something better than eternal pain.

The cub shows signs of growth. You might have sabers soon if you keep growing.

"You fat cat. You might not be able to hold your head up soon if your head keeps blowing up like it is."

Hattie sent him waves of laughter through the bond and they merged into the Time Before.

The plains were free of snow, but the land was still barren. Shafts of straw-colored grass stuck up from tufts dotting the plain.

Okay, so I get this operates the way it operates, but there's still the why *of it does what it does.*

Hattie sat down on the bluff. *The sky is the color it is. Why?*

Because oxygen absorbs every color in the visible light spectrum except that specific color. There's a why *for ya.*

Actually, he'd had to look that up. Hattie caught him before on that one and he didn't have a good answer. So if the sky had a particular color because of science, maybe this place had a why because of magick. And if there was anything that had rules, it was *magick.*

Then you must know why the Time Before works in its way.

Well, no. I kinda hoped if I had an answer, you would, too. Dexx pulled in an imaginary breath. *Let's move past this. How do we operate it? Maybe I don't need the why or how. Not yet.*

It is good to let the things you cannot understand be.

Whatever. How do we travel fast?

Hattie quirked her head to the side in confusion.

You know, like when you're playing a game and you need to get to another part of the world to finish a quest or something. You do it all the time here.

Hattie shook her head. But it was a head shake of patience.

Suddenly, she sank to her belly, her ears perked and flicking forward and back. Whatever caught her attention Dexx couldn't—wait a minute.

Very minute vibrations touched him. It wasn't sound exactly, and it was through the ground, or was it?

There was a disturbance somewhere, and Hattie had trouble detecting from where it was coming. *Your first lesson, cub. We do not want to stalk the creature stalking us. Not yet. How do we leave before it gets us? Hurry. It is not far.*

How the hells should *he* know? *Run?*

She grunted. *We will not outrun this beast.*

Run…faster?

Maybe your teeth will be slower than I thought, she growled. Think *about where you want to be. Make it familiar to you and step to it.*

She was really going to wait for him to do this.

Where do we want to go? Pick a place. Hurry. It's almost here.

The vibrations were stronger, closer. Dexx picked a place at random and leapt.

Hattie flew off the ledge and began to plummet.

Oh, shiii—

The ground disappeared and she landed smoothly on her feet in tall thick grass. The sun was warm on her back and the grass felt rough against her fur. She dropped to her belly again, tentatively sticking a paw out.

This wasn't anywhere he'd seen or been before. First of all, there was *actual* sunlight, and second of all, there was the vision-destroying grass *everywhere*.

Where are we— He cut off as Hattie sent him a warning to shut up.

Okay. What was going on here?

The paw came down silently and she moved forward. She walked like that for*ever*. At least it felt like it.

Two steps. Five. A breeze moved the grass gently and rustled with a soft static. Her foot came down, the fur on her foot soaking up the pops and breaks of the dry stalks.

He wanted so badly to ask what the hells she was doing, but she'd already told him to clamp his trap. His only options were to do just that or leave back to reality. He had some time to kill, so he'd hang out watching a true master of the hunt do her thing.

Another two steps and minutes later, the grass parted to a small clearing. Nothing moved and nothing—wait.

A faint signature lit the other side. It was a blob he couldn't distinguish, but it *was* there.

Dexx waited as Hattie froze. The wind was coming from

159

the wrong direction to pull more information on the blob of heat across the small clearing.

The thing raised its head and looked away. It was anoth—

Hattie leapt out, claws extended, and pounced.

You are dead.

The sabertooth under her turned its golden eyes to her and kicked out with its rear legs. They caught Hattie solidly in the ribs and she flew off backward but her feet caught the ground easily.

Yes. The cat had a smooth male voice. *You are a better hunter. Is that what you want me to say?* He stood and shook himself off, standing even taller and broader than Hattie, but he moved slower and without the precision than Hattie did.

His fur looked a bit shorter than hers with muscles bunching and cording with impressive ease under his skin.

You do not have to be the smallest cub last to the meal. Hattie's words had bite.

The male cat growled low. *You do this whenever you find me.*

Because you have not yet absorbed the lesson.

Who's the big guy? Dexx could plow through tons of rock with a body like that.

This is one of my line. Barre. He lived about the same time as the one who shares your name.

So he'd lived when Dekskulta failed to kill Bussemi. *Before, during, or after?* Oh, shit, he sounded like an ass. *Sorry. What I meant was, nice to meet you. Are you a bond like your mom's mom?*

Barre looked at Hattie with his golden eyes. Was he trying to pry private information from her, or was it a private conversation? She'd never kept anything from him before.

You may not. She sent back to her scion. *When you talk with me you talk with my bond.*

Did she ever have a meeting with the sabertooth when she *didn't* have a reincarnation of him?

Barre turned his head, obviously irritated, and huffed through his nose, but he calmed. *Is he going to bring you back to the long wait like the last one?*

Wait, what? *Hold on. What do you mean "like the last one?" Did my last life kill us?*

Hattie sat and rolled her hips to sit on her side. *Your last life was reckless. Stumbling with the feel and the power he felt as a shifter.*

Fucker. Dexx would give a pretty penny to go back and smack the shit out of him. *Nobody* drove his fat cat recklessly. He wouldn't allow it. *Let me be clear. I would not ever do something like that. I treat her like a queen.*

Hattie sighed heavily. *He is the most reckless of any of the lives we've lived together. But he is also the most protective of any of those he claims as his pack. He is the first defender and would gladly send us to the Wait if the others have a chance to stay longer.*

Aw. She thought he was a nice guy. Sort of. *I am not reckless. I just do what I have to do.*

Hattie chuckled in his head. Could that other saber hear it? *So, are you a shifter, or you just hang out looking cool all day?*

Barre huffed again. *I have been a bond. I am an ancient, but one of the last. I choose not to since it has been reopened to us. I will wait.*

He'd be an awesome sprit shifter. Most likely he'd be stronger than Hattie in terms of brute strength, but as she'd already shown, she was more agile.

But that opened up a whole new line of questions for Dexx since he seemed easier to talk to than Mr. You-shouldn't-be-here. *Hey, how do you choose a bond? Asking for a friend.*

Hattie sent him an admonition. The image was of kittens falling over themselves to fall off a log that might or might not be next to a cliff. *Too eager to explore.*

Barre cocked his head as if to ask if Dexx was for real.

When Hattie just stared back, he huffed and sat down.

When there is a call from a high enough potential bond, the spirits who can hold the bond choose it. Through a series of tests, the final spirit gets to choose.

Huh. How was Mah'se going to bypass the line? *So, what if there's only a few, or* just one?

Then the process is simple. Barre's eyes narrowed in something that looked a little more feral than from a few seconds before. *The bonds have been much weaker than from the time when I held a bond. Almost none of them could handle a spirit as strong as I am.*

He looked strong. Really strong. But could he even hold a candle to Hattie? Nope, his fat cat was the best of the best. Probably better. *How do you know when a prospective bond comes up?* Good question. Did they get a prompt like a video game telling them a quest was available?

We feel a pull. Hat'ai doesn't feel the same thing. You two have been bonded since her first, and somehow you made it permanent.

Huh. Could you somehow, say, make a bond without the pull? Something you *wanted to do without a person being born to it, or bitten by an alpha?* That's what Paige had done. Or Cawli had.

Hattie stood. *It is time to go back to your world.*

What? Time doesn't pass the same way— Dexx opened his eyes to Paige shaking him.

"Are you going to answer me or not?" Her brows were wrinkled in annoyance.

"Um. Yeah. What was the question? I was way gone."

"Have you thought more about giving me the bite?"

Wow. She was like a dog with a bone, though...it had been weeks. "I have. Lots of thinking, actually." Did she know on some cosmic scale that he'd been hunting bonds for her? "I don't know if it's a good idea yet."

"What do you mean, *yet*? It's a good idea, but not now, or it's not a good idea and you don't want to tell me no?"

Dexx clamped his mouth shut. If he had a Twix, he'd

totally be unwrapping that pig and chewing for all he was worth. Instead, he took a swig of his beer and inhaled deeply. Why had time been so accelerated in the little clearing with Barre? "It's more complicated than you're making it seem. Spirits don't just fall into a host. They need time to figure out who's best suited to be your bond mate. I'm pretty sure *none* of them would even want a shot at a powerful person like you." Not to mention she'd already been bonded to a spirit who had died.

"They don't have to *stay*. I would be fine with a...trial period or whatever, so they can try it out."

Dexx put a half smile on. "What, like a risk-free two-week trial to see if they like the subscription? That they can cancel at any time?"

"Sure, why not?"

Dexx laughed. "Pretty sure *bond* means more than trial period. You just don't want to be saddled with a garden slug or a possum or something, am I right?"

Paige didn't answer right away but tapped on her bottle with her finger. After a while, she looked at him. "I miss Cawli and shifting into anything I want. It was fun. I miss having the ability to adapt to my situation and choose the best creature to be, to be able to go wherever I needed whenever I needed it."

"Are you sure there isn't any superiority complex peeking through, where you can look down on all the other shifters who don't keep their clothing and only have the one shape?"

Did Dexx have the ability to shift into anything? *Could we have shifted into anything when I had my magick?*

Hattie was sprawled out in his mind. *You would bring back a kill to try it differently?*

The meaning was *why dredge that up when the magick was already gone?* Dang, he'd gotten better at sifting meanings out of her riddles.

Suddenly, Hattie was on her feet and full to the brim with anxious energy. So much so that Dexx's beer trembled in the bottle.

The two things happened at once. The front door swung open as Leslie charged in, and Dexx grabbed Paige's arm, letting his alpha out and clamping on to her wrist with his teeth.

15

Dexx and Paige jumped up from the couch exactly the same time.

"What the hell are you doing?" Dexx yelled at Hattie.

"What the hell was that?" Paige yelled at Dexx.

"What the hell, you two?" Leslie yelled at them both.

Dexx stared in wide-eyed innocence at Leslie, and pointed to Paige's arm. "No, I didn't—it wasn't me—I wouldn't do—" he stammered, trying to get it all out.

"What was all that bullshit about me gaining too much, then you try to chomp *through* my wrist?" Paige held her arm close to her, bending slightly over from the injury.

"Tell me you didn't just do what I think you did." Leslie slammed the door and hurried to Paige. "What the fuck, Dexx? All right, Pea. Let me see."

What the hell, fat cat? I mean, what. The. Hell? *How did you push me, anyway? Talk to me or I swear I'm gonna*— Actually, what could he do to Hattie? Nothing. But he could level the threat anyway. Concern for Paige crashed back in. "I'm so sorry. Hattie just sort of flooded through. I had no idea she was going to, you know...do that." He pointed helplessly at her arm.

Paige had her eyes screwed shut in obvious pain. "Did you have to bite me so hard?"

Yeah, why did you bite so hard? Hattie, answer me.

She stood at attention, really studying the world through his eyes. *I could not help myself. The feeling came upon me and I had to react. It was much like in my life on the world when I needed to make cubs.*

This isn't anywhere close to being in heat. This is...way different. Just, why? How could he put his thoughts and feelings hard enough to really push his point? Was this like making a cub? Here they were *just* talking about how bonds are chosen and *poof* Hattie forced him into making a bond. *This* will *end with a bond, won't it?*

I cannot say. It would with any other person. But she is different. Nothing small or weak will bond her, and if no one will bond with her then... I must go.

Go? Go where? Don't you leave now, you fat cat. You stay.

Too late. Hattie had left the house.

"Dammit."

"Let's get this cleaned up." Leslie passed a glare to Dexx then shepherded Paige toward the kitchen. "No telling what kind of diseases he's carrying."

The front door swung open again and Leah stepped in just in time to see her mom and Leslie carefully walk to the kitchen. "Mom? What happened?"

Dexx answered before Leslie could make it seem worse than it was. "I just gave your mom an alpha bite. No, I don't know why."

Leah's mouth opened, then closed when he answered. "Is she okay?"

Dexx smelled the distinctive odor of blood. "Yeah. She'll be fine." Would she be? What would happen to a person who had been refused by every spirit in the spirit realm? Maybe, just maybe, Mah'se would consent to take her on as his bond. She would *definitely* be as good a bond as Rainbow would have been. He'd have to see that. Or Barre.

Leah turned to look at her mom and aunt washing her arm off in the sink, then back to Dexx. "What happened? I don't get it."

"It's complicated, I think." He took a breath trying to form thoughts when Tyler, Griff, and Bobby pushed in the back door, laughing at some juvenile joke, no doubt. Mandy and Ashley followed them in with Kammy in tow.

"What's complicated, Uncle Dexx?" Mandy's eyes went straight to the kitchen and Paige.

Leslie picked her eyes up from Paige. "You kids, *all* of you go outside. Don't stop, don't pass go, and definitely don't piss me off. *Move.*"

As one, they turned back around and left through the door they'd entered.

"And you, maybe you should go someplace else." Leslie wrinkled her brow in anger.

Dexx took a step toward the hallway and paused a second to recover. "You may not remember who I am, so here's a refresher. I'm *your* alpha, but more importantly, I'm *her* husband. Snarl at the kids. It's your job. But you pull the teeth back when it's me, okay?" He let a little alpha push her to press his point.

Leslie shook her head like she was trying to keep herself awake. "Yeah. Sorry. I just snapped. Don't know what happened."

"Me neither. You okay, Pea?" He went to the sink to see.

She nodded, but the pained kind of nod.

Her arm bled but the water washed it away easily, revealing his handiwork plainly. A perfect arc of slight punctures showed on the underside of her wrist.

"I'm sorry, Pea. Something just plowed into Hattie and she charged me. It was the strangest feeling. Hattie got all nervous, and it was just weird."

Paige flexed her fingers. "Yeah, you said that. Kind of reminds me of the time *you* got bit, doesn't it? He couldn't help himself either."

Dexx really didn't remember that too well. "I only have flashes of that day."

"Well, I guess the question of you biting me is settled. How soon do you think I'll be chosen?" Paige flashed him a pained smile.

"I don't know. I can't even say you *will*. The spirits over there, they're terrified of you. No person has ever outlived their bond, let alone asked for a second one. If it's anything, it'll be something to behold, though."

"I can't wait. It has to be soon." Paige pulled her arm away from the water, and grabbed a towel. She wrapped it and squeezed.

Dexx snorted, understanding where she was coming from and needing her to be cautious at the same time. "You pushing them to pick you is about as likely as you starting Leah's car. *Ever.*"

Paige groaned. "Is there some way you can ask?"

Dexx had a much better handle on what the Time Before was and how it operated, but one thing he'd learned was that it did *not* have a bureaucracy to complain to. "Funny you should ask. I was *just* tapped to be the president of the spirit realm. I'll push it through right now."

Leslie barked a laugh.

Paige glowered. "You don't have to be an ass."

"Then you'll have to remember that they do things their own way, and you'll just have to suffer the wait. Sorry, but that's the way it is."

"If you two are done, I'm going away." Leslie turned around and left.

Dexx watched her leave. "You think this is the same thing that happened when I got the alpha bite?" The alpha who'd gotten him, though, had been chipped and was being controlled by Sven. That technology had then been transferred over to DoDO and then since modified. Could Dexx be chipped? How would they have done it?

"I think it's an amazing coincidence."

"Babe. This is *not* coincidence. You wanted a bite, I say no, then it happens by magick? No. This is something else. But now you're in line to receive a bond. I really hope it's—" He cut off. He hadn't told her there was a spirit almost *actively* looking for a bond.

"Hope it's what?"

He didn't want to dangle ideas in front of her. She had enough on her plate. "Hope it's a *whole gang* of garden slugs. It would serve you right." Dexx let a smile cover his face, then lost it when she gave him a smile of her own. "I'm sleeping on the couch, huh?"

"Yeeeup." She left, following Leslie.

Dexx blew a breath out. "Women. Speaking of, Hattie? Get your furry butt out here. You got some 'splainin' to do. Come on, fat cat."

He trudged up the stairs to their room. He wasn't planning on sleeping on the couch, not really, but best to be prepared just in case.

In the room, he pulled a blanket from the closet and set it by the dresser. When he stood, he passed a look over the clutter. The amethyst sat in the *shamiyir* bowl, just how he'd left it, except the bowl was repaired. The crack was completely gone. The scorch had been already been cleaned for a while, but now, it was—nothing.

Furiel had said it *had* been used to channel magick. He

never said what type, though. Could be ley energy, or elemental, or door, or blood, or death, or any one of a hundred types. Except it had been *his* in a previous life, so it had been *his* magick. Would he ever have that ability again?

The runes carved into the bowl were shiny and new, but they meant as much now as they had when it was a good pop away from two pieces. And although it felt like it was *his,* it held nothing else.

Oh well. He didn't have it before, and he still didn't have it. He'd keep his clothed shift and be happy.

He set the bowl on the dresser and put the crystal back in it. They were great keepsakes.

A glint of silver caught his eye. The little fob thing that Mario had dropped just before he'd taken the long nap of death. "Hope you're burned alive forever, asshole." There was no punishment strong enough for that man.

Palming the device, he left the room to check on the kids in the backyard.

Tyler had the rest of the kids standing with their hands in the air waving them like they just didn't care. He was a one-kid concert. He sang and made noises and made anyone listening *see.* He projected images *right* into the brain, and he'd quickly become very good at it.

He sang a low note, drawing the song to the end.

Griff jumped in the air, fist pumping. "Okay, Mandy's turn. Do the fire puppet thing." His enthusiasm overcame his balance and he fell over.

Leslie saw Dexx come through the door and a smile lit on her face. "No, I want to see Leah raise some zombies while Tyler sings 'Thriller.'"

Tyler struck a claw-handed zombie pose while Leah scratched the back of her neck, clearly not comfortable with the idea.

That was enough for Dexx. He shifted and sprinted into

the woods. Zombies or any hint that zombies were coming out was his cue to get the hell out of Dodge.

The noises that followed him into the trees weren't laughter. It couldn't be. It didn't matter, though. He wanted a few minutes of alone time.

The grave markers appeared quickly when he was a great cat.

Hattie still hadn't come back from wherever she had gone, but Dexx put that on the back burner. When she showed her face again, he had a few questions.

He shifted back and walked the rest of the way to the stones. Boot's had friendship, Alma's had wisdom beyond even her many years, but Dexx needed Rainbow to lend an ear. She'd been the person he could bounce ideas off of. And her smile never judged.

"Hey, kid. Some shit's gone down. I don't know how to explain it. I mean, *yeah*, I know how to explain it, but I mean string it together in coherent content." Dexx stopped at Rainbow's grave and ran a hand across the top. He turned and sat down, leaning against the stone. "First, and possibly the least, is Merry is plotting something. Shocker, I know. McCree came back to town—no, not the lizard wizard, the dad of that winner. They got something cooking, but they're all about doing their part. For the moment, as long as they're doing what they're told, it's all good."

Dexx took a breath. Then, he took another, sifting through scents on the slight breeze. The day was cooler, being the end of February, but he had a good enough coat for the time being.

"The next is, met your grandma. Sweet old lady. She reminds me of you a lot, because I'd like to put hands on the throat. She hit me with a resulka whammy, and I didn't know it until later. I kinda wish you'd told me about her.

He pulled the device from his pocket and rubbed his thumb across it as he spoke to his dead friend.

"Vampires are in town, and helping reinforce our army, such as it is. They're hard to motivate to *stand down* from converting anyone, and so far, they haven't but they're crazy. Almost like the bloodlust that Tony went through when Merry—"

Was it too much coincidence to think Merry had things all twisted so she could do her thing without interruption? No, but how would he prove it?

"Anyway, we got elves and vampires, and some questionable Australians to help the cause.

"Third is I bit Paige. No, not a fun nibble on the ear. An alpha bite. *That* just happened. I was in the Time Before with Hattie, we got shoved out and Hattie got all antsy, and boom. A chomp. So that's bad enough, but it's eerily similar to what happened to me. I can't think this is coincidence. I just can't."

Dexx scratched his head with a hand, the other played absently with the silver fob.

"Dang, I almost forgot. *Michelle* developed *magick tech*. I know, right? *Michelle*. Well, her grove anyway. It's a cute little thing, her cell phone."

Dexx chuckled, remembering the look on her face.

"She did *not* appreciate my take on her phone. Still, mixing magick and tech is amazing. I think we're on the cusp of some real sci-fi shit soon."

Dexx fell into silence thinking about the melding of magick and machinery, and that got him thinking about Rainbow's grandma, and then to Rainbow and the last time he saw her alive. The shock on her face as the spear of solid shadow impaled her.

A tear rolled down his cheek.

How could he have been so selfish? His own truth that he

dared not admit to was he'd been using her as a crutch. He'd been away from Paige so long that Rainbow became a source of confidence.

Bussemi had broken him, and she'd believed in him. She'd stroked his ego, while Paige had forced him to stand on his own. For the sake of his ego, Rainbow had died.

"I'm so sorry. You really *did* deserve better than me. I wish I could go back and change it."

Cub. You do not. If you value that one, you will learn from the hunt. Hattie's voice resonated, but sadness tinged her words.

Where have you been? He sat up from Rainbow's grave. *What in all the hells happened? And what's going to happen to Pea? Did you talk to Mah'se or what?* Dexx rattled questions off at Hattie before she had a chance to answer. He knew what he was doing. Even as more rolled out from his mouth, he couldn't stop. *Irrelevant* questions poured out. How would Hattie know how to make eggnog?

Hattie waited in quiet as he rambled, her patience everlasting.

"And finally, you scared me. What happened?"

I do not know. I talked with Mah'se. He will not take the bond. He feels the pull, but he will not answer it.

"Will *any* spirit answer?"

I am a powerful member of the ancients, but I do not know how it works. If one of us knows, they have not shared it with me. There will be many who feel your mate's open bond. That is all I know.

How long could Paige hold out? That was if being open to a bond didn't hurt the person. How long had Leslie had an open bond? She'd never even shown symptoms of *anything* wrong, and Robin had blasted his way in.

Crap.

Well, Dexx'd better go make some amends to his wife, if she was still upset about getting what she wanted. He *had* done some damage with that bite. Maybe it would call a stronger spirit—just hopeful thinking.

He pushed his hands to the ground to push himself up. His thumb slipped on the little fob he'd confiscated from Mario.

A silver slash rent the air about fifteen feet in front of him and solidified into a doorway.

"Hey, man," Fox said as he walked through Rick's front door. "I scored some veg."

Rick came out of the kitchen with a towel in his hands. "Great. What all did you pick up?"

"Just some frozen broccoli leaves. I didn't even think that was a thing."

"Yeah, well, me either." Rick gestured to the kitchen island and went back to the pot on the stove. "But when the pickins get slim…"

Fox grimaced as he set the bag down and started rummaging through the meager food supplies he'd scrounged.

Things were pretty…dire. There were no other terms for it. They were on the tail end of a long winter, but February could still bring a lot of hard work for them. These would be the coldest days of the year yet. They still hadn't fixed the electrical grid, so there were loads of people without electricity or running water. The villages were doing better for once because their power grids were at least powered from diesel generators.

But what happened when the diesel ran out?

He had already run his growing list of concerns by Gertie, who had taken over negotiations with Phoebe Blackman, who was a pretty decent person as far as he could tell. The politicians had gotten involved too, which was good because they had access to the infrastructure that was already in place to help the public at large.

"You look glummer than usual," Rick said, setting a thick cutting board in front of Fox. "What gives?"

Fox didn't want to spill, but...he knew he needed to talk to someone. "Wy's leaving."

Concern rippled over Rick's dark features as he frowned. "Why?"

"It's too hard living here."

Rick gestured to the three small containers of veggies Fox had managed to procure from the store. "Can you blame her? All kinds of people are leaving."

Fox got a knife and started chopping at the broccoli leaves. "Do you realize the kind of place we could have if people like her stayed?"

"Right." Rick put another stick of wood in the wood burning stove, conserving his gas for the baseboard heating. "Can you imagine what things would be like if the place made it more welcoming for people like her to stay? Things might actually change."

Fox groaned. "That's the reason they're not." The people here liked things just the way they were and so they were resistant to change. Fox wasn't stupid.

But he also knew firsthand that the people here *could* change and that Wynonna would be a great instrument *for* that. "I don't want to see her leave."

"For Charlie, right?" Rick asked in a smart-ass tone.

"Yeah, asshole." Fox sighed and pushed the chopped frozen broccoli leaves to the side of his board. "For Charlie."

Rick put the lid back on his pot and turned. "Look, if you want my advice..."

As if Fox could make him *not* give it?

"Be the kind of person she's looking for. Right? People

like her leave—not because it's too hard. They came up here *knowing* it would be."

If there were brochures on the state, that would be the headline.

"They leave because they're lonely. And, dude, she's lonely as fuck."

Fox didn't know how that was even possible when the woman lived in a house with amazing people, but...

If the only way for Wy to stay was to get her emotionally invested in the people there, then that was exactly what he was going to do.

After all, she was the first love of his life.

She could be his second, too.

16

A silver-grey film obscured the view of the other side. "Gah!" Dexx stumbled backwards from his half-standing crouch. He almost shifted, ready for DoDO to come through and attack.

Nothing happened.

No DoDO. No demons, or anything else.

The silvery hole shimmered, ready for...what?

A person to come through? Probably.

Slowing his heartrate down, Dexx looked down at the fob in his hand and then looked back up at the doorway, giving it a closer inspection. This had to be how Mario had been able to travel from one place to the next so fast. They didn't *need* door witches. They had technology they could *carry* that opened doors for them.

Cell phone, his *ass*. *This* was what magick and tech should be doing together.

Maybe, if they figured out how to blend Blackman door magick with dryad technology, they could open doorways even inside warded areas so they didn't find themselves trapped. Again. Because that had been horrible.

Nothing came through, but he still had to exercise caution. Just because nothing came through didn't mean there wasn't anything waiting on the back side.

What do you think that is? He knew *what* it was, but Hattie understood.

This might be a trap. Lure the hunters into easy prey.

You really think so? Dexx hoped not, but this was Mario and DoDO they were talking about. Also...maybe the reason this thing worked was because it was limited? Maybe it was only programmed for one location like a garage door opener? That would suck a little more. He'd still take it. *I mean, he's dead. Way far gone, dead. He* wishes *he was ashes dead. The question is what's on the other side? A DoDO stronghold, his bedroom with the hooker still in there, or the daycare he left his mind in?*

Shift, and go through.

The doorway didn't look big enough to fit something the size of Hattie through. Sure, it fit Mario's ego, but that could be infinitely malleable. But the door could be protected, too, just in case Mario had been pursued while using it. The man had been very cunning. Dexx wouldn't be surprised if it was booby-trapped to cut off anything too big to fit. How to test it?

He looked down at the hard-packed dirt of Rainbow's grave. No fucking way. He wouldn't give that asshat any more of his friend. The trees had plenty of branches. He leapt up and grabbed a stout longish branch and snapped it off with a little help from Hattie. Okay, so a *bit* more than a little.

He swished the branch through and swung it at the silver door.

The door resisted and bulged where the tree pulled on the edge, showing that the frame could expand.

Sweet. He dropped the branch and shifted in the blink of an eye and charged through.

The other side was a bit anticlimactic.

It was an apartment. A flat, the Limeys called it. The place was a wreck. The furniture that had probably been top-notch was kindling. Lamps were knocked over and crushed. The dinner table was on its side. No wall hangings, though. Not a picture, not a certificate of assholery. Nothing. Just blank, off-white walls.

The dining room lead off to a hallway, presumably to a bedroom and bathroom.

This was *Mario's apartment.* Did DoDO even know he had one? Well, except that *someone* had found this place, unless this was just the way the man had lived. He hadn't given off the *dirty slob* vibe, though.

Wait. It could be a girlfriend's place. Boyfriend's?

Possibly, but if it was, they were dead or out of country. The place made homeless shantytowns look good.

He shifted back to human and stood there pulling at all the senses he had.

No heat signatures, no active magick. The smell was definitely something horrid, but old. The temperature was low, but not a problem for him.

Moving slowly, Dexx crunched his way across the carpet. Glass and wood made little splinters for unprotected feet.

He rounded the corner to the hallway, which was amazingly free of destruction. The door at the end of hall had to a bedroom or bath—loo. There were two more along the hall on the right. Spare rooms?

He stalked forward slowly to the first door down the hall. He carefully reached out and turned the knob. Yup. The privy.

He went to the next and tried that knob. *This* was the bedroom. Wow. For everything else Mario had been, his bedroom was *meticulous.* It could have been in *Bedrooms Weekly* or whatever they had over there.

Blue and grey were the dominant colors. The dresser looked expensive with a really nice finish, something Paige would have liked but never actually gone to buy because their reality was on the poor side of broke most of the time. Brits had really good furniture. Or money. Could be both.

Dexx'd had enough of the bedroom, though he made a mental note to check it out some more just in case the man had stashed some more of these door devices around with his belt and wallets and stuff. He moved on to the last door.

That turned out to be Mario's office.

A desk sat along one wall, and a bench took up the entire length of the back wall. A drafter's table stood a couple steps away, and *these* walls had hangings. Weapons. Like a lot of weapons. Crossbows, guns, whips…and other things.

Dexx cast around for a light switch. He flicked it on, illuminating the room.

"Holy shit." He'd found the mother lode. The room glowed with magickal devices, on the wall, the bench, every place that had a flat and open spot was covered with collars, guns, *everything*.

He made his way around the drafting table and stopped. There were two neat stacks of papers with dates at the top.

Notes. No, not notes. *Plans* for the invasion of the States. Plans to eradicate paras in Europe, Asia, *Africa*.

Not that these were the actual documents DoDO was going to use, but still, it gave insight into the most notorious organization in the history of the world.

Dexx flipped through the notes, looking at dates in descending order. The first sheet had plans to summon something. The name was in characters, that didn't make sense.

Runes. Overlapping and violent, but runes.

"How am I going to read this?"

The scent of *clean* touched his nose the same time Roxxie

spoke. "You don't. And you never will. Just knowing the name will put you on the list to be...restricted."

Roxxie was still impossibly beautiful with perfect blonde hair, and a leather jacket over a white shirt and pants. An angel wings pin was on the left side of her jacket with matching boots. "Dang angels and demons. Is this information restricted or liquidated? Is Furiel with you?"

"He is not."

"Then how did you get here?" There were only a couple ways, but she'd probably been following him.

"I have to confess I've been keeping an eye on you. I came through your doorway."

"Roxxie, I like you. I really do. You've helped me out of some tough spots and of all the angels I've ever known, I think you have humanity I can get behind. But I also think you're full of shit. If you've been so close all this time, why didn't you help when we were escorting the elves through Kansas?"

"Dexx—" Roxxie inhaled deep and let it go with sad eyes. She looked so genuine. "I'm sorry. I've told you before, and this is true on any oath you would believe, I can only help you so much. I'm not what I was, and even then, things required attention and I did what I could. Of all humanity, you and the entire Whiskey family are the most deserving. I would be with you at all times, if I could."

It sounded so sincere, but if demons had a cardinal rule, it was they couldn't be trusted. Angels were the opposite side of the same coin. They just couldn't be trusted.

Roxxie walked into the room and held her hand out to him.

He took it, and she covered his with her other. "Humanity is...a complicated bunch. You—"

"Yeah, 'cause demons and your kind are so—"

"*You*, humanity, are complicated. The best and the worst

are separated by degrees, but some hold those degrees as far apart as a different plane. The one you call Cardinal Bussemi. He's on the track to completely eradicate you, and all who stand on your side, but what do you want for him? For him and all who stand on *his* side to be eradicated. How far apart are you? Really?"

"But that's different."

"Is it?" Roxxie still held his hand, warmth enveloping him. She might not be powerful, but damn, she should be.

An image passed through his head and something occurred to him. "Hey, what would it take for you to be back where you used to be? Full power?"

"That is beyond me now. To dwell on it would be to dream too large."

"Sure, I get that. Sometimes it's fun to talk about winning the lottery. What would it take?"

Roxxie looked at the wall with the plans for different ballistae through the ages. It looked like she *had* thought about it. A lot. "It would take more power than this world has seen in a long time. And a powerful summoning. One that might be as destructive as the one that claimed Mario Kester."

They'd survived that just fine. "Okay. Then what?"

"I would need a conduit." She smiled briefly, then it fell away. "I appreciate this exercise, but we should not go further."

Dexx nodded, getting to the point. The angel must be torn apart thinking about what she had lost and the impossibility of it returning. So, he changed the subject. "You followed me here. You know what that was, where we are?"

She gently pulled her hands back. "Yes. That was a doorway, a technology fueled by advanced magick. We are in London, specifically—"

The warmth of her hands stayed with him and infused his

body. "Okay, okay, you know a lot." Dexx looked around the apartment. "We could use this place. A hideout."

"We can?" Roxxie turned a full circle and stopped at Dexx. "I would not call it secure."

"How secure does it have to be if *nobody* knows where to look for you?" There was the fact that it'd been hit by something explosive, but if people had already come through to pick the bones, then they had no more need to look in the apartment. Right? This was as off the map as he could hope.

"You speak sense." She moved away, taking in the scene. "Some of these should interest you." She lifted a hand to the wall of guns.

"Why?" He set the stack of papers down and walked to the wall next to the angel. They were pistols of a lot of makes, but then recognition hit him. "Hey, those are mine." He reached out and took his guns off the wall. Two Baby Eagle, a H&K, and a Glock hung in a row by themselves. Those were his favorites. All with him when he'd been kidnapped and brought to England.

He plucked them from the wall and stuffed two in his belt and the third hung awkwardly out of his pocket.

Roxxie had moved to the stack of Mario's notes. "These, you can keep. I will take what you should not know."

"Hey, those are *mine*, too. Discovery is nine-tenths of the law." Why was she stealing his stuff? He hadn't invited her along on this adventure, so all of the loot was his.

"This will not hamper you in any way. It *does* have the potential to harm the ones you love and to kill you."

He didn't need anything else that could harm his family. "Censoring knowledge?" How terrible of an idea was that? If there was trust in the one protecting you? "You do that for the atomic bomb? Swords? All those had great potential, too."

"Consider it a gift, then. Or an apology for dredging up emotions in me I try hard to bury."

Damn. Trapped in angel logic. He probably couldn't stop her in any case. "Why don't you take this place as a gift? Pretty sure it's off the books for now, and we could use it to keep tabs on the enemy."

"Listen to you talk as a warrior." Her smile came back to her face.

His mood lifted. "Warrior, huh?

"No. You are many things, Dexx. You are a fighter, a leader, a loner, a hunter, and a healer. You are not a warrior."

That insult had been carefully wrapped in a burrito of compliments, making it sting a little harder. "Not catching the difference here." He went back to the drafting table and picked up the stack of papers. No way she was getting more.

"For all that you are, you do *not* look for battle. Your vision is not tuned to allies and enemies. You are the one who looks to exist with your people, your pack. I think I will accept this place as a gift. I would like the device as well."

"The apartment, you can have, as long as I can sleep on the couch when I have to. The fob? It's mine. I have a feeling I'm going to need it. A lot."

"You would trap me in here?" Roxxie's eyes looked hurt. Puppy dog hurt.

Dexx smiled. A big fat smile. "You may not be at full *you*, but I don't for a minute believe that you don't have a way to go wherever you want in the blink of an eye."

She returned his smile. "I have to have a few secrets."

"That's what I thought." Dexx pulled the fob from his pocket. "Don't suppose you'd like to tell me how it works?"

"That is not a secret and is something I could share."

"Would...you share it with Michelle?"

Roxxie nodded with a frown. "I could."

"Excellent. I don't want to destroy Phoebe's franchise, but these could be helpful."

"Helpful, yes," Roxxie said hesitantly. "But limited. They are limited, and designed for only a handful of locations."

"And can they be used behind wards?"

"You're talking about the dampers DoDO uses."

He nodded.

Roxxie lifted her face to the ceiling and then nodded, biting her lip. "Yes."

That answer made it seem like there was more going on there than she was willing to say, but as she said, she needed to keep a few secrets. "Okay. Great. I just don't want to get trapped again like we did in Kansas."

Roxxie nodded. "It's a smart move."

Dexx led them to the destroyed front room. "What do you think happened here?" Now that he was looking at it again, it didn't quite look like a home invasion or burglary.

"This was Mario and *it*." Roxxie extended her hand as though she was tasting the air in the room. "It ate his humanity and took him over. Not exactly possession, but not, *not* possession either. They worked together and fought against each other. That is as much as I will tell you, and more than I should have."

She was as bad as Hattie for riddlespeak. "Well, I guess when you talk in circles, it *was* a lot. Together, apart, the only thing for sure was their savage heart."

"Well, Dexx. You have an ear for verse."

"Heh. More like an ear for bullshit." But that also meant that this was probably definitely a good safe house. He just had to figure out how to keep it paid for. He didn't want to hold out hope that it'd be mysteriously taken care of. That only happened in fiction.

If they could figure out this tech, they could get another foothold on DoDO. Dexx had one goal, really.

He wanted to get DoDO off the war map, and he hoped there'd be something in here that would help with that.

A scream of pain filled the night, pulling Emma from her dream. Mal roared to the surface as she shifted partially, yanking the sleeping bag away from her. Fear filled her from Susan's bond, but there was no other information.

Juliet's roar joined Emma's as the polar bear stumbled out of the orange and red tent she shared with Brett.

Someone, Mal said, his words unhelpful but the scent profile that came with the words said that the intruder was female and a non-threat.

Then why was Susan screaming?

Emma walked briskly around the coals of their campfire and pulled the tent flap back to reveal Susan huddled next to her husband, Robert. She was shying away from something in the corner and another scream was bursting to be released. They couldn't afford to bring attention to them, though, so Emma dug deep and roared with her alpha will to keep the woman quiet. For all that she was a rat in animal form, the woman had an impressive set of lungs.

Susan and Robert scuttled out of the tent, careful to stay as far away from the far corner as possible.

Emma was so confused. She *smelled* a woman, but she wasn't seeing one. "Show yourself," she said carefully, shifting back to full human, hoping the partial shift hadn't ruined *another* shirt. Out on the road, trying to escape detection, it was hard to replace damaged clothing.

The shadows morphed and a small woman filled the space where seemingly nothing had before. She knelt there, naked, though she didn't seem fearful or angry.

Which was confusing to Emma. Typically, when another

shifter broke into a shifter camp, there was fear or anger paired with that. "Who are you?"

The woman glanced around and then gestured to the tent opening. "Who are you?"

Emma wasn't in the mood for Twenty Questions. "Are you going to tell me or is this some kind of guessing game?"

"You're trying to escape?"

Emma nodded. "Are you?"

The woman nodded. "You headed to Canada?"

Emma nodded again. "You?"

"We got sent back." The woman clenched her fists and then released them, standing in a stooped position. "Can we talk by the fire?"

Why would Emma invite this stranger to a fire they hadn't built yet?

Smoke and the scent of burning wood told Emma that someone—probably Mason—had already started the fire-making process.

"Fine." Emma stomped out of the tent.

They had a small camp of three tents: hers and Mason's, Juliet's and Brett's, and Susan's and Robert's. They weren't a big pack and Emma was okay with that. She wasn't one for power trips. But it was times like this when she wished there were a few more stronger people in her pack. All she had for protection, really, was her, Juliet, and Brett who were all bears. Mason was a porcupine, and really no help in a fight, and his parents were rats, equally unhelpful in a fight.

"Who are you?" Emma asked when they were all gathered around the crackling fire.

The woman looked around uncertain. "My name is Virginia Cook. I'm a shifter like you."

"Really." Then why hadn't Emma been able to see her?

And why can't I smell her? Mal asked.

"What kind?" Emma demanded.

"Spider," Virginia said quickly and then grimaced, her hands flailing as if preparing for a verbal beatdown.

Emma could well imagine it. She'd already gotten a lot of flak for allowing two rats and a porcupine into her pack. "I... had heard rumors of spider shifters?" She shook her head, careful to keep her judgment to herself. "I didn't think it was real."

"It is." Virginia folded her hands in front of her and then looked back to the woods. "It's a family thing."

"Not all lines are." But bears definitely were, like her family. All bear shifters. But she kept glancing at the woods and there had to be a reason for that. "I take it you're not alone."

Virginia blinked, her mouth open. Then she visibly made a decision and nodded. "My sister and a couple of others are in the area. And, well, Rex smelled that you were bears and..." She frowned at Susan.

Who jerked away as if still remembering the shifter's spider form.

That wasn't going to work. "Remember that you're a rat, Susie? And people are plenty scared of rats."

Robert sent Emma an apologetic look.

Emma waved him off. "I'm not looking to take on stragglers."

"We wouldn't be that." Virginia straightened. "We could join your pack."

"No."

"Yes," Mason said, pushing his glasses up his nose as he joined Emma and took her hand. "We can at least meet you."

Virginia frowned at Emma then at Mason and back again. "We have strengths we can add."

"You're a spider," Emma said, not wanting to insult the woman or anything, but *if* she was going to add more people to the pack, they'd give her power, not just more baggage.

She now understood *why* she'd gotten so much flak for taking in rats and a porcupine.

Virginia smiled.

And then disappeared.

"What the—" Emma searched, throwing out her senses to find the woman.

"Over here," Virginia called.

Emma turned full circle.

Virginia stood beside three other women, two foxes, a cougar, a badger, and a wolverine. "We just need an alpha to protect us."

"No."

"Emma," Mason said quietly beside her. "Let's talk about this."

"This isn't going to fall on you," she said just as quietly.

He stood in front of her and ran his fingers down each arm until he got to her hands. "We need more power. You said it yourself."

She had, but not like this.

"And who are we," he continued, daggering her with his porcupine gaze, "if we turn our backs on them to save ourselves?"

There were times when she loved her mate.

And times when she wanted to wring his prickly little neck. "Fine," she said over his shoulder. "Let's see who you are and why I should add you to my pack." Their stories had better be good.

D exx stepped through the doorway and into Furiel's chest.

Dexx almost jumped back into the doorway. "What the hell, man? I'm getting all kinds of celestial traffic today. What do you want?"

"I *am* sorry." The demon in the business suit held out a hand.

"What are you looking for?"

"The door maker," Furiel said calmly. "Hand it over."

No. No. "No."

"It cannot fall into the hands of the enemy." Furiel sounded reasonable, but the expectation was anything but.

"Who says *you* aren't the enemy? You've done a couple good turns by us, bud, but that doesn't mean much. You're still a demon, and that means I have to watch you close. Closer than most."

"And I have told you. I value my life more than most. I have to take the device."

"Ah, *fuck you*." Dexx went to shift and show the demon why he had a name among the demons, but Furiel was gone.

Dexx looked around the exclusive graveyard for the demon, and he disappeared. "That's right. *Run.*" He pulled the Mario's door device from his pocket.

It wasn't there.

Dexx slapped his other pockets and dug in each, repeatedly. It was gone. That fucker had taken it after Dexx had told him no.

"Faaahhhhh!" Dexx's yell of frustration echoed through the woods.

Dexx sat at the table with the rest of the entire family and the pack, birthday caps on their heads, and a pile of presents in the center of the table.

Nick rounded the corner with a cake and eleven burning candles on top.

Tyler began to sing, and the rest joined in. Never in all the history of singing "Happy Birthday" had the song been invested with memory visions of the birthday girl and the family singing.

Tyler's bard skill was simply the most amazing thing. It worked almost like the siren's call but instead of being manipulated, he helped the rest recall memories in vivid detail.

At first Dexx and the rest faltered when they began to remember all the times Kate'd spent with the Whiskeys, but Tyler put a little more in the song and they picked back up and remembered and sang in perfect harmony.

"...Yoooooou." Tyler hung on to the last word and laced magick through the note filling the rest with hope for the future.

Damn, the kid had grown in a short time.

They clapped as Kate blew out the candles.

Dexx watched for the telltale sign of gag candles that lit again after they were blown out, but they seemed to be the regular sort.

More than one eye watered, but they pegged the happy-meter.

Kate was mobbed by the kids, followed by the adults in rapid succession.

She took it all in stride, with a smile for the well-wishers, and waited patiently for Nick to cut the cake. This was her first human birthday. Dexx didn't know how elves celebrated the day, and judging by her reactions to little things, he had guessed she hadn't had the greatest of childhoods at her old home. He was glad she was making happier memories there.

Mark and Leslie brought out two more and the birthday cake-fest began. Dexx polished off a couple of pieces, tied with Leah, but it was uncomfortably pregnant Margo who took the most at four.

Kate remained reserved and stoic for the song and the cake but began to fidget as the clan watched Margo go for her final chunk of cake. "So, can I now?" Her eyes flicked to the stack of gifts on the table.

Ember and Rai watched with great interest. After all, they still hadn't had their *first* birthday.

Nick glanced at Mark who nodded. "Go for it."

She tore into her gifts with abandon.

Paige stood with Dexx, her arm around his waist, and his around hers. She felt good under his arm. *Really good.* He leaned close to her ear, although they wouldn't have heard a nuclear bomb outside the door at the moment with all the noise. "Hey, you want another one?"

Paige's grin spread slowly over her face. "Sure. You pop it out through your penis, then I'll be all for it."

Dexx lost his grin and put on a pouty frown. "Aw. Can we at least practice?"

"That might be workable. Pay attention. This one is from us."

Dexx was as surprised as Kate at what was under the wrapping. He had no idea where Paige had found the time to get a bike.

The party had calmed down and people filtered away. Nick and Mark hauled two wheelbarrows of gifts back to their house in the woods.

Tru and Leslie wrangled their kids to their rooms, and Leah tucked Rai and Ember in. Paige and Dexx wadded paper into black trash bags ready for Mandy to burn the paper, then the ash to carbon atoms.

Dexx stuffed the last bits in the bag and set it at the back door. He straightened as the smell of sulfur tickled his nose. "Demon." There were only two demons—wait. One demon who could make it through. Balnore wasn't a demon and it was going to take Dexx forever to remember that. "What the fuck you want? You bringing me my door thingy back?"

"I *did* try to express my apologies." Furiel stepped into the light, pulling the collar up on his coat as a soft snow fell. "The time has come for recompense."

"I just want it back. I've got a plan to get that to some buddies of mine to help us with our movement. Don't know if you noticed, but we're fighting a war over here."

"Yes, actually." He held out his hand, and even in the darkened night, Dexx saw it plainly and bright silver.

"I thought it"—he changed his voice to a mocking tone—"couldn't find its way into enemy hands."

"That is true. It might also have been tracked or trapped. I had to make sure it was safe."

"And is it?" They needed a way to win.

Furiel grinned. "It was not attached to a monitoring device, so it is safe to use. As for the how, it does take a magick user to operate it."

Did that mean the dryads could figure out how to replicate it or not?

"All you need is the connection. A few shifter spirits might be able to do it."

Good to know. "You just crack the code to give it back?"

"Mostly. In my time in Kupul, we tried to tie magick to the mechanical, but we did not have the time. I believe we could have succeeded, but instead it took much longer. The runes are a language I can read, and it was not as difficult for me as it would have been for you."

"Hold on a second. You're giving it back, and teaching me how to use it? What's your angle here? Because demons lead with their greed."

Furiel smiled. "We are not above that. I copied the device. We will be making more. Refined, as well."

Dammit. "Okay, fine. Show me."

———

"Walton's crossed the canyon," General Saul said as a form of greeting as Paige stepped into the war room.

The female general had really found her place and had taken to the office. She was still struggling a little with the idea of using paranormals in her army instead of trained soldiers, and that was something Paige was *trying* to get her to understand. Paranormals had skills and abilities.

But her own past exploits hadn't really helped with General Saul's opinions. All Walton had to do was dampen those abilities and take out the portal magick, and suddenly those strong paranormal soldiers were just normal people with sticks and rocks.

Which was a valid point.

One more reason Paige really hoped the bite worked. She

was starting to get a little worried because she'd been bitten weeks ago and…still nothing.

She could only worry about one thing at a time, though. Paige had people looking into the dampening wards, trying to find a way to neutralize them.

But in the meantime, they had to hold the line.

Walton was trying to gain *more* ground.

They'd already lost Nevada, Utah, Arizona, and New Mexico. They were about to lose Southern California, which would be horrible because of San Diego…apparently. Paige had no idea why they needed ships when the fight was on land. But General Saul was adamant they weren't going to lose *any* of the ships in that port.

"We need to send a paranormal force." This was only the eightieth time she'd said that or something like it.

General Saul just studied Paige for a long moment, her cheeks sunk in. "What do you got?"

Well, shit. It was time to prove to Saul that they could add something to the resistance. "Let me make a few calls."

But she was also going to be on the field as support. Just in case.

"I need a general of the para forces, too."

Paige didn't want to, but she sighed. "I could ask Dexx if he wants the job."

"No good. I want a general who knows how to keep people in line. I want Chuck Deluca."

"Let me make a few *more* calls."

Instead of handing the device over to Michelle, he'd given her the plans with the rune instruction manual Furiel had given him. He knew he was likely to put himself in some hairy situations and he wanted a way out. Just in case.

So, he covered two birds with a single stone.

He felt two percent better about himself a few days later, when he walked through the portal with over a thousand vampires, his pack, and Alwyn, as the battle leader to the outskirts of Denver and the destroyed eastern plains. Nobody had time to designate ranks yet, and that was fine with him.

There had been a rash of riots after Paige had created the canyon along the Colorado border with Kansas. It looked like a war zone. Enough city structures remained for good cover, but there were also large swaths of open territory.

Paige had told him and Chuck that they had to have a win here with the paranormal force. He understood why. All that power and here they were hiding behind soldiers and big guns.

And Walton had most of those. And the planes and the missiles and the...fucking everything. So, the paranormals needed to really show Walton why they should be feared, because without that there was no way they were keeping the few states willing to stick with them.

He'd been given the vampires willing to fight and from Britain, hoping to have better luck against DoDO on the American shores. So far, the rabble hadn't bolstered Dexx's confidence any.

But because they had vampires on the field, they couldn't ask the Eastwoods to join them with their blood magick. Dexx was both happy and not happy about it. He didn't like the Eastwoods in the first damned place, but he also didn't like losing.

The Blackmans had proven to be hugely beneficial in the war effort already. The Whiskeys were a really small coven whose magick didn't seem to be as...powerful as the other two covens? He remembered thinking that the Whiskey kids had been a force to be reckoned with and they were.

But consistent? That didn't seem to be the Whiskey way of things.

Blood magick seemed like something that would be a war booster, though, and Dexx liked winning too. However, if they had vampires in the field, there could be *zero* blood magick.

Blood magick made vampires go insane.

So, for a win-win battle scenario, vampires were in because they needed the numbers and the Eastwoods were out.

Chuck had Leslie and other paras who could cast at a distance raising wards and dropping devastating attacks with fireballs and lightning. Frey, Scout, and Michelle each had their own groups of mostly shifters, but Dexx had control of all the redshirts—vampires.

Michelle walked over to him, glancing at Chuck, who was surrounded by alphas and shifters. "I've got something that should help."

Good. Dexx was trying to figure out a way to negate their greatest weakness. Those damned dampers that were capable of stripping shifters and witches of their abilities. If DoDO deployed those—and why wouldn't they?—then they were all sitting ducks. Which was the reason the vampires were going first. Their blood curse had nothing to do with magick.

The groups of fighters mingled in a place they designated *Alpha,* a generally safer place just to the west of the abandoned Air Force base on the outskirts of Aurora.

The civilians pulled back to western edge of the city, and definitely away from any fighting.

Michelle turned back to the field as a convoy of armored vehicles cleared a hill in the distance. "Remember that tech we were discussing?"

"You got the door fobs already?"

"Not quite yet. But I have one better."

"Really?" He had to hope so.

"We can stop the dampers."

That got Dexx's full attention. "What?"

Michelle smirked. "Yup."

Thank the gods. They might have a chance. "They're in place?"

Michelle nodded. "They are. So you and everyone will have their abilities. Should be a heck of a shock to Walton's guys."

Great. "Get in place, then." A thread of excitement went through Dexx at the prospect of potentially winning here.

A portal opened and his vampire soldiers went through. Chuck called it *Victor*. Victor for vampire.

His pack went through as wolves and a hyena, and Dexx went through last.

Then he became nervous.

He stepped out a bit south of the Denver Tech Center. He remembered when those buildings went up, a long time ago.

You will hunt well, Hattie said.

No doubt about that, but I wish I could be with Paige to protect her.

She has enough protection. You have to be the lead hunter here.

Right. Dexx went to his guys, addressing the closest. "We're the line," he told them. "The dryads have neutralizers working against their dampers, so we'll be good to go. Wards and long-range weapons will be taken care of by elementals and witches. Walton has air defenses. That means aircraft, drones, and missiles. We're here for the ground forces. If they come in transports or on foot, we take them down."

One of the vampires raised a hand.

Dexx nodded to him.

"Do we leave them alive?"

This had been one of the dilemmas they faced. Did they kill the humans, or let the vampires change them for reinforcements? After all, if they were paras, would the Federalists let them back to a country that aimed to destroy paras?

"Do what you want. If you think we can turn them to our side by turning them, then, yeah. But I bet most of them would be just as against us if they were one of us. But your call."

How many shifters could we make? Dexx asked.

We could make more shifters than the world has seen in thousands of turnings.

Years. Would that be a bad thing? *The term would be years.*

Hattie huffed in his head.

Dexx looked east. They'd be coming from the east, but they still had too much city between them and Walton.

He motioned for Alwyn who he'd made his second-in-command.

"What's up, Yank?" Alwyn half grinned as he stepped close.

"Any of them giving you any trouble?"

"They're just edgy," the Brit said. "It's like they've all got ADHD all of a sudden."

Probably just nerves. They had to know they were fodder. "Watch these guys. They stay here. I don't see a huge ground force coming without someone noticing."

A portal opened and Chuck came through with several Blackman witches. He had the top spot, the general of the para forces battle leader, but he really focused on the shifters. Probably not a good call, but Dexx'd make the same one.

"We're covering location *Alpha* from *Bravo*." Chuck stepped to the two. "You have Maybelle to open doors for you. I'm headed to *Bravo* to finalize plans with Frey's forces." He nodded to his Blackman witch and they walked through.

Before he had a chance to think about maybe finding a good spot to set up, a lightning bolt lanced from the sky and detonated a missile.

The fight was on.

18

Missiles began to fill the sky.

Dexx returned his attention from vampires who could maybe go into a blood rage and into the more immediate need to not die by missile.

Some were batted from the sky and exploded behind the enemy line. Others were caught in the air and held in place until the rocket fuel gave out. More and more came at them until it looked like a scene from *Braveheart* with arrows darkening the sky. Except these arrows had flaming tails, so they really didn't darken the sky...

Something is wrong, cub.

Cheers from the vampires went up in counterpoint to the distant explosions of the rockets.

Alwyn fist pumped the air. The army might be wasting rockets, but it definitely was too early to celebrate. Modern armies *always* led with a softening attack meant to strike fear and reduce resistance. But one thing was for sure: America's military had been battle hardened by more than forty years of continuous fighting.

Why are they sending so many? Hattie asked.

Why is the sky blue?

Lightning flashed across the sky, destroying massive numbers of the missiles, and still others floated in the air until they were spent and were carried away.

It was impressive, but the fat cat made a good point. What did they hope to gain by shooting all their rockets at a lost cause?

Dexx turned to Alwyn, "Got a question. You think this is all they have?"

Alwyn shook his head. "Pretty sure they have lots more."

"No, I mean, why would they shoot those when we have a defense for any amount?"

Alwyn shrugged. "Maybe they don't know?"

"That's not a bet I would take. So, if they know we have a defense, they do it for another reason."

"Shock and awe. I remember it on the telly."

"Or misdirection. Scan north, as best you can. I got south." Dexx used his enhanced sight, but nothing jumped out at him.

What do you think? They got 'em so they might as well shoot 'em?

Only a fool doesn't watch the stinging tail when the claws snap.

You saying they're blasting us with the missile claws, and swinging in with the big sting somewhere else?

Many have learned that trick from nature.

Damn. So where was the real attack coming from? He needed to get someplace high. He wished his door fob had the ability to take him where he needed to be. He cast around for Maybelle. He found her staying clear of the vampires. "Take me to a rooftop with a view. Please."

She obliged, and they stepped onto a glass roof. She stayed close as she let the door close.

The doorway had opened on top of a glass building with a sheer drop on one side and a progressively curving arch on the other.

"Wow, you sure can pick 'em."

Her smile wavered. "Thanks."

All of Denver spread below him and the wide flat plateau that made up the base of the Rockies.

Dexx quickly found the various locations of the engagement, where the vampires were staged, the shifters, the military units, and the witches.

Nothing seemed to move in the distance. Hattie had the sight of any eagle from their vantage, and nothing showed. From the top of the skyscraper, he could see almost to Limon to the east and Wyoming to the north. The south dipped with foothills, but Pikes Peak showed itself easily.

What was Walton hiding?

The Rockies were a barrier, and everywhere else was wide and open. Actually, the Federalists would be fools to attack Denver. It was too easily defended...

A diffuse trail of dust rose from the south, running west around Castle Rock and ending right around the interstate. A sinking feeling told him he'd found the attack route. They drove across the plains, avoiding roads altogether.

Another trail of dust came in from the north.

"Dammit. Fake a barrage from the west and come in from the north and south."

The feds would be there in less than an hour, give or take. What to do? The missile strike didn't seem to have an end, so he couldn't depend on anyone but him.

The sharp concussion of explosions touched his ears. Those weren't the missiles coming from the east.

He cast around triangulating the location of the noise. To the north, he saw tracers of smoke from short-range rockets or whatever the military used.

Well, shit. *Bravo*. Frey had that position. He looked to the south, then back north. Did Chuck need to know about this?

Yes, but would they have time? Did the feds already have a force in place? He stood frozen with indecision.

Chuck had control of everything on the ground, so he needed to make it work. Live or die.

Frey would have her hands full, but she had the shifters to help.

Alwyn didn't have anyone to help keep the vamps in line.

Frey could be in trouble, but they already had their surprise sprung. If the para forces were going to keep from being flanked, they needed the vampires in place and ready to defend.

Dexx turned back to the door witch. "Take me back."

She nodded, a little pale around the eyes and cut the door.

He stepped out almost on top of Alwyn. "I found the trap. We're being flanked from the north and south. We need to get these guys covering the main roads and blockade anything coming north."

Alwyn looked at him with confusion. "How do you know? Our intel was quite clear."

"Yeah, I know. Now things are different. Let's get our asses moving. We take the vamps and stop anything coming up from the south. We go that way a few miles and there'll be the interstate that splits about four times. I think we can go a little south of that and bottleneck them."

"Miles? That's a long way from here."

"Not by door, but yeah. And we have to keep them *there*. We won't hold out long if they flank us in the city. We take them all, and I'll let Chuck in on the plan. It won't take long. I hope." He asked Maybelle Blackman for a door to Chuck, and she opened a door to Frey's force and stepped through alone.

Merry watched the battle rage from her vantage. She set the binoculars on the desk. Nobody knew she was in Denver except her ally, and he wasn't talking. Her initial reason for coming was to ensure things went to her plan. And for a little fun that only she could have.

She shook her head.

Their battle plan was catching the missiles and using them later? It might have been brilliant if she had thought of it. As it stood, there was a real chance her plans could be overturned and she had too much to lose.

By helping Walton in this critical battle, she'd ensured her long life and had guaranteed her future holdings.

They had a deal. He would honor his side and she would honor hers.

Of course, if he didn't, she had certain...precautions in play.

Her heels clicked hard as she paced the room and pulled out her phone—which was working because it'd been giving to her by Walton himself—and swiped a call to the general in charge of Walton's attack army.

"General—"

"Shut up and listen," Merry said. "They're catching your toys. Now, if you don't want them dropped on *you* in a few minutes, you'll do something else."

"Why, Merry Eastwood," General Hancock said with a sneer. "Are you scared? Don't worry your unnatural self overly much. Only about half of the armament is actually live. We knew the frontal assault was going to be no joy. But you're saying the paras are *capturing* them?"

"A few, yes. And I am *not* scared. I want this over with quickly, so I can bring order back to my city, and repair the damage that slut caused."

"Language. Well, as it turns out, you may be in luck. We dropped a proposal on the assumption every one of the

SSM's would be neutralized. We'll just re-institute it. Don't worry. You'll have your little slice of hell all to yourself in two days."

"You take care, General. Do not forget who I am, and what I can do." Merry snarled at the phone, her grip threatening to crack the screen.

"I'm sure you're very scary in your circles. But I think *you* should remember who *I* am. We could just drop a nuke on your para asses and be done with it all. You read?"

"Of course I read, you idiot. Intelligence is *my* area of expertise. And don't think I won't forget your impertinence. Failure here—" The feel of blood magick stopped Merry in her tracks. She forgot the world around her and soaked the waves of the power of blood.

"You were saying?" The device in her hand spoke words to her.

For over two hundred years, Merry had only felt the sort of power that came to her once before. She had a small part in the Civil War, and maybe helped it along a bit. Thousands died on that day...

The memory of the call of blood faded and she still held her phone absently. She placed it to her ear. "*Do. Your. Job.* Leave the thinking to those with thought. Carry out your orders." She swiped the call closed.

Dexx dodged another barrage of lightning and bullets.

Denver was a big place and finding Chuck and Frey and their troops wasn't as easy as following Google Maps. When he found them, he'd been pressed into service to help push back and stall the rush of DoDO and Federalist forces. How long had he been there?

Not for the first time, he wished he'd kept Maybelle with him.

Was Alwyn in place? Had he been able to bottleneck the incoming military?

He'd have to wait for the answers, there was too much to do here.

He did some quick math between slicing spells and people, and equipment with the *ma'a'shed*. He'd crossed the majority of North Aurora, and Commerce City, and might even be north of that. Rocky Flats?

Damn, he needed to get back. Two agents flanked by six soldiers walked by his hideout. Two whacks with the *ma'a'shed* and a brief change as the cat later and they were history.

Alwyn would just have to hold them off until Dexx could help.

He needed to find Chuck or a door witch, but so far both were as hard to find as a snowball in hell.

One good piece of news filtered across his brain. The barrage of missiles had slowed down, and now only a few every few seconds roared in or exploded harmlessly out over the plains. Hopefully Paige could get the rest of the witches to the ground and they could push back the invaders.

A second group caught sight of him and began the chase.

He slowed considerably for them. An opportunity was coming closer.

Dexx turned at a piece of upturned concrete and launched himself back at his pursuers. They seemed surprised at the flying cat coming at them.

He bowled them over, making sure that the living ones were out of the fight. Broken bones were mendable, but that *really* hampered the will to fight on.

Dexx backtracked for the shifters from Chuck's pack.

They had managed to draw the fight into the city and gain some footing forward.

DoDO had trained well, better than he'd seen them anywhere. They were coordinated and precise. That could be from the American soldiers scattered around, though.

They were better than before, but they didn't have the ability the shifters and other witches had.

They were the best things to happen to the Western states. Bands of four or five had started to take on entire company of soldiers. Their quiet anger had finally paid off.

Suddenly, he realized the noise stopped.

He searched the battle zone with Hattie's infrared vision and saw plenty, but nothing that helped in a meaningful way. Bodies that were dead were cooling, but not fast enough to help.

Dexx shifted and looked around. A few shifters crawled over rubble and around cars sniffing out the living. The image looked bad when they sniffed the air like they did.

Frey stood in front of a pile of DoDOs, all very dead. Her sword could cut through bullets and flesh just the same, but magicks were harder to deal with.

Joel poked his head from a smoking husk of a pickup and threw his fist in the air with a yell. "You did it, boss. Killed these and scared the rest." The little goblin hadn't been hiding, not with obvious magickal burns on his arms and side. "Sent a message to Walton. They come up against a Valkyrie, and they might as well shoot themselves. I bet you just made the most wanted list."

Tarik hauled two DoDOs by their collars and dropped the bodies outside Frey's circle of death. "They stopped firing their wands and stood up. I stunned them only. But they are dead, nevertheless."

"How did they die?" Frey cocked her head to the side.

"I cannot say, except to say *I* did not attack to kill."

Dexx checked the pulse of the closest DoDO. "You know, if they try to kill you, you can try to kill them right back. It's totally allowed."

"I have given it much thought. I am not ready to kill again just yet, but they *would* have been important sources of knowledge. With the right *motivation*."

Yup. The former djinni had a point. They could have been interrogated. But now they weren't worth anything except to build a wall of flesh, and nobody liked that.

"Next time, just tell me when they do something stupid." Frey waved at the bodies with the back of her hand.

"Understood." Tarik nodded once.

"Yeah." Joel nodded vigorously. "You don't need to inconvenience the boss lady with the *bodies*, just tell her what's up. Right, Frey?"

Dexx raised a brow. Was the goblin *ego stroking*? "Did you search the bodies for anything useful?"

"I have not. I did, however, grab their wands."

Ooh, he sounded downright *Voldemort*.

There were other things that needed his attention. "You got this?" He eyed Frey and Tarik.

"We aren't happy-go-lucky cavalier fanboys," Frey sneered. "Yeah. It's covered here."

Joel crossed his arms. "Better get while the getting is good. She's only going to put you down again if you try to stand up." Wow, the little man didn't make much sense.

Dexx pressed his lips together to keep from showing teeth. He popped a *very* disingenuous thumbs-up. "Where's your Blackman?"

"Brian didn't make it." Frey sneered at the dead soldiers. "Bastards shot him in the back."

"Then I need to get in touch with—hold on. Hey, I need to call Chuck. Can you find him?"

Frey pulled a cell phone from her pocket and made a show

of it. "Yeah. I can." She swiped the screen, and a holographic image of Chuck appeared. "We may have *Bravo* cleaned up. I'm sending teams out now to check. And you have an anxious battle leader who's been absent from his team. Dexx needs a ride back to his post."

She could have done without saying that.

When Chuck arrived with his Blackman witch, he didn't look pleased. "I'm coordinating with the dryads. The signal is our best defense against their dampening fields."

"Well, Maybelle had stayed behind to help Alwyn. And the vamps are wigging out, sort of."

The doorway opened. Hopefully he hadn't been kept too long.

19

Dexx stepped out of the door and found Alwyn. A wave of relief passed over his face. "What's the news?" He'd lost time with the fighting at Frey's position, but Alwyn looked to have just finished preparing.

"You never said this place was so sprawling." He waved at the wide plains.

They stood at the major interchange of three interstates, I-25, C-470, and E-470, and the best place to enter the city en masse. There was no traffic, no people, no nothing. The last time he had been there, there was too much of everything. Now it seemed too empty.

Three wolves ran in from the north, where the quiet interchanges met.

They shifted, and Margo walked uncomfortably to them, her brothers and Alex close to her. His pack was very protective of each other.

"I *did* say a few miles, right?" He was sure he tried to give the man at least an idea how much space Denver occupied.

"You never mentioned how far a mile was. Our mile is a bit different."

Oh. Dexx hadn't heard that before. "Well, sorry?" The milling vampires brought him back to the danger hidden by the rolling hills. "How's it looking out there?"

Margo flicked her hand toward the curving interchange. "It's quiet. I would have expected an attack by now. You gave me the impression they were fast movers."

"They were. Left a tall dust trail and everything." Dexx scanned the road and the surrounding hill and plains. More trees dotted the landscape in the south than north of the city, and they could hide a few, but not the number of troops he saw.

"Something isn't right."

A vampire approached Dexx and Alwyn. He was dressed in denim pants and a T-shirt. He looked right at home in the cold, and Dexx's infrared put him a couple degrees above ambient. The guy was huge, with bulging muscles and ultra-wide shoulders. He probably thought he was a real ladies magnet. "Yeah, dude. What can we do for ya?"

"Ramiro. There is something wrong in the air." The guy had a soft accent Dexx couldn't place. It wasn't totally British, and it wasn't full anything else. But it had traces of all over. "Ever since we landed, I've felt strange. Something is poking at my calm. Keeping me on edge. Ever since the day we came in at the docks."

Alex and Garek bracketed Dexx. They knew what vampires on edge could do.

"I'd bet my car it's Merry Eastwood." He hadn't seen her anywhere *near* Denver, but it had to be.

If Paige knew she was there...

Ramiro shook his head. Obviously, he had no idea who that was.

"The Eastwoods have blood magick. You won't have a choice." Dexx turned to Alwyn. "We don't have any of the Eastwoods here, do we?"

Alwyn shook his head slowly. "I have a few witches, but none of the Eastwoods."

"So, if we don't have a blood witch around, there are two possibilities. The other side has a weapon, or vampires are less trustworthy than we hoped."

Ramiro sneered. "*You* are the ones who are untrustworthy. Making promises, then going back on your word at the last minute."

Dexx shook his head slowly back and forth. "We really don't have time for this. Look man, it wouldn't be your fault."

Ramiro started to square up, then relaxed a little when Dexx finished.

"Watch yourself. We're about two seconds away from—"

A faint thump in the air followed a crackle.

What the...

Alwyn looked past Ramiro's shoulder. "Was that an explosion?"

"Dammit. Yeah, it was." That was from the wrong direction. The feds should have been seen way farther east than that explosion. How had they—a black mushrooming cloud marked burning fuel. "Fuck, they took the other way into the city. We have to get there now." How had he been so stupid? The other road in was more restrictive, but less obvious.

Alwyn's eyes went wide with accusation. "*Another way*? Do you know anything about your city?"

"This was the easiest way to get here. Just shut up. I'm working." He grabbed at Maybelle. "We need a door behind a motorcycle dealership about three miles that way. You able to do that?"

Maybelle nodded. "I think I can. I'll be close, anyway."

"Be ready." He motioned to everyone nearby.

"What do we do about our far scouts?" Ramiro gestured to the hills outside the city.

"Leave 'em. They'll join as soon as they can, if you're right about them."

Ramiro sneered, his vampire teeth showing a little.

Dexx opened up a door and stepped through. There didn't seem to be a visible threat, but more sounds of fighting were clear.

The closest vamps and his pack with Joe and Ripley ran through.

Fifty, a hundred, two hundred, almost a thousand Para-West defenders ran through Maybelle's doorway.

This was it. Frey took the northern incursion, and Paige stopped the eastern. Now Dexx's turn.

A slow-moving troop truck rolled around the corner.

Dexx very clearly saw the driver's eyes widen as he saw the last of the paras coming through the doorway and hit the brakes. The soldier on top of the truck swiveled the cannon, pulling the charging rod on the gun.

Alwyn's arms wove in large circles and energy coalesced and as the gun began blasting, Alwyn let the lightning find its mark.

Thirteen vampires blew apart as bullets ripped into them and the truck exploded as the lightning flashed the fuel into a vapor bomb.

Dexx clenched his teeth together. "Fuck." At best, they'd traded fighters. They'd lose badly, if all they could do was a one-to-one trade.

"Alwyn, find a perimeter and push it back, go north. Take the witches and Ripley. Ripley, go ghost dog and frighten them as much as you can, kill gunners. I've got the pack. We're going to be the spearpoint, and go south. Ramiro, bring your guys in behind me and sweep up any that came through. They caught us with our pants down, so I don't care what you do, take them out of the fight."

Ramiro smiled. It looked hungry and something else. Sinister, maybe?

Dexx shifted and let Hattie lead, while he set to thinking. How had the Federalists known to flank there?

Hattie, Alex, and Garek led their force south along the road along the hills and cliffs overlooking the pavement. They passed abandoned houses and the occasional stray, but nothing else for a mile, and farther. Had the feds *all* made it into the city? They went farther until Hattie smelled diesel fumes. She hunched low and crept over a rise.

A line of convoy vehicles had piled up behind a large transport truck cratered, and burning. Mundane soldiers picked pieces laying up and down the road. Black scorch marks fanned out in a flower pattern.

Troops surrounded the exploded rig, and more lined the road, expecting, but not seeing trouble.

Hattie dropped lower to the ground, prowling low and slow.

Dexx broke off his train of thought, coming forward in the moment. The string of military had more than a little DoDO sprinkled in through the line of soldiers.

None of the DoDO tactical black seemed to be watching anywhere as intently as the camouflage green regular military. They really should have listened to his training.

There were far fewer DoDO agents and younger-looking soldiers in this bunch.

This smelled to high heaven. Why would *this* battalion be lesser trained and backed by fewer DoDO?

It didn't matter. They needed to be gone or dead.

Ramiro motioned for the vampires to fan out, stringing their line along the bluff and casting illusions that hid them from the humans below.

Hattie's belly stayed low, scraping on the yellow winter

grass, blending in with the other yellows and browns of late February. *The creatures smell strange.*

They're vampires, of course they smell bad.

Cub, they do not smell like the friend vampire.

Tony? Could just be he doesn't take human blood.

Blood is blood. They have the smell of the foam-mouth bite. They are close to mindless.

Gotta believe they're holding on. They were already committed, so there wasn't any choice anyway.

Merry *had* to be behind the strangeness. One day she'd lie in the bed she made.

Alwyn should have had his perimeter set and ready to push against the feds. If many made it past the roadblock.

Hattie flashed a glance to Garek and Alex. Dexx pushed his thoughts through Hattie. *Flank me and provide cover from anything I don't see right away.*

The hyena and wolf didn't nod or anything, but they got the message. The hyena bristled, her eyes locked on the humans below them, and the wolf's paws raked at the ground in front of him with tiny strokes of his foot.

Well, if the vamps at the end aren't ready, they'll just be late to the party. Hattie, jump.

Hattie barely waited for him to finish before she was in the air, closing on the guys with guns.

The eerie sound of a hyena laughing followed Dexx as she flew through the. He'd seen it affect humans more than seeing the biggest damned cat the world.

The humans had been ready. Their guns were trained forward, and the scared kids had muscle memory. Too bad they didn't have experience with paras. The mainstream media of the Federalists had done a superb job making paras scarier than they actually were. Good news for Dexx and his vampire army.

Shots were fired, and some were even aimed in Dexx's

general direction, but most of the bullets were involuntary pulls of the trigger as they fled.

Dexx plowed into DoDO agents as the humans ran toward the safety of the armored transport vehicles.

Spells zipped by Dexx as he dodged back and forth, covering, then revealing the hyena and wolf as he ran on. His claws dug into flesh as he ripped DoDO agents and a few soldiers apart.

So sad. If only these kids just let us be. I don't like killing our military. DoDO, however…

Hattie bit down on an arm extended with a wand. A hand and wand fell to the ground as another DoDO was removed from the fight.

Merry pulled her Bugatti Chiron past the fighting at the south end of the city by driving the beltway interstate around the less interesting paras. Of course, Dexx would take control of the vampire force. Nobody but him would even think of fighting with agitated vampires she'd driven nearly mad with her own special magick.

The power swelled forward down the road, the magickal energies leeching back into the earth. She pressed the pedal to the floor and jetted on, rushing toward the greatest source of blood.

She found the road she wanted and yanked the wheel. They weren't far, but she stopped clear of any engagement, and parked the car. She didn't need to be a *part* of the fighting. She only needed to be close enough to get what she wanted.

She drank in the power Dexx and his paras created for her. Blood magick energy coursed over her from the ocean of blood he and his band of vampires spilled.

Regular bloodshed trickled with power. The power the vampires made with her magick driving them was *so much more*. It was more intense than *anything* they could do on their own. She'd been sprinkling the vampires with her own blood spice, slowly pushing them to bloodlust. She let her arms raise of their own accord, reveling in the ecstasy of the moment.

Oh, there were so many insults and injuries to repay. She would start with Dexx and his ever-running mouth. Then, she would visit Paige while she grieved over the loss of yet *another* love of her life.

Merry smiled. Once they had been dealt with, Merry would broker the peace treaty with Walton. The entire west of the continent would be hers. She would cede the deserts to the McCree clan with *small* perpetual insurance dues.

Add to that the *massive* price on Dexx. Annelle Rovoski had agreed to pay a massive price *and* the artifact. The amethyst crystal Dexx had so thoughtfully brought to her.

Merry would have settled for the artifact alone, but she could always use a little more money to spread her influence.

And, the butter on her bread, the world would go relatively back to normal. The world economy wouldn't have to shift or be remade because of one woman and her insane and inappropriate crusade.

Merry smiled at the plans all coming to fruition.

The first tendrils of the power helped create the conduit. Merry strengthened the siphon and blood magick slammed into her. She felt the earth, the plants, the very *molecules* comprising all of it.

The sun dimmed as her own power eclipsed the local star.

Merry's fingers curled in fists.

She would pluck out the eye of the saber and show it to him. She would challenge the goddess.

She *was* magick.

The fight had gone well. Hattie trotted down the road following the destruction the vampires caused.

Bodies lay everywhere, but not all of them were dead.

Dexx and his fighters had taken the bottleneck and closed it off. The main force seemed to be strung out behind the overturned transport truck. Better they be caught here than let them get spread out and set up.

Dexx would have smiled, but Hattie had control for the moment, and people pissed their pants when she smiled.

Luckily, things were quiet.

The vampires were efficient in their bloodshed. Dexx shifted and found Ramiro. He'd just finished with another DoDO agent, but the woman still lived.

Dexx shrugged. If they were their own worst enemy, they might fight with the paras instead of against them. "You think she'll fight for *us* now?"

"It doesn't work that way. Vampires will not just—" Ramiro's hands twitched almost constantly, his fingers curled and flexed. He rolled his neck, his face a mask of pain, then snarled.

Dexx alternated his gaze from the vampire's hands to his face. "Won't just what? You with me?"

He hadn't seen Merry Eastwood anywhere near Denver. But she had her ways, and the vampires were acting like they were in a perpetual pre-bloodlust state, and that screamed Eastwood.

So he'd counted his blessings, gave her the benefit of the doubt, and thought, however briefly, that maybe the East-wood witch was turning over a new leaf like Paige had hoped.

"Hey, you still here?" Dexx took a step back, and as he watched, something happened. The vampire, *all* the vampires were growing little seeds of heat inside them. The vampires fell to the ground in a wave, writhing and gasping where they lay. Whatever had them down looked painful at best.

Ramiro began the groaning scream, and it spread from there.

"Alwyn, gather any witches and shifters we got. I have a bad feeling here."

That's when he saw Merry Eastwood.

Ramiro stopped clawing the ground and stood. His eyes went red, and his features changed to feral vamp.

Dexx shifted and smacked the vampire to the ground with Hattie's giant claw. The vampire didn't get up, and there was no way he was checking to see if Ramiro lived. Dexx shifted back and backed up with Alex and Garek.

"Maybelle!" Dexx yelled and ran toward her as vampires swarmed. The witch was bleeding from her arm, leg, and abdomen.

"Tell me we're getting out of here."

"You're damned straight we are," Dexx said. "Alwyn, time to move."

The door witch didn't pause. She opened a door and Dexx and his team ran through into a grove of trees in the middle of a street.

"Michelle," Dexx bellowed.

She ran down the street toward him. "What? What's going on?"

He gulped breath more to buy himself some time to think than because he needed to breathe. "You know those dampers?"

She nodded.

"Did they deploy them?"

"Oh, yeah. Of course they did."

Great. "Did you kill them or just..." He shook his head not sure what else he was thinking there.

"We just jammed the signal."

Even better. "Can you stop jamming the signal in a specific location?"

"Maybe." She narrowed her brown eyes at him. "Why?"

"Merry Eastwood is driving the vampires into a craze."

"Oh." She thought for a second and then turned into a tree in the middle of the war-torn street.

Dexx just had to hope this would work because otherwise, the para army was going to be destroyed by the very soldiers they'd brought to the field.

Merry stepped into the circling mob of vampires, swimming in blood magick.

She pulled at strands of the evolved form of her magick. With this, she had blood slaves who would produce *more* of her magick. This was bliss. The world would tremble once those idiots took each other out and she was left standing in their blood.

Vampires closed in on Merry, the only source of blood nearby. She casually lifted a shield they couldn't penetrate.

So many fools.

All she needed now was the artifact and to find Dexx. He was an issue, but easy to find. He would go back to Paige as soon as he could. Of course, he would try to warn her, but Annelle had that part of the plan. She better not fail.

Merry plucked at the thickening tentacles of blood magick streaming through the air. With this much, she could challenge...oh, *anyone*. That cardinal Dexx cowered from, Walton, the world, even *God* wouldn't dare stand toe to toe against her.

She let a smile spread on her face. Yes, things were about to change.

A prickling sensation touched her at the back of her consciousness and spread through her body.

Her shield thinned and lost strength.

She lifted her a hand. "What?" The magick swirled thick and ready to use, but she was losing her connection. "That's impossible. How—who?"

This had to be Walton. He'd sworn he wouldn't use the magick inhibitors in this battle to ensure she had the advantage.

Why hadn't Paige found a way to defeat those yet?

Irritated with herself, Merry spun and ran with her weakening magick.

She had some control, but it quickly faded. The magickal restrictor generators were being powered up. She shouldn't be affected. She'd been *assured* the restrictors wouldn't—

A vampire slashed at her.

Even before she'd fully realized the threat, she sliced the hand off at the wrist. It was a simple use of blood magick, and her reflexes lashed out.

She ran, fueled by residual magick and adrenaline. Her car was nearby, but far enough away that nobody had seen it.

Merry rounded an outcrop of stone and there it was. Her smile grew again. Once inside the car she could relax. Paras could run fast. Paras could *fly* fast. *Nobody* kept up with a Bugatti.

Walton and *everyone* would pay for the betrayal.

The shiny blue and black car called her on. It offered safety and retaliation. One glance behind her let her know that she had outrun the vampires. Damned things.

She would claim the general, then she would reclaim the vampires and figure out a way to turn those restrictors off. This was her *right*.

Hands quivering with exertion and fear reached for the door handle.

She grabbed it and yanked. The door opened on smooth hinges, just as expected.

She let a smile cross her face as she—

Her nails broke and her shoulder dislocated as she was violently yanked from the car. Her back slammed into the dirt, driving the air from her.

"Fucking beasts!" Merry roared. She sat up, regaining her senses. "You'll all pay for that." Her vision went red with fury.

Cheap knockoffs of a nice dress shoe stepped into her line of sight.

Her gaze lifted to a man dressed in a suit, if it could be called one. He had features from Mexico, but he held himself more cultured.

He had the red eyes of a vampire in bloodlust, but he stood calm. "Stand up." The man talked in the clipped tones of ex-army or police.

Merry stood, anger burning through her.

Faster than her eyes followed, he hit her in the chest.

Her back hit the car as more of the vampires rounded into view.

She could make it! Her chest was on fire where he hit her, but...she could...she...could. Something was wrong. Something vital. Her arms were too heavy to move.

The vampire stood in front of her, his face almost pressed to hers.

"Tony." His eyes flashed red and his teeth fit together in sharp points. "My name is Tony Guerrero."

So? What the hell was *that* supposed to mean? Merry tried to raise her hand, ready to deal death to the vampire.

He held up a bloody hand, something quivering between his fingers.

Disgusting. The animal held a heart in his hand. It pulsed in time to her own...

Sudden realization hit her as she looked down at the pooling blood down the front of her pencil skirt.

He faded as he squeezed her heart like clay.

Merry fell to the side as her shoulder pressed into the asphalt next to her very expensive ride.

Billie Black held her hand to the ward tree. Resonant force calmed her and protected the land. She smiled at the gently shaking bare branches of the winter limbs. In the summer, the leaves would rustle and cascade the ward magick to roll along the ground in soft translucent waves. In the winter, the same magick wafted through the air like the aurora, but in pastel blues and pinks.

When she had been much younger and had had far fewer responsibilities, she had sat at the edge of the magick concentration and had watched. Just like the clouds, she had seen fanciful images of teddy bears, rabbits, and the starship *Enterprise*. Strange, but yes, many times she'd seen spaceships in the clouds *and* in the ward magick.

In mid-fall, however, the shapes always stopped, and the wafting took their place.

The tree spoke to her sometimes. Not with words, but with emotion. Levels of communication above the mere muddied intent of words.

"It would be nice to have a conversation though. Like the

tree people in the books." Billie circled the tree again, trailing her fingers along the semi-smooth bark.

On her next pass, she looked above her to the general store and the bookstore. Every winter the tourists, either para or mundane, went away to wherever they came from, but just like the leaves, they'd be back. Last summer, though, they hadn't. This war had already begun, trapping paranormals where they lived and isolating them.

Some things should have just stayed under wraps. But that was water under the bridge. Nobody could roll back time.

The good news was that time seemed to roll differently in Cheechako. Not the seasons or days, but influence from the outside. Things were slower, more comfortable. *That* was the magick of Cheechako.

She took one more step and froze. The aurora falling from the tree coalesced into an image of a man in red. He stood in front of her and then vanished.

That hadn't been Santa Claus.

That had been the Royal Mounted Canadian Police.

The tree *spoke* to her. It hadn't done that in a while. The last time it had shown her Leslie Whiskey in the form of her spirit animal, the griffin.

The message beyond the obvious was clear, though. They were going to have company.

She cast a look up to the bookstore again. She didn't want to leave, not now. The peace of the tree was a strong draw.

Somewhere in the back of her mind, the tree pushed her on. No branches came down to shove her, just the feeling like she needed to be someplace else, *right now*. Damn.

And the day had been so peaceful.

Dexx stepped through the portal Maybelle created. The witches moved quickly through their makeshift headquarters of *Alpha,* gathering their things.

The dryads had *tried* to release their jamming device in a localized area. The area of the feral vampires.

It worked at first, then suffered a cascading failure that took them all offline, which meant that the paranormal forces were being forced to retreat. *Bravo* was abandoned, *Victor* was lost to the vampires.

However, Walton's forces would be forced out also.

Merry Eastwood had done too good a job of flooding the area with blood magick and the vampires were...insane with bloodlust.

Denver was lost. Probably forever.

"I don't understand." Paige stood with Chuck at the large section of interconnected jammers. "I thought we had this one. What happened?"

A lot of shit, but mostly Merry Eastwood who should never have been trusted in the first place. "Great question, babe. Probably for a later date. Right now, we kinda have to leave. Unless you somehow have access to your witch hands. Then, I'll let you call a magick Uber."

Paige turned a Whiskey glare his way.

Chuck raised a brow.

He shrugged, pushing his head forward. The dryads were still trying to get their damper jammer device working, but in the meantime, it was a full retreat for both sides. And since this was the first super-engagement they'd had against Walton, they needed a plan that didn't include losing everything in the first battle of the civil war.

"Where are we going?"

"I thought about going to Kansas and see if we can get behind those fucking dampers. Hopefully, they're directional, and we take them out at the source."

"Is that a good idea?" Paige moved with exaggerated slowness.

Proving she wasn't scared? Or maybe trying to show leadership by acting confident?

Not Dexx. He was scared as shit, and they had to leave before bad things hit.

"Maybelle, you got a good spot picked out?" She nodded. The door opened to flat plains.

An explosion rocked *Alpha*, shattering windows and breaking concrete like a balsa wood airplane.

Dexx picked himself up, searching for Paige. She made it to her hands and knees, coughing in the dusty air.

Parts of buildings rained debris down, but thankfully, the portal was still there, five inches higher than it had started.

"This place isn't going to be here much longer. *Move.*" He pulled her up and escorted her to the—

The next blast threw them through the portal, fire chasing the wall of air. The two of them rolled over the dead grass of the flat land.

This time Dexx hurt a lot more. Double vision and dizziness prevented him from standing. He cast around for Paige. She'd made it through, but she wasn't moving.

The portal was closed, but Dexx couldn't find the door witch who had been attached to it. He stumbled to his wife. "Pea, you okay? Pea? Hey." He leaned over her chest, listening. Her heart still beat, but it didn't sound right—or did it? Was his own super-hearing getting his in the mix?

"Okay, fool. Calm your tits," he told himself. "She's fine. We just have to make sure." He took a deep breath and listened again. Fast thumps and slow thumps, but different timbres. Two different beats.

There it was. Paige was unconscious, but she seemed fine...for being unconscious.

The door opened again and Maybelle peered through.

Dexx carried Paige through.

The dryads let up a little cheer. That sounded like good news.

Michelle walked his way.

"Hey. You guys have magick here?"

Annelle Rovoski stood over them, her eyes locked on Paige. "My magick is vith me. How is she?"

"If I were a doctor, I could tell you."

What the hell were they going to do? With Paige down, he didn't have a great plan.

Their *military* force had been blasted to bits, and they had no clear chain of command.

Where was Chuck? Lost somewhere in the explosion, or helping someone else.

"*Fuck. Fuck, fffffck,*" he forced through his gritted teeth. He could see red with his heat vision, but it just wasn't the same when his blood was on fire. What the hells was he supposed to do? No Paige, no Chuck, Tuck, or *anyone else* who knew had to run a campaign. *Nothing*.

Dexx took a knee and slammed a fist into the ground.

Okay. He'd had a tentative thought to take out the dampers from the back, to hit Walton's forces from behind. That was still a valid thought. He just had to turn the idea into a plan.

He crouched next Paige, his fist repeatedly hammering the ground. What could he do? Annelle didn't heal. In fact, the only magical healer he knew was Bobby.

Wait.

His door witch stumbled over to him and collapsed to the ground. "Tell me we're nearly done here."

Nearly. "Take us home." Dexx picked Paige up and pointed at Annelle and Alwyn with his eyes. "Stay here, keep Maybelle safe. Lay low, and don't give our position away unless you need to defend yourselves. I'll be right back."

He felt a little bad leaving, but at the moment, he needed to. The house was familiar, but not comforting at the moment.

"Leah! Bobby! I need you *now*." Dexx roared as soon as he stepped through.

Many more sets of footfalls than the two he'd called thundered from upstairs.

Tyler was the first to land at the bottom, and although he wasn't wearing a cape, an imaginary one flared behind him. "Oh, dang. Is she going to—"

"Mom!" Bobby hit the bottom stair right behind Tyler.

Leah mimicked Bobby, rushing by them both to inspect their mother.

"I don't know how bad she is." Dexx needed to set her down. "Bobby, can you heal her? Leah, I have something else for you."

Ember and Rai skidded to a stop, followed by a more sedate Mandy, but not by much.

Bobby pointed to the couch. "I can. What happened?"

Dexx turned around and gently placed Paige on the cushions. "Lee, I need a door. Two doors; one here, one right above a large body of water. Can you do that?"

"Um, no. I don't think so. Why?" Worry creased his daughter's face.

"I think I have a way to make this work out."

Rai stepped in front of Dexx. "We're coming, too."

Ember squared off in front of Dexx next to his sister.

"Not this time." Dexx shook his head.

Rai cut him off. "Yes, we are. And if you think you can stop us, you may try. Or you can let us fix the people who hurt Mom. Who do you want to stop more?"

Dammit. That was his kid for sure. He took two breaths while listening to Hattie.

Your cub speaks true. The problem with cubs is they grow up. They will help the pack, or they will find their own.

Not this time. This is war, not just a random battle. So, he reached into his alpha will and pushed his kids to remain.

Rai looked pissed, but she stayed.

Ember just looked mildly annoyed.

Dexx really wished he had a fresh door witch, but he wasn't taking Leah with him.

Which was fine. "Heal up," Dexx said as he stepped through the door.

The witches from *Alpha* headquarters gathered into a circle, casting a community spell with a seven-pointed star in a protective circle. The magick was already spreading fast, making a large dome that was growing as they cast. They were erecting a ward.

"What are you doing?" Dexx asked.

Annelle broke away from the circle and walked toward him. "They are providing a sort of defense."

"Are you sure they can't track that?"

"Wards are our best defense."

Dexx had to hope so. Can you feel the currents better if you have access to water?"

Too late. Dexx heard the distant roar of high-altitude jets.

He looked up. "New plan, everyone duck!" Dexx crouched down.

Alwyn ducked low following Dexx's lead. He certainly didn't hear or see anything, but if Dexx said it, well, there were too many times he had been right.

Something at the very edges of his hearing tickled his senses. *Could* that be Walton? He scanned the sky, trying to detect something, *anything*.

"Stay still. If anyone has a cloaking spell, now would be a

good time to use it."

Nobody had that. Vampires cast illusions.

"Get inside the ward," one of the witches called.

Alwyn heard them now as he stumbled toward the ward that wasn't big enough to fight them all. "I can hit them with lightning if I can see them."

"Think that'll work? Even passenger planes are protected from hits."

Cock and balls, he was right. "Do we have nothing that can reach them?" Would fire do anything to the warplanes?

"Stand back, boys." The old Russian lady stood up. "I have been bringing men down since this country vas still suckling at the teat of the Old World." She held her hand above the ground steady as a stone. She cast a look up to the incoming jets, then closed her eyes and raised her other hand.

The woman turned a slightly dead shade of blue, the color beginning at her fingertips over the ground, and crawling over her skin to end at the fingers held to the sky.

Jagged ethereal light shot from her fingers lacing the air.

Alwyn doubted anyone else could see the show. She might look just like an old lady praying. He had a special connection to the earth, though. His parents had been druids and had taught him some of their magick.

The blue magick of the rusalka lanced to the sky and the planes. At first, nothing seemed to happen, but then the jets turned nose down and a few seconds after, the sound of the engines stopped.

Several of the shifter paras Dexx had with him stood and cheered, fists raised to the sky and shaking their fists at the falling planes.

Annelle Rovoski herself had a satisfied smile. She turned to look at the other witches, her smile turning superior.

Then the falling planes shot missiles.

21

Billie set the kettle of hot water to the side while she jiggled the infuser and watched the steam rise from the cup.

"Who did you say he is?" Bertie rolled her wheelchair into the kitchen from the store.

"I didn't. The tree showed me an image. He's Canadian. RMCP. Any more than that and I'm guessing." She could be guessing too much already. Assuming in today's world had problems.

"When is he going to be here?"

"Again, if I knew I think I would have—"

A knock drew their attention to the door.

"But I think it could be sooner rather than later."

Bertie gave her a long-suffering look.

Billie pulled the curtain back. Two people stood on the porch, a man and a woman. To set her at ease? Could be anything, really.

She opened the door but stepped out in the cold late morning air. Just because the tree had said she'd have a visitor didn't mean they would be a good thing. It might have been a warning. "Morning." Better not give them any information before she found out why they crossed the border.

"We're looking for Billie Black. Is he home?"

So, they had bad intelligence. They were looking for a man with her name. "Sorry, who are you?"

The woman stood in front of the man, exuding a heavy authoritarian vibe. "Ma'am, we're with the Canadian government. We have information that says Billie Black lives at this address and needs to come with us." She had a slight French accent. RCMP employed French?

Billie stared at the woman. This wouldn't have been legal before the secession, but who could say *what* was legal anymore? "You produce a warrant or good cause, and I'll present Billie Black. Otherwise, you're trespassing in a foreign country, and where I'm from, that's invasion."

The man pushed his partner back. *That* guy looked like the one from the vision. He had intelligent eyes, and they rolled hard when the woman tried to bully her way. "Sorry to bother you, ma'am. Here's the deal. We have knowledge that a Billie Black lives here. We were sent to bring him back any way we could."

The woman crossed her arms swaying back and forth like she was judging how much force she could use for the *any means necessary*.

Billie raised her magick, ready to force the Canadians off her porch and run.

The woman shifted her way again. "Are you going to cooperate?"

"No." Billie wouldn't be bullied. She'd never stood for it before and that hadn't changed just because the world was on fire now. "You better be going."

"Cindy, *shut up*. I have to apologize for my partner. She has notions of Americans and won't step away from them."

Billie wrinkled her eyes and pressed her lips together.

"Have you held up your actions in front of a mirror? You came to *me*. You threatened *me*. I'd say if anyone's been pushy, it's you, sister. Last chance."

"We're being invaded," the man said quickly. "We came here because we think Billie Black can help. At least, we've heard it said…by people."

Now they were gettin' somewhere. "Well, why don't you tell me by who? After that, I can get him a message." These two watched too much American TV. Clearly a classic good cop, bad cop routine.

"Maybe if we take you with us, he'll get the message faster?" Cindy sneered.

Billie thought all Canadians were supposed to be nice. "Or maybe take off, never to be found. That would throw a wrench into your plans, wouldn't it? Who's invading? And where?"

The man inhaled deep, then blew his cheeks out.

Oh, good. He'd had enough of the game, too.

"China. Through American lands on the East Coast." His face fell. "We need Billie to help secure our borders and push them back."

"That sounds sincere. But you still haven't said who told you."

"Juliet Yazzie. Her clan used to be one of the strongest in the Northwest, but they've splintered, but some of them have a lot of influence."

"Juliet Yazzie?" She didn't know anyone by that name.

"We already tried to get in touch with the Whiskey witch clan, but they are exceedingly difficult to get in touch with. So, we asked around, and Billie Black was the next-best name. And we need him."

Billie gripped the door, prepared to slam it in their faces.

Bertie cleared her throat behind her. "That's not who we are."

235

It wasn't. "You"—she said, pointing to the man—"can come in. You"—she said, her finger swinging to Cindy—"can stay out here, or wait in the car. I don't do bullies."

Cindy's eyes went red hot.

"Any questions?" Billie smiled sweetly at the man.

"Um." He looked to the porch again and shifted a foot. "We kind of have to stay together? Technically, she outranks me, but the mission is mine."

Shit. If she let them in, the bully won. Sort of. "Okay, how about this: you both can come in. If she says anything, even a peep, we move this out here."

Cindy opened her mouth and inhaled.

But the man held up his hand. "That sounds like a deal we can live with. Lead the way."

Dexx worked his arm and swiped at the debris in his hair, staring at all the paras who had followed him to this field with only a small scrap of an idea of a plan. Only dumb luck had prevented death. None of his paras had been killed, but several had sustained injuries. A few of them might still die.

He couldn't just go off with an idea of a plan anymore. Battling demons, sure. Fighting against rogue shifters? Sure. Bring an extra gun and some spare ammo and things were peachy.

But this was war and Walton had some damned big weapons.

He turned to his door witch, who was sitting up, blood sliding into his right eye. "Let's get out of here. They won this round." Just like that, Dexx had lost his first battle. His big guns were hurt, and the rest needed to be supported and he needed some fucking tanks.

The doorway opened up on the Whiskey front lawn.

He sent the paras home who could walk.

He needed to get better quick, or this war would be over before it began.

Paige wobbled from their porch and set to doing what she could. Tarik had a line moving as he healed most people.

"*Fuck.*" Tarik *healed* people. Dexx had forgotten all about his demon healer. Dexx balled his hand into a fist and looked for something to hit.

"Something wrong?" Leslie asked politely, but her eyes were a violent orange fire.

"Yeah. I don't have the background to fight a full-scale war."

"None of us do. But if you want the job you fought for, you can't whine about when you get it."

"Yeah. Next time will be a little different." But he'd need to get smarter first.

How do we do better next time?

We will learn, Hattie said. *They attacked from the sky, and we forgot to look up.*

Great advice. You going to keep an eye on the sky if we get to fight again?

Do you not have what you need to protect you from sky attacks?

Dexx stopped. He did. He had the ability to cover the sky. He'd even seen it in action. Leslie was his weapon of war in the sky. And Robin loved to fight and gain superiority wherever he roamed. Good thing the manticore was already dead and couldn't come back for however long it had to stay wherever it was.

"Are you okay?" Paige finally let the last of the minor wounded go and it was his turn.

"Just fine. For losing like a thousand vampires. They all went into a blood frenzy. I think it was Merry."

"Merry? What makes you say that?"

He shrugged. "I saw her out on the field and then the vampires went super bloodlusty."

"Like they do with blood magick?"

He nodded. "I'm the reason the dampers went back on line. I had to take away her ability to cast."

Paige nodded, looking away. "That was a good call, but I wish there was another way you could have warned us."

"We need better communication. I really miss phones."

She snorted. "I never thought I'd see the day."

"Me either." Dexx let his head fall. "Today was not the win you wanted."

"No." She leaned into him. "But we learned some pretty important stuff."

"And if we live long enough, we can put that all into motion."

"Exactly." She let her head fall on his shoulder. "You kicking yourself for losing like you normally do?"

No. "Probably."

"Do you need to hear how amazing you are?"

"When *you* say it, it just sounds like I'm a moron."

"I still love you," she said like that was the answer to the universe.

"Times like this, I don't think you do." But he felt better just being beside her.

"I know." She sighed.

"I think I kind of suck at military leader thing."

"Me too."

"Demon hunting is so much easier."

"And I really thought it'd prepare us for...this." She shook her head which still leaned against his shoulder.

"Same."

"But it...didn't."

Seriously. "No."

"We need more generals."

"We need Chuck to do more in the field."

"He should probably not be in the field." Paige sighed. "General Saul has been pressuring me to stay out of the battles. She might be right. First with Nevada, then Kansas, and then this."

"Yeah."

They were quiet a long time.

"Do you think we're going to win?" Dexx asked quietly.

Paige didn't answer immediately and then she shook her head. "No. I think we picked the wrong fight."

That thought was terrifying, but only because it rang with a truth that hit Dexx hard.

"I thought getting more power would help us win," Paige said. "I've had this feeling that we're just going to lose for weeks now. Months, maybe. I don't know how I ever thought this was something we could do."

"We have to *find* a way," Dexx said, taking her hand in his. "The thought of our kids being led away in chains…"

She nodded like a rocking child. "We're not smart enough for this."

"Well, I'm not."

Releasing a long breath, she leaned deeper into him. "We gotta find people who are, then."

Yeah. They did. Because Dexx couldn't afford to lose this.

And neither could anyone else who'd decided to join them.

Paige let Leslie do the last little bit of perfecting the arranging of the table. Bobby and Kammy were only going to turn three once. They didn't look like three-year-olds anymore. They didn't even look like they were the same age anymore, but…it was still their third birthday and…

They all needed something to celebrate.

Paige hadn't felt anything from the bite and she was starting to feel a little relieved. Maybe she had been ignored. Maybe the ancients had decided that this was all just a big mistake and they were going to let her continue on her dull experience without the aid of a spirit animal.

Dexx had the kids entertained in the garage. A ping-pong table came up for sale, or something and he *had* to have it. So, the first annual Ping-Pong Para Championship was underway in the garage.

She watched for a few minutes while Dexx and Tru explained the rules and showed them how to play, then they were all cheers and good-natured trash talk. Dexx had taught them well.

Leslie and Paige had control of setting up the birthday table. Nobody remembered, except the parents, of course, so it was the first surprise birthday most of them would know.

Streamers hung from the ceiling lights out to the walls and a big Happy Birthday sign stretched along the back wall.

Paige stifled a lump in her throat. Her baby boy wasn't three. Technically he was, but he had the body of a teen. The sadness threatened tears, but she pushed it away. She missed all the fun baby years. Then again, she missed the terrible twos, threes, fours, and fives.

Leslie stood back with her arms crossed. "I think that should do it. You couldn't ask for much more for a Whiskey surprise party."

"Not for *any* surprise party." Along with the regular banners, streamers, and party favors were floating globes of magick, streamers of vines, and spelled food. Yup. It wouldn't be Whiskey if they didn't have a little something extra in the cake.

"I can get them if we're ready." Paige nodded to herself at the laden table of gifts. Mostly clothes, now that they had a few coming in, but there *were* a few things toddlers would like. Bobby didn't get any of those. He had a Bluetooth headset and phone coming. Something he could use *if* things calmed down enough to *have* those things. But Dexx *had to have* it for Bobby. Boys.

Leslie nodded. "Yeah. Yeah, I think we can call them in now. You get 'em, I'll guard the table."

That had been a story. Back when Paige and Leslie had been little, Alma had made Leslie a cake—a chocolate cookie cake—and they went for an outing before indulging. In the excitement, someone forgot to close the door completely and the neighbor's dog nosed his way in and ate the entire thing. They found the dog and the crumbs on the floor, and the neighbor found them standing over the dog. The dog made it, but never set foot near the house again. Alma did something she never talked about after that.

Paige walked down the hall to the garage, sounds of a fierce ping-pong battle filtered through the door. Sounded like both sides had a cheering section and, of all things, a commentator.

"…and a smash return by the Tru Heart back to the Man-Cat, and he picks up the save, and pressing his advantage back to the Tru Heart. Yes folks, this is the battle of the century, in the remote hamlet of Whiskey Gardens, today's coverage is brought to you by the best in the business."

Wild *tok-tok* noises of the paddles whacking the ball back and forth met her as she opened the door.

The kids ringed the sides of the table, leaving the ends open where Tru and Dexx had stepped way back flinging their arms as the ball sailed from one side to the other.

Paige leaned against the doorway. Nothing was going to force her into that mess.

Tru fired his shot, Dexx responded with a fierce backhand, Tru reached out and pounded it back to Dexx.

Dexx wound up and hit it back, and Tru squared up and... lightly tapped it to the table where it barely made it over the net. Dexx rushed forward, paddle extended, and...missed. The ball bounced once, twice, three times before it rolled off the edge.

"And the winner is Tru Heart! Better luck next time, Man-Cat. We have some lovely parting gifts for you."

Paige slow-clapped. "Very nice. Time to put the game away and come inside."

A chorus of groans met her. Not all of them were kids, even though the adults had a hand in keeping the kids occupied. She tipped her head at the biggest groaner.

"But I was just about to slaughter him. Just *one* game?"

"Not unless you want to answer to Leslie." She smiled sweetly.

That brought him around. "Oh, yeah. That."

Paige nodded. "Yeah, that." She stood aside as the kids and Tru tromped by, the older kids relating plays they liked best or referencing other games, Tyler, Bobby, and Griff animated in the retelling.

Dexx leaned his head close to Paige. "She got it the way she wanted?"

Paige answered in low tones. "Not exactly what she wanted, but she worked super-well with what we had. Let's move or we'll be late." The followed the kids being sure that *all* of them were bracketed in. Tru disappeared around the corner into the dining room and as the first kids walked in, the adults yelled, "Surprise!"

Every kid jumped.

Bobby and Kammy had no idea. They hadn't had a birthday they remembered, but they *both* would this time, with Bobby being around thirteen, and Kammy rummaging around people's thoughts.

They went into a round of "Happy Birthday," while Tyler blended his special magick in.

Mandy lit the candles with a flare and everyone tore in.

Dexx made sure his piece had as much frosting as he could scrounge from the plate. He gave her an innocent look when she mentioned it.

So. These were the good times in the middle of a civil war. She'd take it.

The Federalist States had been quiet for a few weeks, and while it made her more than a little nervous, she made the most of the unexpected truce.

The kids were into their second pieces and Dexx had polished off a third when someone knocked on the door.

That put an end to the birthday celebration faster than she could have thought. "Keep eating, I'll see who it is."

It had better not be news of an attack. It had better not be—

Ishmail ran his hands through his hair. "Hey, I know it's a personal day, but..."

She sighed. "What?"

"We think China's invading Canada."

22

Geneneral McCormick walked into the Oval Office and waited patiently while the president signed papers. They could have been any papers, from another executive order on down to signing the receipt for lunch. Probably not the lunch order though.

Walton was unstable. That much was undeniable. Pressing legislation through by way of executive order wasn't lawful. But if nobody stood up to tear it down, then the difference wasn't measurable. McCormick had signed up to protect the country. He'd protect it as best as he knew how.

With the country divided as it was, it kept the president under, not exactly control, but at least focused. The secessionist states took the brunt of his mania and hopefully at the end of the current administration's term the madness would end.

Would the others concede and join the Union again when someone else took Walton's place? They couldn't win, and after the loss of Denver, they had to know that.

President Walton looked up. "Oh, good. You've decided to join us."

"I came as soon as I was requested."

"You took longer than I expected, but no matter. I'm hearing rumors about the rebel states. Please tell me we're taking ground back miles at a time."

McCormick couldn't. "If I said we were, I would be lying. The truth is the para forces are equal to our own. Not in training or arms, but the powers they have neutralize ours quite effectively. We've basically come to a stalemate. We can go no further, and neither can they."

"But Denver was a win."

"We can't take Denver, sir. It's flooded with vampires in a bloodlust. The best we can do is contain them to the metro area and hope they burn themselves out."

President Walton frowned. "What happened to the inhibitor emitters? I thought those had them pretty well cornered." Walton's hands steepled under his chin.

Paige Whiskey and the people who followed her may lack experience, but they were empowered and emboldened. They were also unafraid to try new things. "They were and continue to be effective, but they have found a way around them. Once they get behind our lines, we become vulnerable. And the more we use them, the easier it will be for the paras to find them, and perhaps take them offline permanently." It might be the best if they did. That was unconventional warfare at best, and at worst it was cruel. Those people were Americans, and they had rights. Never mind they seceded only *after* the mandate forced registration.

He wouldn't want to register on a list just because he was different. The other side of the coin was that paras had abilities that other people did not. The mess was tangled, and several consecutive bad decisions had been made along the way. Walton hadn't been the first to make them. He just wasn't making them any better.

"I see. It seems to me that we are thinking too small. If

the inhibitors aren't working, why couldn't we take another route? Something a little more permanent?"

That sounded ominous. "More permanent? We have the inhibitors in satellites now?" That tech wouldn't work from space.

"No, we can wait for that. No, what I mean is *permanent*. The nuclear kind. If we can't bring them to heel with manpower, then we do it with firepower."

What the hell? "Sir, you can't do that. Firing on your own country like that? That would be the height of treason."

"It would be if it was still part of *this* country. As it stands, they've declared themselves a completely *different* country, and *that* is one we can bomb. They have no UN charter and as far as this country is concerned, *they* shot first."

"That's a tortured way to look at it, sir, and you know it. Dropping nuclear warheads won't solve your problems. Even if you managed to hit only the paras fighting, you would irradiate huge sections of land you weren't aiming for. You'd be hitting countries we're *allied* with."

"Maybe. But who cares about Canada anyway? The paras will probably try to talk Canada into a peace treaty, too. Hell, they may even invade. No, what I'm proposing is more of a preemptive strike that'll keep the good and decent Americans from harm. We may have to move cities back a little, or evacuate some smaller communities, but even that's better than what we have now. They shouldn't be that close to the border anyway."

"Sir." McCormick shook his head.

President Walton looked McCormick in the eye. "Get brass together. I want limited options drafted for my approval immediately."

That wasn't how this worked. But if McCormick wanted to continue to make a difference, he'd have to stay close. "Of course, sir." And maybe with the support of remaining military leaders, he could find a way to avert a complete disaster.

Leslie watched Bobby and Kamden on the floor playing with a few of the toddler toys. The boy might look thirteen or so, but he hadn't been that big for a long while yet. He still had some of the wonderment of a boy his *actual* age. Whatever had caused him and the twins to grow so fast had tried to get Kammy, too. She wouldn't have that, not *her* kids. They were going to grow up like the Goddess wanted.

Mom, why do you want to stay small forever?

Dammit, the boy could claw through her mind too easily.

You will stop that, right now. Robin boomed through her head, sending Kammy into giggling fits.

Stop it, both of you. Leslie glared at her son and sent the griffin the mental equivalent. Sometimes she felt like she had *all* the children around her. Even those who should know better. She cast a look toward Dexx, but he was in deep conversation with Paige and the bear clan leader who somehow showed up after cake, so the look was wasted.

She wanted no part of the war talk, so she sequestered herself away and watched the kids play.

Tru came up behind her and put his hands on her waist. She grabbed his hands and pulled him closer. She loved him for everything he was and did. Just a regular human, and that he somehow kept up with the entire family was its own special magick. Anyone else would have either melted or run away in complete madness.

He nuzzled her neck. Damn, he must be angling for some quality time later.

"I wish they could stay cute and small forever."

Leslie smiled against his nuzzling. "Except for self-entertaining and diapers, I agree."

Tru huffed a laugh against her neck. "Too true, my lady." He squeezed her in that way he had. "Do you ever think maybe we should have let him grow like Bobby and the twins did?"

"No." Her tone went flat. All the things that went into making good humans happened when they were learning to walk and talk and developing fine motor skills. "Kammy is going the long way. If I have to take him to the middle of Bum Fuck Egypt, he's going to grow up like we did."

"Of course he is. Whatever made the others grow isn't still happening, so that part's over. I was just wondering."

"But to answer the question I think you're really asking, yes. It would be easier in a way. But not all the ways."

"Spoken like a Whiskey. I love you."

"I love you too. Think we could go for a walk and have Paige and the biggest child watch the littlest child?"

"Only one way to find out." Tru pulled his chin from her neck and turned to Dexx.

Ishmail didn't go into great detail on their source, but if China was moving in on Canada then…

There was nothing they could do to help. There just wasn't. They couldn't even keep Denver, though thanks to the flood of blood magick and the vampires now loose in the area, no one wanted the metropolis.

Leslie called to Dexx from her spot with Tru. "We're going for a walk. Watch the kids."

Dexx furrowed his brows and jerked his head back. "You must have me confused with another alpha. I don't do that."

Leslie raised a brow. "No, I don't have you confused with

anyone. In this house *I'm* the alpha, and you can watch the kids while I walk with my husband. That is, you will because you like Paige's boobies. Get it?"

Where was a Twix when it could really come in handy? "I guess it's a warm night for a walk. Why don't we watch Kammy while you and Tru go out and enjoy it?"

"Thanks, alpha Dexx. I think we will. Mighty nice of you to offer."

Dexx gritted his teeth. Damn the complicated living arrangements. Truthfully, the boy wouldn't be a problem, but that she always had him doing menial things made him chafe.

To keep you from growing beyond yourself. Hattie always seemed to have Leslie's back.

Shut up, fat cat. Keep your comments to something useful.

Then you might want to come with me to the Time Before. You have duties you have neglected.

What now? He had fifty things pulling him in fifty directions. Did he need *one more?* He glanced at Emma. She was the brains of the outfit there. Maybe not brains necessarily, Mason was a school teacher after all, but she had way more, well, not timidness.

Mason was a good guy, just not very aggressive.

What do I have to do there? He didn't leave the stove on, or a messy bed that he could remember.

You will have to see.

Dammit. *Fine. Be there in a—*

The world formed into black and fog and a tree lit from above with the softest grass that could be imagined. Hattie met him and they stepped into the Time Before as the big cat.

—second. You drive. What are we supposed to be doing here anyway? They could spend a year here, and still be back before Leslie and Tru.

They melted into one creature and Hattie took another step and the Time Before appeared around them.

Okay, now I can get behind this. The landscape of the bluff and the plains had altered considerably. Green shoots of grass waved lazily in the light breeze and the temperature felt like the heat of the day easing into evening.

A few spirit animals grazed without care, occasionally lifting their heads and chewing the soft stalks.

How come you bring me here when it looks like this? I could hang here under the almost sun and laze the day away.

You are not here to watch others eat. You are not here to eat others.

Dexx sighed in Hattie's head. *Then why did you bring me here with all the things I like about being alone? Nice weather, no people, soft grass to lie in, what else could a guy ask for? I mean, you're already here, and Paige can't be, so that's the one downside.*

You have a promise to keep. Hattie took a step and the landscape changed to the plains under the bluff.

I do?

She took another step and they stood in a familiar protected stone circle. The one that Cooper McCree bound Mah'se to the Earth by way of the Time Before.

And there lay Mah'se. Flat on his side, head twisted awkwardly because of that enormous rack on his head.

Shit, we have to help. Dexx pushed to take their body over.

Hattie resisted and kept them where they were. *We will. You must be gentle. Do not speak until he's ready. He is very weak, and I would keep my friend here.*

Was he dying? Was Hattie really that attached to the spirit? *Why are you so invested in him, anyway? As I recall, you're always the one saying things like* this is the way it is *or some other bullshit.*

I have my reasons. Help me keep him here. The pleading in her sending was sincere. She'd never sounded like that before.

Is he like a…boyfriend?

He is like a companion. *One that I would like to keep around.*

She'd never sounded so straightforward, either. *Well, then lead the way. I'll take your lead.* If this was important to her, it was important to him. And they were sort of bonded forever, so it was probably best to help her as much as possible.

Hattie circled wide, and made sure Mah'se saw her. She made another pass, and circled closer. She didn't speak, just made sure he saw her. On the second pass closer she stopped, and paused for a minute and sat.

You have come to see me die?

She looked away, in a very human type gesture of dismissal. *No. I am here to make you strong again.*

You are too late. I think I want to commit myself to the passing.

You would not dare. You gave yourself to guarding the land. Would you leave the lesser spirits alone?

Mah'se snorted. A puff of dry dirt floated away on the air. *They don't need me.*

Maybe they do not. I do like the company.

You have your bond. You've made that clear often enough.

Dexx couldn't hold back. Too much pity-me-because-what-I-want-went-away going on for his taste. *You know, if you wanted to move on, we could just end it for you. A little bite on the throat or over the nose, shouldn't take too long.* His eyes would have been narrowed if he had his own body.

You are not welcome here. Mah'se's words were level, but lacked heat.

I hear your words, but I don't feel your sincerity. Don't be such a guppy. You have a friend who cares about you so much, she brought her best friend who you don't like to help in any way he could. But you know what? Maybe she doesn't deserve a bad friend like you. Come on, Hattie, let's move.

Hattie didn't move, but Dexx shoved his way forward. He struggled for control of her, and the result was a non-moving cat. The upshot was she couldn't move either.

What would you know of loss? You have no idea what I'm going through. Mah'se shifted his head away from Hattie.

Red-hot anger flared in Dexx. Hattie lost control of the spirit form.

Hattie's claws extended and slammed to the ground on the sides of the elk's head, and growled in his face. You *are an asshole. I lost her too, and I knew her a hell of a lot better than you did. What would you know about* any *of it? I put friends and family in the ground, people I loved who I'll* never *get to see again, and I miss every day. I came with Hattie to pull you out of your pity party, but I think you should wallow in it. Just don't drag my bond down with you. Fuck off.*

Dexx yanked his claws back, digging furrows into the earth, and willing them back from the Time Before. He blinked at the lights in the room. Emma and Mason were still sharing a look as the door slid shut behind Tru.

Don't ever ask me to help with that crybaby. He wants to stop living, let him.

Hattie's heart broke.

He was going to be mad for a while. He needed seat time with Jackie, or a beer. "Babe, I think Emma and Mason should get some rest. Do we have an open cabin, or do they need a hotel?"

Emma turned to Dexx. As an alpha she probably felt him seething. "I have plenty of places to stay, but thank you for the invite." Her eyes asked what was up, but he shook his head only enough for her to tell that he wasn't going to talk. "We'll talk more in the morning."

Paige blinked at the sudden end to the conversation. "Um, okay. You can come by the office any time. There's usually someone there early. Just tell them I sent you."

Emma grabbed her stuff and led Mason out. He waved, and Dexx tipped his head up, returning the goodbye. They closed the door behind them.

"You want to explain what that was all about?" Paige turned a Whiskey eye on him.

"No, I do not." Dexx drew in a deep breath and let it go. "It's a long story. Sorry."

"Well, I think you should start—" She dropped her head and braced it against her hand. She squeezed her eyes shut.

Dexx put a hand to her shoulder. "You okay?"

"No. My head is going to explode."

23

Dexx woke up early the next morning. He'd forced a gallon or so of water down Paige's throat after her migraine attack. She'd really been ignoring her need to drink anything besides coffee. It was either that or the bite wasn't going well, so he hoped it was the water. Water he could deal with.

She had tossed and turned for a few hours, but the fluids must have balanced her out eventually. Her soft breathing wasn't labored, and her heart beat slow and steady.

Dexx slipped from the bed and dressed. In the low light, the amethyst crystal glowed a soft purple. He really needed to do something with it. Whatever it was he was supposed to do with it. Dekskulta didn't ever outright say it was to kill Bussemi, but he *had been* the topic at the time, so that left options thin.

Down the steps and to the kitchen, Dexx paused at each of the kids' rooms, listening to them sleep.

He'd never thought of himself as a dad, but he kind of liked the gig. It still scared him silly, though. He'd never admit it to Paige.

He only hoped he could train the kids to take care of themselves. He couldn't let fear stop him from letting them launch. Leah was only a few years away, but the other kids— he barely knew them.

The coffee could wait, for a while at least. Jackie needed a visit. Almost totally done and all she needed was the hood attached and oil. Maybe gas.

Cab sat in his own spot, quietly away from the other, more *normal* cars. With everything else he couldn't admit to people, the car kind of grew on him. Like a cancer, slow and insidious. Not that he'd ever give Jackie up.

The rapidly stabilizing weather meant pleasant days to drive. Truthfully, he could drive her now.

Tools. Okay. Time to get the party started. He didn't actually *need* to finish Jackie, but the nervous energy the fear had needed to be used.

Hood went on. Normally he couldn't have done it himself, but shifter strength and all...

Gas, oil, and a final check over. She was ready, but he couldn't bring himself to start her. He leaned against her fender, face in a palm, while he put some thought into his feelings.

Why would he be afraid of starting her up?

Like something made him afraid of things he'd never been scared of before.

Damn, things felt off. Out of control. Or something else was.

He heard feet coming down the hall to the garage. Paige. Her distinctive gait paused at the door and it opened with a soft swish of the door molding along the floor. "Babe?" She didn't have a trace of sleep in her voice.

"You need something?"

"I woke up and you weren't there. Got worried." She stepped into the garage with bare feet.

Good thing Chuck had heated the floor.

"Couldn't sleep any more. Thought I'd stick her together. What do you think?"

Jackie gleamed in the light of the garage. Like Cooper McCree had never happened.

"She's beautiful. You going to start driving her again?"

"Not yet. Too much going on for the attention she needs."

"That doesn't sound like you. Usually, that car is the only thing you live for."

"So now it's something else. Shouldn't we get ready to meet Emma?"

"Oh crap. I forgot." Paige turned for the door.

"Hey," Dexx called her back. "How's your head?"

"Actually, it feels good. No headache. Not even a little behind the eyes, like I normally have after a migraine."

"That's good." And a little worrisome. It probably wasn't just a migraine.

Paige padded on her bare feet over to him. "Hey." She held her arms out for him. "Come here."

He wrapped her up and she squeezed her back. "I like the way you feel."

She puffed a laugh against him. "I like the way you feel, too."

Liberally dosed with caffeine and stuffed with eggs, they both headed to the office building across from the house. It wasn't huge, and the architecture wasn't ultra-modern, but it was furnished well, all paid for by Chuck's interests. They'd probably have to pay him back at some point.

But it was time for work. Dexx walked her to her office. "How are we going to win this?"

She shook her head. "I have no idea."

"That's not boosting my confidence."

"Mine either," she said as her booted feet crunched in the gravel. "We'll figure out a way."

"We've *got* to start working smarter."

"Oh, I agree with that. How, though?"

"Fuck if I know."

"Same." She gripped his hand tightly. "I'll talk to Saul."

"Are you thinking of helping Canada?" Dexx didn't want to *not* help, but they weren't doing great on their own.

"How?" She opened the door to the office building and led the way through the waiting area. "Let's win a few first and *then* start helping other countries."

Look, a few losses under their belts and they were already thinking smarter. Dexx stayed with Paige a few more minutes, not quite ready to go to his own duties. He felt like a failure and he really didn't want to face Frey, who had no issue with getting in his face about it.

The door opened and a Hispanic woman with her hair pulled tight against her head, and a tall broad-shouldered young man walked in. He looked familiar. She did not.

The man had a feel to him, dangerous in an undefined way. She had hotness rolling from her in waves, but she moved like any nerd he'd ever known. Ethel moved like she did.

The kid—Dexx snapped his fingers. Ah. His dad was at that superpower meeting. The one they voted to allow a civil war. Dragon spirit.

Hattie didn't want to fight, but she wasn't backing down either. She was alert and ready. Nervous.

Are dragons scary? I haven't seen them shift. It would be cool to see, right?

Hattie wasn't playing. *Dragons do not shift. They do not want to or cannot willingly shift. But they have power.*

Hey. We *have power. We do.*

They call me the greatest of the first. That is not completely true. Dragon shifters existed far before my time. We might fight one to a stop, but we could not win.

What about Leslie? She shifts into a griffin. Can't be that hard for a dragon.

Cub. You know little.

The woman held a hand to Paige. "Mrs. Whiskey."

Paige took her hand while the woman introduced herself. "Ms. Pierce, has there been a development?"

"I'm afraid so. You see, the water's being poisoned."

Dexx straightened. "What?"

"Right now, all I can say is that the water has some sort of pollutant introduced in it and it's targeting paras. In the short term, it affects a shifter and their spirit."

Paige stood up straight. "Where did you find this? Who's doing it— ever mind that, I'm pretty sure who. What evidence do you have?"

"Did you want to give her a chance to answer, or should we write this down?" Dexx crossed his arms, Then, he faced Zoe. "And you can talk to me. I'm local law enforcement. *Captain* of Red Star Division." He cast Paige a withering look.

"Either of us will be fine." Paige returned Dexx's look.

"Well, I suggest we spread the word as quickly as possible to prevent any serious long-term damage."

"What *is* the long-term damage?"

"I don't know. But I *do* know that it isn't good to be drinking the water."

"What do suggest we do?"

"We have to warn people not to drink the water. I don't have a cure figured out yet, but I should have one soon."

Dexx put a hand up. All the women gave him the exact same half-lidded look. "Wait, is this all water, just city water, just well water...how much is safe and what isn't?"

"I—that's a good question. It's in the public city water, for sure, and I think over time it will filter and dilute out. Any lake-fed rivers will also be affected, but I'm sure well water is fine."

Paige narrowed her eyes at Zoe. "*How* do you know this?"

Brack suddenly straightened, and for the first time Zoe looked unsure of herself. "I...found out."

"How?" Paige pressed.

"It's too long to—"

Paige doubled over and fell to her knees, holding her head with her hand. Was this the poison?

Dexx dropped to a knee. "Pea, you all right?" He looked up at Zoe and Brack. "Is this the poison?"

Brack shook his head.

Zoe knelt on Paige's other side. "No, this is different. Unless she's been mega-dosed. Has she been swimming in the city supply?"

Dexx's turn to give a look. "Swimming lessons conflicted with our little civil war, so the instructor cut them short."

"Ah. Yes. Well, then I think we can rule out extreme exposure."

This wasn't poison. Dexx was almost positive of that.

This was the bite.

And it wasn't going well.

Bussemi walked through his palatial house in the Italian Alps. The mountains were as close as he could get to the place where he grew into manhood so many thousands of years ago. Could it have been millions? There simply was no way of knowing. The demon had taken thousands of years of his consciousness and subdued it.

Time meant nothing to the demon. And even after all this time, he still didn't know its name or even if it was just an extraordinarily powerful demon. It slumbered, but barely. If Bussemi made any move to take more of himself back, it would wake and take control again.

It was never supposed to be like this, but it was.

What they needed was for Dexx to come out from hiding. Under his ward, he had more protection than should be possible. Normal demons from any of their realms wouldn't be able to penetrate, but not even the demon could stretch his influence under it. They didn't succeed in stealing his body, not completely anyway, but they had a toehold, and if they had a toehold, the battle was lost. All they needed was time.

Bussemi reached a large ornate door at the end of the hall and waited for it to swing open on silent hinges. The long table already held a few occupants.

These were the people who shared ownership of the world. Nations, banks, the rich and powerful thought they controlled the world. None of them did. *Bussemi* and these few owned them. The *world*.

"Why are we here?" The tall gaunt man sat at his usual chair when meetings were called, but those were few.

"You are here because of the pact we made together to come when one of us called. I trust you remember that?"

"I may remember more than you, but that still does not explain *why* we are here today."

Bussemi would burn the man to a cinder when he owned the Colt body. "The pawn we set in motion. Has he delivered the package?"

"The pawn." Waugh folded his hands on the table. "*Your* pawn. *Your* piece. *Your* problem. If you are asking if I know if he's fulfilled his role, then yes, it is done. Since you've pulled me into your schemes, why are the Whiskey witches and the Colt boy so necessary to you?"

"That is my business. What you need to know is that I will hold up my end of the bargain."

"Yes. You will." Waugh stood up and vanished through a doorway.

The rest stood and disappeared as well.

Soon, he wouldn't need to deal with *any* of them.

Bussemi's fingers worked the symbols to open a scrying window. The ward prevented him from poking through and influencing Colt. When he emerged, however, he could push, cajole, and sway. All without the man's knowledge. Then the power of one of the first magick users would be his.

Curious that he refrained from using the magick since he fought with that upstart Kester. Where had Kester found so much ability from? Questions he would drag out of Colt when the body was his.

<hr />

Annelle Rovoski paced back and forth in her mansion. The remains of her latest servant lay broken in the corner. She'd send for a new one in the morning.

Dexx Colt and that *witch* of his were becoming more of a pain than she originally thought they could be. Never mind she'd been given a mysterious warning to leave them alone. She would get her revenge. Young Annika should have been here. Learning the ways of ruling the lesser beings of the world.

Could the warning have come from the rumored cabal that ruled above her? No, surely she would have found them out hundreds of years before.

Merry Eastwood was her closest rival for power, and she was missing. All to the good. Thomas McCree might have to be dealt with, but as yet he was still malleable. But he might be an unusual ally from the desert lands to the south. If he wanted them, he could have them as long as he didn't look north.

The traps and contingencies were set. Once the Whiskeys were together and unguarded, she would exact her revenge.

They turned her Annika against her. Somehow, they turned her. And then killed her.

A familiar tingle sent her to her knees and head bowed.

"Yes, mistress of the currents. I hear and obey."

"The mother rusalka seeks action against the Dexx and the Dexx people?"

"Yes, mistress. He has taken from me and I will take from him."

"The Dexx has been our champion. Has the mother rusalka known this?"

"It does not matter. He has taken from me and I will take from him."

"The mother rusalka will do the action without our assistance."

"Yes, mistress. I do not require your help. Only permission."

"The mother rusalka will do the action without our assistance."

"Thank you, mistress. The help I have employed, will they be against your wishes?"

"Our assistance will be withheld."

"As long as I will not be held back, that is all I ask."

The currents withdrew and left Annelle with the warmth of her absence.

As long as the mistress didn't prevent her from moving forward with her plans, that was enough permission for her.

Dexx Colt and his entire family would not survive the week, either by her hand or her bounty hunters'.

Leah sat in the extra room reserved for plants in Wy's family house in Alaska. The sun *finally* had heat and the room wasn't the coldest anymore.

Fresh grass shoots poked through the patches of snow left over from winter, as the rest of the yard tried to dry out.

The northern country spring wasn't as bad as she'd thought it would be, though it was taking forever. Leah was still a little mad that everyone else in her family was looking at green grass and she was still staring at snow with dirt patches and...more snow. It'd just dumped more earlier that morning. But it wasn't as bad as she'd thought it would be.

Or that's what she was saying on the outside, because Alaskan people were crazy and didn't like hearing her complain about how it would *never* be spring in Alaska.

Leah was trying to become an adult.

She had to go home, but not for a few hours. She took a cookie from the plate and absently chewed as her homework shrank.

Gertie glanced at her from her book, foggy-eyed from the story. The couch across the room sat under a large window, letting a wide sliver of sunlight warm the back of her head. "What was that, hon?"

Uh, nothing. Leah hadn't said anything out loud. Wait. Had she? "It feels good in here."

"It does, doesn't it? We'll have to turn the fan on to get air circulating before long. Summer is hot." She dropped her face back into the book. "Then the mosquitoes will be out. Haven't found a really good ward against them yet."

"What?" Leah whipped her head around, but Gertie was firmly planted in her book again. Mosquitoes or cold, which would be easier to put up with? Good thing she had door magick and she could pick her poison.

Her phone buzzed as she worked on the last question of her homework. It was so good to have that back. Leah hadn't realized just how cut off from the world she'd felt without it. Granted, when she was home, she had to share the phone with the twins, but...when she was in Alaska, it was all hers.

Mandy wanted to know when she was planning on going back to the house. "Oh, crap. What time is it?" The sun didn't seem to have moved in the sky, but it was already past six. "Dang it, I have to go." She turned to Gertie, but she wasn't there. Her book was closed, and a bookmark stuck out from the top.

That woman was like a ghost. Leah slammed her books closed. In a few moments, her bag bulged and she shrugged her coat on.

She rushed into the kitchen, snagged another cookie, and opened a portal home. She stepped through to smells of cooking and the sounds of her cousins and siblings talk-arguing.

Kate slammed her last card of Uno on the stack.

A flurry of cards flew across the table as Rai showed her losing face. Leah was glad that she wasn't the *only* sore looser

264

because she was soooooo tired of getting ragged on about that. Seriously.

Mandy sat at the end of the table, scrolling through her phone.

The dryads had most of the kinks worked out of the phones and stuff, which meant that pretty soon, they might all get phones and tablets and computers and internet and working TV and online games and all of that back. Soon.

Ember came over to her with a smile on his face and swiped the phone out of her hand. "My turn."

Which would be super-cool.

"Sorry, lost track of time. So what's new?"

Mandy looked up from her phone and shrugged. "Not too much. We're stuck here waiting for the next raid, or battle, or whatever." She shrugged, but her face said she was a bit scared of the fighting.

"Where's Mom and Dad?"

Mandy shrugged again, but Tyler answered. "They're out waiting for the water poisoning. We don't know if it's soon or already done. But they don't have enough water bottles for everyone." He shrugged as Bobby gathered cards.

Wait, poison? "When did that happen? Who's poisoning the water? What water?"

"Zoe says she can cure it," Tyler said with a dreamy look on his face.

"Wait. Who's Zoe?"

Mandy rolled her eyes. "The scientist working on this."

"She's pretty," Tyler said with a lovelorn expression on his face.

"She's also old," Mandy said.

Kate frowned. "You define old weirdly."

So, for an elf, Zoe was probably in her thirties?

"Anyway," Mandy continued, "the more you drink, the worse it is for you. And some people won't recover. She says we should be fine since we're on a well. Which, by the way, if we have a well, why doesn't it work when there's no power?"

That was something Leah knew. "There's a pump that's electrical."

"In a well." Mandy's voice said that was dumb.

"It's in a hole." What part of this wasn't she getting?

"Where water belongs."

She couldn't be this slow, right? "And the sinks are...up the hill." It was basic physics.

"Ooohhh," Mandy said, the light dawning.

Yeah. That didn't hurt at all.

"I feel dumb now," Mandy growled at her phone.

Aunt Leslie walked out of the kitchen, a wooden spoon in hand. "Dinner in five. Get cleaned up and find the table."

Mandy took over and directed the cleanup, and soon the game was away, and the table was clean enough to eat from.

"Where's Mom and Dad?" Leah spooned up the chowder and wiped her bowl with a piece of bread.

"Out."

Dying? In trouble?

Bobby dropped his spoon and stood. He glowed like he did when he was smaller. "Dalles, Wallula, Arlington, and Little Crater. *All* of them have been tainted. The city won't last."

Dexx took another call. This one was the same as the last, a para had been sickened by the water.

This wasn't Dexx's job. He'd been reduced to a battlefield nurse, trying to keep up with the calls for help. "Yes, ma'am, we're aware of the situation and we're doing our best to deal with it."

"When is this getting fixed? Are we all in danger?"

"Ma'am, all I know is we're dealing with it as best we can right now." Dexx hung up the phone. He remembered being really glad when they were back, but now? He had really mixed feelings about it. It'd been a little freeing not constantly being attainable.

He ran his fingers through his hair. "You sure Zoe's got this all figured out?"

Paige had her head in her hands. Both of them had been at it for hours with Red Star and her staff, trying to keep the population calm. "She's confident she can manufacture an antidote soon." She had her eyes covered and talked to the table.

"Another headache?" Dexx pressed his leg against her side and rested a hand on her shoulder gently.

She ducked her head against his hand. "Yeah. It hurts a lot."

That had to be an understatement. If she was in normal pain, colorful words would have been pouring out of her mouth. If all she had was *hurt* to describe the pain, it must be intense.

"Go get some rest. I got this, babe. You need some sleep, and we have more than enough to cover the phones."

"No, I have to stay. There's nobody else to do it." She lifted her head slowly and turned to Dexx. Her eyes were bloodshot and half closed.

"You going to try to play the *sick mom* card? You know, the wife gets sick and still finds time to cook a soufflé, but when the dad's sick, the world has time to stop? Be the dad, babe." He'd been up and moving plenty of times when he should have been strapped down, and Paige had too. But this time, she didn't have to.

"That's not what I'm doing."

"It is."

"Is not. It's just that I *have* to."

Dexx pressed his lips together as he shook his head slowly. It was like this new baby nation was her new kid. "No. No, I don't think so. We really have this covered, and I doubt you could call your witch hands right now. So, I get to pull rank and get you into a bed in a room with no light. You're going to rest, and every time you get a migraine, or I *think* you're in migraine territory, you go to bed. And you stay away from any engagements too."

Paige opened her mouth to argue, perhaps pulling the leader-of-the-free-states card, but Dexx wasn't going to let her finish.

"You won't be any help if we have to take care of you and fight a raid, or whatever it is they do."

She began another protest, but she stopped and covered her eyes with her hands. The nod was very slow and forced. Her scent was rolling sadness and self-loathing.

"You get to rest a bit. You've pushed yourself way too hard." He didn't want to think about how this might have something to do with the bite going bad. "It's all good, and I got this. Zoe has the cure—" Or a treatment. He couldn't remember which. "And soon we'll be back in business. So, for now, you walk out of here, or I'll carry you to the house."

That could have possibly been the weakest argument in his entire life, but she only nodded again.

She had to be in blinding pain. She stood with his help and walked slowly toward the door.

"Hey, we're going to step out for a minute. Be right back."

Frey nodded, and Joel mimicked her once he made sure Frey acknowledged him.

Sidekicks.

Dexx finally wound up carrying Paige to the bed and gently laying her down. He pulled her shoes and socks from Paige's feet and covered her with a thin sheet. She was already hot to the touch, and socks might make things unbearable.

Paige laid an arm over her face and passed out.

She will *make it, won't she?*

She is strong. Hattie didn't have a strong, confident tone to her voice.

She is. But how long can she go on like this? Does this at least mean spirit shifters are looking at her?

Hattie didn't answer.

Dexx pulled the curtains closed to pitch black for an ordinary person. He still saw things well enough to get around.

The amethyst crystal called to him. Not exactly calling him, but the crystal suddenly seemed to want to be held.

He reached out to grab it, but hesitated. Why would it be calling to him? Could he use it to help Paige somehow? And did he *really* want to *give* her more power when he'd been upset about her power grab through shifter spirit? He grabbed it and it…nothing.

Not completely nothing. It still wanted him to hold it, but it felt, well, it felt comfortable. Satisfied that it had him close.

Aw, dammit. Now a stupid *mysterious crystal* wanted his attentions? Hell—dang it.

Dekskultas was an ass, maybe even an asshat, but his intentions had been in the right place. If he'd made it to help Dexx, then it really was meant to help him. And if the thing had a touch of sentience and knew what it was supposed to do, then it might help him to activate it. All he probably had to do was say his name and the name of the city it came from. It worked that way with the *shamiyir*, but letting that sort of power loose all at once…was suicidal at best.

Closing his eyes and letting his head drop back, he slipped it in his pocket. Then he snapped Jackie's keys from the dresser, and they went next to the power stone.

Why were all these things coming all at once? He wasn't

one for a notepad, but damn, he needed to write it all down to keep up.

Paige turned over with a sigh in her sleep with the absence of excess stimulus. She might have mumbled thanks, but it was just sound, not words.

Dexx debated returning to the office. Paige was the diplomat, the politician. He wasn't. if they had an enemy stand up, sure, call him and he'd take care of it. But poisons? Poisonous president? Hard pass. But Frey was there, and he *did* say he was coming back. That didn't mean he'd be back right away though.

Shit. His feet walked him back to the office and the phones before he finished debating with himself.

Joel stood as tall as his toes allowed him and was trying hard to stare down Rocco. His little hands were fists behind his back. It reminded him of a little kid refusing to accept the fact that playtime was over.

The gargoyle stood with no expression on his face, his posture relaxed. "I meant no disrespect. You may certainly brew a new pot for yourself and Ms. Van Sant."

"Damn right I will. Nobody screws up coffee. Not while I'm here." Joel huffed around Rocco and into the next room.

"Did, something happen?" Dexx watched the goblin through the door carefully measuring and pouring.

Rocco met his eyes. "I offered to make a pot. Not even to anyone in particular. But he thinks he is the only person who can make one for Frey."

Good. She had a groupie. Maybe he'd fill the void she had. Doubtful, but it could happen.

Frey didn't notice anything since she was turned around, a landline phone stuck to her ear. She nodded a few times and finally turned around to hang the phone up.

Dexx tapped on her desk. "A little free with our sidekick, aren't we?"

"What, Joel? If he went off on someone, they deserved it. Where's Tarik?"

"It's not my day to watch him, but for a cool Grant, I'll go find him."

"The fuck's wrong with you? I'm not going to pay you."

"Oh. I thought you wanted to know where Tarik went. My fault. Don't let the captain's badge get in your way."

Frey shook her head with narrowed eyes. "Seriously. What the fuck's wrong with you?"

"Seriously just messing around." Frey's relationship with Dexx had deteriorated to the point where she wanted to clobber him, but she clearly held some resentment toward him. Could be he killed her favorite flying horse when they were in the djinn's death games.

Or she thought she still deserved to be in charge, when she *clearly* had no business with that much power. Not yet.

"Someone named Zoe. She said she found a cure for the water and wants to deploy it. I was going to vet her with Tarik. So now I need to find him."

Dexx grinned. "Just you two? No pitter-patter of little feet three steps behind you?"

Frey didn't even blink. "Of course, there will be."

Wow, so Frey really liked the positive strokes coming from the hanging-toothed little guy. Well, if that's how she liked it, who was he to stand in the way?

Dexx sat at the desk ready to take the next call.

Paige dreamt. She knew somewhere in the back of her psyche that she was sleeping and the images were her subconscious dealing with things. But that didn't stop her heart from racing as the ghostly images of her kids and kids everywhere accused her of using them as cannon fodder.

She wouldn't ever feed children into the chipper just to win, never. Or had she been doing just that?

Sure, the kids hadn't been any more than bruised from their various encounters. Of course, most of those would have likely killed other kids or even most human adults.

That didn't sound as good when it was thought out loud.

The vague blobs strafed her and pushed her to the ground. Each one accused her.

Leah's ghost folded her arms and looked down at her. "Killer. How can we trust you?"

Bobby sank to his knees. "How can *you* trust you?"

Ember stared at her with pained eyes. "Would you sacrifice us to survive?"

Rai shook her head. "We are not your sacrifice."

Paige ran. She tried to anyway, but her legs were too heavy. They didn't move right and every step took her full concentration.

One step. Push hard and lift the other leg.

Fear and sadness assaulted her. They were right. How could she press her children forward to die in an adult's war?

She couldn't. She *wouldn't.*

Tickling on her face made her wince. She threw up her hands to defend herself but they wouldn't move.

The tickling at her face came again.

She jerked her head away from it.

The tickling came again, and this time something soft and insistent patted her face.

With a start, she sat up in bed with a gasp.

She twisted her blurry eyes to her tormenter.

Wynonna's little rainbow cat sat on her pillow, looking up at her with one blue eye and one violet eye.

She had never been a cat person, and that little ball of torture cemented it.

"What the hell? Get out."

The cat stood up then jumped off the bed and trotted out the door.

At least one thing was clear in her head. Her kids would not be fighting again.

And her migraine was already fighting to come back.

25

Dexx's finger scratched the table while his cheek rested in his other palm. "I wish I could just go to sleep for a year."

The poisoned water had affected paras in Troutdale for three days, and for three days, he'd had to collect barely functional people for recovery. They still had more than a few spare houses thanks to all the times Troutdale had been blockaded and attacked. So, they were thankfully easy to find. Not that they were easy to get to. Or easy to staff.

So far, about three thousand paras had collapsed from the poisoning, and most were slated for a full recovery. A few would never recover. They had been the weakest shifters, and Dexx was a little glad that Emma had taken Mason and the rest of her pack away from there. He just hoped that where ever they were, they were away from the poisoned water.

Joel speared him with a stare. "Frey goes out from daylight to dark, and doesn't complain. Now *that's* a leader we can follow. She's pushing through her exhaustion, and we as, supposedly, the stronger sex can't wait just to go nap."

The goblin's hero worship of Frey was really starting to

get old. The funny had worn off about eighteen thousand phone calls ago.

The one good piece of news he'd heard since this had all started was that Texas and the Southern states were on a land grab, and the Federalists were in full flight. Oklahoma, Missouri, and Tennessee were now part of the Confederate States. Or the Southern Alliance States, because Dexx was hearing both names and it was starting to get really confusing.

The news came from Wynonna, through Leah, to Paige who usually already knew thanks to Lovejoy, who preferred to keep this information to herself, and then spread around to perk morale. It did, sort of. Walton was on the run, but ParaWest was poisoned. Good to balance the bad. In a way.

"You go, boy. Sing the praises of Greta Man Sant." Frey's real name, with a flare. Van Sant was her *actual* name, but it poked daggers into Frey and Joel when they heard it. "I've known Frey a lot longer than you have, and I gotta ask. Does she let you sleep at the foot of the bed? Do you warm it up for her when she's brushing her teeth at night?"

Joel's face twisted indignantly as Dexx went on. By the end, his eyes looked like they could catch fire. "You watch what you say. And no, she won't let me."

Dexx snorted a laugh. *His* morale was raised.

Yes. He was a bad, bad man. "Dude, you gotta stop. You really *asked* to warm her bed?"

"Yeah, why?"

Dexx's head sank to the table as he beat on it with his fist. The laughter settled after a minute, and he picked his head up and wiped the tears from his eyes. "Oh, man. Thanks, Joel, I needed that." Though, he probably wasn't really laughing at the goblin. It felt more like a release valve letting off some pressure.

Joel growled.

Dexx stood but he steadied himself against his desk. A few chuckles popped out, and when he spoke, the last of the giggles came with the words. "Okay, bud, I got to get moving. Bad guys need monitoring."

"My Frey can handle that, you morsel."

Dexx waved a mock salute. "Keep your feet warm." He left the phone banks and headed to Director Lovejoy's office.

Stef Lovejoy wasn't a director in the FBI anymore, but she still did most of the things a director might do. Plus, she worked with General Saul on the military side of things.

He knocked on the doorframe and stuck his head inside.

Stef had papers strewn across her desk and one held in front of her. It had her complete attention.

He rapped on the frame again, and softly called, "Knock, knock."

"I'm busy. Make it fast."

Dexx stepped into her office and leaned against a chair in front of the desk. "I was going to the house, and I figured I could get some of the latest and relay to Pea."

"I'm not finished, but I have enough to give you. Should I expect Paige to be increasingly absent?

Dexx hesitated, and stumbled over his words. Did Stef think Paige was abandoning her? "Well, I don't think—"

"Hold it. I understand she's busy. *I'm* busy. Everyone is busy. I'm not trying to accuse her of anything, I just want to know if this sort of information-sharing will be more common."

Oh. As a mushroom, he'd be the *last* to know. "I don't have a clue. I just thought I'd be nice. Pea likes to have her fingers in the pot all the time, so I'd guess no. She'll be here for the next update."

Stef set the paper down and looked up at Dexx. "We have twenty thousand paras that could be considered to be middling level. The breakdown of those is eighty percent shifters, twelve percent witches or magick users of various sorts, and eight percent mythos. Those are the vampires, elementals, and people who don't *use* magick as much as they *are* magick or magickal in nature. And one angel, who is severely disabled."

Uh, what was this report, and would Paige understand this, because he wasn't quite getting it. "Roxxie? When did she join up?" Being disabled was going too far in his opinion. She just had limitations on her powers.

"She came to me a few days ago. The way she spoke, I thought she'd have told you already."

"She's busy, too, I guess. Did she say where she was staying?"

"I have her address in London. Did you want me to get a message to her?"

"No thanks. I have that covered. Thanks. Is that everything?"

"Not by a long shot. Have a seat." She motioned to the chair he leaned on.

Had he volunteered for something accidentally that looked a lot like work? Damn. He'd made his bed, he might as well lie in it. "Shoot. Got nothin' but time." He smiled at her glower.

Her scent spiked for an instant then came back to normal. Stef inhaled and shuffled a few sheets around. She pulled one out and read from it. "We effectively have two borders. Since we lost Nevada and Utah to Walton, our border is almost twice as long as it had been."

"Why did they even go back?"

"Stability," Stef said simply. "We can't offer that, but Walton's promising it. Back to this, though. If the Confederate States continues on, they might be able to take those states back and keep Arizona and New Mexico from going back to Walton. It's not ideal, but I'd rather have those states with the Confederates than with Walton."

"Why aren't we fighting to keep them?"

"We just don't have the resources to promise to them."

Didn't they though? Why weren't they trying to negotiate with the power of the Blackmans and the artifacts in the library? He realized those artifacts had been stashed away for reasons, but if they could be...

What? Used to retain power, all the evil they might potentially release to the world would be okay? He had to trust that Phoebe and Reece knew what they were doing. "And what are we calling Walton's states?"

"Well, he's still calling it the US."

"Right? But what are *we* calling them?"

She shrugged. "Federal States?"

"Federalist States," he offered.

"Yeah. I don't know. Anyway. I would rather a non-aggressive neighbor."

"I don't know, they seem pretty aggressive against the Federalists."

Stef bobbed her head. "True, but they just seem to be carving the Federalists up, not us. And I'm okay with that."

Dexx settled in. This might not be so bad after all. He didn't *like* being a mushroom. "Okay. So, let's consider them frenemies. What next?"

"We have garrisons—you might call them bases—at the biggest invasion threat locations. Outside Denver, which is now held by the vampires, San Diego, Green River, Anchorage, Sioux Falls, and the big island of Hawaii. Those are the ones we can't lose because we already lost Salt Lake and Las Vegas. Those were heavy losses for us. San Diego would be... another big one."

They had bases in all those places? No wonder Troutdale didn't seem to be growing a population as much as it should have been. "And they all volunteered to be in our *military?*"

"They came to fight. Most did, anyway. There are more civilians, but they understandably wanted just to live in the free states. The others understand they'll have to fight."

Freedom wasn't free. And to be free, sometimes they'd be called on to kill. The less glorious part of taking power from the tyrant who wanted to rule the world.

"So, all we have is paras in our bases?"

Stef crooked a small smile. "No, those are just the paras. We have a little over two hundred thousand *non*-paras in each of those locations. Most of those are actual military who decided they heard an illegal order given and refused to stand with Walton. Of those, we have twenty-three high-ranking generals, and two former Department of Defense."

Dexx really didn't know what that meant. "We have Hawaii?"

Stef nodded. "Barely. The Chinese have had their eyes there ever since this all started and now it looks like we have to send resources there. Half of the Pacific fleet went there, and the other half went to Alaska."

"We *really need* Alaska? That place is good for ice and darkness. What use is it?" Dexx curled his lip.

"Well…" Stef laced her fingers and leaned forward on the desk. "Its strategic placement, for one, keeps a barrier between Russia and the Northwest. Another thing is the vast resources. Everything from paper production to oil and gas. Precious metals are just about everywhere, as I understand it." Stef rolled her hand and sat back. "Maybe it's just so big they're bound to have a bunch. Anyway, they're a buffer, and they have things we need. Ice or not, dark or not."

Okay, now he felt like a mouse turd. Leah had spent a lot of time up there, and she always mentioned the cold and dark. He'd never heard the resource part of it.

Stef sat back in her seat, her hands folded primly on her lap. "You really want to keep going? This stuff isn't just a point-and-shoot video game. Real people. Real lives. And it's *very* complicated."

Should we listen? It's boring and riveting all at the same time.

Hattie's ears had been forward since they'd walked into the office, and she seemed more than willing to sit through the lesson. *In other lives I have listened while you sent others to die in ambushes and in many together. You have not yet taken the alpha of the many. This is where we need to be.*

Dexx wiggled his butt into the seat a little further. He wanted to be an alpha now, and this was his responsibility. "I do. You have a map so you can point out what's what?"

The meeting with Stef took over an hour, and she'd filled his head with numbers, strategies, and outcomes. She was right. There was a lot more to the secession than he'd thought. And it eclipsed anything that Paige had told him. Was this the kind of shit she neglected to tell him about, why she was always so tired? No wonder she had headaches stacking up.

He opened the door to the room slowly. Paige might still be sleeping, and there she was, groggy, but rising from unconsciousness.

He'd timed it pretty well, getting to her just as she woke up. "Hey, kitten." He left the door open for some light for her to see by. He sat on the edge of the bed and held a glass of water out to her.

"That's my line." Paige's arm went over her eyes as she blew out a breath.

"Sure, but you've taken a few of mine, so payback."

"Pff." She puffed out another breath and sat up. "Is that coffee?"

"It is not." Dexx emphasized the words. She didn't need coffee, not as much as real water. She could go back to sleep and coffee wouldn't help.

Paige grimaced but took the water. "How long have I been asleep?" She grabbed the glass gently.

"Almost five hours. How are you feeling?" Trick question, of course. She couldn't hide her scents from him, but her words might try.

"I could use the world's biggest jar of wine, but I feel great."

Fifty percent right. She could use wine, maybe, but only to put her back to sleep. "I got the rundown on the warfront, if that's what we have. Education is time consuming."

"Who did you talk to?" She made a face, then started drinking the water. She *had* to be thirsty. The smell of sweat hung lightly in the air.

"Stef."

Paige finished the water with a breath and handed the glass back. "Now get me a coffee. Double tall, double strong, double quick."

"No, I think we should go a little slower. Relocate to the couch." He reached his hand out to help her up.

Paige batted his hand away and swung her feet out and to the floor. Her hair stood out at odd angles, and her face had the telltale signs of drool. She stood up and shuffled toward the doorway, slow and steady. She seemed to regain more use of her body as she went along.

Dexx loomed over her as she flopped to the couch. Exhausted.

"Nice. Now someday, we'll stretch our legs and make it to the woods."

"I wish I had a spirit. I never hurt like this when I could shift."

"I think that ship has sailed." Had it? *I'm right, right? It's been too long. Right?*

Hattie flicked an ear at him. *She has not been chosen. The door remains open though.*

Damn. Well, he *had* bitten her. "Okay, moving on. Our forces are as prepared as they can be, with limited comms and resources and such. Chinese, Russians, and a few others are making noises, but as far as we can tell, only the Chinese have a friend in Walton."

"Is that all?" Paige sat back, her eyes closed, but not because her head hurt like it had. She was just overtired.

Not even close. "For now, yes." Dexx pressed a small smile on when she picked her head up and looked at him.

"Good. Now there's something I want to talk to you about."

No fun conversation ever started out like that. "What did I do this time? I haven't broken *any* part of the city in like...months."

A portal opened as soon as Paige started.

She ignored it. "Our kids. They stay out of the fighting."

Leah walked through, hugging books to her chest and her eyes wide. "What?"

Dexx glanced up at his daughter. "Where is this coming from?"

"This isn't going to be a negotiation," Paige said firmly. "I know you think you can sidestep me or reason a way through it, but I'm standing firm on this. No kids anywhere near anything that looks like fighting."

Leah closed in on Paige, next to Dexx. "Is this how you want to treat us now? Be good strong humans, but only when you give us permission?"

Dexx agreed with Paige, but he also agreed with his daughter. But he had to form his alliance quickly. He couldn't expect anyone to stay out of it who didn't want to, and he believed in the power of his kids. All of them. "I'm with Leah on this one. You've taken her right into the thick of things and on a whim you cut her out? No. I'm going to need some evidence that we can even keep them safe. If the fight comes here, our kids have the most powerful spirits we have. Excepting Leslie, and Robin still isn't used to the world."

"*I'm* the most powerful witch in the world right now, and I can keep us *all* safe." The look on her face said she didn't believe what she was saying.

Dexx crossed his arms and scowled hard. "Did you fall out of bed? You're on the injured reserve and fuck if *I'll* let *you* on any battlefield. At your best, you'd be a heavy hitter, but right now, Bobby could take you down with a spitball."

"I have more ability in my little finger—"

"*Mom.* This is *so* unfair. All you've done since you got me back from Grandma is tell me how good I am and that my power is mine and not a bad thing, and now you tell me it's actually *yours?*"

Ouch. If that didn't hit Paige right in some feelers, she had none.

She sat up, pain in her eyes. "That's not what I said. I don't want you hurt or worse. I got us into this, and it's up to me to get us out again."

"Back the truck up, Pea." Oh, Dexx wasn't letting her drive *that* bus. "You tried to keep this under wraps, it was *Sven* who blasted it all out in the open. So don't even try to take the blame. We did what we had to. DoDO isn't your fault either. They would be mine, if it was anyone's."

Leah cocked her head at Dexx, a question on her face like she didn't have words.

"My first life I had the opportunity to kill Bussemi and I didn't. Then, I brought DoDO to our door when I captured Alwyn on their first demon hit. It's all pretty stupid."

"And now you're proving my point." Paige stood, and

looked just as fierce and steady as she always had. "You didn't know what you were doing, and things got worse for everyone. Let me take care of things. You'll be safe."

"No, babe. You can play martyr all you want, but no. You will *not* tell them how to live their lives after you've trained them to be self-sufficient."

Leah put on her Whiskey face and crossed her arms like Dexx. "You can't stop me. I'm in. And I'm learning things you never knew. I won't take on all of DoDO like you did, but I have a fight and I'm doing it."

Paige looked at them both, her mouth working.

Dexx didn't know what else to say. "Coffee is in the kitchen. I'm going out for a while."

Leah nodded. "I'm going with Dad."

26

Jackie burbled to life, the first start-up since her resurrection, and the garage door opened up letting the late April sunlight in. The car rolled out slowly, ready to take on the sort of drive only Dexx knew. His heart pounded nervously for the maiden voyage. Not *just* for the maiden voyage.

Usually, Paige had well-thought arguments, and rarely tried edicts. But this time had been different. No real case. Just a mandate.

He kept the speed slow until they hit pavement. Dexx mashed the throttle and the noise echoed through the forest.

Dexx pressed hard into the seat, glad he had the steering wheel.

Leah didn't move, or *couldn't* move, but her eyes looked like great big snowballs.

He let off the gas before the first big curve and eased through. That normally took much longer. It was time to be more adult. He backed out of the throttle and merely went into town speeding only slightly.

"You look scared. You go way faster than I do." Dexx glanced at Leah. She sat very still in her seat.

"I might have leaked a little." She swallowed hard.

"You better not have. This is a *new* car for all intents and purposes." Dexx slowed down even more.

Leah shifted in her seat and looked at him uncertainly. "No, I'm good. What do you mean, I'm faster than you?"

"Portals move you almost instantly, right?"

"Dad. It doesn't work that way. You don't have the feeling of moving. I open a door and step through, I don't break ludicrous speed."

"Good thing for your wardrobe. Plaid…"

Leah cracked a smile.

"Can I take you somewhere? Ice cream or a cemetery?"

"Why would I go—oh. Zombies. Sure, let's go there. I know you'll make friends." Her smile went predatory.

"Ice cream it is. Do we have any open?"

"I heard one in Portland opened up. I think." Leah curled her lip.

In the end, they had to settle for finding a park and sitting on a bench, enjoying the sunset and the spring air.

"Hey, Dad. Guess what tomorrow is."

He was pretty happy just chilling with his daughter on *this* day. "One of them that ends in Y, right?"

"Ha. Ha. Good dad joke, Dad."

"It's in the manual. Got it off Amazon before the world imploded. I think it was the thirty-second revision of the medieval printing. Got some good ones in there."

Leah bashed her shoulder against his and made a guttural sound.

He grunted back at her.

"Can she really keep us from fighting?" She turned worried blue eyes up to him.

"When the dust settles, I think she'd be able to pull it off.

I see where she's coming from, though. If I could, I'd keep you safe from all the world's evils too. But since I've lived through a bunch, I don't think I can." Dexx cracked a smile. "I want you to live long and prosper. Go further than I ever could hope to reach. I think that's the goal of any good parent, to slingshot you farther than them." His own father was a complete failure. Dexx would not be.

A car pulled into the park and stopped next to Jackie.

"Daddy-daughter date is over." Dexx leaned back, elbows on the table to wait for Paige.

She got out of the car and passed a look over them.

"She chased us down?" Leah cocked her head at Dexx.

"Yup. She's never done that before. She's either really pissed or super sorry."

Paige closed on them slowly. Sort of like going up to an unfamiliar dog. Gentle and deliberate, showing no aggression. She stopped at a tree, lightly touching the lowest branch. "Is this a private party or can anyone join?" She hinted at a smile and waited.

"Sure." Dexx cracked his own smile. "This is a safe space and you'll have to have the talking stick."

Paige dropped her hand from the tree and closed in on the picnic bench. "I—" Paige started, but closed her mouth, and took in a large breath. "I want to say—"

"How nice. All of you here outside your protections." Annelle Rovoski stepped from behind the same tree Paige had stood next to seconds ago.

"Annelle?" Paige turned to the old woman. "What's going on?"

"*Da*. You took something from me. Something I loved. Now I vill take something from you. Something you love."

A demon stepped from behind the tree, holding a small struggling figure.

Bobby.

Paige stepped forward, her witch hands suddenly out and *glowing* black. "Let him go right now."

Dexx stood from the bench.

Leah sat, frozen, circulating looks to everyone.

"Stay your hand, vitch. Or I vill kill the boy right now."

Dexx sat on the edge of shifting, barely holding Hattie in check. "No, you won't. You kill him and your last look at this earth will be my fangs closing on your head."

"*Shedim*, you are predictable in your wrath." The demon laughed. "You will do no such thing. This boy is insurance of sorts."

"He's not as good as you think," Dexx said, wanting his son back. "As soon as you hurt him, you die. You'll get to go home, but the way things have been lately, your portal may not show up. I've been noticing not all of you get to go home like you used to." *Wait for my signal. We're going to do this, but I want to talk them into letting Bobby go first.*

Hattie pulled back a bit, easing the pressure off Dexx, but ready to shift at an instant. *Do not wait until it is too late, cub.*

Not me. These two are already dead. "What the hell, Annelle?" he asked the old woman. "I thought you were on our side."

"Foolish mortals."

Foolish mortals? Where the hell did bad guys pick that shit up? As if she wasn't mortal too.

Paige kept her hands out, ready to attack. A thread of earth dove into the ground and streamed out of sight. "There must be some mistake."

"No mistake. You took Annika from me. I take something from you. This is the vay of the vorld, but vhen I take from you, I vill take everything and make you vatch."

"Annelle." How many times did he have to say he was sorry? Dexx took a step forward. "This won't end well for you. You have to know that. Demons, by and large, are untrustworthy as a whole, and if you've made a deal with one, you're on the losing side of things. We won't steer you wrong."

"I had Annika on the right path. The one I started in her youth, and you took her away vith your magicks."

"You're wrong." Paige took a step forward. "We helped her be who she was—"

The demon yanked hard on Bobby.

His legs swung like loose flaps in the wind.

The demon shook the boy again. "Enough. I came here to collect the bounty on the hunter's head."

Annelle's smile had no warmth in it. "Then do it."

The demon made no move, but a change in the air signaled three more demons who landed in a large circle around the Whiskeys.

"*Shedim Patesh*. This is your last day in the world."

"Then you don't know me that well." But a part of Dexx was glad to have a fight he could actually win. Finally.

"The Old One has your rock. He waits for the stone to be filled. You cannot win this one, hunter. We have the high ground, as you say."

"Careful, that high ground isn't as steady as you think it is. You want a fight, you got one. Me against you. I'll take those odds, but you let the boy go, and you let the girls go, too."

"You take us for fools? We will not give up our best shields."

Dexx leaned to Paige. "Can you send these guys back?"

"Not with Bobby there."

Dexx tipped his head to the side. "Then we do this the old-fashioned way."

Another demon appeared next to Annelle and the demon holding Bobby. "You are free to try." The demon's skin lit with fire and he hunched over, holding his hand over the ground in front of him and made circles. "*Ahn toor aka uun*."

"Ye—" Paige doubled over, holding her head.

The demon holding Bobby chuckled. "One down. Our high ground is looking better all the time, hunter."

"Leah, take your mom home." Dexx kept his gaze on the demon holding Bobby. "Add a layer on the wards if you can and stay there. You need to tell others what happened."

"No, I'm going to stay here. I can help."

"You know what I said? Well, that's what I'm doing. You know who they are. You'll get revenge when you're ready and they aren't. Now move your ass."

Leah reached down and touched Paige's shoulder.

Dexx leaped at the demon holding Bobby, the *ma'a'shed* already growing as he pulled it.

Bobby dropped to the ground alongside the head of the demon. The body toppled backward.

Dexx shifted to the cat and swiped at the old woman. She crumpled to the ground and didn't move.

Hattie rounded on the other demons and stopped.

The last demon finished his incantation.

Dexx had never seen this spell before, but he'd heard of it. The ground charred and then turned a low shade of orange, then brightened to gold then a bright yellow. The earth blistered and popped, releasing a molten pool of metal that floated next to the demon.

The demon reached out a hand and took the glowing blob. His scream shook the earth and tore leaves from the tree. He fell to his knees, his hand still in the molten metal.

What was going on? Dexx turned his cat body around to run. He took two jumps before a cage of fire rose in front of him, and around the demons.

The demon rose to a knee, the glowing earth turned a dark orange as it cooled.

"You will stay. You will fight. You will die."

Probably. Dexx shifted back to his human form and raised

the sword. If he could buy some time for Paige and the kids, then he'd do it. Though, how was he going to get Bobby out of there?

Bobby sat on the ground, his blue eyes searching for a way out.

"Bobby. Get up and get out." Dexx stepped between him and the other demons. "I'll be home after a bit."

"Dad?"

Dexx tapped him with his foot. "Get up and get out." He waved the sword at the demons, trying to keep an eye on all of them all at once.

The metal demon had almost made it to his feet.

Dexx crushed his teeth together. "I'll be *home* after a bit."

The metal changed from soot-black into bright silver. It was a sword that resembled a *mavet ma'a'shed,* except it glowed bright silver like an angel bade. A *mavet ma'aka'el.* It refracted the last of the dying sunlight.

"The *ma'a'shed* won't help you, *Shedim.*"

Dexx tapped Bobby again, this time harder.

Bobby turned over and jumped to run away but stopped at the ward. "I can't get through."

"Fuck. Then stay away from them. Use whatever power you have and keep them away."

Annelle twitched. "I am stronger than I look, remember?" Her arms cracked and stuck out and bent in odd ways. They pushed the old woman up and she definitely didn't look better for the wear. Her teeth were sharp, and her hair went lank and stringy.

Shit. She went full rusalka.

She motioned to the demon with the sword. "I have released the hold on the bounty. All you have to do is win. Now take his life."

Dexx barely raised his sword in time to stop his head from joining the other demon's.

The shock numbed his arm instantly and the *mavet* dropped to the ground, a knife again.

Okay, time to take stock. Bobby was still in grave danger. Dexx had a knife he could never hold on to, his shift, and his sharp wit. What would his best chance be?

Change. Let me out.

Dexx didn't even hesitate. He let Hattie do her thing.

In an instant, he was the cat with her in charge, and she already had a good head of steam going.

Annelle threw out her arm and Hattie stopped in place. "I vant you to see your death, thief. My little Annika vas going to be my heir. My legacy. She fell under a spell you put on her. You killed her. My life is now to kill you and all you love."

Dexx really needed Leah. Why had he told her to go home and stay home?

When had any of his kids actually done what he'd told them to do?

Annelle changed again, taking more blue coloring on. "You see, the mother currents are strong in me." Her voice was layered with many tones, almost like a demon's.

Oh, shit. Yes! The currents owed him one. One request, no questions asked. He cast through his mind trying to figure how he could call on her when—

The fiery cage bowed outward and ripped, the rest dimming slightly as a figure walked in. Dexx couldn't tell who it was at the corner of his eye.

The ground erupted with ice and encased the demons, holding them in place.

Annelle Rovoski turned and shrieked. "You said he vas *mine*. I vas to do vith him as I vould. You vear her face. You know my grief. You handed him to me."

The figure stopped in front Dexx.

A perfect likeness of Rainbow Blu studied him. "This is

the Dexx. Release the Dexx and release the Greatest of the First."

"No," Annelle screamed. "He is mine. You agreed to let me have my revenge."

"We have directed our daughter. Release the Dexx." She blinked once and Hattie settled on her feet. Hattie went back to the Time Before, shifting Dexx right there on his hands and knees.

"I want to—"

"The Dexx will make no sounds."

Dexx's jaws clamped shut, but not by his own will.

"Mother, vhy do you do this? He must pay—"

"The Dexx has championed our daughter. We have granted the Dexx a boon. The Dexx has not requested the Dexx boon."

"I want it to be extra-special."

Rainbow looked into his eyes, her study of him seeming to pass deep into his soul.

"Dexx."

The voice was soft, almost a whisper. Rainbow's voice.

"Rainbow?"

The soul search ended and the currents stepped away from him. "The Dexx has been granted a boon."

"You vill set him free?" Annelle's voice broke into shards of pain.

"We have granted the Dexx a boon, and our daughter has taken an action. We are in a quandary."

"Please, Mother. Let me take him. I vill do it in the old vay and give him directly to you. He can be vith you forever."

That didn't sound like a plan. Not one that work for him, anyway.

Movement from the side caught his eye. Bobby slipped out of the cage where the currents broke it or ruptured it or whatever she had done.

A flash of white came through just after Bobby left. The cage repaired itself and the fire reignited.

"The Dexx does wish to be granted a boon?"

Dexx snarled a curse. "You know what I want. I'll take care of the rabble by myself."

"The Dexx is refusing the boon?"

"No, I'm—"

The demon with the earth metal broke free of the ice, throwing shards everywhere. He swung at Rainbow, but the currents disappeared before the blade struck her head off.

Dexx jumped back avoiding the tip of the sword.

Annelle raised her arm, freezing Dexx in place. Her other hand went out to the demons, stopping their charge forward. "No escapes this time. No help from friends. You all vill die."

Dammit. Only Rainbow had ever been able to control him like this, with the power of the currents to help her. And Annelle. Nothing else had ever held him for long without paying for it. Not demons, not sirens, not *Bussemi*. Only the damned rusalkas had been able to treat him like a puppet.

"Let me go, water witch." The demon with the sword struggled to free himself from her control.

Annelle circled him, leering and trailing a finger along Dexx's skin, sending shivers of cold cascading down his body. "I vill go after the rest of them vhen I am done vith you. But you have a resilience I have not seen in my many years. But not to worry, I vill take them, and I vill offer them to the mother."

"You slimy bitch." Dexx struggled to break free of her hold. He hadn't been able to when Rainbow had been in full rusalka mode, and Annelle was a bit more powerful. "You can't take me in a fair fight, can you?"

"Who said this is not fair? You vould use your power against me, and you vould consider that fair?" She smiled, her long-dead face pale with deep black eye sockets more malevolent the wider she went. "Or ve agree to not use powers and ve fight as people. Is it fair for a young bulging man to fight an old voman?"

Can we break free? With Rainbow we were separated. Can we break her hold?

Hattie struggled, pouring power against the rusalka. *It will take more time than we have.*

Annelle's smile showed pointed teeth and the hatred poured from her. She jerked once, and the smile faded.

Mandy walked through the fiery cage as though it didn't exist, holding a hand of white flame in front of her. "You should probably just let him go."

"I think I vill no—"

Mandy double-tap shrugged as if she wasn't super-sure this was the right move and then shoved her ultra-hot hand at the old woman's chest.

Annelle jerked again, her chest lighting from within. Mandy stumbled backward as Dexx and the demons were freed of the rusalka's hold.

27

Bussemi watched Dexx Colt. He'd been *allowed* to see the world through his *own* eyes.

The scrying pool saw the Whiskey family from a distance above them.

They couldn't see exceptionally well, but the important parts were all there.

Dexx Colt looked about ready to die. Oh, the thorn could *die* of course, but he wouldn't permit the *sheneshae* to desecrate the body. Once Dexx was dead and the *kadu* was full, he would rend the creature and the other demons to pieces too small to see. And with the demon gate closed as it was, they would find real death.

The bahlrok ran a finger, *Bussemi's* finger, around the edge of the scrying pool.

An elder hell-demon folded space and stepped out.

Should we go? Bussemi didn't have control of himself so that left begging, and *he* wanted Dexx's body.

"We will go when I can be sure there will be no intervention. I went at your urging, and was turned away. That will not happen again."

That meddling *thing* kept them from harvesting Dexx. Some of the old entities had long memories. Dexx Colt had too many things watching over him, even in the end days.

Of course not. I meant only to be ready in case the man-killer became over-enthused with her kill.

"That is none of your concern. Be grateful I let you see at all."

The woman sent a powerful call to the force deep in the earth. She would be a powerful ally, one not to be underestimated. Not even by the bahlrok.

Thank you. Cursed beast. The plan had *never* been for it to supplant him from his own body. It was supposed to strengthen him like the other shifter spirits had. He had miscalculated.

The image fuzzed as the elder demon pulled magick from the earth.

"Gah!" The bahlrok lost control of the scry and quickly set the spell again. When the image cleared, a child ran from a rent in a demon cage, the magick weaves disrupted.

The scry flashed white. This was not a disruption, but a concealing spell, hiding something from the pool.

The cage repaired itself but only seconds had passed when a portal opened, and one of the little Whiskey girls stepped through trailed by another.

The second girl glowed with earthfire and matched the resonance of the cage. She walked through with no resistance and hurled pure earthfire at the *sheneshae*.

The creature never had a chance. Her bones turned to ashen powder before she knew she was on fire.

The four demons and Dexx Colt reacted and attacked.

Bussemi-Demon leaned forward, ready to open a portal directly on the spot when Dexx breathed his last. He smiled in anticipation just as the scry pool exploded into shards, a large piece striking him in the face and chest.

Magick bled from Bussemi's body.

The bahlrok coughed and repaired the damage quickly. It growled low and long. "Angel."

———

Dexx didn't waste time as Annelle Rovoski opened her mouth as if to scream. He spun on the closet demon. It happened to be the one with the shiny new appendage.

Contrary to the prevailing belief in DoDO, demons were rarely ever caught off guard, and this one wasn't any different. He caught Dexx in mid-flight by the neck.

Dexx shifted in the demon's grip and raked a back foot from stem to stern down the demon.

He opened up but no guts spilled to the ground. Demons had different physiology, but that didn't mean he wasn't injured.

Hattie continued the drop and spun, keeping momentum, and leaped to the next nearest demon.

That was Mandy out there, and she'd never gone up against a demon. How she got there was going to have to wait.

Annelle Rovoski exploded into dust, momentarily obscuring Mandy behind the cloud.

The next demon drew a *ma'a'shed* and began the swing that would hit Hattie center mass.

Oh, shit this was going to—

"*Hold.*" The voice attacked the entire park with vibrating power. The pure essence of it filled Dexx with peace and frightening power.

Lightning lit the cage, banishing even shadows in the darkening evening. Tendrils of electricity touched the cat and seized her muscles into cramps.

Hattie landed hard, and after a few seconds, she could

breathe. Hearing came seconds afterward and finally their vision cleared enough to see the tree split down the middle and smoldering.

Dexx and Hattie pushed themselves up with weak limbs.

He recognized the voice, but she couldn't have that much power.

The big blue blur covering his vision faded slightly, at least enough for Hattie to make out the shadows of demons imprinted on the pavement and burned into the grass.

The demon cage lost cohesiveness and faded from the top to bottom, leaving the area in natural dusk.

Hattie shifted them back into human.

Dexx stumbled to the prone form wearing all white on the ground, her heat signature almost equal to the surrounding area. "Mandy, get over here. Light us up," he yelled over his shoulder.

Fire arced overhead and split into seven more arcs, lighting the park like a sports stadium.

Roxxie lay crumpled on the ground, her face grey, her lips blue.

"Shit. Mandy, get over here, now."

Two sets of feet padded up at a run.

"Dad, are you okay?" Leah asked, out of breath.

"Fine," he said, so incredibly grateful his kids didn't know how to obey. "Mandy, heat the ground. We have to warm her up." He didn't know anything at all about angels, but they always had a strong heat signature. And an angel with almost none couldn't be good.

Mandy set her hands on the grass and heat radiated away from her.

Dexx felt for a pulse but couldn't tell if there was one or not. "Leah, listen very closely. I need you to open a portal. We need to port directly to a bed, and she can't move. Not an inch. Not anything. I don't know if moving her will kill her, so she *can't move*. Can you do that?"

Leah still pulled in air from the run, so she didn't answer right away. "I—I haven't ever tried to open a doorway so precise. I usually just tear a hole to get to a place. I try to get my doors within a foot or two, but it's never been important."

"Well, it is now. We have to get her inside and stable. Mandy, warm her slowly. Take the cold from the ground. We can't risk it pulling any more from her."

"Okay, Uncle Dexx." Her voice wavered.

"Gentle. That's the name of the game. God, gods, or goddesses, whoever's out there, I'm asking for a little help. Keep her alive. I'd consider it a real favor."

The air around Dexx began to warm considerably and swirl in a gentle breeze.

"I don't know if I can." Leah knelt next to Dexx, inspecting the angel. "I can't sense her, so she's not dead, right?"

"Who knows anything about angels? I just hope we can keep her alive long enough for her to recover on her own."

Leah reached out and slipped her fingers around Roxxie's. "Hold on." She closed her eyes and froze in place. The ground turned granular and dissolved into a doorway. Mandy and Leah's room appeared around them, then the doorway lifted above them and closed. Mandy dropped the two feet to the floor, but Dexx felt no movement at all. Leah's bed shifted with the weight of the three of them. Hopefully that wouldn't have been enough to send Roxxie into shock.

Dexx let a slow breath out. "Nicely done, lion. Get Leslie in here. And check on Mom. Is she all right?"

"Dad." Leah's eyes filled with tears. "I'm scared."

"Me too. Tell me about your mom. Is she asleep or worse?" Keep it cool. People only freaked out when everyone was freaked. "Leah, Mandy, look at me. We can fix this. One step at a time. Take a breath and stay with me. Mandy, check on Pea. Leah, throw sheets in the dryer. High heat."

Mandy would be better to stay and warm the room, but Leah wasn't a reliable person to check on her mom. "If anyone passes Tyler, I need him here. Posthaste. I could use Leslie, too." Oh fuck. "Where's Bobby?" How could he have forgotten Bobby?

Too many things all at once.

"I got him. Before… He's downstairs. I think."

"Grab him too. Get everyone in here. This is going to take us all."

Mandy gestured with her hands, something that looked like a motion spell, and a fireball appeared above Roxxie, the heat reaching her like a campfire. She turned and ran out the door.

Leah backed toward the door. "Sheets. Got it."

"No, wait. Get the kids. Hurry."

Leah nodded and ran.

"Come on, Roxxie. Stay with us."

She had gone way above and beyond. Too far for an angel with barely any power left. Without her connection to heaven, she'd been a powerful human. And that attack in the park was at least as powerful as Paige could have summoned when she had Cawli.

"You stay. You stay right here. You're one of us. A Whiskey. I'll make sure you get a permanent spot at the table. You stay and I'll forgive anything I think you might still owe us. Just don't go."

The angel, of course, didn't answer.

Is there anything we can do?

Hattie stood, her nose down like she could smell exactly how much life the angel still had. *Cub, sometimes there is nothing to be done.*

That's not a good answer. I don't accept that. I reject that. We can help, I know it. I'm not letting another one die for me. "I'm *not* going to do that."

"Do what?" Leslie stepped into the room, her eyes already glowing orange.

Dexx looked up, his eyes filling with tears. "Fix her, please."

Leslie passed her hand over Roxxie's body but didn't touch her. "She's beyond my ability. If she was stronger, maybe." She put a hand on Dexx's shoulder. "I'm sorry."

Several sets of feet stormed up the stairs.

The room filled quickly.

Dexx unfolded from the bed in time to meet Bobby rushing through the door. He grabbed the boy up in a hug and squeezed him tight. This was the reason why Paige didn't want the kids in the fighting.

But this was also why they needed to be. Mandy had saved his bacon.

Which... come on! He'd finally been handed a fight he could win, and he'd needed to be saved by two girls? On one hand, that meant that the enemy was getting more powerful to beat him.

On the other, it meant they didn't have a fighting chance in hell of winning.

"You okay, Bobby?"

The boy nodded in his chest. His smell was shaky, but okay.

"Hey, you wanna try to heal an angel? You *are* a prophet. Should be easy, right?"

Bobby passed a gaze from Dexx to Roxxie. Then he held his hand over Roxxie's still form. He stood there for a long time. He shook his head. "I'm not feeling anything from her. At least, I don't think I am. People are different than angels, right?"

"Uh, yeah. I guess. Can you try?"

Rai and Ember pushed past Leslie and stood next to Bobby. "We got you, big brother. Anything you need, we'll funnel it through you."

Dexx did a double take. In everything that had happened, he had never known the kids could channel power. "You can do that?"

Rai nodded. "Something we learned in the *Vaada Bhoomi*. It's like what a generator does, but it has to be tailored to the user. Bobby's a natural conduit, so it's pretty easy."

Whoa. Rai sounded about thirty times her maturity. Where had that come from? "Okay then. Do it."

Bobby gathered his golden light around him, holding his hands over Roxxie, the tendrils of magick falling to extend over her.

Rai and Ember lit with magickal energy too, a deep red and a fiery orange. As the energy passed to Bobby, it changed to the pure gold that surrounded him and flowed into Roxxie.

He stood stone-still and the light intensified around each of the kids. One minute, two. Five minutes on and the glow around the three became painful to look at. As one, the glow faded from them all, and finally nothing.

Roxxie didn't look worse, but she didn't look better either.

All three kids huffed big breaths like they'd run a four-minute mile.

"She—I can't." Bobby shook his head. "I think I felt something toward the end, but it would take more power than all of us together have. It's—she's just so weak. It's like we have to climb a wall to push a door."

Rai shook her head. "No." She took in another breath. "It's a block. We have to break the block then pull her close."

That sounded like how Roxxie had described what Sven

303

had done. He'd pushed the angel realm away and had closed a gate.

"So, do it. Fix her."

Bobby nodded and put his hands over Roxxie again and began again.

Leslie slapped his hands down. "Leave." She stared at the kids. *All* of them. "Get out. Your dad and I have to talk."

They shuffled to the door but left it open and huddled just outside the doorway.

Leslie rounded on him and slapped his face. Hard. "Who the fuck do you think you are? They're *kids*. They worship you, and you'd kill them by pushing them to do something impossible. Do even know how much power they pushed through themselves just now?" Her eyes turned a dangerous shade of orange. The mama bear had awakened.

Dexx shook his head. "I'm trying to—"

She slapped him again. "Listen to yourself. Push *harder*, do *more*, no matter that they aren't even adults. *You're* the one they look up to—*trust*. You have no idea if they even *can*. You push too them too hard and they end up like her or worse. Burned out or dead. That what you want? Pea is down there, helpless. Goddess alone knows what's going on with her, and you're up here with a *dead* angel trying to breathe life back into her? *What. The. Fuck. Dexx.*"

She raised her hand again, poised to strike.

Dexx straightened, pushing his alpha into an aura around him. He growled and let Hattie come through a tad, though her words were hitting him where it was needed. "You want to keep that hand, you'll put it down. No, I *don't* know what I'm doing. Just trying to help a friend who might have given her life to save mine."

"Your *kids* come before a friend. Your *wife* comes before a friend. Family first. We might just survive that way."

"Family. Yeah. *That*—" He paused and jabbed a finger at

Roxxie. "*Is* family. Maybe not by blood, but so what? We've made family out of non-blood before, and we're doing it now." Dexx's mouth curled into a snarl. "You got that? She's *family* now."

Leslie stared at Dexx, then at Roxxie. The fire left her eyes, but they still glowed with power. "Then *we* will try it. Leave the kids out of it."

Dexx nodded once. "Fine. You and me."

Leslie lit with green faerie fire and placed her hands over Roxxie, almost the same as Bobby had.

The spell form had a name. Memories flooded into his mind. Powerful witches millennia before cavemen scribbled on cave walls used it. It was old and not for mortals. But she was too weak, even with a griffin to push the power.

Dexx's pocket warmed against him. He pulled out the amethyst. It sparked inside with a life of its own. Dekskulta said he'd know what to do with it when the time came.

"*Ae auun Dekskulta ya ae auun dhu kupul.*" I am Dekskulta, and I am the key.

He crushed the crystal in his hand.

28

D exx crushed the crystal as easy as pulling a flower petal apart. What had been indestructible before was more fragile than a snowflake.

The house, the kids, and Leslie disappeared.

Dexx floated in darkness and, in his hand, was the crystal, a fiery furnace with the light of the sun. The still form of Roxxie lay in front of him.

"You have the First Brother in front of you?" Dekskulta asked.

Dexx would have snapped his head to the voice, but he couldn't move. "No, why?"

"How did you access the power? It was keyed for you to destroy him and the beast."

Dexx'd never felt anything from it other than immense power, more than everything combined. "You said I'd know what to do with it when the time was right. It told me the time was right."

"It did not." Dekskulta's voice vibrated with disapproval. "You were to use it to kill the First Brother and the beast within him. You were to save us all with the power inside. They gave their lives for this. For *you*."

Roxxie lay in front of him, and he couldn't move. "Yeah, I'd rather use it to keep a loved one alive than to kill an enemy." He would find another way. He had to. Also, the crystal *had* told him *this* was the right time. Not when he'd been fighting Bussemi. Now. Trying to save Roxxie's life. "Bad guys are a dime a dozen. Someone who loves you with all your flaws intact? Well now, *that's* a whole different ball game."

"I cannot believe you."

Something Dekskulta said struck at him. "You said, 'they gave their lives.' Who gave their lives?"

"Friends. People and beings I trusted. We had a vision. Of a world free of the threat of the First Brother and now you've ruined it all. For nothing."

Dexx remembered the short introduction of some of those who had died to create the crystal. One of them had been an angel. "If one of your trusted lot was an angel, then your purpose may not have been as pure as you thought."

"It does not matter." Dekskulta nearly whispered. "You released the power and now, all is lost."

"I reject your asinine thinking and substitute my own. Roxxie is family, and we haven't always seen eye to eye, but she's sacrificed for me, and now it's my turn."

"I had hoped to see the destruction of the First Brother, but instead you doom us all." Dekskulta traded his sorrow for condescension.

"If you don't like it, get the hell out." The crystal vibrated in Dexx's hand, slow at first, but as Dekskulta berated him, the vibrating worsened.

"I had high hopes for you. I see I was mistaken in trusting you to finish my—our work."

"You know, the more you talk, the less I like you. You're a

douche. I have a life to save." Dexx firmly put Dekskulta on ignore and concentrated on the raw magick quickly growing out of control.

Now what to do? It grew more unstable by the second. It quivered, ready to explode or dissipate into the ether.

Rai said there was a block to overcome. So how could he fix that?

Overcoming a block was...easy?

I don't suppose there's any use in asking you?

Hattie wasn't in the space, wherever he was with Roxxie.

He took the total and divided it into two pieces. Just one of those could have had powered his magick for years of high-intensity usage. He could...keep some. He'd have his power back, and maybe he could help Paige. She could identify with him easier and he with her. They'd have the—

No.

With one half of the power, he infused Roxxie's body. Or he tried to. Something pushed against him. He pushed harder.

It resisted, but bent.

Well, if something bent, it could be moved. Or broken. Oh, please don't let it be her life force.

Dexx refined the power, formed it into a point. The power blunted and splintered against the block until it stopped.

He needed more. He pressed harder.

There was another shift.

More power.

Push.

For Roxxie.

Dexx strained, the beginning of a wordless growl escaped him.

Another shift.

Dexx slammed the power with all he had.

Roxxie jolted, her eyes wide, her arms flung out as she screamed.

Six spears of light jetted from her body, lighting the darkness. Shadows writhed at the edges of the spears of light.

The thing that had been blocking her shattered and her connection to her home was open.

Roxxie felt distant, far away.

He sent the other half of the power through her and grabbed at the distant part, anchoring the power.

The crystal visibly weakened, fading.

Quickly, Dexx called the anchor back.

Now, instead of the block forcing the power back, the anchor dragged at him, like he was pulling against a current.

"Fuck you will. You're mine, bitch." Dexx growled as he pulled harder, straining to bring the anchor closer to her.

He wasn't strong enough. There wouldn't be enough of the power left to finish.

He moved to pull harder, and he felt...something. An absence. It gently tugged at him. Insisted he pay attention?

Now what?

He spared a whisper-thin thread of power down the hole and—he found another end. It *wanted* an anchor.

Dexx set the hook and thickened the power going to that end. It flashed and pulsed power back through him to the other side.

The strain lessened, and he relaxed. Both ends fed on the magick ending at Roxxie, mixing and pulsing back to the origin points.

She inhaled, grunted, and went limp.

Dexx struggled with the two points but they scooted closer and closer. Then he felt something click and stabilize.

The power of the crystal thinned and evaporated into both anchor points.

The darkness lightened and formed back into Leah and Mandy's bedroom.

Roxxie jerked again and flashed with magick. She looked at Dexx and smiled. "You beautiful human." She closed her eyes and relaxed into unconsciousness.

"Dexx!" Leslie picked herself up from the floor. "What in the sphincter of hell are you playing at?"

He wasn't entirely sure.

"What did you do?" Leslie passed her hands over Roxxie, then held her finger to the angel's throat. She pulled her hand away, her eyes in a hard gaze at Dexx. "How?"

He sighed. "If I told you, I'd be lying. I have no idea what happened." He had a strong suspicion, but the details didn't make a lot of sense to him.

Leslie took Roxxie's wrist. "She's...alive?"

Dexx pulled up his heat vision and Roxxie's signature was as strong as the last time he'd seen her. "Looks like. I don't—"

The kids, all of them burst into the bedroom, surrounding the bed.

"Can I keep her this time?" Tyler took the free hand and gently rubbed Roxxie's fingers.

"No." Dexx and Leslie said in stereo.

Rai and Ember exchanged a look. "How did you have that much raw magick in that stone?"

Leslie passed a glance over them. "You saw?"

The twins nodded.

Rai squinted at Leslie. "How could we not?"

One thing had gone right. He just had to hope it had been the right thing to do. The crystal might have been created to defeat Bussemi, but it hadn't wanted to do that and he hadn't figured out how to make it happen. So...maybe what he and Paige needed to focus on was gathering stronger, smarter, more capable people to them, because they were in a fight so much bigger than them. "You guys take over. I have to see to Pea." Dexx disengaged and left the throng surrounding Roxxie.

He made it down two steps when a wave of vertigo passed over him. He grabbed the railing and held on tight. *What the hell?*

Cub, I am weak. What happened to us?

I, he paused. They'd processed a lot of raw power.

Hattie nodded. *I am feeling tired. This does not happen. It can, but we have bonded long enough that it should not.*

"Sh. Be quiet." Dexx took the stairs one at a time, slowly. He didn't find Paige on the couch. Sonofa— He turned and slowly made his way back through the dining room and kitchen and...up the stairs again. By the time he made the top stair he felt about as strong as a toddler. He crawled to his door and managed to turn the knob and crawl to bed and climb in next to Paige.

He barely noticed as her cold feet and legs clung to him before he passed out.

Chuck Deluca swiped the call closed. Merry Eastwood was dead. Final confirmation might never be made, but the source was reliable. Tony wouldn't lie, not on something like this.

Faith walked in the dining room, smooth and stealthy.

"It seems the Eastwood coven has lost their matriarch."

Faith raised her brow. "They have? How do know?"

"Do you remember Tony Guerrero?"

"Yes, I do. The vampire who replaced Paige as the captain of Red Star for a while."

"That's him. He just called and said he 'disposed of a problem' and that he has a set of shiny new wheels."

"Wheels? I don't understand."

Chuck rubbed his chin. "Merry never went anywhere without having a car or a driver to get around. Sounds like her."

"I wouldn't put it past her. What's going to happen to the rest of the coven?"

"Oliver took control while Merry was absent, and he should be able to control it again after her departure."

Faith moved to the couch and sat. "Do they know yet?"

"I can't say. They might suspect, it's been weeks since she disappeared, and every day she doesn't show is further confirmation."

"Has she done this before?"

"Not in my memory. She always had an iron grip on the coven before and she can't control the women without being intimately present."

"Good point. So, what do *we* do?"

"We make a show of doing nothing." Chuck sat easily next to Faith, close enough to touch her leg. "And very quietly move to acquire her assets. We need more for the war effort." That was an ancient way of thinking of things, but it was as accurate now as it was then.

Footfalls announced one of his pack. Richard wore a nice suit from a tailor in Portland who'd moved right after learning of the high concentration of paras in the area. "Sir, I have news."

"Yes?"

"We have a credible threat on you. We should get you to a secure location."

"Of course. We'll leave in an hour."

Richard shook himself. His spirit was a mountain goat, and easily startled, but he was a good man, one Chuck implicitly trusted. "Of course. I'll let them know to expect us."

Faith stood. "I'll get the kids. We can spend some time together before you leave. How long do you think you'll be?"

"I won't know until we can neutralize the threat. But I hope to be no more than a few days."

Threats were nothing new. He'd been through attempts on him before, and he'd never been one to run, but the McCree witch had put fear in him, fear he'd never known before. And being a figure in the secession from the United States made him some powerful enemies.

"Get the kids. We'll hunt for a few minutes and get some quality time in before I leave."

Faith smiled, her scar pulling as it always did.

Chuck sighed once. He should call Dexx in. No single shifter had the power and ability Dexx Colt had. And he'd voiced his desire that Chuck stay high alpha forever. And he had uncanny tracking skills.

Time for Colt to be a hunter again.

Dexx woke in the morning, refreshed and ready. No, not really. He didn't feel weak, at least not like he had the night before, but he could have slept for another year or so.

Paige pushed at him to roll over or get up or *something*. She wasn't talking, just pushing at him, so he rolled out of bed and looked around.

Why was he weak, though? He...he got in a fight with Pea, and then he and Leah—

"Oh shit. Jackie!" He charged out the door, thankful he'd dressed the night before, and ran down the stairs, thumping against each one until he hit the bottom.

Mandy and Leah sat at the table eating cereal. The really good kind with cinnamon and sugar that crunched even when it was soaked with milk. "Doorway. Now. Jackie."

Leah dropped her spoon. "Oh no."

"Oh yes. We have to get her, *right now*."

Leah looked down at her bowl, and at Dexx. "Can I finish breakfast first?"

Dexx started to say no but stopped. Jackie would survive a little longer. But he was really hoping he'd regain his strength soon. Leah nodded slowly and shared a look with Mandy. "Tyler's in love again."

"*Roxxie?*"

Leah nodded.

"Hmm. She still here?"

Leah nodded again. "She's still upstairs."

Dexx went back up the stairs to Leah's room, going a bit slower than his normal self.

Leslie sat in a chair next to the bed and Tyler sat on the other side.

Roxxie's smile lit the room and passed a sense of peace over him. "I'm better, thanks to you. You healed me. You repaired the gate. I'm free."

Molly Hammond sat straight up in bed from a dead sleep.

The whisper of a voice echoed in her head.

The time nears. Prepare, the Other will be released and he will bring his plans to bear.

Molly nodded. She had no idea what that meant, but her master always let her know when something was up. She still didn't know who the voice was, only that when the time was right, she'd have a hole in her memory, and life would just go right for her for a while.

It didn't stop Bow from dying. Dexx Colt could have been a friend, but he was just too stuck on himself. Men were often that way. Way too observant and cluelessly oblivious at the same time.

Molly bowed her head, even though she had never been instructed to. "I serve."

You will spare the life of Dexx Colt if you have the opportunity. If you do this you will be bestowed a wonderous gift.

Molly bowed her head again. "I serve."

The presence left her alone in peace, in the darkened room.

The voice had *never* asked her to do anything, just to prepare for something. How would she know if she could save Dexx's life, anyway? She never had control of her actions when she was serving. Or memories. How would she know if she could save Dexx's life or not? And why should she? He was the instrument of death of the person she loved most on the planet.

She almost growled and punched her pillow. If she was to save that bastard, then she would. After all, she was the herald, and it was hers to serve.

D exx's eyes blinked rapidly. "I what?"

Roxxie leaned to Tyler and patted his hand. "Thank you." Then she swung out of Leah's bed and stood. "I heard you. I heard everything. I would be honored to be accepted as part of the Whiskey clan." She smiled. It was pure and made the room more peaceful.

Dexx had meant every word. She'd more than proven herself loyal to the family. It was time to honor that.

"Your sacrifice. The *mavet mogroch*, the crystal you carried with you. You used the power within to save me and bring the gates back into alignment."

He groaned. Those gates being unaligned had been what had kept the demons at bay. "Please don't say something like angels and demons are coming back."

"If you do not want to hear it, I will not say it."

He let his head fall back. So, he'd managed to use the crystal to fix Roxxie and bring back angels and demons, which could, in effect, create whole new problems. Was he trying to make things easier for Walton?

"So, the vicious cycle's been kickstarted again?" Leslie turned flat eyes to Dexx. "How comforting."

Except that angels and demons were familiar ground for them, so maybe they could find a way to use this to their advantage. Right? "The only thing I can say is that it felt... right. We just have to figure out how to make this work is all." But how? There had to be a way.

Roxxie placed a hand on his shoulder. "You honored me. I will not forget. I will never forget what you did for me, and I will honor the sacrifice of perhaps the most powerful object in creation. I know I've never seen anything close."

Damn. It would have obliterated Bussemi. And he used it to...restart the conflict between angels and demons.

He had to make sure it had been worth it. "You wouldn't be able to help me kill him, would you?"

"Help, maybe. Kill him for you?" She shook her head. "The thing that possesses him is quite powerful."

Okay. He just needed a plan. He could work with that. "Thanks. You need a ride or something?"

Roxxie's smile was amused. "Thanks, but I think I have to check in. I only waited so I could thank you in person. The greater likelihood is if we know the gates are open, the demons know this too."

"Hey, I want you to remember something. You *know* not all demons are bad guys, right? Furiel?"

"You are not wrong. But in all the demonkind realm, they are not in the majority. Conversely, not all angels are the helpful kind either. I remember Genael. But if I can, I will speak for those who need to be spoken for."

Maybe *this* was the reason the crystal had asked him to heal Roxxie. Maybe he was healing *this* rift.

"Walk me to the door?" She held a hand to Dexx.

He needed to find the win in this one. "Yeah. Okay." He took her hand and she teleported them to the front door.

"Damn it. You wanted to *walk*, remember?" His stomach roiled, but it was empty, so the porch was safe. This time.

"I wanted to tell you in confidence. Please keep this to yourself."

Dexx quickly sent his senses out and felt for eavesdroppers. The kids were on their way, but he had time. "Shoot. Are you sure you're okay?"

"More than that. When you used the crystal, you didn't just heal me. I'm not just any angel now. My power might rival Michael's."

Dexx furrowed his brow. "Do I even want to know?"

"What might interest you most is that I might be on even footing with the archangels now. I had a small squad before. Now I might command a Host."

"How much is a Host?" Bringing that to the battlefield might be a strategic advantage.

Roxxie's smile hid secrets. "More than a few. But I will say this: any angels under my command would necessarily act more like me. I suppose it would be like you are. An alpha."

Alpha. That reminded him. "This is my pack, with certain caveats. If you're in the family now, I'm your alpha."

Roxxie's smile widened in genuine pleasure. "You catch on quick. Thank you, again." She grabbed Dexx in a quick hug and kissed him on the cheek, then poofed away.

A feather, bright as sun-kissed snow drifted toward the porch.

Dexx caught it in the air.

Hmm. For being as open as she was, she still hid secrets. Maybe he could weasel more info from her in time.

The door burst open and Tyler flew out in front of the other kids. "Aw, man. She didn't say goodbye."

Dexx held the feather out to him. "Yeah, she really did."

Tyler took the feather and beamed. "Wow, this is so cool. I can feel it vibrating, like, with good stuff. Wow."

Leah was in the back of the pack, peering out.

"*Now* can we go get Jackie?" Before anything else happened.

Leah opted to ride back with Dexx after they'd collected the car, and when they got home, Paige was waiting for them in the garage. Dexx parked Jackie right where she'd been when they started out last night.

Page wore a sad look. "We still have a conversation to finish."

Dexx's stomach fell. Were they *really* going to start this again? "We can if you want. But my thought is this: the kids are going to wind up in the fight sometime because they're *our kids*. Whether now or later, and I'd like to teach them how rather than wait for them to learn on their own."

Paige nodded. "They probably will. I only ask that we try to keep their exposure to as little as possible and still teach. I'm scared all the time for them, and it would kill me if I had to bury any one of us."

"Me too." Dexx nodded. He'd already lost more than he could stand. "And maybe they'll save us again. Like last night."

Dexx had exactly one hour of peace after he and Leah parked Jackie.

Hattie filled his mind with her presence. *We must go.*

Go where? Because I'm having a pretty good day just hanging with the fam.

The alpha calls. We must go.

Dexx mimicked her. *The alpha calls. So?* We're *the alpha, remember?*

Irritation flowed through the bond. *And we answer to a higher. Your alpha calls.*

Can't we just leave a message and he can call us back?

When you refused to take the alpha's place you made us beneath him. And when our alpha calls we go.

Dammit all to hell. "Pea. I gotta go. Apparently, Chuck needs me to see him or something."

She frowned at him. "How do you know?"

"Got the alpha bat-phone in my head. Hattie says we have to go."

"Is everything all right?"

"It's a bat-phone, not ESP. I'll send a message as soon as I can."

Paige shook her head. "Sure. Get going. I got things—"

An urgent knock on the door drew her attention. It opened and one of Paige's people walked in carrying that stupid clipboard against her chest. "News, Mrs. Whiskey. The Chinese army's invaded Canada *and* Hawaii. Russia has moved against Alaska's west coast last night and they've taken hundreds of miles inland."

"Everyone's in the war room?" Paige asked on her way out the door.

There went the whole day. "Where're we going?" Hawaii might not be bad this time of year. Early May was a good time, right?"

"*You* are going to see Chuck. *I* will take care of this." She pecked a kiss on his cheek. "Love you."

"No, I can't leave you here—"

Paige turned the Whiskey look on him. "*You. Are. Going. To. Chuck.* I have this under control." She turned to look at the kids. "You. Guys. Are. Staying. Here."

Leah turned up her lip.

Tyler robot-armed as he spoke. "We. Are. Not. Robots."

"What if you get a migraine again?"

Mandy snorted and joined the robot talk-off. "You. Can't. Tell. Us. What. To. Do. If. You. Are. Not. Here."

"I'm gonna kill 'em." Paige shook her head at him. "What if I do? You can't help me there. Stop making me repeat myself three times. This is getting old."

She was still being considered by spirits. What if they never chose? What did the migraines mean? That she was or was not being considered for a bond?

This will get us nowhere, Hattie said. *She is right. We must leave.*

Shit. *Let's go see our* alpha.

Of course, they had to take Jackie. After so long without her, and a brief dip into depression, she felt way too good after that first drive.

So Chuck summoned him like a vassal. So what?

He'd taken a nearly dead angel and had made her better than before. He'd even reversed the damage Sven had done to the world. If moving the gates was damage. That had yet to be seen. Though a part of him was starting to see how everything worked together, even if he didn't like it.

Okay. So, fixing the gates to fix his friend had been a fifty percent win. He should be happy for that. Crap, even *Thanos* had taken fifty percent as a win.

Dexx let his hand slide over the steering wheel like he was stroking a favored four-legged member of the family. Jackie had put a piece back into him he'd thought was gone, that he hadn't remembered was missing, anyway.

So what could be so important Chuck sent for us by—what should we call it—alpha phone?

Hattie huffed at him and hung her head in a very human gesture. *You do not help in the hunt unless you get the best to eat.*

Translation: I kind of ignore you unless it benefits me first. Am I close?

Yes.

Well, that kinda hurt. Did that make him self-centered?

Maybe.

As a bad thing?

Maybe...not?

You are the alpha of a small pack, she continued. *Our pack should grow and be the alpha pack of this region.*

Why is this so important to you? Dexx took the turn from the highway to the side road to Chuck's *very* large house. To say it was a mansion might be too little by a room.

You are one part of a much larger whole and that whole is what is most important.

That made a little sense, something he was definitely starting to understand. He couldn't go in with half a plan and alone anymore, and his family just kept growing. *You ever going to run out of rules to uncover?*

Only if you listen harder.

He was. He was. Dexx leaned on the throttle and let Jackie roar, making his self-centered heart feel a little happier.

Jackie rolled down the paved drive along the perfect landscaping to the circle drive in front if the house smooth and less rumbly than she had before the improvements.

One of Chuck's pack opened the front door of the house and stood there. He had the strangest look on his face.

The man was familiar, probably a regular around the house, but he wasn't anyone special.

Okay. That sounded bad, but Chuck's pack had hundreds of people in it. Maybe even thousands when all the members of all the packs who answered to him were taken into account. Dexx wasn't going to remember all those names.

The shifter headed to the car.

Dexx cringed at the muted red and blue printed stripes on the guy's shirt. Fashion wasn't his gig, but if the guy could pull it off, more power to him. Dexx killed the engine and set a foot out, waiting to hear if he was being sent off some-where else or if he was needed for a meeting or what the deal was.

"You're Dexx Colt, right? I've seen you around."

Dexx's pride swelled a little. "Yeah. Here to see Chuck. I think he's expecting me."

"Chuck's gone. He went to a secret location, but Faith is here if you want to talk with her."

Okay. So, what exactly had the message said? That Chuck needed Dexx to find him or that he was needed at the house? It'd been pretty vague and Hattie wasn't offering any help. *This had better not be some damned test.*

It is not, she said, equally confused.

He sank into the seat with an exhale. "I think I'm supposed to find him. Don't suppose you can direct me there?"

"No. Like I said it's secret, and I'm not an alpha, so I wouldn't be able to track him directly."

Dexx resisted the urge to pound on the steering wheel. *Does this mean I can since I am an alpha?*

Perhaps, she said, though she didn't seem certain.

"Thanks. I think I know where to go. Tell Faith I said hello." He pulled his foot in and shut the door a little more vigorously than he needed to. He managed to keep his foot out of it until the main side road. He left an impressive amount of rubber on the road due to his frustration. This *felt* like another damned test and he was sick and tired of *being* tested.

Hattie played happy paws in his mind until he turned sour attention to her. *You are testing me, aren't you?*

Perhaps, but I have learned that, in this lifetime especially, no one can tell you what to do. You must figure it out on your own.

Sometimes she could be so irritating. *Okay, big trainer kitty, how do I find the calling alpha?*

Turned out, finding Chuck wasn't hard. Not hard at all. Dexx just had to apply the proper concentration to the sensation of seeing that little movement out of the corner of the eye.

Soon, he turned into the parking garage of a nearly abandoned business building in Portland.

He drove up the levels until he found Chuck's big ol' Suburban, alongside a couple other GM products. Of course, they were all black. Ew. No fun.

Jared met him at the elevator doors. "You made good time. Most new alphas would be hours. You picked up on it impressively quick."

So, this *had* been a test. That...conniving... "Yeah. I have kids."

"Let's meet the others, shall we?"

The doors burst open and Chuck, with *every* alpha Dexx knew of, ran out.

"The house!"

S omething big crashed upstairs, so Faith went up to
see who and what had died this time.

The kids were playing a frantic game of tag, just
like always—when they weren't jumping from the furniture.
This time, it appeared that the large dresser she'd asked
Chuck to secure to the wall had fallen over.

"Sorry, Mom," Will said as he pounced on Aaron.

"Clean it up later," Joseph grunted as he joined Will.

Aaron shrieked as he was attacked, but that quickly
turned into a roar as he fought off his dual attackers.

She'd had Chuck build the room for the destruction their
four boys could cause.

The Whiskeys had their hands full with toddlers and
babies growing to almost functioning teens in just weeks.

Faith preferred the old-fashioned way. Slow and steady
made for good alphas.

Joseph and Will had Aaron pinned and were threatening
to let spit drop on his face.

Fred, who'd somehow come up with the nickname Skeet,
waited in another corner to ambush them all.

All four of the children were developing nicely, their spirit wolves were alphas, and were much bigger than other pack members of the same age. Every one of her boys would have large packs and push the boundaries of their region out.

Faith smiled. Their influence would grow. In time, the Eastwoods might be supplanted by Faith and Chuck's pack. Portland and the area had seen the end of the Eastwood era, and soon the Deluca era would rise to replace it.

Skeet jumped in and bowled them all over. That started the fight for dominance all over again. One of the others would wind up on the floor and the others would torment him for a few minutes. The fight for the lead alpha never ended with those four.

With Chuck the leader of the paranormal military, he was a constant target, and this latest threat was just another inconvenience.

Chuck had good instincts Faith rarely second-guessed, but she didn't agree that calling on Dexx Colt would be a good move. He claimed to be just a normal guy, with no designs on being the regional high alpha, but she'd seen the inner conflict whenever he came close to Chuck. The man might not want the regional high alpha spot, but his shifter spirit might.

And Faith had plans to create a better region, plans that didn't involve Dexx, who couldn't find all of his resources to *use* effectively in battle. As a regional high alpha, every day was a battle, though not always one that looked like war. Sometimes, the carnage lay in empty cupboards and broken shoes.

Not that she distrusted Dexx. He'd been the instrument that saved Chuck, and worked harder than *anyone* to keep him high alpha, but how long would that last? Was he only biding his time until he found weakness? No, Chuck had been weak before and Dexx had protected him. Maybe he wasn't lying, then.

Robert quick-walked down the hall to her. "We have movement outside."

When Chuck was out and they were in the middle of a war? Faith didn't trust the wards Paige had placed over their grounds. Paige might have been a shifter once, but she was still a witch and she was the only person who had survived the death of her shifter spirit. That wasn't a thing to trust. "Rouse the barracks."

"Already done."

She had fifty members of the main pack in an outbuilding just on the outside chance of an attack on the house. They'd learned, after being attacked twice, that it might happen again even with the help and support of Whiskey magick. "Good. Don't let them be seen right away." Faith was sick of this cat-and-mouse game. "We draw them in, just like we practiced."

Fifty paras repelling an attack should send a strong message. The Deluca pack had teeth. Literally. "Boys," she called, using her alpha will a little to pull them out of their play and to let them know that things were getting serious. "Come with me."

"What's going on, Mom?" Skeet had the sharpest mind of the four, but he wasn't the largest.

"Someone is going to try to bully us, I believe."

"I don't like bullies." Will showed his teeth, and his spirit subtly shifted the boy's looks. He was the protector, but also not the biggest.

"We're ready." Joseph *was* the biggest. His wolf was almost as large as any full-grown shifter already. The boys just had their seventh birthday.

The first blast that shook the house took them all off their feet.

Magick. "Son of a bitch." Faith got her feet under her. That sounded like the bedroom.

She reached for the phone they'd been given to share. It wasn't there. She'd left it…charging in her bedroom. She brushed off her pants and stood. *How many? Can you tell?*

Carina, her wolf spirit, didn't reply immediately. *I can't say. I can try to find Sorakos. He will tell the high alpha.*

Do it. That felt magickal. She had to hope that the Whiskey ward she'd disparaged just moments earlier continued to hold.

Another blast rocked the house, but it didn't seem to have made much of an impact. That was a good sign.

Robert crouched as he came into the room. "Get down. Don't stand in front of the windows."

Faith looked over her shoulder. Nobody should be able to see in the windows, or grab an infrared of the interior. They'd been specially designed and manufactured per her specifications. She wasn't going to allow her family to be put in danger.

The drywall cracked as an explosion in the foyer took out the front door.

If the wards were holding, and she had to believe they were because they really had protected the town for a long time, then how…

The acrid smell of gunpowder filled her nose.

Magick and artillery, Carina said.

"Boys. The saferoom. Now. Robert, you too." Faith pointed to the room opposite her bedroom. She led the way to the far door as pack members backed down the hall, facing someone coming up the stairs. One by one, they took on the invaders and, just as quickly, died.

There was no way her boys stood a chance against someone that powerful.

"To the master of this house," a man's voice called in a

refined British accent, "I ask you to come out and give your-self up. You will be treated with dignity until your time comes."

Faith couldn't believe a word the man said. He'd already destroyed lives and property. "Get to the saferoom."

The sounds of scrambling feet told her that her order was being filled.

She faced the man as he entered the bedroom.

He paused with mild surprise.

He looked Middle Eastern with the cheekbones and color-ing, but there was nothing else about his appearance that told her who he was. "I will not be threatened in my home."

She raised her hand to smite him.

Her shifters ran up the stairs, howling and yipping to take lead.

She smiled. She was an *alpha* and it was time to show this man what that meant. She raised her face to the ceiling and called to them with her human voice, imbuing it with her alpha will. *Kill.*

The magician glared at her and shook his head. "You will regret that action, wolf. You will wish you had agreed to lay down arms."

Faith seriously doubted that.

A blonde-haired woman with a severe braid running down her back stepped forward, her eyes glowing blue.

"Angela," the man said conversationally, "try to keep her alive. She'll make a good hostage."

Angela dipped her head to the side and smiled.

Faith snarled. There would be no hostages.

Dexx and Jared raced ahead of the others, soon leaving them so far behind he couldn't see them.

Jared's phone rang as soon as it was apparent Dexx would reach Chuck's house long before anyone else. "He says it's DoDO."

"Great," Dexx said, feeling a touch stupid for having just been there. "Just let Faith know we're on the way. Hold on —" Dexx yanked the car around a normally easy corner, but going over a buck forty made it mostly slippery.

Smoke rolled from the tires as the rev limiter dropped cylinders and pulled the power back. Once they had traction again, the pedal was held to the floor.

"Good—oh, crap. I'm gonna die." Jared mumbled mostly incoherently as they raced past intersections and through the sparce traffic. The drive from Portland should have been a twenty-minute ride. At warp speed.

Dexx made it in a little under seven minutes.

Jackie ripped down the driveway, and as the trees gave way to the wide landscaping, Dexx saw a column of smoke mushrooming from the house.

The ward tree was still in place, however.

How in the hell had DoDO managed to make it through Paige's ward to do this much damage?

As Dexx pulled up, he noticed a metal ring around the base of the tree.

An inhibitor? Was that even a thing?

Well, they'd shown they were pretty ingenious when it came to disabling their strengths, and Paige's ward trees were one of the greatest defenses they had, so...

Dammit. They probably should have prepared for DoDO to find a way around those wards, and maybe Paige did but... she wasn't exactly in the fight.

Dammit. Of all the times for him to give her the bite.

And for the ancients to hold out on her, as if they didn't understand how much she'd sacrificed for all of them. He didn't have time for that little rabbit hole, though.

DoDO agents ran around the outside and a few darted inside, but the fight was already lost. They were casting spells indiscriminately and fires were spreading quickly through and around the mansion.

Shifters and agents littered the ground, most of them still.

Dexx jammed the brakes and would have skidded to a halt if he hadn't added the latest in anti-lock racing binders.

The DoDO agents still standing didn't seem to think he was a threat, or maybe they hadn't heard him roar into the complex, so none of them paid the two shifters any mind until a sabertoothed cat and a large grey wolf tore into them.

Hattie, tell Chuck we're here, and to get here quick. Dexx ripped through two agents with Hattie's claws. They went down spraying blood and organs everywhere. They were already dead, but their limbs moved like they hadn't noticed.

The magick they'd been throwing left them as they hit the ground.

We're outnumbered. And tell them to get the tree unbound when he gets here.

Jared did his best, taking on three DoDO agents and besting them one at a time.

Dexx went for the front door, since survivors were likely to be inside, and *somebody* was putting up a fight. He sent his alpha aura in front of him, commanding non-alphas to back down. It worked in humans, sometimes.

A few agents *did* stop, but not enough. Parts of the house burned as fire elementals pushed flame in front of them. He took those agents out first, but the fires they'd started still grew, giving him and the remaining survivors one more thing to dodge as they fought to live.

He reached the stairs that led to the second floor and shifted into human form. He took his *ma'a'shed* out and took off the heads of two men preparing to take their assault up the stairs.

He took the steps two at a time, taking out any DoDO he could reach. Any that he couldn't, he pushed at them with his alpha aura. Sometimes it worked but mostly they paused only long enough for him to get further in the house.

Dexx followed the sounds of crashing and fighting, taking out two more agents before he stopped.

Sir Sayyid Maxwell floated in front of him, his fists glowing a warm yellow with motes of black lazily wafting through the magick. "Mr. Colt. I told you you were a disgrace. You proved it in my country. Are you here to prove it in yours? Lower your weapon, or I shall be forced to punish you further."

There was no way Dexx was about to do that. He smelled the angry fear pouring off Faith in the other room. "No. I will, however, kill you. Unless you let me by." The man was dark-hearted evil, and Dexx *knew* that. But somewhere deep in his psyche, he *really* wanted to just follow the man's orders. He pushed his will out to the man to stand down.

Sir Sayyid twitched and dropped his eyes for a second as though trying to remember something, then he looked back up to Dexx.

Something big crashed in one of the bedrooms. *Faith. Hold on.*

"That was a nice try, Mr. Colt. You never made it long enough to learn who the directors of the department are. Now, I'll just have to show you." Sayyid's hands flared with magick, and he spoke a word. "*Gravitare.*"

The floor beneath Dexx bowed and cracked under him. His sword weighed a ton, probably literally, then Dexx bowed under the weight of his own body. He dropped the sword and crashed to the floor. He couldn't breathe. Couldn't move. His eyes started seeing spots from the pressure.

Oh, shit.

The floor popped once more and crashed to the floor

below. As soon as the floor let loose, the weight lifted. Dexx shifted into the saber and ran.

Sir Sayyid's magick followed him through the hallway to the room. "Mr. Colt, don't run. You'll only make more work for yourself in the end. Give up now. I shall grant you the mercy of a quick death."

Fucking fucker. The guy was a monologuer and they needed to find a way to get that inhibitor off the ward tree. Dexx didn't know *how* it worked, but he did understand that any magick users inside the wards would be damaged by their own magick, which was exactly what Dexx needed.

He ran outside to see about getting that inhibitor off, but there were already shifters working on it.

DoDO wasn't stupid, or whoever had designed it wasn't. But Dexx didn't know that he'd be able to provide any more help on that front than the shifters trying to pry the ring up in the first place, so he went back into the house to keep Sir Sayyid occupied.

This is stupid. He understood why Paige wanted her shift back. What he wouldn't give to be able to use the power of his shift and some magick in this battle.

Fiery debris fell from the ceiling, forcing Dexx to dodge into a room on the left.

The room looked like an office. A very big, very expensive office. A heavy desk of polished rosewood with flat-screen monitors that seemed too big to be just for QuickBooks sat to one side. The other had a selection of custom knives in a glass case.

"I know where you are. You can't hide from me." Sir Sayyid's voice was getting closer.

Damn. The man spoke words of power. He didn't need a wand or complicated gestures. Spell-work like that was rare, and always powerful.

What's their weakness?

I would not know, cub. You should not be caught.

No shit. What would their weakness be? Dexx stepped into the Time Before, knowing he could search for a solution while no time on Earth passed.

"Hattie. I need your help." Dexx stood next to the portal tree in his imagination.

She appeared and they merged and materialized in the Time Before on the bluff overlooking a verdant plain, animals eating the grass in lazy pulls.

I know I'm kinda playing a bitch card, but I need a minute to think. He needed to be smarter, but it was becoming apparent that wasn't his strong suit.

You should not be here. Mah'se lay on the ground, watching the grazers. He made no move, and his words had no heat.

Mah'se, you're a chihuahua. Shut up. Make a difference in the world instead of whining. That was it. Dexx needed to *use* his full range of power and stop whining. He needed to heed his own advice.

Mah'se's dark eyes swung toward them, but Dexx stepped back to the real world.

Sir Sayyid's magick licked the edges of the doorway.

Dexx grabbed a knife from the case and palmed it. He might not have magick, but he had two powerful hunter forms, one with claws and teeth and the other with knives and weapons.

Sir Sayyid floated in a few moments later like a complete douche.

"I'm sorry. I'm sorry." Dexx held his empty hand up. "You win. I know when I'm beat, but don't kill me. Just leave me alive...please."

A crash from the ceiling dropped burning dust around the room.

"You have a trick. I have seen your movies. I know you're planning something."

Dexx wasn't going to say he was original by any means, but yeah. He had a slight semblance of a trick up his sleeve. "No plan. Just...if I die, your boss gets my soul in the *kadu* and I don't want that. Not yet."

"You were always meant to die."

"Sure, but could you, you know, spare me? Let Bussemi have the honor?"

Sir Sayyid smiled. "No. I will enjoy this."

What a douchecanoe. Dexx just needed his moment, that time when the man was about to throw magick, when he allowed himself to be vulnerable for a split second.

A crash and a scream from a room above caught Sayyid's attention.

That's what Dexx was waiting for. He leapt, his knife in hand.

Sir Sayyid turned his attention back to Dexx.

Not in time. He jammed the knife into Sir Sayyid's chin and into his brain. Dexx gave it a twist and tossed the body down. "Yeah. I had a plan. Dumbass."

Dexx ran to the flaming hole in the house and recovered the *ma'a'shed*. The flames were quickly gaining on the house. "Faith," he shouted. "We gotta get you out of here!" He ran up the stairs, raising his arm to shield his face from the heat of the rising flames. Angela Hopkirk held Faith with a magickal noose with one hand, and with the other hand, she threw a limp child to the ground.

No!

Faith's mouth opened in a scream, but no air came out. Her fingers scrambled at her neck, trying to pull air.

Dexx didn't even think about it. With the *ma'a'shed* in hand, he sliced Agent Hopkirk's back as a burning beam crashed across the large bed.

Faith fell to the floor.

Angela dropped to the floor, trying to scream.

Dexx put a boot to her chest, the *ma'a'shed* at her throat. "We don't murder kids," he whispered.

She smiled through her own blood, clutching his ankle. "You don't kill kids. I'd destroy Hitler as a babe if I could."

The *ma'a'shed* ripped across her throat before he had a chance to even think about it.

The house was falling down around them. He turned to Faith.

Dead eyes stared back at him.

Dexx sat against the freed tree trunk and let the tears come. Another person he couldn't save.

Another person who'd counted on him to save them and he failed.

Failed. After everyone he'd lost, and *sworn* it would never happen again, it had happened. And not just to one. *Five more.*

When Chuck arrived, he fell to his knees and wailed at the burning remains of his home.

Dexx didn't have the energy to do even that. This was the reason Paige didn't want the kids to be a part of this war.

And this was the reason he couldn't stand by her in this argument. Chuck's kids and his alpha mate had all died in their home under the protection of one of Paige's ward trees.

The lawn filled with shifters and fire elementals who managed to put the fire out.

Chuck let himself be led away.

Jared took a knee and rested a hand on Dexx's shoulder. "What happened?"

Dexx shook his head and pulled out his phone, sending

Michelle a message to send one of her dryads over to see if they could find a way to neutralize the device. If they couldn't protect the ward trees from this new tech, then Troutdale wasn't safe. The Whiskey house wasn't safe. None of the other towns Paige and Billie Black had protected with these trees would be safe.

Jared took in a deep breath and set a hand on Dexx's shoulder. Then he stood up and went to talk to the others gathering around.

The attack on Chuck's place sent shockwaves through the para community.

Dexx didn't see Paige for days afterward while she scrambled to keep the para forces together. General Saul deployed the twenty-three high-ranking generals to various locations to help with morale. She took Paige to the border forts to give speeches.

But through the succession of losses they'd sustained, Arizona and New Mexico had decided to go back to Walton and Southern California was in serious discussions to do the same.

This revolution wasn't going well. Too many people were dying without any positive outcomes. That had to change, because they couldn't back down. What would that look like? More para kids dying? More para families being torn apart?

He needed to talk to someone, but he also couldn't burden anyone with the heaviness in his heart. He wasn't feeling like they'd win. He knew he needed to. If he couldn't feel that, he couldn't inspire it, and then what would people be fighting for? To die their own way? Before Walton and his goons could do it for them?

Dexx folded the rag and left the house to visit the forest graveyard. He sat against Rainbow's headstone, letting his flow of consciousness take his mouth wherever.

After about an hour, he felt a little better, though he wasn't sure he was able to inspire anyone to stand up and fight a losing war yet.

Dead leaves crunched not far away.

Dexx scrambled to hit feet and relaxed a fraction when he saw Chuck approaching.

Chuck's steps came even and slow. He saw Dexx and said nothing. He just walked closer.

Hattie went on high alert, though she didn't tell Dexx why.

If it were him, if Chuck had been the one sent to save the Whiskeys and had failed, Dexx would have been enraged and would have needed to fight. Would Chuck react the same way?

The regional high alpha's face didn't provide any answers, his dark expression unreadable. "We need to talk." Chuck stopped by Boot's grave, reading the inscription on the stone.

"Look, I—" Dexx cut off as Chuck raised a hand.

"When I said talk, I think I should have said *I* need to talk and you need to listen."

Dexx closed his mouth. He could do that.

"I don't blame you."

Dexx wasn't sure whether he did or didn't. He'd been there. He should have fought harder, been smarter. But he had been.

Sir Sayyid had just been smarter.

"I blame myself and DoDO. You warned us all about them enough."

Dexx had certainly tried. "They surprised us with the inhibitor on the ward tree."

Chuck nodded solemnly. "We should not have relied on it."

The Whiskeys probably shouldn't either, but they did.

"The dryads are working on something that will protect the ward trees against something like that again."

"Good." Chuck sighed heavily and closed his blue eyes for a moment. "You'll be one of the best alphas in our region when you decide to take your place."

Him *taking his place* had been what had allowed DoDO in in the first place. "I don't want that. I want to just be me. I got a pack I never asked for, but I won't give it back, and I'm not looking to make it any bigger. Certainly not after—" He couldn't say it out loud. The image of Faith's dead gaze flashed across his inner vision. "I don't want more."

"Faith never believed you. She never thought you were content to stay where you were, an insignificant pack alpha."

Dexx squared up. "You think I *let* her—"

Chuck held up a hand again. "*She* never believed. I didn't say anything about *me*. You are many things, but a calculated killer isn't one of them."

Dexx wrinkled his brow. "I don't know. I put some people in the ground with plenty of calculating." More without it, though.

"Coldblooded killer, then. You show a very tender heart." Chuck motioned to the graves. "Your loyalty to your pack proves who you are."

Dexx had no flippin' idea what Chuck had come for, but it couldn't be about his loyalty to his pack. "Why are you here? I'm sure if you wanted to kill me, you'd be digging a hole right now."

Chuck laughed. It was a cold, dead sound. "You couldn't lose in a fight between the two of us. Your spirit is the strongest of the continental alphas. I couldn't win."

"That's some bullshit, right there. *You* are the region high alpha. I got some lucky shit happening for me sometimes, but outside of that, it's all clumsy cat."

Chuck's eyes held Dexx's and something pushed through.

His self-deprecating need was being turned aside so the strength of what he hid beneath shone through.

And that scared Dexx a little.

"I *am* the regional high alpha," Chuck said quietly, stepping closer. "I *chose* to be the alpha. But I also know that if a certain big cat challenged me for the spot, that cat would have it."

Dexx didn't *want* it until he could prove to himself he was worthy. There was so much more responsibility that Chuck shouldered, and he did it with the kind of experience Dexx simply didn't have, no matter how strong and powerful his alpha spirit was. "Then as a prospective challenger, I will challenge the challengers, and make sure *you* stay there. You want it, and I want you to have it forever." No matter if Chuck *still* wanted it? How would Dexx be reacting if he'd lost Paige or Leah or Bobby or the twins? Tyler or Mandy or Kate or Kammy? Tarik or Michelle or Ethel?

Frey? He could possibly lose her.

No. He would still feel bad, even though she was an extreme irritant.

"I want *you* to take my place."

Fear stopped any smartassed thing Dexx could say.

Chuck smiled. A genuine smile. "There's a legend among the alpha spirits. The details aren't important, but the core of it is that the mighty sabertoothed cat and her bond mate rise up in every lifetime to make a powerful difference in the world."

Maybe Dexx's other lives. He didn't feel like he was meeting expectations in this one. "Sorry to disappoint. I only do what I can. Lately, it hasn't been enough."

Chuck nodded solemnly. "I want you to succeed me. If the time comes, take the regional alpha position. Make a difference again."

Dexx didn't know when or if that would ever happen.

"I'm just me. I don't want your place, and my magick is gone. I'm a guy, and my spirit is a fat cat. We help as much as we can."

Chuck nodded, and turned away from the graves. "I don't know how much longer I can do this."

Dexx didn't know what to say. "You'll do what you have to for as long as you can because that's who you are." And how big of a dick was Dexx for forcing Chuck to keep fighting when he'd lost so much?

But Dexx *knew* what Chuck refused to admit. Dexx wasn't suited for big leadership positions. He was an alpha. Sure. A great leader? No. It didn't matter how many people said it however many different ways, Dexx's *past lives* maybe have been great leaders, but Dexx was just...an okay one.

"This place is peaceful. I may have to ask if my kin can be buried here."

Dexx opened his mouth to protest, but Chuck was already leaving. Looking at the three graves was plenty enough to remind him of his failures. He didn't need small ones to put a finer point on them.

He stood there thinking about the avalanche of his feelings and never heard Pea sneak up on him.

"I hope you're over yourself. You did what you could." She had a Whiskey look on her face.

"I'm—" He wasn't sure he could withstand one of Paige's frank pep talks. "I'm always too late to make a difference. No, not always. But it seems like it. I mean, Boot. Alma. Rainbow. Faith. Her kids. Why?"

"Okay. I'm going to play the part of your ego booster. When I'm done, you're going to knock this stupid shit off, you read?"

"Huh?"

"Dexx, you're the biggest, best shifter on the planet."

Oh. It only worked if he believed she believed it, and he didn't.

She cupped his face and stared deeply into his eyes. "I don't say this enough. I know. I'm harder on you than I should be. I know. My love language is…" She rolled her eyes and sighed. "Hard."

He agreed with his eyebrows.

She clunked her forehead to his. "If I have a million dollars to bet on one guy, you're the guy. I literally live in the presence of a super-shifter legend, and I'm in awe every day." Her fingers curled around the back of his head. "I don't know what I'd do without you to stand beside me."

That was what he needed to hear. "Shut up. I hate you." But the smile that crept over his face said she'd hit her mark.

"You feel better now?" She slipped her arm around him.

"I hurt less. But I feel the pain moving to my pancreas. I think I have gas." He started them moving toward the house.

"I love you."

She felt good beside him. "She fought hard," he said quietly as they walked slowly toward the house.

"Faith was a fighter."

"So are you." He pressed a kiss to the side of her head.

She leaned into it. "Okay, so while you've been sulking, and I *let* you sulk, shit's been happening. The dryads *do* have a protection for the trees."

"That was fast."

"They're dryads and it's a tree." She shook her head and shrugged. "Canada is losing ground to the Chinese. One of the Asiatic states is parked off the Hawaiian coast and is lobbing shells inward, and someone's moving on the Confederate States."

Maybe that would take some of the heat off them for once. "Are we going to help? Send some people in?"

"Wouldn't that be nice? *All* the paras move to the aid of the rest of the country? Then poof—where'd ParaWest go?"

"General Saul's been telling you stuff again? That sounded tactical to me."

"Yeah." Paige took in a deep breath. "We need to play smarter. I've got twenty-three high-ranking generals and two members of the Department of Defense and most of them are still with me."

"Even after losing Arizona and New Mexico?"

"Yeah." She shimmied a little. "They'll probably be back, but *only* if we start getting our shit together and showing that we're capable of doing this, standing up as a nation."

"It's a lot different than running a police station."

"Fuck." She rested her head against his shoulder, tugging his arm tighter around her. "And oddly the same? Everything's just bigger now. There are a lot more people."

"Fuck," he repeated. "Sooooooo many more people."

Paige stopped and looked up at him. "We're going to win."

"You feel comfortable letting the rest of the world fight amongst themselves?" Paige'd been the worst at letting others fight their own fights.

"No." She dropped her gaze to his chin. "I'm not. I hate it, but I *can't*. Not with these headaches coming at random."

"Still?"

"Yeah. The attack on Chuck's house reminded me that I can't leave *us* vulnerable. We're so thin, it just doesn't make sense."

Paige hadn't had a headache in days. Or at least he hadn't seen her in the room with all the lights off. "How *is* your head? It's not going to roll off your shoulders or anything, right?"

"It's fine." She turned and continued toward the house. "I

think with all the concentrating on all the things, I'm doing fine."

Or maybe she'd been passed up by all the spirits, and she could move on with her life.

And if she could, he *had* to. "I still feel like I failed. Like *I'm* a failure."

"You aren't. You just can't win 'em all. We all feel like it though."

"Thanks, Pea. It's going to take a while, though. And you're right, I suppose. I'll put on my brave face and my big boy pants. I just suck at the whole superhero thing."

The house came into view through the trees, and the office building peeked through the forest farther down the yard.

"Good thing you're not a superhero, then. Not even a hero. You're just...Dad."

"Ow. I may bleed out. *Just* Dad? I'll have you know that being a dad is more than just cake for breakfast and watching the kids' heads snap back in the car. It's a lot of really tough questions and...keeping them from eating you alive."

Paige had a superpower. Super-snark mixed with super-odd humor and super-tough love. Dexx's perspective fell into a place much closer to normal. Not that he felt good about the Delucas. He didn't. But he had others to live for. He loved them all the way to the end.

They walked into the house—well, the chaos contained in the house. Tyler had the girls in some sort of tizzy and Bobby watched like he wanted to join in. That might not be the best idea for him, though.

The television played the local station. Tru and the dryads had been working to get things back to normal again. They had intermittent internet thanks to the satellites, because the actual internet had been taken down. The information infrastructure everyone had taken for granted was gone. But the parts and pieces of it were houses, to large degrees, all over ParaWest. In central California and Colorado for two, but there were others. Many others.

It was something to get used to again, having television when it'd been cut off or wildly unreliable for so long.

Leslie stirred a pot of something on the stove, but it smelled like dinner, and flashes of magick light careened off the walls.

Tyler led the screaming girls on a chase up the stairs and thumping down the hall. The sudden quiet seemed a little unnatural and welcome all in the same breath.

"Hey, Les, need something?" Paige stood at the spice cabinet, ready to pull something out.

"Yeah, I need…"

The cartoon cut out suddenly. "We interrupt this broadcast for a very important message from—"

Dexx turned to the television. Really? A special announcement?

"My fellow Americans, secessionists, and loyalists." President Walton sat behind his desk in the Oval Office. "I apologize for breaking into the broadcast, but I have a very important message to deliver."

Dexx headed into the living room. He didn't think the Federalists even *had* access to the ParaWest network.

"This country wants to heal, *needs* to heal. I'm calling for a halt to aggression. On all sides. The fighting amongst our own is pointless, and the…"

Dexx called into the kitchen. "Hey, guys, you might want to get in here right now and see who's on TV."

Paige walked in with a frown. "What?"

"Walton." He gestured to the screen. "He wants to"— Dexx mimed a stiff hug—"come together."

Leslie poked her head out. "Fucker." Then she disappeared again.

"...have devastated large tracts of land. Peaceful, intelligent people who have no dog in this fight have been killed or dislodged from their lands. They just want to live their lives, to have regular lives with regular jobs and kids and a white picket fence."

"You believe this shit?" Dexx hooked a thumb toward the TV.

Paige frowned at her phone in disbelief. "I...can't believe this."

"I don't buy it either."

"...certain instigations, which I was not informed of. We can't go on fighting like this, like playground children. So I'm putting down my arms, my aggressions. I'm begging the rest of you do so, too. We can come to an arrangement with concessions."

"Oh good. Concessions." Dexx turned away from the TV.

"It hurts to—" The speech cut off mid-word.

Paige leaned back from the screen.

"Let me add my voice to the peace talks." Cardinal Bussemi talked with a slight accent that didn't necessarily belong to any place in particular.

"What the hell?" Dexx asked. He spun to the TV and Cardinal Bussemi stood at a pulpit, a life-sized Roman Catholic crucifix behind him.

Paige shook her head, her eyes wide.

Dexx wanted to run, but he couldn't. He stared at the TV, rapt and repulsed all at once.

"There may have been misunderstandings. There were certain individuals in my employ, and I regret they acted on an impulsive word. This is my fault, and I cannot fix the mistake."

Paige raised an eyebrow at Dexx.

He had to agree with the sentiment.

"The best that can be said is the parties were avenged by you already."

Intense emotions swirled in Dexx's head. Intellectually, he knew Bussemi was a piece of shit who needed to die. In every fight before, Dexx and Hattie had lost.

What was going to make it different this time? Something had to. They couldn't afford to lose again.

"I know you're watching, Dexx. I can see you, looking lost and frightened. Your bride, not as much, but she's nervous."

Dexx whispered to Paige. "Can he do that?"

Paige shook her head slowly.

Bussemi nodded.

"I can. Consider this my personal entreaty to you. I wish for peace."

Phoebe Blackman held her hand out to the Governor of the ParaWest State of Hawaii. "Deal. You get unfettered access to me and my coven for doorways. We defend the islands against invaders and other aggressive interests and in return you grant my coven the island of Lanai, with all interests transferred to the Blackman Trust in perpetuity. This cannot be voted on or refuted."

George Hannah nodded and took her hand. He looked almost ill, well, absolutely ill, but he had big interests eyeing the islands that *nobody* could keep as safe as the mainland.

Sure, part of the Pacific Fleet had moored at the base, but where paras were concerned, they didn't have much chance. She'd leave conventional fighting to the conventional fighters.

The Eastwoods had taught them a valuable lesson in their

years of using the Blackmans. Carry the biggest stick on the block, and don't take any guff.

And in this yard, they had the biggest stick. No, not yet. She needed a Whiskey. Just one. And with her, she'd bring a few more powerful paras. All she had to do was set the right seed out.

3 2

L eah found her dad at the table, trying to wrap boxes with the color newspaper comics. Who did that? "Hey, what're you doing?"

"I'm trying to relive my youth. We used to wrap *everything* with the funnies. Ember and Rai are gonna be *one* tomorrow. I got 'em a little something."

"That's *tomorrow*?" Wow. Whoops. Another thought hit her, too.

"Wow, a year since Great-Grandma died."

Her dad dropped his head. "Please. I'd consider it a huge favor if you didn't mention certain things on their birthday."

Right. One of the best things that ever happened to her mom and dad came on the heels of one of the worst things to ever happen in the world. "Sorry. Mum's the word. So... what'd you get them?"

Dexx raised his head with a smile. "A present." He tapped the box with a finger. "Got 'em *both* one."

"Yup. I see that." He was so proud, but wasn't this what parents were *supposed* to do? "Good going, Dad. We're all pretty impressed." Or something. She wasn't sure what she was supposed to say.

"Smart aleck. Put your finger here." He pointed to a spot with a fold of paper sticking out. "You back for something *other* than your siblings' birthday?"

"Well, I'm glad someone *told* me."

"Not actually our job."

It totally was!

"But you're welcome. So, what'd you find?" He slid the tape past her finger and pressed the paper flat.

Frankly, she'd been busy. Doing double duty between here and Alaska was keeping her on her toes, but...you know, she kinda liked it. "I think I found a way to use the ley stones with our magick."

"Ley stones." He frowned as if trying to search the sock drawer for... Leah didn't know. Pants.

"Yeah. Those things me and all of us have been studying with Wy?"

"Oh, right, right, riiiiight."

Her dad, sometimes. "Yeah, anyway. Those sigils—the markings—"

"I know what sigils are," he said grumpily.

How was she supposed to know? "—are like tuning forks kinda, and we can merge them with our wards."

"And that's a good idea, you think?"

"Do I?" Was he serious? "Oh, I don't know. Like, they were only placed there by *aliens* before dinosaurs roamed, but sure, maybe not. Anyway, *Dad,* if we merge our wards with those wards, we'd not only have more *power* but we'd—I think—be able to pick out individuals. Use them defensively and *offensively.*" She shrugged. "So that, you know, what happened to Chuck never happens to, you know, us."

"Now that would be a trick." He pushed the packages toward the middle of the table. "How did you find this out?"

"Okay, so…"

Leah became way too animated as she told Dexx about the ley stones and the Whiskey wards. Seemed there was a… resonance. That was the word she used. Resonance. Aw, she was growing so big.

"The problem is, I couldn't test it. Not really."

"But isn't this a magick you can work?"

"You'd think that, wouldn't you?" Leah bit the end of her thumb in frustration. "But no. There's something special with Mom, I guess? I don't know. Anyway. I tried. I failed."

She looked a lot like her mom when she got irritated. "You want to tell Mom?"

"Tell Mom what?" Paige walked in, tossing papers to the table. "What's that?" She motioned to the packages on the table.

Wasn't it *obvious*?

"See, Dad," Leah said, getting up with a smug look on her face, "I'm not the only one."

Paige moved her gaze back and forth. "Stop playing games. What are you two talking about?"

They could talk ley wards later. "The twin's birthday is tomorrow."

"Dammit." Paige's lips thinned and her jaw clenched.

"See?" Leah gave him the vindication-snark head wiggle. "I wasn't the only one."

"Again. Not my job to inform you when your family is having birthdays, but you're welcome. Got a little something, and if you're real nice, I'll put your name on the tag. *After* mine, of course."

She mock glared. "I'm a shoe-in for Mom of the Year. Again."

"Don't worry, babe. I heard this year they were going to hand out consolation prizes for all the not-winners."

"Shut up. What did we get them?"

"A present." Leah folded her arms and flatly stared Dexx.

He gave them a shit-eating grin. "Yup. A present."

Paige daggered them both with a slight smile as if telling them they were both jerks. "Have you at least told Tyler yet?"

"Of course. Got him working on a playlist right now." How many times had Dexx been on the receiving end of the last to know? Way too many. He could have a bit of fun with the kids' birthday. Besides, he was better with dates anyway. How much was he willing to bet that she'd completely forget their anniversary? For at least the first six years.

Paige scowled. "You're not even going to give me a clue?"

"Okay, fine." Dexx was such a sucker. "I asked Ollie and Michelle to get me a couple of those new smart phones. This way we can keep track of them, and they look cool next to the other kids in school, or wherever they are."

Paige leaned on the table with her fists. "I...I don't hate it. Are they holographic ones?"

"I don't know."

"I'll tack a tracer to them so we'll find them anywhere."

"Mom, that's like spying or something." Leah stared down at the phone she was still sharing with Mandy. "What if you did that to me? I'd be plenty pissed."

"That's not how you earn it." Dexx needed to see about getting her a new phone too. Her birthday had already passed, but maybe he could just *get* her one.

"I'd be upset." Leah's visible upset probably had less to do with the injustice of the tracker than the fact that she was still sharing. "I'd leave it because you'd be spying."

Okay. Maybe not.

Paige leaned toward Leah, fists still on the table. "You know they're turning *one*, right?"

Leah's expression folded. "Oh. I guess I just don't remember that. It seems like a long time ago."

"Not to us. Just a couple weeks, and presto, here we are." Dexx motioned to the packages.

"Oh, hey, Mom, I want to talk about using the ley stones around here."

"How many are around?" Paige went from stony, disapproving mom to interested research assistant in almost a heartbeat.

"A lot, and we're still finding more. They're everywhere."

"Define *everywhere,* Lee."

"I can't be sure, but I think global." Leah held out her hands. "Okay, so we've verified where we could. We didn't go into a dangerous situation because, you know, we didn't want to get yelled and stuff, but in all the places we looked along the ley lines, there are these stones. So, that's a thing."

Dexx watched the two interacting. Not too far in the past, Leah had been working on cars and not completely enjoying Paige's company. If he had the choice, he'd keep them on good terms. Cars could take the back seat to a mother-daughter relationship.

"And one we kinda already knew."

"Yup. But...verified, soooo..."

"So, what did you want to use the stones for?"

"Well—" Leah took a breath and shook her fingers out. "Okay. I think we can use them to work with our wards. I just don't know how."

Paige's eyes narrowed in thought. "Are you sure?"

"Not a hundred percent, but I think we can turn them into an offensive spell. One that could potentially hunt out bad guys when they're inside *our* boundaries. Not like bank robbers or anything, but like people who want to do bad things. I kind of want to try it on DoDO. Get some revenge for Chuck."

Dexx raised his brows. Leah wanted *revenge*? "Kind of putting the cart in front of the horse, aren't you? Shouldn't you find out if you *can* first?"

"This is all theory. It just seems like we can. It's kind of all tied up in magick theory and...it's stuff."

Dexx *could* have had this conversation with Leah, too, if he had his magick. The Mario demon had taken that from him. The jerk. Dexx got up from the table and let the two of them discuss magick. Good. They needed more common ground.

Dexx found Leslie in the garage, leaning against her car, staring at the driveway. "Hey, kitchen witch extraordinaire, you look like you haven't quite figured out that *one* taste in the soup."

"I just got a call. Phoebe Blackman. She just offered me...a job."

"A job?" Uh, what? "Don't you already have, like, a whole bunch of those?" Dexx took a folded cloth and ran it over Jackie's fender. He'd swear he could hear her imaginary purr.

"Yeah. But she's offering something nobody else is."

"Money?" That was a joke. Since the secession, real money was something of a joke. And ParaWest hadn't had the resources to make a currency yet.

"Peace and fucking quiet. I just have to do a job first."

Oh. That hurt a little. "Yeah. Like that's a thing anymore." What would they do without Leslie? She was a fixture in all of their families. What would the kids do if they separated? They were less like cousins and more like siblings right now. "There's no peace anywhere."

Leslie leveled a look at him. "Ever hear of a place called Hawaii? Seems like she has a whole island all to the Blackmans and she offered me a place to stay for as long as I want. Me and whoever I want to bring with me."

"Obviously Tru."

"Maybe." She sighed and nodded. "Maybe not."

That didn't sound good. Not even Leslie-not-good. "What are you saying?

"I'm sure that you and your spirit are perfectly happy together, always making decisions together and having the time of your *lives*, but Robin is a handful, even when he's cooperating, or I have him under control. Sometimes, I just need some space to run him. I don't have that here."

"I think you have us confused with the shifter haters we're currently at war with."

"You don't get it. Even here, I have things to deal with. Responsibilities, people demanding my time. People who want me to do stuff just because they want an extra pair of hands, or they won't because it's easier if *I* do it."

"Whoa, hold on a minute. *I* don't ask *anything* like that."

"No, Dexx. You would never *ask*."

That...stung.

"I don't know anything about cars. You'd probably ask if I did, though."

"You know, now that you mention it...I wouldn't ask even then. Can't be sure you wouldn't spit in my seat or down the gas tank or something."

"I would. I totally would." She smiled at Dexx. Not completely warm, but not just teeth either.

Was she asking for a heart-to-heart? He sucked at those. Recitation of *Star Wars*, and it was on. Real substance? Ouch. "I can't pretend I know what's going on in your head. I know I have a helluva time with Hattie, and she's generally on my side. But I can say this with certainty: you aren't alone, and you have a spectrum of experiences to draw on. You've got friends."

Leslie nodded. "I know." She smiled and held her arms out.

Dexx walked in and hugged her back, pushing out his

alpha will and sending some comfort to her. Being an alpha felt a lot like being a dad to adults.

Leslie gently broke away. "And there's something else."

Shit. The other shoe-drop.

"How do you know teaching the kids to fight is the right thing?"

Oh, damn. Whatever he'd thought she wanted to talk about, this was *way* down the list. He inhaled deep and let it go slow. "I don't. But Pea and me think about the same way on this. If they can't take care of themselves, then *we* have to do it. What's the right move ever? Before Leah, I never wanted kids. Ever. But when she came to live with us, something changed. Then I wanted them to be better than I was. That meant passing my knowledge and, well, that means fighting. You got them doing laundry and cooking and other stuff, so at least they have a rounded home education." Words fell out of his mouth. He had *zero* idea what was coming out next. But Leslie looked like she heard what she wanted.

She nodded. "I think I'm going to take Mandy and Tyler with me. Tru needs to stay here with Kammy until we make the islands free of danger."

"Free of danger? What's going on?" He gave her his just-kidding smile, and she gave him her flat stare.

"Other countries attacking."

"So, not a vacation."

"Not currently." She shook her head. "If anyone can handle it, Mandy and Tyler can."

He didn't know what kind of advice she was looking for. "I've been watching him. He's got a good head on his shoulders. Impetuous, brash, and eager. Roll 'em together, and I don't know. You got Tyler. Mandy is full of fire. You just got to bring it out. Annelle Rovoski found out the hard way."

Leslie nodded. "I just wanted to keep them away from all of this."

"Sure. We all did."

A whisper tickled his mind. "You might grow up soon after all."

That was enough.

"Thanks, Dexx." Leslie gave him a single-finger gun salute.

Awkward.

Tru, Mark, and the kids came back a couple of hours later, and the festivities began.

Somehow, Leslie had made *two* cakes, each a different flavor for the twins. The last of the frosting had just been dotted on the cakes when the twins burst through the door followed by a tired Mark and Tru.

They stopped when they saw decorations hung for another birthday.

"Whose birthday?" Rai asked, her eyes narrowing.

Dexx stood up with the rest of everyone else and started, "Sur..."

The rest picked up and helped finish, "...prise!"

Ember and Rai had both experienced birthday parties, but not their own. Ember let a mile-long smile crack his face, and Rai's eyes filled with tears.

"Happy birthday." Dexx held his arms open for either one to take the hint. They both slammed into him.

Hugs went all around.

Happy birthday, indeed.

They both enjoyed the phones which were super-cool holographic magick-enhanced versions of regular phones other normal kids got. Which meant that he'd have to totally get one of those for Leah. Great. More hugs went around.

Leslie brought out the cakes and Mandy lit the reused

candles Dexx had found, and Tyler magicked the singing of "Happy Birthday."

Dexx looked around at the rest of the table as they sang. This was the best birthday ever. Best family ever. They had problems, but still, they were amazing when they were together. He was proud to be the alpha. *I don't want more than I have right now, fat cat.*

She hmmed at the back of his mind.

The singing stopped and the good feeling lingered, gathered and flowed around the room. Margo and the pack, Paige and the Whiskeys. Perfect.

Paige smiled at the twins, raising the knife to cut into the first cake. "Okay. Let's start with Rai. What cake you want first?"

"How about one of each?"

Paige rocked her head to the side. "Yup. You're Dexx's kid for sure."

Rai laughed and shared a glance with Dexx.

Paige lost the smile and stared past them, confusion on her face.

It took Dexx a second to realize something was wrong.

The knife dropped and she collapsed.

The spell Tyler had woven broke. The sound of scraping chairs backing up followed by the mad rush of people moving to Paige filled the large room.

Dexx knelt next to her, one hand under her neck as the other gently touched her face. "Babe? Pea?" He listened for breath or a heartbeat but there was so much noise pollution preventing him from hearing *anything*.

"Stop moving! I can't hear."

Everyone went still, including Kammy.

Dexx returned his attention to Paige. "Babe? Come on, Pea, this isn't funny."

Nothing.

No heartbeat. No.
Paige was dead.

Paige looked around the cavern in confusion, the walls and the large, clear pool familiar to her. This was the cavern of shifter ancients. What was she doing back here?

Lights swirled over the water of the lake swooping and darting and dancing.

That was a neat light display, but…

If she was here, then this had to be some kind of judgment? Like the last time, though, before she'd been taken to the desert to find her way here. She didn't remember that this time. She'd been…

"It's the twins' birthday," she said out loud. She didn't know how to get out of there, but had to find a way. "Hello?"

A smooth deep voice rolled over the water. "You have been denied a spirit."

She let that statement roll over her.

The mammoth formed above the water, powerful and regal.

Okay. If she didn't get a shifter spirit, that was fine. She had discovered she really needed to learn to lead from the rear anyway. So, this would be…

A small voice reminded her that some people died when they were rejected by the spirit realm.

Well, she couldn't die.

Why?

Because she was Paige freakin' Whiskey. That was why. She had things to do. People to lead.

To their deaths.

She closed her eyes and tried to calm down.

"You are too dangerous to house another spirit," the mammoth said.

She kept her eyes closed as her reality crashed down around her. The migraines that had been going on for weeks after Dexx had bitten her? They made sense now.

"Against my blessing, many have been asked. None want to try."

Because he hadn't given his blessing?

"Cawli was powerful and you killed him easily."

Paige forced her eyes open and raked her hands through her braided hair. "I didn't kill him."

The mammoth shook his head. "A spirit is the responsibility of the host. You were lacking in your protection. We forbid you to have another."

A thought hit her. Spirits outlived humans because they were *spirits*. They were virtually immortal. "Spirits *can't* be killed by normal means."

"He is dead and you are not. There is none who will take you."

And as frustrating as it was to hear, she had to be okay with that, something she'd learned in law enforcement. She could do her best, be her best, present her best case, which wasn't much this time. This mammoth had the final say. "You're right. I didn't kill him. But I did put him in a situation that was dangerous to us both. He died valiantly saving...countless lives."

The mammoth raised his head, his hairy trunk splashing in the water, sending up glowing splashes. "Mah'se, would you take the bond with this human? You are, after all, suffering."

Paige licked her lips and looked around for the elk.

His image appeared majestically over the lake. He met her eye calmly and serenely, something pushing at her.

She didn't understand what he was trying to say, though,

so she held her ground and met his stare as calmly as she could.

He looked toward the mammoth. "I will not. She is powerful and unstable. I feel her connection to the bond mate I had chosen, but this one is too much. Her energies are in wild flux and I fear for my wellbeing."

The mammoth turned back to Paige as the great elk dissipated in a flash of blue sparkling light. "Mah'se is a very powerful spirit and the only one of the ancients willing to take your bond."

Well, this was it, then. "Okay. I am...sorry to have wasted your time." Would she be okay in the real world? Would she die? Would something else happen with this rejection? He raised his trunk like an arm. "According to the pact of the bite, you must be chosen or die."

Fear gripped her gut and refused to let go. She thought of all things she still had to do. Not just winning the war. Being with her kids. Watching them grow up. Helping them with their homework and their first dates. Walking any of her kids down the aisle.

"You have not been the first to be refused, Paige Whiskey, and you will not be the last."

What else could she do, though? What fact could she bring to this trial? What ancient or animal spirit could she plead to?

The mammoth's trunk rose. "I pronounce you—"

"Stop!"

Paige searched the cavern, trying to figure out who had spoken.

The voice was hard and commanding. Like the hardcore drill instructor in army movies in boot camp. A bright horse with a glowing horn on his head appeared over the lake.

"A unicorn?" Paige pressed her fingertips to her forehead.

Weren't there rules about those? Like, only virgins being able to hear them and stuff?

"I will take the bond."

Tentative relief rushed through her, though she wondered at what she was signing on for because...she didn't really know a lot about unicorns.

"Eos, you will not. I have spo—"

"You did not allow *me* to speak."

Oh. Well now, that was said with power.

The great mammoth let his trunk fall to the water.

"And now I do. I will take up the bond."

"There are reasons," the mammoth said, "that you are not allowed into the world of men."

Eos bowed his head, his horn nearly touching the water, reflecting his glow off the surface. "I do know this."

The mammoth released a whuff. "You feel a connection to this woman?"

"I do."

"You accept her bond?"

"I do."

"And her magick?"

Eos looked over at Paige and nodded, his long mane bouncing. "If she accepts mine."

He came with magick? "Uh." Maybe this *was* a bad idea, but...if it kept her alive to protect her kids? "I do?"

"If I die," Eos told the mammoth, "you may do with her as you wish."

"Now, wait a minute."

The mammoth nodded gravely.

The unicorn charged.

Dexx knelt next to Paige's body for several seconds. There was no sign of life, not even a skipping heartbeat. Bobby could heal injuries, but not death. The currents couldn't bring the dead back or they wouldn't.

Paige...couldn't be dead.

But the seconds ticked by.

"Isn't someone going to do CPR?" Leslie asked.

Right. Gods. What was *wrong* with them? Would CPR even work if the ancients had decided she wouldn't survive the magick bite he'd given her?

He reached for her chest, finding her diaphragm and going up her ribcage three fingers. He folded his hands in a daze.

Rai stared at him, her mouth open.

Leah reached for her mom's hand.

Bobby just stood there, staring like he didn't know what to do.

Ember took a step back, a knowing look sinking into his dark eyes as he frowned, his face twisting in pain.

Maybe she just needed a little time. Dexx could give her that. Keep her heart pumping, keep oxygen flowing to her brain.

Paige arched her back hard on the floor, her arms extended with a ragged inhale, then collapsed, unconscious.

Nobody moved, or barely breathed.

Dexx listened for the sounds of a heartbeat.

Paige took a breath, slow and shallow. Then another. Her heart ticked a beat like it was tired, and then picked up the pace.

Dexx closed his eyes and sat back. "She's alive."

That seemed to cut tight strings and the gathering sagged as one.

Leslie kicked into gear. "Get back, all of you. Pick her up. Let's get her to bed. Everyone else, finish your cake. Happy birthday. Your mom's alive. Whoo-hoo!" She threw imaginary confetti and then made a cheering gesture with her hands.

Nobody moved, not even Dexx.

"*Git.*" Leslie's Texan drawl came out loud and clear.

It was like that one sound unstuck the glue holding them all.

Paige wasn't much of a burden even without his shifter strength normally. What had happened? Had she been rejected? Was she going to live? Were there conditions?

Hattie rushed into his mind. *She has been chosen. I do not know by whom, but the spirits are not happy.*

Relief swelled through him. *You can't tell? Or they won't tell* you? Because that was a big distinction. *Was it Mah'se?* He could live with Mah'se taking Paige's bond. Hell, he'd tried to force that bond. Well, as far as he could.

I do not know.

The spirit elk would be a strong choice, and as a guardian, their two personalities should blend well together.

It worried him that Hattie of all people couldn't figure out who had accepted the bond.

If it wasn't Mah'se, who was it?

Dexx toed open their bedroom door and put Paige on the bed, pulling the covers over her. She still hadn't awakened, but she was breathing easily.

Can't you go through the process of elimination? Who was there before, and who isn't now?

Hattie smiled. She put all the snark a sabertooth could manage around those two huge fangs. *Spirits take a bond all the time. You want me to count the grass and find the one stalk that isn't there the next time I count?*

That's not what I'm asking for. I just want to know if she's going to be okay.

The simple way is to wait for her to wake. Then ask.

Dexx squeezed his eyes shut. *I kind of want to know now. How long will she be like this?*

The stronger the bond, the longer it will take. When the griffin took the bond, there was a considerable wait.

Only a day, remember?

Leslie opened the door and joined Dexx. "Robin says the one who took the bond was a strong one."

Dexx released his breath, almost like a sigh, but more manly. He scrubbed his fingers through his hair. "Of course it would be a strong one." So, sitting around being a nattering ninny wasn't going to help at all. "Does Robin know who or what it is?"

"Nope." Leslie shrugged, stepping back to push kids back out of the room with her butt. "The whole spirit plane is being pretty hush-hush over it, I guess."

"Super-slug? Power crab? There can't be so many powerful shifters that we can't figure this out."

"Is that your only concern? Who her bond is?"

"No." Well, kinda. He needed to know who he'd have to

deal with in the pack, which Paige would be a part of again. Would he need to grow his numbers even more to allow this one in? That'd been the reason he'd been forced to take on more shifters into his pack when Leslie had been chosen. Or was Hattie strong enough to handle whoever'd joined them? "It's a steaming pile of shit. Why right now? I mean c'mon, Les. Why wait until the world is *right* on the edge, then pow, give it a little push?"

"Because they know you'll try to make some snarky comment and play it off. Maybe they want to see what you do."

"You aren't helping."

"Okay," Leslie said, slapping her hands against her thighs, her eyes flashing amber. "Maybe this has absolutely nothing to do with *you,* so maybe you should just shut up and *wait* with the rest of us."

Dexx bit off his reply and took in a deep breath. "You were out for a day. We need to expect Pea to be down for at least that long. We got a super-secret shifter, and I have a feeling it's not a slug. Although that's what she deserves. Wanting another shifter bond. That's just... I don't know. I'm a little concerned."

"We all are." Leslie put her hand on Dexx's shoulder. "Just have faith. Pea will do what she has to. In the meantime, let's go finish a birthday party because Paige isn't dead and...huzzah!"

She was right. He was worrying to worry. Paige was going to be fine. They were going to be fine.

They just needed to start winning some freaking battles.

Leslie's phone buzzed in her pocket as they headed down the stairs, the kids fighting with each other verbally and physically.

"Someone important?" Dexx asked. It was so *nice* to have phones again. "Could be your boyfriend for a booty call."

She looked at the screen and then at Dexx. "Could be *yours*, and he's calling me because you won't answer your phone."

Leslie always had a comeback.

She answered the call, but didn't put it on holographic display. Maybe it wasn't that kind of phone. "Hey, I'm kind of in the middle of something important. Could you—" Leslie stopped talking and stood in the middle of the staircase, listening and nodding, her expression grim.

Dexx plied his super-hearing, but he couldn't hear the other side. Leslie must have the volume down a lot.

"I need an hour. I have some goodbyes to make."

Dexx stood up. "Les, what did you do?"

Leslie closed the screen and put the phone away. "I told you. I got an offer. I just took it."

What? "Not now. We have problems right here. *Pea* needs you." He pointed toward the room they just left.

"Too bad the *entire* world doesn't give two shits about us and our problems. Phoebe needs my help and we're going."

Why did it sound so final? "Where?"

"Hawaii." Leslie turned around and left the room.

Bussemi watched the Whiskey witch fall to the kitchen floor through his own eyes, though he still lacked any sort of control.

"The woman is dead." The demon closed the scry pool and stood. "The time is now. I will assemble every one of my forces. We will remove the paras, and take the world."

Remember. I get—

"Nobody cares what the deal *was*," the bahlrok sneered. "I do not need you any longer." The demon shut Bussemi off from his own body but let him watch the world through his own eyes.

Bussemi pounded at the walls of his mind, trying to break through, to use the power he once held. That power had faded and had been added to the beast. Bussemi was a ghost living in a body that was no longer his.

The beast opened a portal to their chambers in the Vatican, retrieving a deep red cloak. Picking up his staff, he walked from the room and past the guards stationed there.

The two jogged a step to keep up with the old man.

The beast had years of practice with the old man's voice. There wasn't anyone alive in millennia who would have even known the difference, if there was any. "Call every single member of the Office. The paras are weak, and we move now."

"Yes, sir. Should we notify their president?"

"Do feel free. We are allies, are we not? Invite the foreign governments to start their attacks. Tonight, we take the para threat and destroy it."

"Yes, sir." Both guards split to take care of their orders.

Bussemi watched the world pass by. He could wish the paras put up a fight and last for days.

But there was no way out for Bussemi. He'd sealed his fate and this was it.

It was not the revenge he'd pictured it to be.

Dexx got a call moments later. "Hey, Chuck. Everything all right?"

"No. General Saul just called. We are being invaded in force. I need you to come to the base and take command of a company."

Hadn't the president *just said* he'd wanted peace? "I think we should think about this for a minute. The last group of *soldiers* I had all went crazy and we lost the entire Denver metro area."

Chuck paused on the other end. "Do this. We lost thirteen scouts, and before each one went dead, they said they saw DoDO uniforms."

Dexx let his head fall. "It's my kids' birth—" *Fuck*. Way to stick his foot in his mouth. "I think Paige was just chosen. She's unconscious. I've made her as comfortable as she would be awake. I don't know how long she'll be out."

"It will take as long as it takes. There's nothing you can do. But you *can* take command and destroy the people who took my family."

Okay. That was a heavy burden.

"Dexx, I have been ordered elsewhere."

"Why? You're the best leader we got—"

"By an alpha higher than me. I can't go against her wishes. And I don't particularly enjoy the thought of pushing you to take command."

Dexx breathed in. He could do this. He just had to work smarter, use the assets of his team. Find a plan, follow the plan.

"Dexx, I need this of you."

He couldn't really ignore that plea, could he?

"You get to be a captain's rank. Should be something you're used to."

"I don't need a fancy title."

"Let me put it this way. I'm the general. You're a captain in my command. And I've just given you an order. Now, move."

"What do you need?"

"We think the *entire* DoDO fighting force is massing outside of Denver. You destroy those, and you effectively destroy one of the threats to our existence."

That was something Dexx liked the sound of. "Such a sweet-talker." Dollars to doughnuts, Bussemi wouldn't be there. With Sir Sayyid and Agent Angela Hopkirk gone, DoDO'd lost a significant part of their command structure, but they still had Director Harris.

"And we have a surprise for you."

Dexx could hardly wait. "And that is?"

"Get here posthaste. And I'm sorry I ruined the birthday party." The phone clicked off.

Dexx could have sworn he heard a catch in the man's voice. Chuck couldn't be blamed for having raw feelings.

Dexx ran up to their bedroom really quick to check on Paige. He touched Paige's cheek. "I have to go. I'm going to take DoDO down for good." With a plan. He'd go in, assess, and come up with a plan that didn't involve self-sacrifice, dying, or defeat. "I love you."

He wouldn't need Jackie, so he left his keys in the *shamiyir* the crystal had mended. It still felt empty, so he'd filled it with keys.

"Take care of her for me."

When he made it downstairs, his door witch hadn't arrived yet, so he went to the kitchen, following the sounds of the kids.

They were eating cake, but it was a pretty sad little party. "Hey, guys. Why the long faces?"

Leah tipped her head toward the stairs. "Aunt Leslie's taking Tyler and Mandy somewhere."

"Yeah. I heard. Good news is you guys get to hang out here."

Kate swished her hair. "She isn't being truthful. I can tell *you* aren't either."

Dang kid was too smart by half. And he hadn't said anything yet. "Well, I *do* have to go take care of something. But it shouldn't take too long." Hopefully.

"You aren't going to have cake? Ember thinks you'll like it." Leah pointed her fork to the mostly missing cake with the deep purple frosting.

"I'll have some when I get back." Dexx loved sugar, but wasn't a fan of cake. "Don't want to be heaving a food baby around." And it would taste like ash if he had to pretend to have fun in front of the kids. "Okay guys, sorry for busting up the festivities, but I have to go."

Leah was the first in line for a hug. She held on tight.

Dexx bent a little to gather the twins. Ember and Rai came in together and he stood, both of them clinging.

Rai whispered in his ear. "Tell us where you're going. We can help."

Dexx only shook his head.

Leslie watched him get ready. She inclined her head, saying her own goodbye silently.

Tell Robin to watch their six, he told Hattie. *She better be okay.*

Hattie nodded and her spirit went to the Time Before.

Dexx made sure he had his *ma'a'shed* and then walked down the long hall to the front door, stepping onto the porch to await his ride.

Leslie met the Blackman witch on the back porch with Mandy and Tyler. Tru was pissed and he had every right to be. She'd accepted Phoebe's offer without consulting him, and now she had their two oldest going into a warzone. She'd watched this fight between Paige and Dexx less than a year ago, and here she was following in her sister's footsteps. She'd have killed people for doing less to her kids.

"Hi, I'm Maria." The girl couldn't be any more than fourteen or fifteen. Just older than Man-Pan. This world was fucked for making kids fight.

"Take us to Phoebe." She didn't trust her voice to say more.

Maria opened a doorway and gestured for Leslie to step through.

Phoebe Blackman stood at a railing on the porch of a ranch-style house, watching the sun set over the ocean. "Thank you for coming. Because of you, our chances just increased."

Leslie released a long breath, hoping she hadn't just made the biggest mistake of her kids' lives. "You know my son and daughter? Tyler and Mandy."

"I think I've seen them, but never been introduced. I would give you the tour, but the fleets are already engaged. They need your help immediately."

Leslie raised her chin. If they were going to have *any* peace, they'd have to make it, and that's exactly what she intended to do. She spoke in the smallest whisper. "Show us where."

34

Tyler crouched behind the scrap of what used to be a car.

The Blackman witch, Andrea, had taken him and a bunch of other people to a city somewhere. They had to still be in Hawaii because it was just as warm as when they showed up the night before.

His mom and sister were somewhere, but the bad guys sent a couple rockets in and they had to split up.

The sky was getting light on the one side, so that meant sunlight would soon help them see. Although before they got separated, Mandy and his mom had done a pretty good job making it easy to see.

"Hey, kid, move back here. You don't want to get your head blown off." The soldier pulled at Tyler's shoulder.

"Oh, sorry." Tyler slipped back a little farther. "Do you think they know where we are?"

"They know we're here. Just can't pinpoint us because the fire is throwing off the infrared."

Tyler nodded. Dexx had told him how Hattie could see

things with heat, so that was pretty easy to understand, but not visualize. "And they have us pinned down, right, sir?"

"I'm a petty officer. We work for a living."

"Petty officer?" Try as he would, he couldn't see where the bad guys were. If he could see them, he could pulse a blast at them. If he could just keep them distracted for a few moments he could get them to a better hiding spot.

"First Class Naval Aircrewman. We operated radar and such."

Tyler grinned. "Really? Radar? That's co—" Tyler flinched back as several rounds of machine gun fire smacked into the ground around them. One or two hit the ground close to the car, but behind them.

"They're zeroing in on us. We have to go." The petty officer kept his hand constantly on his helmet, pressing down.

Shadows in the dark moved, but it could have been his imagination. The moments of gunfire and bullets ricocheting into the dark wasn't, however.

The guy was scared. *Tyler* was scared. But he'd gone up against demons before. Mostly sort of from the side, but he'd done it.

"We, uh, we can't go. They have the high ground." The aircrewman pointed to the building right about the second floor.

"I used to play a lot of hide-and-seek and capture the flag and stuff with my uncle."

"So? This is real life. You can get killed out here."

"That's what my uncle said. You know what he taught us when you don't have *the high ground*?"

The petty officer put a falsely patient look, like his mom did right before she made him do the dishes. "No. What did he *teach* you?"

They pulled back as a smattering of bullets bounced off the pavement, one thunking into the shield car.

Tyler swallowed heavily. Finally, he realized his mom had brought him into a warzone.

"He said bring the high ground down." Tyler closed his eyes and made an image in his head of what the building looked like. Then he drew in a deep breath and hummed. He had to start it low and work higher from there. When he found the right note, he could pour on the power. Then the building would fall. Simple.

At first nothing happened. Not a big surprise since he hadn't quite found the right note. When he hit the right pitch, he could *see* the outline of the building in his mind, like if he had his eyes open. As soon as he felt it, he raised the power. Hard and fast. Just like Dexx told him.

The car shifted away from the blast and the building shook like a giant rammed it.

Dust and broken windows rained down into the street and alley.

He took another breath, holding the right pitch in his mind and blasted again. This time the walls cracked, and it fell partly into the building on the far side.

Anyone in *that* particular building would be holding on to anything nailed down to keep their feet.

Tyler sat back and smiled at the Navy guy. "See? Make it *not* the high ground."

The guy swallowed hard and stared at the building. "Holy shit."

"Nah. It's a gift, but it's not religious."

"How did you do that?"

"It's a gift. Magick. I'm a bard."

"Isn't that a singer or something?"

"Not when you're a Whiskey."

Leslie flew as high as she could and still make out roads and vehicles. And invaders.

The first rockets that had split Tyler and her apart had been dealt with.

With extreme prejudice.

Mandy had gone missing just after that, and Leslie had to hope she was okay, or things might dissolve soon after.

Kammy, can you hear me? She sent out the call every few minutes, just in case her little boy could help with communication. Also, Kammy's voice had been more constant in her head than Robin's had been for the past few years

She scored the water for enemy soldiers.

Flying as an albatross, she'd been nearly undetectable.

She went for a little more height. She needed her magick and that only came in human form. After she'd gained enough altitude, she shifted to her human form and went into freefall.

She called air and lightning and struck at the boats carrying soldiers and small support boats with machine guns.

She shifted back to an albatross, easily finding an air current to ride.

The boats were sinking. She didn't have time to sit around and watch. It wasn't like watching the *Titanic* go down, but it wasn't super-fast either. Two small boats drifted too close together and sank as one.

A third, sleek boat raced for the shore, filled with more soldiers. She regained her altitude, and then transformed again, sending lightning to the railing and through the engine to the fuel tank. The explosion was intense.

She fell a thousand feet, maybe more, then shifted back into a bird. A seagull this time, speeding toward the ground and the Blackman witches sending troops wherever they were needed most.

She landed gracefully, taking a breath. She'd been in the air most of the night, blasting everything she didn't recognize.

That had been a problem, when the night hid the invasion force as well as it had hidden her, and several times she'd had to give her position away to verify her targets on the ground.

"That's the last of that wave."

Phoebe stood in a makeshift tent just on the side of a larger building they'd managed to secure early on in the fight. "The sunrise should be in about an hour. General Ashe said the support went back to the fleet."

Did that mean they'd won?

Phoebe directed her coven to open doors, sending groups of soldiers out into the pre-dawn night.

Leslie sat on an overturned barrel. "I'm out there all by myself." And she was winning without any DoDO devices limiting her shift. "The Chinese sent regular humans. Why would they do that?"

"Simple. We're outnumbered. Probably by thousands, so they thought they had the advantage. Also, they have a lot of ammunition."

Most of which was now at the bottom of the ocean.

Phoebe smiled at Leslie. "I'm glad you're here. You single-handedly swayed the odds considerably. *You.* All by yourself."

"I did." And that bugged her. The enemy had access to way more people, way more technology. As far as she knew, spirits didn't care if the human they chose to bond with was of high moral standard or not. Cooper McCree and all his buddies were proof of that.

An imposing man joined Leslie and Phoebe.

"Ah, General," Phoebe said. "I think we're—"

"It's Admiral. Not General."

Phoebe shook her head. "I don't see the difference."

"It's a rather large difference, but since gunfire is being exchanged, you can just call me Hastings."

"Fine. *Hastings*."

Leslie chuckled.

"I think they're going to do something. Something we don't expect."

Leslie stood from her seat and went to find water. Let them talk about how to kill people.

Every time she ever fought demons or people, she hadn't had a choice. This was the first time she'd *looked* for someone to fight, to *kill*. Normal humans.

Maybe Man-Pan had been right. War on the invasion-level scale was too much. Why was that every government's response to other governments? Kill the other guy.

Blessed Mother, she hoped the kids were okay out there.

She found the stack of water bottles still in the shrink wrap in the supply tent.

She snagged one, ripped the top off, and angry-chugged.

All for a place to relax her guard and let Robin be a griffin.

Mandy stood at the shore, watching the waves come in. The tide was almost nonexistent, but the waves rolled in exactly like it did Troutdale.

The morning sun was bright and warm, and inviting.

The exact opposite of how her insides roiled.

Her mom and Phoebe and the rest of them had expectations of her. Expectations that she might not be able to carry out.

Honolulu spread out behind her, a place she'd read about and watched on TV. It looked great, but it felt like... She didn't know, but it wasn't happy.

She'd been told the invaders were either Chinese or Koreans, and she was supposed to kill without remorse.

Could she do that? Annelle Rovoski had been a special case. Her uncle had been in danger and she had been...*so mad.*

In the end she didn't think she—

The waves that had been so steady stumbled.

Mandy cast her gaze out toward the big breakers. They seemed fine, but unnatural bubbles rose closer to shore.

At first, she didn't move. Elementals could cause that. She swallowed hard.

She wasn't Leah, or Tyler, or the twins. They were all fighters, and she'd tried to stay away from anything resembling a fight, but it had found her.

Water slid from something rising from the ocean floor. At first her mind flew to Godzilla rising, so as the head came from the water she had trouble recognizing what she was seeing.

It wasn't one head. It was *two*. And as they came out, pieces fit together.

Dogs. Two of them, and massive things. They might not have been Godzilla, but they weren't sweet puppies.

Mandy started backing up. Her urge to run warred with her urge to stand still and remain unseen.

The pair of monster dogs stood twenty feet or so at the shoulder, and their eyes were a deep black. They walked up the surf to the beach and flanked Mandy, who stood still, but quivered.

Were they the enemy? Were they friends?

The closer dog lunged at her, jaws wide with large teeth.

Mandy dodged out of the way and felt her fire form and spear out.

The flame took the dog-beast in the mouth and blew out

the back of its head. The beast fell, wreathed in oily black smoke.

The other dog stood for a moment, staring down at its buddy.

Mandy's moment of hesitation was gone. She held her fire in her hand, ready to unleash again. In all the years she'd played with the fire, she had never once used it as a missile, or an explosive device.

Her fire had just done something she'd never practiced.

That scared her more than the dogs.

The monster growled, deep and menacing. The dry sand farther up the beach vibrated into little sand rivulets, and messed with her eyes.

She swung her fire out and collared the dog with flames and tightened. The monster's head fell to the ground a moment before the body joined it.

"Oh, crap. Oh, really big *heaps* of crap." Dexx and Leslie had the market on creative swearing, so Mandy had a lot of practicing to get to their level. She could start—

She was rambling in her head. She knew it. But things stopped making sense as soon as the dogs had come up from the waves.

She backed up, finally able to move.

More things split from the water, rising to the land.

In the distance, little dots moved along the horizon. Boats. Soldiers were coming.

Mandy let her fire wreathe her body, the flames comforting her in a way.

Another dog-thing and a man emerged from the water.

She didn't wait for the dog to hit land. She formed her fire into a blade and cut the thing in half. She poured power into the heat, burning the thing from the inside out. The pieces turned to ash as it fell over.

She hesitated burning the man as he walked closer. He was naked, like all shifters were.

"That's not a man. He's not a person. He's not a real person."

He was muscular and lean, and his smile was gleaming white against his wet slicked-back hair. He could have been a model on a beach shoot. He reached out his hand, palm up.

He didn't seem threatening. He wouldn't hurt anyone.

"He's not a person. He's a bad guy. Don't believe him." It wasn't working. He was unarmed. He wasn't *doing* anything threatening.

The man took another few steps up the beach. He lost his smile and turned to look behind him. He turned back to Mandy and waved his hands in front of him in the universal plea for non-aggression. He started talking rapidly and pointing behind him.

He said one word over and over though. "Kaiju."

Mandy shook her head. "What? I don't understand you." If only *someone* else was there. Even Tyler. He would know what to do.

She liked to hang out with her friends. It was Tyler and Uncle Dexx who liked to fight. Except when Tyler let her secrets out. She liked Josh. *Still* liked Josh, but he said he wouldn't tell, then he made fun of her, told people, and she—

The man walking up the beach did the *exact* thing Tyler did on that day—the hand motions and everything.

The man's eyes went flat and he began to make motions with his hands.

Mandy pushed her hands out in front of her, then spread them apart keeping them linked with fire. The expanding arc burst forward like a shot. It even boomed like thunder as it burned through the air.

The man exploded, spraying the water with bits.

She could have barfed.

She held on as she looked out and the boats were nearer.

A trail of smoke left one of them in a hurry. A rocket. She could deal with those.

She followed the smoke in the sky and found the rocket zooming to the beach, or maybe to the city.

It didn't matter. She sent a fireball to intercept the incoming missile. It exploded with noisy satisfaction.

The wave spilt again and a submarine on wheels drove out.

"Oh, crap." Mandy ran from the beach looking over her shoulder.

Doors flopped open and people swarmed out. Men and women, all weaving spells.

Lightning, fire, and earth spells sped toward Honolulu, destruction following.

Tyler led a group of over fifty soldiers. By ones and twos he gathered a force.

His original four or five guys kept the rest in line, but really, what was he doing leading a bunch of *trained* soldiers?

The sun had just crested the horizon, and soft thuds drew his attention. "Guys, I think something is going on over there." He pointed past the last wall of buildings before it gave way to picturesque beaches.

"Can't be. That's just beach over there." The Navy petty officer had been the guy to relay the messages to the group and help Tyler rack up enemy kills.

He tried not to think about the guys he couldn't help anymore. He really needed to talk with Uncle Dexx. That little nervous ball in his gut was really tight.

"The beach is there?"

Petty Officer nodded. "Yeah. I been through here with my buds a lot the past couple months."

"I don't want to sound like a total dumb kid here, but why aren't we defending the beach?"

"Because they're all over in the city already. Duh."

"It sort of seems like there aren't a whole lot here. Shouldn't we be like, in way more battles than the two or four people teams we've found?" He'd seen plenty of TV. And Dexx. If he wanted to draw attention away from something important, he'd do something just like that.

"I'm going to the beach. Can you guys spread out and stay hidden?"

Navy Guy made motions and whispered instructions to his friends.

The soldiers crouched and soon it was just them again. "Wow. That's pretty cool—"

Several more booms caught his attention. Okay, that wasn't his imagination. He was going to the beach.

He ran forward, hoping anyone with a gun couldn't target him well. He rounded the last of the buildings and stopped. Broken palm trees and sand led to the actual beach and dead whales littered the beach. As he looked, his brain filled in details.

Those weren't whales, and the beach wasn't empty. A person stood out there. Fire erupted and streaked into the sky. A boom meant a rocket had exploded.

Mandy was down there. "Come on, guys, let's go get her."

Then a submarine *drove* up the surf to the sand and the floors fell away and people jumped out and sent lightning and fireballs.

"Crappy balls. Shoot those guys."

35

Bussemi's body shuffled without his permission down the long hallway. The bahlrok would personally be leading the entire fighting DoDO force.

His first-in-command, Director Harris, had inherited the post, and from what Bussemi knew of the man, things would not go entirely well. There was a reason he'd only managed to make it partway to the top.

They were only a distraction anyway. The bahlrok had made the organization as a means to an end. Now that end was at hand.

"The spies have the target at Echo location. He has a total of three hundred sixty soldiers under his command, and he is the only para."

"Where are the secondary targets?"

Bussemi would have blinked in shock if he were more than an unwilling passenger. The bahlrok had *secondary* targets? When did *that* happen? Had he been pushed into the blackness?

Things were far more degraded than he'd thought, but there was absolutely nothing he could do about it. Would he honor their agreement and give him Dexx Colt's body? He couldn't even communicate with the beast until he had permission.

Director Harris began to answer.

The world stopped around Bussemi and the hallway lit with an unnaturally bright light and in the center, a woman floated. The herald of the *Other*.

"Hold."

The bahlrok stopped, unable to disobey. "Release me," the demon demanded.

The woman ignored him, but spoke to Bussemi unhurriedly. "You are free to move against him. Ghir'Uuhz, your time has come."

If this was the entity Busemmi knew only as the *Other*, then the woman was a mortal being used as a herald. He knew nothing more than that, though. Bussemi and the bahlrok had tried, of course. Many had been caught and tortured, and spells had been placed upon them, but the *Other* had proven resiliently resistant to discovery.

The bahlrok smiled as the herald vanished, and let the world resume as though it never were.

Bussemi smiled, too. He finally knew the monster's name: Ghir'Uuhz.

It was time to turn the tables.

Dexx waited in front of his scraggly band of troops.

They stood at rigid attention, all of them a carbon copy of the last.

He inhaled deep and scrubbed his hand though his hair.

Okay, they weren't scraggly. They were perfect examples of military training. Every single soldier was armed to the teeth and loaded with the explosive tips of the missiles they'd captured in Denver. Their eyes held death for anything in front of them. Hopefully they hadn't gone to Stormtrooper Academy.

The only good news was Alwyn had managed to talk someone into reassigning him to Dexx's command.

Dexx waved one of the soldiers over.

He obeyed immediately, and stopped three paces away. "Private First Class reporting for duty, *sir*."

Damn. He had *those* guys. "You nervous?" The kid's scent spiked with fear.

"Sir, no sir. Sir, we are locked and loaded and ready for action, *sir*."

"Awesome. Look at me."

The soldier obeyed and for the first time his face matched his scent.

"Good. Now that we have that covered, you aren't going to fight like this are you? In neat rows."

The kid shook his head. "Sir, no sir."

"Knock that shit off. I'm not a *sir*, no matter *what* that other guy said. I'm Dexx, and if you want to survive, we're going to do this smart. And that means you run and hide and plink at good targets. You read?"

"Sir, the private does not."

Dexx opened his mouth to explain, and Derrick stood in front of him.

"You ready? The report is Denver is wiped out. They're mobilizing westward. The report has them sweeping through the downtown area. No paras."

Dexx shook his head. "No, we're not—"

The doorway snapped open wide enough for ten across to fit through.

Dexx closed his eyes. Well, at least they had a plan this time. "Okay," he nearly whispered. "Kid, I want you to stay near me for comms. Move out."

The private made a motion and as one the entire battle group moved. As they closed in on the gate, they shrank together and fit through cleanly.

Death waited on the other side.

Dexx and Alwyn were the last two through, but Derrick didn't come through with them. Three hundred sixty-one guys were on their own. They had to repel the might of the feds and supposedly the Chinese all by their lonesome. Small favors had them fighting humans only. If DoDO was around, the story would be very different. They could use mundane tactics, and mundane solutions.

Dexx looked around, the sun still climbing to the noonday peak, just coming to the top of the tallest trees in the area. Houses dotted the residential street and a four-story building rested on the corner of a larger road intersecting the small street.

It looked like a lot of Denver Metro, except there were no people to clutter the city. It was quiet. Too quiet for the houses crammed together. At least there was plenty of cover behind cars and trees and houses.

"Here goes nothin'." Dexx grabbed Alwyn's shoulder. "Find cover. Up high if you can." To the private he said, "Get these placed around. Remember, we want maximum carnage with *no losses*. Then, get them out of sight. I'll go scout around and lead bad guys back here. Be ready. Oh, the first person to shoot a sabertoothed cat gets eaten by said cat. Is that clear?"

The soldier nodded and went to relay orders.

Dexx shifted and ran toward the buildings of downtown Denver. Ground moved fast under Hattie's paws. She crossed streets and parking lots, all quiet, and for the most part intact.

Where are the vampires? Denver should have been swarming with them. Or at least pushed ahead of the sweep.

Hattie slowed as the buildings became taller, and the streets wider. The city had a completely different feel without people to make it a congested feast for vampires.

They stopped when they had a large round hotel in front of them. Not quite downtown, but it was close.

Vehicles. Not civilian with the roar of diesel powerplants. He'd found Walton's soldiers. Well, that's what he'd come for.

The air changed and a spell formed. Dexx leapt to the back side of the hotel.

The first shot smacked the ground to his side, followed by a crack of thunder. The gun had to be a fifty caliber. Debris from the hotel crashed to the ground.

Dexx would have shivered, but Hattie had control. That shot could have torn him in two. Maybe.

He felt more of the spells forming, lightning being the go-to attack.

Let's go. They had the enemy's attention. Now to get them to follow, but that shouldn't be a problem.

As fast as the ground moved when they into the city, it *blurred* on the way back.

Whoever was back there hounded him as he headed back to the trap.

Hopefully, the entirety of DoDO would come out and stand still for an incoming barrage of bullets. Might as well wish for a set of wings, too.

The sounds of vehicles in pursuit coming from all directions pricked his ears.

He made the final straight back to his guys when DoDO agents poured through doorways in front of him. Damn it all to hell, DoDO wasn't supposed to be in Denver. All the paras were defending the border fort somewhere else.

They had a mole in the ParaWest army.

Spells ricocheted from all directions. Fireballs and ice and lightning seemed to have no target, except the ground.

Dexx ran through houses and under trees using as much cover as he could to deflect spells and elemental attacks.

He found the smallish street and tore off toward his guys waving his arms. "Guns up! Right behind me."

A fireball hit a yard of long brown grass and lit the yard on fire. Dammit, that would be a signal soon.

Small arms began to return fire. Lightning speared into the DoDO ranks. Well, at least one of them. The rest weren't visible yet.

Dexx shifted and turned on a dime to attack the closest DoDO agent.

The woman's eyes bulged as the big animal that shouldn't move so fast slammed a paw to her face and crushed her to the ground. She might live.

Dexx dodged back and forth as the fog of war set in.

The yard that caught fire lit the house and smoke rolled high into the air.

DoDO and foreign fighters, the Chinese, closed ranks, creating a free-for-all. All he could hope for now was his guys took out as many as possible.

Alwyn kept up his attack from wherever he'd found his high ground, and he couldn't tell if his own guys had a good shot at anything.

They must have, because bullets and spells reduced significantly.

Dexx took cover in a shallow ditch and shifted back to human once the fire had been suppressed.

Every few seconds, a burst of shots went off on one side or the other.

Oh good, they'd discovered trench warfare again.

Dexx felt the lightning form. Saw it materialize above him. He could have pointed exactly to the person forming the spell. But he couldn't have done anything about it. The final weave of the spell completed, cut the power, and released the bolt.

The world turned dark in contrast to the light of the form that appeared above him. The lightning stopped in a long, jagged arc aiming straight at him.

"He comes. In a body not his, he comes. Prepare yourself for the end. One will survive the day, the other will know the permanence of death. He comes, prepare yourself. Ahkuun, the first brother, comes."

"Molly Hammond?" There was *definitely* a woman in the bright center of the flare.

The figure seemed to hang in the air and stare at him, then nodded once. "You will fail, or you will succeed. Today."

The flare darkened and the world started again. The bolt of lightning struck the flare and bounced away, exploding against the tactical gear of an agent. The feet smoked at the ankles, but the body didn't exist.

The first brother? Oh crap, Bussemi was on his way? Oh, *fuck*.

Dexx shifted and ran toward his camp as a sabertoothed cat, his mind scrambling for a plan that didn't involve dying alone. *We have the* ma'a'shed, *but the last time we went toe to toe, he had us.*

Hattie didn't send waves of confidence. *We will stand. We will win or we will not.*

Yeah. Molly said that much. How do we fight him?

Cub, stop. Change us to your form and stand ready.

We need a plan. Because doing the same thing over and over again wasn't helping.

Cub. Hattie didn't leave room for argument. The cat shifted and Dexx stood for a heartbeat and pulled the *ma'a'shed*. Turning it into a *mavet* seemed so simple compared to when he first transformed it.

He swung the blade through spells, and somehow bullets went around him. So many seemed to pelt the ground around him, or houses behind him.

The troop carrier vehicles had finally caught them. Chinese poured out of carriers, some not even waiting to disembark before shooting.

Dexx swung through every spell he saw coming, but somehow bullets weren't a thing.

Hattie sat down in his mind, very calm, and very still. *Go, cub. You take the spell casters. I have the others.*

What the hell did that mean?

For as much cover as his guys had, the feds and their friends had as much cover. They hid behind parked cars and laid in ditches and hid behind houses.

Fireballs hit wooden structures and soon smoke signals went up in multiple places.

If there were vamps in the city, the call to dinner had been made.

Then he felt the change in the air. The sudden pressure from ley magick mixed with natural and unnatural magicks.

The bahlrok had arrived.

"Dexx Colt." The voice rang out along the city and made the spells and automatic gunfire seem like whispers in a library.

Dexx hid behind a sizeable tree. *Fuckohfuckohfuckohfuck.*

"Dexx Colt, now is the time to face me." That voice sounded familiar in a way some dreams feel familiar, like a place he should have known. But that wasn't the voice he remembered from Bussemi.

He chanced a look around the tree. The man was tall, over six feet and broad in the shoulders.

That was his first brother. Ahkuun, simply translated meant *forked stick*. Memories flooded him as the name and the face came together.

He'd leaned evil from the very start and Dexx'd leaned the other way. He held Bussemi's staff in his hand, and planted it into the ground.

An expanding ring of force ripped through the soldiers on both sides. Then the explosives detonated. Anyone on the ground ceased moving. Whether they were dead or very, very calm was yet to be seen.

Had Dexx been the only survivor?

Dexx withstood the blast, Hattie's protection seemed to pass that around them like the had been moments before.

Nothing moved. Nobody else around. He was alone with Bussemi, and his…bahlrok.

The one silver lining to all of it seemed to be he lost three hundred soldiers. China may have lost thousands.

He backed around the tree again, scared shitless.

"Face me or watch your family die. I will kill them all. I have the power. The *Other* has pulled your protection, and now is the time."

Dexx let the convulsion of fear ripple through him, squeezing his stomach painfully, then forced himself to relax.

Molly had told him to prepare. Fine.

What did he have *this time* that he hadn't before?

Well, he had the power of a pack, and Robin was still a part of that pack. Paige's new shifter was part of it. He had more power as a shifter this time.

Okay. Great. What else?

He wasn't alone. He had people.

Yeah, and they were dying. What else?

He had allies. Powerful allies, like an angel.

Who wasn't there. What else? He needed something. He wasn't *dying* there. What else did he have?

Nothing.

This time he had all he needed. Himself.

He stepped from behind his tree and let his sword hang casually at his side. "Someone call for an ass-whooping?"

"Cavalier in the face of the final death. You will be a suitable host." He stroked the *kadu* at his neck.

Dexx felt the pull like fine iron to a magnet. His arm raised without his permission. Dammit. He lowered his hand with effort.

"The thing I will make you experience. For*ever*."

We might not win, but please tell me we can make it expensive to win. Be the alpha, and his cost will be high.

Good enough. He raised his sword and began to walk forward.

Tyler scoured the beach, arcing the wave of sound toward Mandy.

She might be a girl, but sometimes she was kind of smart. She sent a column of fire swirling around her, attenuating the sound waves through the semi-solid heat waves of the fire.

The invading Chinese soldiers didn't have the Whiskey abilities.

His mundane soldiers strafed the beach below, puffs of sand or blood at the end of each bullet fired.

The combination of the bullets from his band soldiers and the stun wave of his bard abilities, the invading wave of Chinese went down.

Tyler had seen demons fight. Tyler had seen demons die. But he'd never seen people torn apart by bullets. That was what Aunt Paige had fought so hard against. He understood why now. It was horrible to see.

Hi, Tyler. You feel far away.

Kammy! Oh, am I glad to hear you. Tell Mandy to run my way.

Kammy could link him and Mandy, and get her away from the beach and the danger.

You tell her. It isn't easy to do this from so far away. Are you in trouble?

Plenty. Just stay with us. Mandy, run my way.

The air pressurized with concussive blasts from beyond sight, and a faint wall of sound rolled after.

It hurts, Tyler. Keep us together, Kammy. I know you can do it.

Mandy heard and ran away from the beach, sending waves of fire behind her, obscuring her flight from there, and kept the heat high enough to melt ordnance flying in.

The beach was *swarming* with Chinese. More of those wheeled submarines pulled up the beach and other less experimental boats powered up the surf disgorging soldiers, shooting as soon as they had a line of sight.

You two get away from the beach. Do it now, Tyler's mom told them in her most stern mom voice.

Tyler obeyed immediately. "Run! Mom's coming in. Run *fast*."

His soldiers disengaged and ran to keep up with him. Somehow in the night, he'd earned instant obedience from them.

We're going, Mandy's still got a little way to go.

Move your asses, that beach is going to be glass soon. Leslie's voice came in loud and clear, and she only sounded that way when *everyone* had messed up bad.

Crap.

Tyler ran. He'd never been a runner, but his mom sounded *really* bent out of shape. And when she was mad, things didn't go right for a long time for *anyone*.

Mandy caught up, passing soldiers and still trailing fire behind her.

They left the palm trees and the street along the edge of

the beach, all the way to the first line of hotels following the contours of the beach.

He stopped when he passed the back edge of the fancy hotel.

The screech of the griffin was the last thing he heard before—

He'd thought Mandy's fire had been hot. He was wrong.

The wall of fire that landed on the beach turned the sand sunlight-bright in an instant. Then a crack of thunder followed lightning so thick it looked like a train of solid light.

The fire went out instantly as the trees blew away as ash in the wind made by the heat. The pavement was charred halfway to the far side, but not one single life form moved on the beach. It glowed white-hot and steamed were the surf rolled up the beach.

Mom? Kammy voice was in his head, and probably Mandy's, too.

Something's wrong with Mom. She feels different. She might be taking a nap.

Tyler scanned the sky looking for the griffin, or for *anything*. "There." He pointed to a speck in freefall.

"Where?" Mandy searched, her eyes darting back and forth. "We have to help her."

The speck grew to a tiny person. That was their mom, and she wasn't shifting into a bird or anything.

"Mandy. Can you shoot fire that high? We have to make a cushion."

"No, that would fry her."

"Trust me. Heat rises. Sonics have weight. We can do it. But you have to trust me."

Mandy's face crumpled, but she shot the fire into the sky.

Mommy? Mommy, are you okay? Kammy rang loud and clear in their heads, his link strong no matter that he was three or four thousand miles away.

Tyler sang a pure note and climbed the frequency past audible into supersonic. He warped Mandy's fire into a ring with a depression in the middle slowing her fall, but it wasn't enough. She still fell too fast. He pushed more into the sonics, condensing the flames into plasma, bleeding flames continuously along the bottom of the cushion.

Mandy made the flames larger.

Tyler compressed the heat.

Leslie slowed, slowed more.

Tyler turned the sonic waves and she floated down, but started to fall more to the side coming at the kids and the hotel.

He made the motion to cut the fire and brought his mother down the last thirty or so feet with his magick alone. The world greyed at the edges and turned into pinpoint, then went black.

36

Dexx didn't run, but he didn't walk slowly toward his brother either. He wasn't alone this time, and that *had* to count for something.

It still wasn't a plan, but this wasn't a massive battle with thousands of other soldiers. This was him and a bad para. And that was something he'd trained for decades to do. As long as he didn't lose his shit, he'd be fine.

He had a griffin in his pack and that made him...stronger.

He had wolves, a hyena, and a bear in his pack, and that made him...stronger.

He had a thunderbird and a rajasi in his pack. They for sure made him stronger.

He had... Okay. He didn't know what Paige had bonded with, but he was starting to feel more strength from her through their mate bond because she wasn't fully back in the pack yet. As she awakened and grew stronger with her spirit animal, Dexx was gaining in strength.

And there were the others in his pack, his family who weren't shifters. They were witches and a Valkyrie and djinn and normal humans, but they still made him...stronger.

As a shifter and as a man.

That would have to be enough.

Dexx Colt wasn't alone.

Dexx stopped outside of sword range, raising his weapon. His *mavet* vibrated with the need to kill the beast in front of him.

All Dexx had to do was to keep the sword in his hand, and he might have a better chance of winning.

Bussemi-demon pulled out Dexx's *kadu,* and it pulled at him, begging him to hold it with an intensity that made it hard to think.

"You make things so easy. Easier than killing that broken girl."

Broken girl? Rainbow hadn't been broken. She had been secure in who she had been. Unless he meant Bruna.

That was the last straw. Dexx's insides were twisted in knots from the need to hold the *kadu* and from the torture of remembering Bruna and Rainbow and the endless list of people he had lost over the lifetimes he didn't even remember.

He swung his sword.

Bussemi casually knocked it aside with his staff.

Dexx remembered that thing. It was the staff that hit harder with every swing.

"Surely that's not the best you have."

Well, *shit.* It was the best he had with all the *things* crammed up in his head. If only he had the *kadu* somewhere safe. Where nobody could find or harm it ever again.

Hattie, can you help me focus?

I cannot. Something holds me.

Bussemi.

Dexx swung again, and this time Bussemi only leaned a little to the side.

"I suppose I will just have to—"

A blast of ice laced with lightning slammed into Busse-mi's chest, hurling him into and through a small house.

The noise in Dexx's mind stopped suddenly and the insanity that came from the *kadu* vanished.

"The Dexx has asked for a boon."

The currents? That was the thing that was different this time than all the others?

He'd befriended a rusalka and had gained a friend in one of the most powerful elements he'd ever encountered. Of course.

"We have granted the boon." The currents stood next to Dexx wearing Rainbow's face.

Wait. If this was the thing that would make a difference, he needed to make it count. Like, take away Bussemi's staff or... ill Bussemi or...something more than hit the demon with lightning ice once. "Huh. I don't remember asking for one."

Cub, I am free, but I feel it reaching for me.

The currents held up his *kadu.* "We will keep this safe forever. We will wait for the Dexx to come back. Perhaps the Dexx will take an action for us."

Hold on, girl. Having the currents keep his *kadu* safe was more than just a boon. "Yes, but can we discuss this later? Kinda busy right now. Unless you can kill Bussemi?"

"That is not ours." The currents turned to leave. "Dexx." She disappeared.

He felt a cool touch on his mind and heard a whisper that didn't sound like Hattie. *The beast returns. The Dexx will stand ready.*

He lifted his sword and waited for the demon.

The house exploded outward in all directions, pieces of furniture and walls and wood raining in pieces no bigger than pebbles.

Bussemi swept his staff angrily in front of him. "Your friend will pay for that," he roared. "I will kill you and bring you back so you can watch their suffering."

"Well, that's one way to go through therapy. Another is to hold the talking stick and talk nicely to the nice young man in the clean white coat."

Bussemi narrowed his eyes. "What did you do? You should be paralyzed with—" Bussemi looked down at his chest where the *kadu* had been. "You."

Oh, yeah. This was the best boon ever. "You bet, you slimy, worm-ridden piece of filth."

Bussemi's face contorted in rage and he rushed forward.

Dexx met the first swing of the staff and quickly drew on Hattie's strength. His arm was numbed, so he tried to tighten his grip. Dexx brought his sword around again barely parried the full-armed swing.

Cub. I am being pulled away.

Again? Really? How?

Bussemi was working spells so fine Dexx could barely see them. That's how.

Dexx shifted—or attempted to. His legs turned into feline legs and his head widened and stretched, but most of the transformation had been blocked.

There wouldn't be much fight as a partially shifted cat. He turned and ran, the tip of the staff tugging at his shirt.

Dexx shifted all the way human and ran as fast as he could, pulling every ounce of power from Hattie he could.

Bussemi growled. "Run, little insect. You are going to die this day."

But what if he didn't want to? Dexx darted behind a house and to the back yard. He had to put some distance between him and Bussemi.

He needed a few minutes to think.

He had the power of his pack, and the currents had helped him stay in the battle by protecting the *kadu*.

As soon as he lost sight of Bussemi, he turned a sharp right and jumped. Hattie had enough power to give him that he barely found the roof with his toes. He leaned forward and caught the rough roofing and scampered low to keep his shadow down. He moved around the house, keeping the roof between him and Bussemi.

"I will find you. You cannot run, not like that. I already have you in the snare, and it will lead me to you."

"Yeah, I know." Dexx whispered and let the *mavet* return to the demon knife. He had moments before he would be found.

He cast around for the spell, and where it attached to him.

Nothing, nothing, nothing—there. Fine strands attached to his feet through the ground. Clever. Son of bitch. "Sorry, first mother. I hope you know what I mean."

Dexx ran the knife through the tendrils and cut the spell.

He felt Hattie return, pressing to shift. *He will not keep us apart. Take him as the alpha.*

Shh. I will. Calm your thoughts. We take him smart.

Hattie's aura flared in his mind and spirit. She was *powerful*.

You been hiding this from me?

It wasn't magick, but it wasn't *not* magick.

We are the alpha and you have powerful spirits in your pack. Something tickled his thoughts, but it was nebulous. He let it hang out, returning to Bussemi.

"You insolent—" He blasted the corner of the house with his staff. The roof on the far side curled and began to cave in.

Dexx dropped off his side and waited, gathering his power, pulling the energy he could from his pack.

"You are proving to be a major nuisance. Congratulations. Only Dekskulta and our first brother ever bothered us this way."

Overconfidence and monologuing. Gotta love the combo.

Bussemi's staff peeked around the corner as he searched for Dexx.

He raised the sword and prepared to slash as a bolt of lightning cracked out of nowhere at Bussemi.

He reacted far faster than Dexx could have and caught the lightning on the end of the staff. "You very stupid boy. Did you think you could hurt me with *my own magick?*"

Uh, no he hadn't. Where had that lightning come from?

Bussemi swiped the staff away and the bolt slammed into the corner of a building. The explosion was bigger than it should have been. He must have amplified the power somehow.

The staff swung back his way.

No time like the present. Dexx took all the power from his pack, including the power Hattie was able to offer up, and swung the *mavet* down into the staff.

In all the time that Dexx had done stupid things, leaping in before he fully understood things had been a favorite.

The wave of kinetic energy ripped the house and the two houses on either side apart like a bomb.

The good news was Dexx was no longer in sight of his first brother. The bad news was that he couldn't hear, and his body was numb from the tips of his hair to five steps away from him in every direction.

He'd come to learn in all his years that when he hurt, he wasn't dead. He had doubts, until the pain cascaded around him, removing the numbness and confirming he still lived.

The wordless scream of rage he heard sort of dashed his hopes that his first brother had been killed in the explosion.

He rolled over, making sure that nothing pokey could stab him in sensitive bits. "Damn," he groaned. Could he have just taken it away from the guy? Probably not. Oh well. At least it was off the field, so there was some good in that.

More good news, he'd held on to the *mavet ma'a'shed*. Now he didn't have to go searching for it in piles of rubble.

And he'd discovered that having the power of a powerful pack really was a benefit in a sword fight.

"I have lost my patience with you. You are dead when I see you."

Dexx rose and found Bussemi tossing rubble from his path.

"You want some, I'm right here, you saggy excuse for a ball sack." Dexx made the Neo come-hither motion.

Bussemi felt the explosion of the staff through his body. Not as much as he would have if he'd been in control, but enough to know the bahlrok, Ghir'Uuhz, no longer had complete control over him.

There was power in names, and the monster—Ghir'Uuhz —hadn't fortified his defenses after the herald had said his name earlier. The monster must have missed it. Or disregarded the slip. It didn't matter.

He had the monster's name.

And a sliver of control. He pulled magick to him.

Bussemi slung spells at Dexx, each one a killer. The *mavet* hungered for the blood in the man or the monster or *something*. Maybe it remembered it had been beaten before and it wanted revenge. The sword was never the same after it ate Mario and his demon buddy.

Slicing spells wasn't as hard as trying to jab it into a person who had a sword himself, but after a while, it became a heavy chunk of steel, even powered by his pack.

Dexx's first brother paused in the spells and opened a pocket dimension, pulling a sword of his own out.

He had to be fucking kidding. Seriously! Where Dexx's sword was midnight black with a bloodred edge on both sides of the split blade, the bahlrok's blade was the brightest polished silver with no clear edge. It just sort of rolled into infinity.

Bussemi charged.

Dexx had learned a few things since they last time they'd crossed swords. When Dexx was able to parry aside the heavy blows, he switched to lighter swordplay, with more finesse. More grace. He tried to keep up, and he did, if only barely. The way the man swung wasn't the same way Frey had taught Dexx, but it was close enough that he could use what he'd learned.

Dodge to the side, swing up to the left, spin down to the right, raise the flat, twist left...on and on it went.

Dexx learned to fight Bussemi as he turned up the skill little by little.

They fought for minutes, or hours. It was hard to tell. Bussemi *had* been too slow a couple times, and he oozed blood from a couple spots. They hadn't healed like they should have.

That was interesting.

Then, it happened. Bussemi missed a swing.

Dexx parried, and it happened again.

Was he about to win?

Bussemi siphoned off power from Ghir'Uuhz. He hadn't gotten a lot, and it hadn't been fast, but the longer he had, the better the siphon went. He formed a sleep spell and cast it on himself. On his body at least.

Two could play at double-crossing.

There it was. A missed swing.

What are you doing, worm? Ghir'Uuhz demanded.

If I can't have him, then I won't allow you to either.

The battle with Dexx Colt continued on the outside, as though nothing happened, but Ghir'Uuhz now had *two* battles.

Then, it happened. Bussemi won.

One, two, three parries, then he had the rhythm. On the fourth, Dexx reached over Bussemi's blade and slid the *mavet ma'a'shed* into the demon's chest, all the way to the hilt. "Motherfucker, that's for Bruna."

Bussemi's eyes widened in disbelief and pain. Blood spilled from his lips and he twitched like a fish out of water.

Dexx yanked the blade to the side, severing Bussemi's spine and letting whatever gore that wanted out to spill. The blade came out clean, soaking up the blood eagerly. The sword felt different in his hand. Subtle, but there was a slight...awakening.

Bussemi fell to the ground, the light in his eyes fading.

Dexx took a deep breath and lowered the tip of the *ma'a'shed* to the ground but not his guard. After so many thousands of years of fighting this fight, he didn't think for one second that it would end this easily, even powered by the greatness of his pack.

The sun was way west, casting longish shadows of trees and houses toward the plains.

How the fuck long had they been swinging swords? Where were his guys?

Bussemi shriveled and melted away, the gore reforming and glowing with an orange intensity that he'd seen before. The time Bussemi turned into that horned, hairy beast.

"Dammit." Dexx backed up. How could Bussemi live after that? Then he noticed that the *mavet* hadn't stopped humming for the creature's blood.

"Dexx Colt. You will die for that." The bahlrok raised the sword, upsized for the massive creature.

Okay. This was going to be a bit tougher, but he'd fought big demons before. He just had to keep his shit together and remember that he wasn't alone.

The bahlrok tensed. Like he'd tried to move his arm, but nothing happened. He tensed again, and still nothing.

"Dad," Rai called, gritting her teeth with her hands gripping something he couldn't see, like invisible rope. "Get him now, I don't think I can hold him long."

Ember had his hands pushed out hard to the monster.

Dexx wasn't going to ask. He *wasn't* alone. He *had* a powerful pack and he had two incredibly powerful kids.

Who were there and helping him fight this damned demon.

And if he thought hard enough about it, this might be the very reason they'd aged so quickly—to be the forces to help him finally defeat Bussemi and to end this ageless battle once and for all. It was a shitty thing to think, but there it was.

Dexx picked up his sword and charged. He had a perfect, unmoving target. There wouldn't be a better shot, and then he swung.

The blade smashed into the armor and blew him backward. Just like it had the first time he'd done it.

"Lee! Help!" Rai called.

Leah raised a stone above her head and made motions with her other hand.

Dexx read the intent, to bind the bahlrok. That spell was probably the most powerful earth-bind that ever had been developed. A memory from Dekskulta.

Black tar oozed up from the ground and lashed the bahlrok as he stood, one arm struggling to swing his blade. It wrapped his legs and arms and throat with inky blackness that seemed to feed on his energy.

The tar blackened and glowed silver.

Bobby glowed a brilliant gold and shot spears the same color, stabbing into the beast.

It twitched and howled in pain.

The *kids* were beating the bahlrok? *By themselves and in under a minute?*

Well, they'd all known the kids were powerful and capable of handling themselves.

The monster growled, his face contorted in a snarl.

The golden glow of Bobby's magick darkened and the silvery blackness of the tar turned pitch black. Cracks formed and the earth-bind spell shattered in all directions.

A shard of darkened gold energy flew back and blew Bobby off his feet. He skidded along the pavement, smoke trailing him.

Oh, shit.

"I am the god of this world." The bahlrok broke free and swung his word at the boy. "I will rule forever."

Dexx roared in anger and charged at the swinging sword.

The world slowed and stopped, for the briefest moment and forever.

Ember glowed with the deep red of his rajasi and collapsed.

Dexx's and Hattie's minds were scooped up and set aside.

Leah was thrown backward as the magick of the earth-bind rebounded back into her, pain flaring inside.

Bobby's magick blasted apart, and a piece hit him in the chest, lifting him off the ground and tossing him backward.

They were losing.

Leah pulled herself up, looking around. This wasn't fair. They'd decided to all come and make sure their dad didn't die fighting some stupid freakin' demon and that was exactly what they were going to do.

Because... yeah.

But even that pep talk did nothing to help her get to her feet.

Rai wasn't anywhere to be seen.

That *thing* was free. It had *broken* the spell and it was going after Dad.

"I am the god of this world. I will rule forever," it roared, bringing the sword down.

Leah's dad rounded on it and swung his tiny sword at the huge monster.

Then the world slowed and stopped.

Ember glowed and his rajasi flowed outward and surrounding Dexx, lifting him off the ground and placing him in the center of the form's chest. Like her dad was now *wearing* rajasi spirit.

Whoa. What the heck?

"He is the godhunter," the rajasi said. "I am the godkiller." The sound rolled like thunder, hurting Leah's ears.

And then the swords met and time flowed right again.

Peals of thunder ricocheted through the sky.

Leah clamped her hands over her ears and still, she couldn't hear anything but the fight.

She'd seen her dad in the last seconds, fighting with the

human version of the demon, and he'd looked good. But this was impossible. She had no idea how to even help.

Houses were crushed underfoot like they didn't exist. And when they went through one, the house *didn't exist*.

Her dad looked like a tiny figurine operating the larger glowing structure of the...whatever it was.

The bahlrok worked his blade just as fast, just as masterfully, but neither seemed to be winning. How long could they keep that up?

She ran to Bobby, who was still smoking and lying still. Her dad and the monster moved away, but were still too close for comfort.

"Bobby, are you okay? Bobby?"

His upper lip twitched. "Pog," he whispered.

"Oh crap." He had so not used that right. "I thought you were—"

"I have a secret." His blue eyes stared into hers. "Ghir'Uuhz."

"What?"

"That thing's name. Where's Rai?"

"I—I don't know."

Fire laced the ground around the two, and a wall rose between them and the fighting giants.

Mommy says I shouldn't be holding the talking open. But I am anyway.

Leah didn't care. *Kammy, where's Rai? Where's Ember?*

They aren't there. Rai has Ember here. No, just Ember is here. Rai's—Rai is back there.

Sometimes, Kammy was sooooo three. *We need Rai. Bobby needs Rai.*

A magnificent bird made of entirely lightning landed inside the wall of flame.

"Your work?" Leah motioned to the wall.

Rai shook her head. "Ember. Where is that idiot? He hurt my dad and my brother."

Bobby sat up. "His name is *Ghir'Uuhz.*"

Rai shook her head, as if unsure what to do with that information.

Leah used true names to call souls through portals. "Use it? Don't demons and things protect their names like super close?"

Rai shrugged as if that was as good a suggestion as anything and took off in bird form. She landed on a nearby roof and turned back into Rai. "Ghir'Uuhz," she yelled.

If only Tyler had been there to amplify her voice.

Rai tried again, louder this time. "Ghir'Uuhz, I have something to tell you."

The two stopped for half a heartbeat, the bahlrok's eyes open in shock. Well, that was a distraction, but now what? And what could Leah do to help? She gathered her magick to create a door to save her sister if she had to.

"Die, asshole."

Ghir'Uuhz roared defiance and swung his sword wildly, attacking the flaming rajasi.

Leah hoped her dad was still in there and that he would be okay. She'd get them both out of there if she had to.

Rai gathered up a *ton* of lightning, her face making an ugly face, and then released it on the demon.

Dexx knocked aside two powerful strikes from the bahlrok inside his... *magick power armor?* He stood inside the construct, battling the possessor of his now dead first brother.

The rajasi that had stolen his body, released most of it back, but it was all Dexx fighting.

411

His head swam with the torrent of power the rajasi fed through him.

Dexx lanced out with a simple forward poke and scored a hit on the monster's shoulder. The blade of strange rajasi magick cut the flesh of the bahlrok as easy as a knife through cake.

The beast answered with dragon flame from his mouth.

Dexx dodged, and another house was engulfed in flames.

Who are you?

Fight, the rajasi said. *You are the god hunter.*

The bahlrok reached his bullwhip arm back to strike.

Dexx pulled a tree from the ground as easy as pulling a weed and flung it.

The tree shattered against the arm tangling the strands in the branches. In a second, the tree was mostly ash, but it did what Dexx needed it to.

Dexx came in behind the tree and grabbed the bahlrok by the wrist and chopped down.

The beast howled in pain as his hand fell to the earth with the spiked whip.

Dexx raised his sword barely in time to meet the incoming swing. Thunder rolled out from the clashing swords, shaking leaves from trees.

They fought, matched skill for skill, the rajasi's power and strength not yet enough to overcome the dog-faced monster.

We can't win, we're too evenly matched.

I am the god killer, the rajasi said. *With my power, we can defeat him. Fight.*

Magicks came at Dexx, blinding, trapping, killing, tempting, goading, drowning him. The attacks were non-stop and deadly.

Dexx countered each one as they formed, still catching the sword against his own.

Jedi masters had nothing on that thing. The entire council would have died in a second.

Dexx had a rajasi.

The power was so big. He burned and froze with the power. He could create universes and destroy matter. He *knew* everything.

But he only matched the bahlrok, strike for strike, and the *one* lucky hit he'd managed to get in hadn't seemed to faze him at all.

The bahlrok picked up his intensity and fought faster, slinging magick Dexx'd never dreamed of.

The rajasi fed him with the power to repel with more intensity, urging him to fight harder, to think outside the box.

A faint buzzing tickled Dexx's thoughts, but he ignored it, kept it out.

The buzzing grew.

Dexx swung harder trying to dislodge the sword from the balrok's hand, but he held on, and counterattacked, pushing Dexx back through a house.

The buzzing in Dexx's head grew insistent, demanded he pay attention to it. Dexx spared a thread of energy and examined it.

Uncle Dexx, be ready. Kammy's voice was strained. He was in pain. A *lot* of it.

Ready for what?

"Girh'Uuhz."

Dexx heard and *felt* the sending. Kammy supercharged Rai's voice.

What the hell was Rai doing?

Thunder cracked as the swords hit. The beast swung back for another attack and paused.

"Ghir'Uuhz, I have something to tell you." Rai spoke

413

confidently, like Paige or Leslie, a true Whiskey witch. "Die, asshole."

Strike now, the rajasi commanded.

Dexx swung the sword. Somehow, the *mavet ma'a'shed* found the beast's throat and took his head off. The sword drank the beast's blood.

The magick explosion threw Dexx from his feet, and the world went white.

37

D exx stood beside his bed, Paige and Ember both sleeping.

They could be only sleeping by the way they were breathing easy and deep.

A tear rolled down his face. After everything they'd faced, he'd finally won against Bussemi. The bahlrok and the magician were both dead. They couldn't be resurrected. Dexx didn't want to lose his wife and his son.

Bobby was burned out.

Kammy was burned out.

Ember, was... Ember was not good.

Before he had time to take another breath, he was no longer in his room, not on the planet.

He was on a plane. Not the kind that flew, but one with a sky and ground the same color blue, and the ground was flat and featureless. *That* kind of plane.

The currents appeared in front of him, all at once the same color and completely different. "The Dexx does not like our place. We will take the Dexx to the place."

"No, it's—"

Fine. The room was the same one they'd taken him to for a one-night liaison with his family.

"Come on. My wife and kid could be dying right now. Maybe *two* of them." Bobby wasn't so hot either.

"The Dexx must be. The Dexx has query."

"It's not that important."

"The Dexx has no better place to be in this time."

"Ah, yes, he does."

The currents shook her head.

"Fine, yes. Yeah. I guess. I know what I want my boon to be."

"The boon has been granted. There will be no more unless we say."

What? "I didn't ask for the boon. But I am *now*."

"The Dexx asked for a boon. The boon has been granted. The Dexx will be silent. The Dexx will see our guest."

The room expanded and Ember walked in.

"Ember! Are you okay?" How was...he here?

His form shifted and a deep red glowing lion stood in front of him. "I have broken laws," the lion said in a faint Indian accent.

Dexx shrugged, not quite sure what was going on here. "Me too. You get over it the first time you accidently blow a building up. Or blow out the window of a guy trying to run you off the road. We all do."

"I have broken laws deeper than mere human trifles. I must return to the pool, and I will likely never again be seen on your plane."

"What—why? You were doing your job. I would have done that years ago if I could have."

"You were not my bond. We tried to grow our bond vessels to contain our spirits. But..." He sighed. "I would have killed your son. Ember would have died before the year was out. We do not leave our bond for another. That is not allowed."

Dexx curled his lip. "So why *did* you, anyway?" Except maybe to save Ember? Dexx didn't understand what was going on.

"The boy could not properly hold my power, the power I pushed through you to kill your god."

"He wasn't a god." But he had been damned hard to kill, so what did Dexx know? "And so you broke the law, saving Ember's life, and my life at the same time. While also killing Bussemi. That all smacks of planning."

"There were many considerations we made in choosing your offspring. But I was the one who broke the law, and I am not dead, so the punishment will be mine to bear. Your son will be chosen by another."

"You mean he's getting a different spirit?" What the hell was going on with the Whiskeys and spirits? "So, he'll be able to shift and everything?"

"He will be granted a spirit. I have seen to that. I am plainly alive, so the restrictions do not apply."

"Cool." Right? This was good. Ember was safe. He'd be alive. "Then..." Dexx could save Mah'se. "I know one he could have." Words tumbled out faster than he could think what he said. "Mah'se. He's a bit rough around the edges, but I think he's a good cat. *Really* loves his job."

"Cat? I remember Mah'se as an elk."

"Doesn't matter. Cat, dog, rhino, good intentions, whatever. I think they'd make an excellent—"

"The choice has been made." The rajasi shook his fiery head. "Mah'se is not the boy's bond."

"Oh." Dammit. Would that elk ever find a bond? "Mah'se's my friend. He's Hattie's friend. I'm just trying to keep him from dying. I just—Ember has a bond? Who is it?

No, wait. Don't tell me. It's a wolf. Got plenty of those on my team. It's a wolf. Am I right?"

"You were closer with the cat. I must leave now, but I wanted to thank you. Hattie chose well. You *are* a good champion."

"The Dexx will query."

Dexx jumped for the ceiling. He'd *completely* forgotten about the currents. She wore Rainbow's face again.

"I don't understand. What do you want me to do? And don't repeat the same statement with the same words. I'll be the same amount of confused." That sentence even came out sounding confused.

"The Dexx *kadu* will remain with us forever. The Dexx *kadu* will be safe for all time. The Dexx will return again."

"Yeah, I *know* that part. No, my original boon. I want—I want my friend back."

"We cannot raise—"

"Yeah. I got that. I get that you already granted me a boon and it was a great one. Not one I'd thought to ask for you. It's still awesome. You're awesome. But..."

She stood there, waiting.

He took in a deep breath. "Can you honor my friend by looking like her, um, by wearing her face? For as long as you have my *kadu*. That's what I want. So she's never forgotten."

"Dexx." The blue lady spoke, but it was Rainbow's voice.

"Bow." A flood of emotions ran through him as he watched the blue lady shift her form, the long hair growing into a poofy afro, the sharp cheekbones softening, the eyes growing bigger, the lips softer, the shoulder straighter.

"That is not a boon," Blue Rainbow said with a soft smile.

Dexx hid tears behind a quavering smile. "Gods, I miss you."

The room disappeared, and the blue lady turned and

became a quickly dissolving mist. "I know." Rainbow's voice echoed softly through the blue expanse.

"Bow?" Dexx threw the question out there as his bedroom blinked back into reality.

Paige's eyes opened. "Eos."

Dexx took a knee by the bed and held Paige's hand. "Hey, babe, you made it."

"Eos." Paige said again, her brown eyes holding Dexx's.

"That's not funny. Are you okay?" He had a million questions, not the least of which was who Paige had been bonded to.

"What—no. Eos. I need coffee."

Why did she keep repeating that? "I told you, that's not funny."

Paige's brows drew down into a frown. "Why do you keep repeating the same thing over and over again?"

"Why are you?"

She rolled her eyes and shook her head, sitting up. "I need coffee. How long have I been out? Did I miss anything important? Are we in open warfare? Where's General Saul?" Paige sat up and held a hand to her head. She swayed back and forth and braced herself on the bed. "Caffeine."

"That's a lot of questions." He passed a look over Ember, and *his* eyes opened. "Oh, jeez, *thank you.*"

"You're making man-sense, I get that, but I haven't understood a word you've said at *all.*"

Dexx pointed at her. "Same."

Ember sat up. "I feel strange."

Paige turned to Ember. "Em, why did your father let you get into my bed?"

"Oi vey. Guys. Stop."

"My rajasi is gone." Ember looked at his hands as though it was for the first time.

Paige nearly levitated from the bed. Maybe she didn't

need coffee after all. "What happened? Dexx, did *you* do something?"

"Calm down, Pea." Dexx pulled Ember into a one-armed hug, holding Paige in the other. "I know," he whispered to Ember. "He told me."

Ember began to cry into Dexx's neck.

"You want to bring me up to speed?" Paige asked. "While we walk for coffee."

Ember clung to Dexx, which was fine, since Dexx didn't particularly want to set him down.

"It's a long story. Long enough for a book, but the short of it is, I killed Bussemi with the rajasi's help. I guess what I'd really needed all those years were our kids. They're fine." Mostly. He still needed to check and make sure Bobby was. "DoDO is...destroyed. Bussemi isn't with them anymore. The field agents they'd deployed against us are decimated. Leslie's in Hawaii with Mandy and Tyler and they did...amazingly. We still have Hawaii thanks to them. Bobby may never glow again, and my *kadu* will never again be the target of nefarious plans."

"How much of that did you make up?" Paige tossed a cup to the coffee maker and clumsily stabbed the single-cup serving in the holder.

Dexx set Ember down. "Also, more good news. You've be chosen by another spirit, since the rajasi broke some laws, and he's going to prison. I think."

"I don't want another spirit. I want *him* back."

"Dexx, can I?" Paige had already had a sip or eight of her coffee, and the wheels had begun turning in her head. "I know what it's like, losing your spirit shifter. It's like that hole in your heart won't go away. And it doesn't."

Ember sniffed snot up his nose and wiped his eyes with his shirt.

"I promise you that after a while you'll learn to stay away

from the hole, and when your spirit comes, she'll build some walls around it and you can go there to relive your memories."

Fresh tears leaked from his eyes. "I feel weak."

Cub. Hattie called to Dexx. She sounded like she was calling him on the phone. *Tell your cub that Barre will be with him soon.*

Dexx's jaw hung open. *What did you do?*

I am the alpha. I did alpha things. Tell your cub.

Oh. Dexx closed his mouth and reached out a ruffled Ember's hair gently. "So, remember a few minutes ago when I said you had a spirit shifter coming?"

Ember nodded, his eyes filled with tears.

"On a scale from one to ten, how cool is Hattie?"

"Pretty cool, I guess." Almost no excitement coming from a boy who could *literally* shift into any animal he wanted. Dexx tried a different angle. "If Hattie was the only animal you could shift into, would you take her?"

Ember shrugged. "I guess. But couldn't I still be able to shift into anything?"

Well, probably. "Well, I guess you'll have to find out. Hattie just told me that the spirit who's taking your bond is her great-grandson. His name is Barre. And I think he's bigger than Hattie."

Ember's eyes went distant as his thoughts went internal. "I'm going to have an ancient?"

"I guess so. I think he was one of the last."

Ember let a weak smile grow. "I hope he's nice. The rajasi was nice."

At least he didn't hate the idea of Barre right off. Having an ancient was a big thing. The only thing bigger were a few of the impossible mythos. Like— Dexx snapped his head up to Paige. "Why did you mention Eos?"

"Why did you say it wasn't funny?" Paige set her cup down and crossed her arms.

"Because he doesn't exist. He's a myth among the shifters."

"How do you know that?"

"From my first life. Things are hazy, but I think he asked Hattie about the spirits, and there were a helluva lot less of them back then. And she told stories. Eos was a myth. The spirit that didn't exist."

Paige raised an eyebrow. "Was he a unicorn?"

Dexx shrugged. "Yeah. There was supposed to be two, but something happened. Then there was *one*."

"Was he black with hooves of fire, and lightning in his eyes?"

"Buh-i-ohno," Dexx shrugged.

"Does he look like this?" Paige stepped backward into the open area of the kitchen and shifted into a black and brown bridle-colored horse with a twisted spike protruding from its head. A long flowing black mane slid down one side of its neck, and a long black tail flicked back and forth.

"Oh shit. Paige, what did you do?"

Leslie stood at the rail on the porch of Phoebe Blackman's ranch house on Lanai island. The sunset threw long shadows across the land and to the ocean.

Tyler hadn't been seen since they got back, no doubt reliving the tales of the fight with his newfound friends.

Mandy'd sequestered herself in her room, and wasn't answering any attempts to talk.

Phoebe held out a glass filled to the rim with a cabernet.

Leslie took two large swallows. "Did I do the right thing?

I listened to Dexx. Let my kids endanger themselves. That was two steps away from suicide. Did I *do* the right thing?"

"My family is big. I don't have an exact count right now, but it's big. The thing is, even with all that family, we *still* don't know what's best for everyone." Phoebe shrugged and shook her head. "Because they're all different."

"You're kind of proving *my* point." Leslie took a more sensible sip.

"Some of our kids are daredevils, and we never know who will deal with danger on their own or shut down. But we don't stop them from trying. Did you go too far, launching them into a war with a foreign country? There were children in the Revolutionary War. So, maybe, maybe not."

Leslie smiled and took another sip. "Yeah. I'm the mother who protects her kids. Not dangles them out as bait."

"There's a certain protection in that, too."

Leslie treated Phoebe to a Whiskey glare.

"Only in that you train them to protect themselves."

"Goddess, you even *sound* like him."

"He may talk more sense than you want to give him credit for."

Leslie shook her head slightly. It was medically *impossible* for the man to speak sense.

"But," Phoebe continued, "I didn't come out here to talk about our brother-in-law. I came to tell you the documents were signed and ratified. This is a Blackman island, and you have a chunk of it. The deed goes into perpetuity, and so does your slice. Congratulations."

Phoebe smiled and offered her hand.

Leslie shook it and smiled. Then she finished the glass and held it back to Phoebe. "More?"

President Walton walked through the double doors from admin to the immense hangar. Fighter jets and bombers were parked in neat rows with razor precision.

The grey jets were fine to look at, but the object of his visit was the menacing black one.

The colonel beside him was dressed in his finest dress uniform, and why shouldn't he be? The president of the United States was visiting. "This here is the newest of the new. Capabilities of a fighter, payloads of a bomber, luxurious as a passenger jet. But you're not here for that."

The man simpered, even though he acted almost like an equal to Walton. He'd have to be disabused of the thought. The president should be feared and respected. He *had* no equals. "What's the range?"

"She's got long legs, sir. She can get to the West Coast and back, no refueling, and silent running. She can deliver the knockout punch wherever you want to send her."

"How many nukes?"

"Two. But we're in the final stage of adding more."

"How long after I give the signal will it be airborne?"

"You give the word, she's up before the conversation is done."

That would serve. There was no room in his world for the abominations of nature. And Paige Whiskey was on the top of that list. He *would* take back America from the vermin that infested her lands.

He would go down in history as the president who reunited a dying nation.

THE END

This concludes Book 6 of the Whiskey Witches Para Wars.

Join us for the next book in this saga as Paige struggles to create a solution to end this war, Dexx masters his alpha abilities, Wy realizes what it means to belong to something bigger, and the rest of our amazing characters struggle on their individual paths on the most challenging adventure the Whiskey witches have ever faced.

Be sure to order it now!

Pre-order now at: https://fjblooding.com/product/breaking-whiskey/

We hope you enjoyed *Eye of the Saber*.
Be sure to visit my site, fjblooding.com, to sign up for our newsletter, get free books, join the forum discussions, and find out more about on our latest books!

And please leave reviews where you buy books. You can also leave reviews on FJBlooding.com.

ABOUT THE AUTHOR

Shane Wolfram lives in his hometown with his amazing wife F.J. Blooding. Frankie let him take over Dexx's story one deadline-ridden night and he's never looked back since. He hadn't quite realized what he'd be jumping into when he volunteered, but he's grown as an author and is enjoying the journey.

They live with his twin brother, his wife, their two kids, and during their long summer days, he gets to spend time with his two amazing daughters. He loves working on cars and letting my bestselling wife write his bios, newsletters, and articles for him while he crafts amazing Dexx books and naps with the cat.

Enjoy!

Follow us on Bookbub!

https://www.bookbub.com/authors/f-j-blooding

Shifting Heart Romances

by Hattie Hunt & F.J. Blooding

Bear Moon

Grizzly Attraction

Here's the reading order to make it even easier to catch up!

https://www.fjblooding.com/reading-order

Other Books by F.J. Blooding

Devices of War Trilogy

Fall of Sky City

Sky Games

Whispers of the Skyborne

Discover more, sign up for updates and gifts, and join the forum discussions at www.fjblooding.com.

WHISKEY MAGICK & MENTAL HEALTH

Sign up to learn more about our books and receive this free e-zine about Whiskey Magick and Mental Health.

https://www.fjblooding.com/books-lp

CPSIA information can be obtained
at www.ICGtesting.com
Printed in the USA
JSHW020926010523
41064JS00001B/9